JUST
THREE WORDS

Praise for Melissa Brayden

Waiting In The Wings

"This was an engaging book with believable characters and story development. It's always a pleasure to read a book set in a world like the theater/film that gets it right…a thoroughly enjoyable read."—*Lez Books*

"This is Brayden's first novel, but we wouldn't notice if she hadn't told us. The book is well put together and more complex than most authors' second or third books. The characters have chemistry; you want them to get together in the end. The book is light, frothy, and fun to read. And the sex is hot without being too explicit—not an easy trick to pull off."
—*Liberty Press*

Heart Block

"The story is enchanting with conflicts and issues to be overcome that will keep the reader turning the pages. The relationship between Sarah and Emory is achingly beautiful and skillfully portrayed. This second offering by Melissa Brayden is a perfect package of love—and life to be lived to the fullest. So grab a beverage and snuggle up in a comfy throw to read this classic story of overcoming obstacles and finding enduring love."—*Lambda Literary Review*

"Although this book doesn't beat you over the head with wit, the interactions are almost always humorous, making both characters really quite loveable. Overall a very enjoyable read."—*C-Spot Reviews*

By the Author

Waiting in the Wings

Heart Block

How Sweet It Is

<u>Soho Loft Romances</u>

Kiss the Girl

Just Three Words

Visit us at www.boldstrokesbooks.com

JUST
THREE WORDS

by

Melissa Brayden

2015

JUST THREE WORDS

© 2015 By Melissa Brayden. All Rights Reserved.

ISBN 13: 978-1-62639-335-6

This Trade Paperback Original Is Published By
Bold Strokes Books, Inc.
P.O. Box 249
Valley Falls, NY 12185

First Edition: April 2015

Credits
Editors: Lynda Sandoval and Stacia Seaman
Production Design: Stacia Seaman
Cover Design by Sheri (graphicartist2020@hotmail.com)

Acknowledgments

In writing *Just Three Words*, I had a blast returning to characters I've grown to love and to a place I love to write about. Sometimes it's hard to believe this is my job. However, I am more than aware that there are numerous people responsible for bringing this book to life and giving me the chance to do what I enjoy.

Many thanks to Bold Strokes Books and the whole fantastic team, who have shown my books a great deal of love and thoughtful care. I'm beyond lucky to work with you.

My family puts up with a lot—whether it's me staring off into space for extended lengths of time, canceling plans in order to meet a deadline, or stopping them mid-sentence to write down something awesome they've said to me (that is now going in a book). I'm blessed with the best group of cheerleaders ever.

Working with my editor, Lynda Sandoval, is not only educational and fun, but inspiring. The passion she's shown for the books we've worked on together makes me excited to get up each day and write more. And that's everything.

Thanks to Nicole Little, Georgia Beers, and Rachel Spangler for their continued love and friendship. I don't know where I'd be without them in my corner—both in writing and in life.

Alan and I have known each other since we were thirteen years old, and no one else on the planet gets me the way he does. I'm reminded on a daily basis how lucky I am.

Lastly, thank you to you, dear readers. Thank you for spending a little bit of your time with my books. I'm so very grateful.

In memory of my snuggly writing partner, Tucker Benjamin.

PROLOGUE

It was the kind of night that felt important. While that wasn't a thought nineteen-year-old Samantha Ennis voiced out loud to the three girls in her company, it was definitely a tidbit she filed away for herself.

There was a gentle breeze brushing the streets of Greenwich Village as they walked to the Cornelia Street Café. It was close to midnight on a Thursday, and the neighborhood was still very much alive with college students and hipsters and even the occasional gutsy tourist. Samantha sent a sidelong glance at the other three girls next to her. They dotted the narrow sidewalk to her left as they chatted about anything and everything. Hunter and Mallory she'd gotten to know over the course of the last year, as freshmen at NYU, but Brooklyn was the new addition to the group. Yet when she'd arrived at the first meeting of the school year of the LGBT Student Interest Group, Sam had a feeling that the fresh-faced blonde in the ponytail was a keeper. And after the foursome spent the past few hours planning the group's upcoming film series at a nearby coffee shop, it felt like they'd found their missing puzzle piece. The four-way synergy had been palpable as they'd spun one idea for the film series into another in a planning session that just felt somehow ordained. But it wasn't just their ability to work well together. They'd had the best time, too, laughing and getting to know one another better, which made the work feel fun. And after all that, they were certainly deserving of the late-night junk-food meal they sought.

If there was any justice in the world.

Imminently, that meant chocolate waffles at the Cornelia Street Café at Hunter's suggestion.

"You guys, I'm gonna pay for this later," Mallory said, tucking her long dark hair behind one ear. She checked her watch. "I have my first chem test of the semester tomorrow morning and an essay on the relevance of *Hamlet* on contemporary themes of modern drama due on Monday. I always prepare for that kind of thing. *Always*." And she did. Mallory Spencer was the most together person Sam had ever met. If there was a task at hand, Mallory led the charge to sort it out. In fact, she was president of the LGBT Student Interest Group they all belonged to and only a sophomore, the youngest president the group had ever elected.

Hunter slung an arm around Mallory's shoulders. "And if I know you, my very studious friend, you're going to get an A on the boring test without so much as cracking a book for five minutes and then dazzle your prof with the Shakespeare thing you described shortly thereafter. Even after you've scarfed down some amazing food with us."

"I could maybe help with the Shakespeare," Brooklyn offered, still seeming a little timid around the new group. "I'm not an expert, but I've read *Hamlet* a million times. I know all the angles."

Mallory smiled. "I knew there was a reason I liked you."

"And I can quiz you on chemistry before class tomorrow," Sam said. "I CLEPed out of that one."

Mallory shook her head at Sam. "Seriously? You really do rock at anything numbers related."

Samantha shrugged, but felt the blush brought on by the compliment the second it hit her cheeks. It was true. "Everyone has something they're good at."

Fifteen minutes later and they were seated around a table at the small café as sounds from the live music in the basement made their way up the stairs. Surrounded by waffles, whipped cream, and chocolate sauce, Samantha found herself in sugar rush heaven. She raised one hand, placing the other on her heart. "And then God said, let there be chocolate."

"Damn right he did," Hunter said, slowly licking chocolate off her thumb with the sexy finesse only Hunter could master. A waiter on his way to the kitchen paused to take in the visual. A girl at the next table did the same. Samantha smiled to herself. Hunter Blair was equal parts beautiful and sexy. While her father was from Ohio, her mother was Hawaiian, giving Hunter an exotic quality that only turned more heads.

Toss in her extra-added charm and she snagged the attention of anyone on two legs. To say she did well with the ladies was an understatement.

Brooklyn placed a chocolaty bite in her mouth and shook her head in wonder. "I love chocolate at any time of day, but there's something about it late at night that makes it extra decadent."

"That's so true," Samantha echoed, relaxing happily in her chair. "Midnight chocolate just makes everything seem easier."

Mallory nodded. "Doesn't it? I'm gonna slam-dunk that exam. Pass the whipped cream and sprinkles. I'll need seconds."

"See?" Hunter bumped Mallory's shoulder and supplied her with the heaping dish. "I might even attempt to speak to my asshole father when I go home next weekend."

Samantha raised her glass of milk. "To midnight chocolate and its ability to make the world a little easier."

"I'll drink to that," Brooklyn said.

Four glasses met in the center of the table and Samantha felt excitement move through her. She passed a glance over each of the three smiling faces and knew innately that these girls were going to somehow matter to her.

"I'm glad I met you guys," Brooklyn said. They didn't know a lot about Brooklyn Campbell just yet, but they had a whole school year spread out in front of them.

Hunter nodded. "Likewise."

"Ditto," Mallory said triumphantly.

Samantha smiled. "I think this was all meant to be."

CHAPTER ONE

Ten years later

Friday afternoons in May didn't get much prettier than this. An even sixty-eight degrees, a soft breeze, and sun shining for days. As a result, New York City seemed to move at a slower pace. People lingered with their friends on street corners, drank their iced coffee at outdoor cafés, and luxuriated in the first warm temperatures the city had offered up in months.

Samantha glanced at the door to the Ground Support Café in Soho for any sign of Libby and then double-checked her text messages to be sure she'd gotten the time right. She had.

They'd agreed to meet at one p.m. for a late lunch, as Libby had taken the afternoon off from her sales job across town. But it was twenty minutes past, and Samantha hadn't heard from her. While not always the most conscientious about time, Libby made up for it in other ways. Just thinking about her, Sam felt the beginnings of a blush. In fact, each time she saw Libby she blushed. And when she kissed her, Sam felt like she was hovering somewhere above the universe. Just seeing her name on a text message made her stomach flip-flop.

And she would be arriving any minute. Right?

Instead of watching the seconds tick by, Sam adjusted to Plan B. Luckily she'd brought work along and turned her attention to balancing Soho Savvy's accounts for April. Music played faintly from the café's speakers, and departing customers smiled politely as she turned to her laptop. As the bookkeeper, money manager, and all-around numbers ninja at the boutique advertising agency she owned with her three best friends, she found it important to stay ahead of the monthly budget. As she stared at the spreadsheet in front of her, tick-tacking new entries as she went, she lost herself. This was not unusual. Numbers carried a powerful allure for Sam, and when she started working with them, something clicked into place. They made sense to her in a way real life didn't always. In the numbers world, the results were hard and fast. The solidarity of that was highly gratifying. Thrilling even, if she was being honest. You could depend on numbers. Count on them.

"There you are, honey bear. I'm so sorry I'm late." Libby Weatherup slipped into the booth across from Samantha, and all was right with the world again. She wore a medium-length blue sundress and carried a handful of packages that she crammed in the tight space next to her, creating a proverbial hill of shopping bags. Mt. St. Retail. Sam had first met Libby in the elevator of Sam's building. She'd been carrying packages then, too. Sam had thought Libby was one of the most gorgeous women she'd ever seen, and after finally getting up the courage to ask her to coffee, things had progressed. Libby moved to Chelsea just before their relationship became official, and life had taken off from there.

"It's okay. I didn't mind waiting. You've been shopping?" Sam asked, closing her laptop. Libby was always complaining about her cash flow. Before answering, Libby leaned across the booth and kissed Sam hello, which left her momentarily speechless. Libby had the most perfect mouth. She daydreamed about it often.

"I did. But before you say anything, I thought through each and every one of these purchases like you advised me to and came to the conclusion that I could afford them because"—Libby took a deep breath—"I got the promotion."

"You did? Whoa." Sam covered her mouth in happily surprised mode. Those really were the best kind of surprises, the ones you weren't expecting. It wasn't just good news, it was great news. Libby had been pulling some killer hours lately to prove herself worthy to her boss, and Sam had said a silent daily prayer that her work wouldn't go unnoticed.

Libby sat a little taller. "You're looking at the newest full-fledged sales rep for Lioness Shoes. No more assistant duties. No more junior account rep status. No more second fiddle. Life just opened up."

Sam broke into a smile. She couldn't have been happier if it had been her own success. "I don't know what to say. Wow. This is fantastic. I'm so thrilled for you."

Libby beamed back. "I knew you would be. You're the one person I couldn't wait to tell, who I knew would understand. You're so smart and together and you've helped me get my ducks in a row, Sam. You know, it was your advice to chase down my goal that did it. Thank you."

The declaration resonated. Libby appreciated her, and that meant something to Sam. The smile tugged again, and her heart soared. "You don't have to thank me. I just know how awesome you are and what you're capable of."

"Aw, honey. You are just the sweetest." Then a look of apology crossed her face. "And I made you wait. I'm sorry. Maybe I can make it up to you later?"

"I'm sure we could find a way." Sam melted into the daydream before shaking herself out of it and shifting her glance to the packages. "So this was a bit of a celebratory shopping trip, then?"

"It was. I decided spring was noticeably absent from my wardrobe. And when you're a full-fledged sales rep in fashion, you have to stay up on trends." She pulled her shoulder-length blond hair into the shape of a bun and let it fall again in a way Sam found endearing. It was sort of Libby's thing, playing with her hair, shaping it into different styles absently. *Le sigh.*

"You have a ton of spring outfits that you happen to look great in. In fact, I don't think I've ever seen you duplicate one."

"Yes, but they're all very *last* spring, which is a problem." Libby eyed the closed laptop next to Samantha. "Working again? You never give yourself a break. And you deserve one."

"When you run your own firm, it's not exactly a nine-to-five."

"I get it, but I'd much rather see you reading whatever book you're toting around in that bag of yours today. I love it when you read. It's adorably nerdy how caught up you get in your stories. What do you have today?"

It was true. Samantha loved to read and devoted most any free moment she could find to some epic tale. Classics were her favorite, and more specifically, the great romances. She'd read *Pride and Prejudice* upward of fifteen times. She wasn't really particular about the settings or the time period, however. If there was a romantic tale woven in there somewhere, she was in. She reached into her bag and showed Libby her copy of *The Princess Bride.* She'd found a second edition on eBay and splurged. "I spent this morning before work with Westley and Buttercup."

Libby smiled. "I've seen the movie. Maybe I can borrow it when you finish."

"As you wish." Sam smiled, but the reference seemed lost on Libby. "At any rate, it's an easy one to get lost in. I had to force myself to stop earlier."

"You're such a romantic."

Samantha shrugged. "Something about two people destined to be together despite the obstacles they face just never gets old."

Libby sighed—the good kind, too. "I like that."

"Well, that makes two of us." The familiar Libby tingle arrived right on cue, and after basking in it for a moment, Sam refocused. "So tell me about the rest of your day."

"I met Tanya and a friend of hers after work and we went shopping in Chelsea. There's the cutest little boutique that just opened up. Oh, and Tanya wants us to celebrate my promotion tomorrow night at Splash, so don't make plans."

Sam set down her raspberry iced tea. "But tomorrow is the movie in the park with my friends, remember? They're running my favorite, *The Way We Were.* I've been looking forward to it for weeks."

Libby's face fell. "Oh no. I forgot about the movie. I'm sorry, honey bear. I told Tanya I was a definite to celebrate, and she's been having such a rough time lately after the breakup with that horror show of a chick, Heather. Do you remember Heather? *God.*" Sam opened her mouth to answer, but it had apparently been a rhetorical question. "I don't think I can back out on Tanya now. Maybe we can rent the movie next week? Just you and me. On the couch. Alone. Your friends will understand, don't you think? It's my promotion, after all. Kind of a big deal for me, and I want you there."

The overly hopeful expression on Libby's face rendered Sam helpless. She really was wrapped around Libby's little finger. Not that she was complaining. It was a pretty gorgeous finger. She sighed as the disappointment at not seeing the film washed over her. "If you promise that we'll actually watch it together."

Libby raised a victorious eyebrow. "Thursday. My place. We'll snuggle up on the couch with popcorn. I might even feed it to you. You have my word."

❖

"I can't believe you're not going to be there." Brooklyn sat atop the kitchen counter in the loft apartment they shared in Soho. Samantha and Brooklyn had been roommates for the past six years since they'd graduated from NYU and first opened Soho Savvy with their best friends Hunter and Mallory. "Who am I going to quote along with? We're the quote-along team, you and me. That's the best part. I may die."

"You won't die. You're just being super dramatic."

"I will. I might actually die," Brooklyn said, blinking back at her.

"Okay, no. Do not shoot me Bambi eyes. You know I can't take them." It was true, the Bambi eyes killed her soul.

Brooklyn blew out a breath. "Fine. No Bambi impersonations, but I'm in the depths of despair. Please make sure that's noted for posterity."

Sam thought on this, scurrying to find a solution. "Mallory loves the film. She can probably quote with you."

"But not like you and I do. No one's as good a Katie as you."

This was true. Sam batted her eyelashes, channeling Barbra Streisand. "I don't have the right style for you, do I?"

Brooklyn slid off the counter, not missing a beat. She stalked over to Sam, dropping her voice an octave. "No, you don't have the right style."

"I'll change."

"No, don't change. You're your own girl and have your own style."

"But then I won't have you." She brought a hand down in front of her face theatrically and bowed her head. "And, scene."

Brooklyn snagged an apple from the bowl on the counter and tossed her layered blond hair. "That was magic. We're magic. And now I'm even more bummed that the magic ends here. Don't desert me, Sammie-Sam."

It killed Sam to flake out on Brooklyn, but she didn't see another way. "It's an important week for Libby. She got that promotion and she wants to see her friends tonight to celebrate. Apparently, her best friend Tanya is having some kind of crisis."

"I get it. Just makes me sad," Brooklyn said. And she really did look the saddest of the sad.

"I know, but how many times have I gone somewhere without you lately so you and Jess can go off and stare into each other's eyes for hours on end?"

Brooklyn took on that dreamy, faraway look she got whenever someone mentioned her girlfriend, Jessica, who also happened to be the CEO of Savvy's biggest competitor. Luckily, they'd crafted little ways to work around the conflict of interest. "That's true. You've let us do lots of staring."

"And to her credit, Libby came out with us two weeks ago."

Brooklyn nodded. "And spent the whole night entranced by her phone. I think we bore her. I should try jokes. People can't resist my jokes."

"It's a fact. You excel at joke telling. But she's not bored with you, Brooks. It's just how she is. She's very social and wonders what her friends are up to. I get the feeling she was one of those ultra-popular girls in high school. Her social calendar is everything."

Brooklyn narrowed her gaze in speculation. "I can see that, yeah."

"In some ways, and I say this only to you, I can't believe she's with me. Think about it. Little miss stay home and do homework on a Saturday night in high school. I was salutatorian and had approximately two friends. Is it wrong that I feel somewhat accomplished at landing someone as amazing as Libby? Holding the attention of the popular girl?"

Brooklyn passed her a look and pulled her into an embrace. "It is wrong. It's backward, actually, because you always sell yourself short. And that wasn't a short joke, even though you're pocket-sized. You, best friend of mine, with your luscious auburn hair and shockingly green eyes, are worthy of Libby and a lot more, if I'm being frank."

"If you're Frank, then who do I get to be?"

Brooklyn cocked an eyebrow and grinned. "Funny. You're a very funny short person. I have to go stare at my gorgeous girlfriend for a while now because there's never enough of that."

"Kiss her cheek for me. But stop there."

Brooklyn looked wistful. "Not sure that's humanly possible, but I'll try." As she slid the loft door open, she practically collided with Mallory.

"Tell her she's awesome," Brooklyn said on her way out.

"Have I told you today that you're awesome?" Mallory said as she glided easily into the room. Mallory Spencer had a way of gliding. It was enviable. She looked elegant today in her crisp navy business suit and heels. Her dark brown hair was fastened with a clip in the back and her blue eyes sparkled with unfettered confidence, which signaled she'd just come from a meeting with a client.

"Nope. This is your first reference to my awesomeness, but I'll take it. What's new, boss?" Technically, Mallory wasn't her boss, but she was the glue that held Savvy together. Due to her polished persona and ability to organize the group, she acted as their CEO. She was also the face of the company, as she could schmooze with the best of them. It was a testament to why Savvy worked so well. Each of them brought a different strength to the table. Brooklyn was the creative force behind their ad campaigns, Sam did the books and managed the money, and Hunter was responsible for all the graphic art and web development. Together, they composed the well-oiled machine that was Soho Savvy. And after recently landing the Foster Foods account, they were getting lots of recognition.

Mallory seemed to hesitate. "I know it's after hours, but I thought we could chat about funds for a second."

"Sure. What do you want to know? Wine?"

Mallory checked her watch, the consummate rule follower. In good news, it was after five. "Definitely. Red if it's open." She slid into a chair at the table to the right of the kitchen as Sam poured two glasses of Cab. "How much wiggle room do we have in our monthly budget?"

Sam considered the question, tilting her head from side to side. She delivered the wine and took a seat across from Mallory. "There's room. Business has been on a big upswing lately and the steady cash flow has added a nice cushion. I'd like to keep it that way if possible. The idea is eventual expansion, and we'll need the capital."

"This came today." She slid an envelope across the table. "The building is raising our rent."

Unfortunately, this kind of thing was quite common in New York City. Sam took the envelope and checked out the news. It wasn't good. In fact, it was more the crawl-under-the-table-and-whimper-softly variety. "This is a twenty-five percent increase!"

"I caught that. Apparently, the rest of the world is picking up on what it is we like about this place. Soho real estate has become extra trendy and thereby extra expensive. Can we handle it?"

Sam sighed. "Let me crunch some numbers and explore a few options. We *can* afford it. It's just a matter of if we want to." And then another horrible thought came crashing down on her. "Is this a building-wide shift?" Savvy's office space was located just five floors below the loft she and Brooklyn shared. Before waiting for an answer, she scurried to the island where Brooklyn usually dropped the mail. And there it was, a duplicate envelope from the company that owned the loft space. "No. No. No," she said as she ripped into the envelope. But the verdict was the same. Her and Brooklyn's rent would jump exponentially in the coming months.

"Sorry, Sam. It's the same with my place." Mallory lived several floors up in a larger loft space of her own. "I guess we all have some decisions to make. Why don't we take some time with this before coming to any rash conclusions?"

But Sam already knew where her heart was, and it was with their apartment. The Savvy office. Their building. The operative word was *theirs*. And call her sentimental, but she didn't want to pack up and walk away from it all. She liked that her morning commute consisted of a short elevator ride down to the office, and what other building in New York, besides an artist's loft, offered that kind of zoning freedom? More importantly, there were memories attached to these walls. Valuable ones. Each room meant something to her for a different reason. It was home, and leaving just wasn't an option.

"We have to make it work, Mal. I think Brooklyn and Hunter will agree."

Mallory nodded. "I suppose we need to find out pretty quick. Midnight Chocolate?"

"Definitely. This is major, so right away. Tonight. I'll set it up."

Midnight Chocolate was their go-to method for solving any and all of life's problems. Inspired by that first night together in the village, they'd latched onto the practice and it had never let them down. Chocolate, wine, and pajamas could take down most anything, and at midnight, the combination had a way of producing some very honest conversation. A fail-safe that never let them down.

Sam crossed her proverbial fingers that they'd come to the same conclusion. It was too important not to.

❖

"Okay. Now take a few deep and cleansing breaths as you move into Downward Dog." Hunter Blair followed the yoga instructor's directions and extended forward onto her hands, feeling her muscles lengthen in the most wonderful way. With just that gentle tug, the stresses of the week began to wash off her one at a time. Yoga could be counted on to wake her body in a way that nothing else really could. Simply put, she loved it. "Hold there. Draw your belly button toward your spine. Keep your leg muscles active, alert."

God, she needed this. The soft sounds of the background music floated past her and through her, completing the experience.

"And now walk your feet in slowly toward your hands."

It occurred to Hunter that April, the yoga instructor du jour, had the most calming voice ever. She generally attended the six o'clock class, but the eight thirty was taking on new and attractive meaning. Given this sexy turn of events, maybe it was time for a change. Nighttime yoga seemed to have a whole separate appeal. A happy accident, due to the fact that her schedule had been wildly off-kilter lately.

In an annoying development, her sublet was up on the studio apartment she rented in the Meatpacking District, and because she'd procrastinated, she now needed to figure out something fast. Unless, of course, she was okay with being homeless on the streets of New York. As it turned out, she wasn't. Unfortunately, her laid-back attitude had come back to bite her once again. It was a lesson she hoped she'd learn one day. Unfortunately, the damage was done and apartment hunting was eating up a ton of her time, and the little things, like her twice-a-week yoga class, were falling by the wayside. Annoying, especially since she'd yet to find anything.

"Inhale as you extend your hands over your head. Exhale as you bring them down and to your heart. Namaste."

"Namaste," Hunter answered back in unison with the group. The class was over, but as was her custom, she took a minute on her mat, ending her session with some final cleansing breaths. By the time she stood, most of the other students had filed out.

"I haven't seen you here before." Hunter glanced up to find the instructor, April, addressing her.

"No, you're right. I generally hit up the six o'clock class, but I thought I'd try something new. I enjoyed it. Thank you."

April, of the short, layered hair and fantastically toned body, flashed a smile. "I'm glad you came. Maybe we'll see you here again."

"I'd like that."

"I'm April, by the way." She extended her hand and Hunter accepted it. Firm handshake. Impressive. Kinda sexy.

"I remember. You told us at the start of class. I'm Hunter."

"Interesting name. I like it."

"It was my grandmother's maiden name. Thanks again for class. See you next time." Hunter picked up her bag, tucked her mat under her arm, and headed toward the door.

"Do you get out much, Hunter?"

Aha. She turned back and studied April with interest, very familiar with where this was all heading. "On occasion. What about you?"

"I get out, too." April looked thoughtful and then, as if she'd made a snap decision, grabbed a pad. "I don't normally do this, but…what the hell." She scribbled something down, ripped out the page, and handed it to Hunter. "In case you're ever looking for company. I never do this, by the way. Did I already say that? God, I did. And now I'm awkward. Perfect." Her hand flew to her forehead. It was cute.

"Not at all." Hunter flashed the smile she reserved for moments like these and beautiful girls like this one. She held up the piece of paper, her eyes lingering in a way that prompted April's lips to part subtly. It was kind of a gift. "I'll hold on to this. You have a great night."

"You, too." She could feel April's eyes on her as she walked away, heard her exhale quietly as Hunter pushed open the door.

Getting hit on wasn't anything new.

She'd attracted attention from both sexes since she was sixteen years old and first came into herself physically. Genetics had been good to her. She'd be lying if she said she didn't enjoy the attention, and maybe even encouraged it. As a result, she'd obtained a reputation as a flirt in the lesbian community. A player, some called her. Who was she to argue? She happened to enjoy women and spending time with them. Not exactly a crime. She preferred the no-strings-attached model to all of the coupling up everyone else seemed so intent on.

Life was too short for boring.

But she had rules. She didn't lead women on, and she didn't make promises she couldn't keep. Those things were important to her. She wasn't into hurting feelings. Ever.

By the time Hunter hit the sidewalk, night had descended on the city. She pulled the ponytail holder from her hair and let the jet-black strands fall loosely down her back, giving it an effective shake. She shrugged into the long sweater and held it tightly against her five-seven frame, grateful that it would keep her warm against the chilly night air.

As she walked, Hunter took a deep breath, enjoying the savory aroma wafting from a street vendor's cart she passed. She loved the city at night. And New York had a vibe like no other place. Something about it just felt so dynamic, like there was something important happening around each and every corner. It thrummed with a pulse all its own, which was one of the reasons she planned to live in Manhattan for as long as she could.

Typically, she spent her evening hours at a bar, a club, or in the company of a beautiful woman. Talking, flirting, or, once in a while, a more intimate exchange. She smiled, wondering what the night would bring. She liked to keep her options open.

As the light changed and the Walk sign flashed, Hunter checked her phone and was greeted with the usual string of text messages crowding her screen. She skimmed them briefly. Melanie. Tricia. Kara. Deanne. Her dry cleaner. Nothing overly important, except the last text: a note from Samantha calling a Midnight Chocolate. Huh. That snagged her attention. She wondered what was up. Her three best friends were the most important people in the world, and no one called a Midnight Chocolate unless there was something pressing at hand. So it was decided. She'd be there. The rest could wait.

Hunter paused at the corner a moment, typed back her acceptance, and headed down the stairs to the subway to catch the C train home. Her studio was quiet when she arrived home, and her one and only roommate, Elvis, her terrier-corgi mix and the coolest dog on the planet, jumped down from the Barcelona chair he'd been sleeping on and turned in half a dozen frenzied circles at her feet. He really was all about the celebrating. She leaned down to pat his head and scratch his stomach, which earned her a few well-placed swipes of his tongue across her cheek. Instead of getting up and carrying on with her evening, she decided to chill on the floor with him a little longer.

"How was your day, Elvis? Sell any stock?"

He whined back at her.

"That doesn't sound good. Maybe the market will be stronger tomorrow. Don't lose sleep over it, stud."

He pawed her knee for more petting. She could oblige. She'd found Elvis locked in a small dog run at the city pound four years prior. He was an hour and a half from being put down. One snap decision later, she'd busted him from death row and had an instant new partner in crime. Elvis and Hunter taking on New York. That's how she'd come to think of them. Elvis was the best decision she'd made in her life.

"All right, sir," she said and placed a kiss behind Elvis's ear. "We need to start organizing some of this stuff for a quick move."

She surveyed the studio. Dark, sparse, and quiet. She had her design desk against the wall, and various images she used for creative inspiration were pinned to the boards around it in a haphazard conglomeration. Her sketchpad stood on an easel next to the desk and her acoustic guitar was propped in the corner. She didn't have a lot of furniture, but that was on purpose. Hunter wasn't really someone who lounged a lot. Too much to go out and do in the world. So the black Barcelona chair and the sculpted blue love seat were enough. Above the sitting area, the walls were adorned with metal art, some she'd purchased and some she'd created herself. As her eyes drifted across the brightly colored twisted metallic brambles, she stared down at the platform bed and all of its glorious memories. Many a night she'd enjoyed with various women, faceless in her mind now, but important all the same. It was a very specific kind of space. But it was hers and she'd be sad to see it go.

She began to take down the printed images from above her desk and organized them into piles of those to keep and those to trash. There was something cathartic about the process. Like maybe she was ready for a new place and this was just the fire she needed to get out there and find something a bit more mature. She was getting older, after all, which was cool in a whole separate way. In a year and a half, she'd be thirty. Maybe it was time for her to settle down some, find a different rhythm. Buy some matching dish towels. She laughed out loud at the thought. Probably not.

"One step at a time, right, Elvis?"

He glanced up from project rawhide in what seemed to be agreement.

And that's when it hit her.

This feeling that overtook everything, causing the smile to fade from her face as it grabbed hold. She wasn't at all into premonitions and she certainly didn't have the ability to predict the future, but signs and inklings had always been very prominent in her life and she'd learned to pay attention when they struck.

She sank into her desk chair and closed her eyes. Though she couldn't put her finger on it, it felt distinctly like something big was about to happen. Like that ultra-still scene in *Mary Poppins* right before the weather changes. She didn't know what it was, or what she should do to prepare, but something out of reach was on its way to her.

That much she knew.

CHAPTER TWO

It was five minutes to midnight when Samantha opened the wine. A bottle of red for herself and Hunter, and a bottle of white for Brooklyn and Mallory.

Generally, the wine opening was Brooklyn's job, but she'd been a little MIA lately. Sam had waited until a quarter to midnight, but her roommate had yet to show. *Cut her some slack*, Sam reminded herself, *she's in the pretty and sparkly land of new relationships*.

In actuality, she could relate.

She lived there too lately and it was awesome. She reflected on Libby and her gorgeous hair and sparkling blue eyes and smiled when she remembered her promotion news from earlier. It felt good to be in a relationship. And with Libby, no less, who was clearly a huge catch. She sighed happily. She should pick up some daisies for Libby tomorrow, a congratulatory gesture. And maybe there'd be some other extracurricular activities later that night.

The loft door slid open at record speed as Brooklyn, clearly doing her Roger Rabbit impersonation, raced in. "Sorry, I'm late. I'll get the wine. Oh, you got the wine. Excellent. I'll get the Oreos."

"They're already on the coffee table."

"Malted milk balls?"

Sam nodded. "Check."

"And the—"

"Done. M&M's. Chocolate-covered pretzels. Ice cream toppings, including hot fudge. And two kinds of ice cream in the freezer. All assembled and ready for consumption. Voilà." She handed Brooklyn a glass of white wine.

"Oh." Brooklyn stared at the wine and seemed to let her brain catch up before turning and surveying the coffee table in wonder. "We always prep for the MCs together. And I made you do everything. I'm sorry I was late, Sammie."

"'Sokay," Sam answered with a smile. "You're in love. It's what happens. Plus, it wasn't that much work."

Brooklyn eased onto a bar stool at the counter. "You're the greatest of the great, you know that? And dependable. I feel like I can always count on you."

"Don't forget the cute one. I'm also that."

"Duh. Just look at you. Five feet two-inches of adorable."

Adorable. Cute. Dependable. Those were words she was comfortable with and used to hearing. They were the adjectives people often employed to describe her. Given, they weren't as exciting as *alluring* or *mysterious* or *sexy*, but she was fine with that.

As she carried a second tray full of treats to the coffee table, she caught her reflection looking back at her. Medium-length auburn hair, which she then tucked behind her left ear instinctually, and dark green eyes. You'd think she was of Irish descent based on the color combination, but her dad's family was from Poland and her mom had Native American ties. So it was really just a fluke of her parents' combined DNA. No one else in her family had auburn hair, and since she was an only child, there were no siblings to compare with. Her height, however, was a direct pass-down from her mother. No female relative on that side of the family had ever bypassed the five-five mark. All in all, Sam knew she was a decent-looking girl, pretty enough, but she'd never thought of herself as a major head turner. She was the type who kept her head down and got things done. And there was nothing wrong with that. In fact, others respected her for it.

"So are you going to tell me what this is all about?"

Sam turned to face Brooklyn. "The MC? Definitely. Once the others arrive."

Brooklyn pointed energetically at the sliding loft door and their two friends entering together. "Now?"

"Almost. You're kind of five years old right now, you should know this."

Mallory rounded the island. "Brooklyn's five?"

Sam nodded. "She is. Super impatient."

"But a likeable five-year-old," Hunter said and kissed Brooklyn's cheek.

Brooklyn grinned at the compliment. "Aw, I can live with five, then." She studied Hunter's look. "But I have to hate you. Since when do you have all-black cool pajamas? Why don't I have all-black cool pajamas?"

Hunter shrugged. "No one is stopping you."

Samantha poured wine for the new arrivals. "We're not as cool as Hunter. It's a cosmic rule and thereby fruitless to try. We'll crash and burn a fiery fashion death."

"Thanks, Sam," Hunter said, kissing her cheek, too. "You're my favorite."

"Easy come, easy go," Brooklyn sighed.

But it was a fact of life. Hunter was blessed with the gift of effortless style. She could take an outfit that would look extreme or tragic on someone else and make it chic and sexy. Even dressed down, Hunter managed to look gorgeous. While the three of them came dressed in a variety of plaid pajama pants and tank tops, Hunter came in slender fitting black crop sweatpants and black cami top that elongated her slender torso and brought out the sleekness of her five-seven frame. Her hair was down tonight and fell in luxurious dark waves down her back, but it was a surefire bet that she'd wear it in an entirely new and equally impressive style tomorrow, and then change it up daily to keep the world guessing. She was a master of diverse hairstyles. The sum of it all was that Hunter snagged the attention of pretty much everyone when she walked in a room, and it was fun for Sam to watch it happen.

"*Jane Eyre*?" Hunter asked Sam, lifting the battered book from where it rested on the end table.

Sam lit up. "Yep. That was last week. Finishing *The Princess Bride* now."

"I have a feeling they're going to end up together," Hunter said dryly.

"And what's wrong with that?" Sam asked.

Hunter regarded her. "Nothing. If you like boring and predictable."

Sam's mouth fell open. "I can't believe you just said that. There is nothing boring about happily ever after."

Mallory tilted her head and looked to Samantha. "Do you ever worry that all of these romances you read will set you up with a false notion of what to expect from real life?"

Samantha smiled at Mallory being Mallory. Realistic and levelheaded. Sam had always been more of a dreamer type. It was why she and Brooklyn got along so well. She liked living on the optimistic side of life as long as it made sense to. "If you would just agree to go on a few dates once in a while, maybe you'd find your Princess Charming," Sam said.

Mallory considered this as she sipped her wine. "While exciting in theory, that sounds like a lot of work, and I happen to have very high standards."

"Yeah, yeah," Samantha said, nodding. "I've heard it all before, Spencer. But one day, love is going to smack you in the face."

Mallory shrugged. "Well, I hope it's a bit more gentle in its execution than that."

In comfy pajamas with wine in hand, the girls settled around the coffee table and all of the fantastic, delectable goodness that came with Midnight Chocolate.

Samantha decided to jump right in. "So I'm sure you're curious as to why I called an MC, and I'm afraid the news isn't great." She located the notice from the end table and passed it to Hunter for reference. "As Mallory is aware, we received notice from the building that they're raising our rent. And not just any raise, a major hike that will affect our bottom line quite a bit."

"Whoa," Brooklyn said. She accepted the notice from Hunter and leaned back against the couch from her spot on the floor. "What does that mean for us?"

Mallory jumped in. "Essentially, that's what we have to decide. How important is the loft to Savvy's continued success?"

"The loft is part of us," Hunter said. "It's where we make everything happen. That space is important, at least from a creative standpoint. You agree, Brooks?"

"Absolutely. I like to stare at the little gray spot on the brick when I brainstorm. The little gray spot sees me through. The gray spot inspires me."

"Okay," Mallory said, smiling at Brooklyn's confession. "It's our home. And the little gray spot is important."

Brooklyn held up a finger. "It's landed us lots of accounts."

"But it doesn't mean we can't make the next place our home, too," Mallory said. "Find you a new spot on the wall to stare at. We have to keep our heads about us. This is a twenty-five percent increase, and the rent in this neighborhood was already incredibly steep."

"Do we have the money?" Brooklyn asked, dropping the notice and turning to Sam.

"We do. But it will definitely cut into the plans we have."

"No. This isn't right. They can't do this to us," Brooklyn said. "We should draft a letter. Mallory, draft a letter. You're scary."

"Thanks, I think," Mallory said. "Unfortunately, it's gonna take more than a businesslike letter. If we want to stay, we have to fork over the cash."

"Then let's do that," Hunter said. "Seems like a no-brainer to me."

Thank God someone else thought so. Sam sighed in relief internally. "I agree with Hunter. I want to stay. The money will be rough, but I can see what kind of magic I can work in other areas. Maybe there are cuts to be made elsewhere."

Brooklyn squeezed her knee. "I have faith in you, Sammie Sam. You're a numbers badass. I'm with them," Brooklyn said, pointing at Samantha and Hunter. "Let's do it. Let's stay."

Mallory raised her wineglass. "A four-way agreement. It sounds like we have a plan. That wasn't so painful after all. And hey, there's chocolate."

"Calorie-free chocolate," Brooklyn said, twisting an Oreo. "There are no calories if consumed after midnight."

"There is one other thing to consider, Brooklyn," Mallory said, sitting a little taller. "This affects rent for the three of us as well. It's a building-wide increase."

Suddenly the Oreo stalled in midair. "Oh." Brooklyn swiveled her focus to Sam. "Of course. I don't know why that didn't occur to me."

"It's okay," Samantha said. "I did the same thing. The building wants to know by the end of the month if we want to sign a lease for another year. I know I don't want to leave, but you live here, too. You have a say."

Brooklyn's eyes were wider than usual, that much Sam was clear on. She looked caught, like an innocent rabbit backed into a corner by some hunters. Brooklyn's gaze moved to Mallory and then Hunter before settling on the coffee table. Okay, something was definitely up.

"Brooklyn, what is it? Is there something on your mind?" she asked.

"Not exactly. But…well, the other day…"

Mallory stepped in. "Brooks, you can tell us."

"I know. I just…"

"Say it fast," Hunter offered. "Whenever I have trouble saying something, I find it's best to just race through it."

Brooklyn nodded and took a breath. "Jessica asked me to move in with her."

And there it was.

Samantha sat back in her chair. "Oh. Okay. Well, that's great, Brooks."

But it wasn't.

It was horrible.

She knew it would happen at some point, the way Brooklyn and Jessica had taken to each other, but she figured it'd be down the road a ways. She was great at deluding herself, it seemed.

"Are you going to do it?" Mallory asked.

Brooklyn squeezed the bridge of her nose and then raised her eyes to Sam. Clearly, this was hard for her. "I was leaning that way. It seems like the next step in our relationship. I sleep over there so much as it is, and now with the lease in question, I think it might be the perfect time to take her up on it, make it official. What do you think, Sam? I don't want to leave you in a tough spot."

What was she supposed to say here? *You're my best friend. Please don't leave?* Instead she did the mature thing despite the desperate pang of sadness that was already settling. "I think you should do it." And while she tried to muster a supportive friend smile for Brooklyn's sake, it was quite a challenge. She didn't want her to move out. They were Brooklyn and Sam. This was Brooklyn and Sam's *place.* That was the way things were. This was life as she knew it, and she didn't want it to change.

"Really?" Brooklyn asked, hope now present in her eyes—all the more confirmation that she was doing the right thing.

"Really."

Mallory sent her a sympathetic gaze, one that said she understood what was racing through Sam's head. She had always been the one in the group capable of seeing the big picture, and she surely knew what this would do to Samantha. "Does that mean you'll look for a new place, Sam?"

She glanced around the loft. The idea of packing up her things and moving somewhere else was enough to make her physically ache. She couldn't do that. She simply could not. She loved the loft. "I don't want to leave," she said candidly. "I guess I need to advertise for a roommate to make up the other half of the rent."

Hunter had a thought and raised her hand tentatively. "I think I might have a suggestion." All eyes were on her. She turned to Samantha. "How would you feel about rooming with me?" The words were out of Hunter's mouth before she'd fully thought them through, but honestly, it wasn't a bad idea. Sam needed a roommate. She needed a roof over her head.

"Whoa. Really? You'd consider that?" Sam asked. But there was a smile on her face, like someone had just thrown her a life preserver. "I mean, I think that would be great. The idea of living with a stranger is kind of terrifying."

Hunter nodded and continued to mull over the possibility. "It would certainly shorten my trip to work every day. And I can vibe with this place. I've always liked it here."

Samantha bopped herself in the forehead. "That's right. I totally blanked that you've been looking for a place."

"Perfect timing," Brooklyn said. "The way that matched up."

Mallory nodded. "It really is. Almost like it was meant to happen this way." Hunter thought of the feeling that had come over her back at her place and couldn't help but wonder if that was the case. Life had a funny way of laying a path out in front of you.

"What's your timeline? How soon do you need to be out of your studio?" Samantha asked her.

She winced apologetically. "End of next week."

Mallory stared at her, mystified. "You like to cut it close."

Hunter smiled and sat back against the couch. "Correction. I like to keep it interesting. It's just how I am."

Brooklyn blew out a breath. "I'll call Jess and get it set up. Sounds like we have some work to do. But later, okay? Pass me the hot fudge. The chocolate and I need to have a fancy love affair."

❖

By the next day at work, Hunter still wasn't sure why she'd done it.

It'd been an impulsive move, offering to share the loft with Samantha. But there was something about the timing of it all that made it seem somehow meant to be. The logic was simple. Samantha was one of her favorite people on the planet. She needed a roommate. Hunter needed somewhere to live. Surely there was something to that. Why shouldn't they live together?

Maybe because she hadn't lived with another human since college and was about as independent as they came? But she could learn to cohabitate like a mature individual. And shouldn't that be the short-term goal? Aspiring to new heights of maturity? Adult behavior firmly in practice? Well, within reason anyway.

She was proud of herself for snatching up the opportunity, actually. This could turn out to be a really good thing. When she thought about it, Sam was the most organized person she knew. Maybe some of that order and structure would rub off on her.

"Hunter, do you have the color layout for the Foster account?" Mallory said, pulling her from her contemplation.

She blinked up at Mallory, replaying the question over again. "Um…yeah. I emailed it to you maybe fifteen minutes ago."

"Perfect. I'll take a look." But Mallory wasn't done. She perched on the edge of Hunter's desk and lingered a moment. "So we're gonna be actual neighbors, you and me. I have to say I'm surprised. This is kind of a big deal. You infiltrating Soho full-time."

"Seems that way. Tell me, do fifteenth-floor dwellers hang out with eleventh-floor dwellers? Are there gangs? Secret handshakes? I feel like I have a lot to learn about the higher levels. My experience level stops at the sixth floor, and I want to be prepared."

Mallory grinned and snagged a paper clip to unfold. "Oh, there's a lot to learn. And I can't promise the hazing won't be intense. Elevator bunny ears, cryptic notes slipped under your door, window washers with a penchant for flashing. Gear up, Hunter Blair, it's on."

Hunter shrugged dryly. "Sounds like another one of my Thursdays."

Mallory threw a glance over her shoulder toward Samantha's desk. As Sam had yet to return from lunch, she pressed on. "So are you going to do okay with a roommate? I mean, Samantha's the ultimate sweetheart, but you've lived on your own for years. And she does like things a certain way. Order and structure and all that. A little like me. Not at all like you."

"I'll be fine," Hunter said. "Plus, Sam is in Libby-la-la land lately. I mean, have you seen her? She stares at nothing and smiles. Draws hearts on her Post-Its. It's textbook and a little sickening. The way I figure it, she probably won't even be around that much."

"You actually have a point there. Plus, you guys have always gotten along great. Maybe no wild parties for the first month, though? She may not recover."

Hunter leaned back in her chair and grinned. "No promises."

"I had a feeling you'd say that. Shall we reconvene for any necessary tweaking of the Foster layout after lunch?"

"I'll see if I can pencil you in."

Mallory backed away, palms up. "That's all I'm askin'."

Hunter turned back to the multitude of lines and shapes on her laptop and lost herself in the drag-and-drop action of Photoshop, a program she'd mastered five times over. Images and their arrangements, their composition, had always intrigued her. The way a slight shift in color was capable of inspiring a whole new emotion in the person taking it in.

Hunter could stare at a painting for hours and still continue to see it in new ways. Dissect the shadow. Examine the contrast. Decipher the meaning behind the curvature of a line. She had no formal artistic training other than her graphic design degree, but the visual arts always intrigued her in a way nothing else did. Her job at Savvy was the perfect outlet for that. As an advertising agency, they worked with a variety of clients and products, and that allowed for a diversity of artistic approaches, styles, and design conglomerations. She loved her job, and she loved that it challenged her in new ways every day.

She flipped open her MacBook Pro just as her phone buzzed in her back pocket. She smiled at the photo of her mother indicating the incoming call. She clicked over. "Hi, Mama. This is a nice surprise. Did you get bored with your other two children?"

Her mother chuckled. "Hi, my baby girl. How's your Friday?"

"Peachy. Two more hours of work and then there's a movie festival that my friends want to go to in the park. *The Way We Were*, I think. One of those old ones you would love. I plan to tolerate it."

"Robert Redford. Barbra Streisand. It's fantastic. Give it a chance."

"Don't I always?"

"No, you don't. But speaking of always, I haven't heard from you in over a week, *nani kaikamahine*." Hunter smiled at the term of endearment meaning "beautiful daughter." Her mother was born and raised on Oahu, Hawaii, and met her father when he was stationed at Hickam Air Force base nearby. Though her parents now resided in Dayton, Ohio, the islands were never far from her mother's mind. Growing up, they'd visited Oahu once every other year or so, but it was hard on her mom, being so far away from the rest of her family.

"It's been a busy week, Mama. I've been meaning to call."

"Mean harder next time. We miss you."

"You do?"

"We were just talking about how long it's been since we've had a Hunter Jane sighting."

Even though her parents were still married, Hunter knew the term "we" was limited to her mother, her older sister, Claire, and her younger brother, Kevin. Her father...yeah, not so much. The guy wasn't overly warm to any of his children, but he had a special kind of aversion to Hunter. And it was fine with her. She wasn't his biggest fan either. Mutual apathy at its finest. While he had never been the kind of dad who attended her soccer games or took her trick-or-treating, when she'd come out at sixteen, it had been the last straw. The slim thread that existed between them was severed. Her sexuality must have made him wildly uncomfortable, and he pretty much quit engaging with her altogether. It was a big deal if the two of them said hello when in the same room. So her father was an aloof asshole. It was a part of life. She certainly didn't lose sleep over it. It wasn't like she was the first one in history with that problem.

"Maybe I can make it home for July Fourth. Claire will probably plan something for everyone not even remotely related to the holiday, and I can't miss that." Her sister had a habit of missing the point a lot.

"She's already talking about a sixties-themed BBQ party."

"Of course she is."

"It would make me very happy to see you on the Fourth, but I was actually hoping for sooner than that. How about your father's birthday?"

Hunter took a breath and tried to figure out how best to navigate this one. Her mother was always in perpetual "heal the family" mode.

She couldn't fault her for trying, but if there was one thing she knew for certain, it was that she and her father were never going to be okay. And her presence on his birthday was a really bad idea. "I don't think I can make it. That's in just a few weeks."

"You can make it if you really wanted to. For me, Hunter. I don't ask a lot."

It was true. But this was too big a request for her to wrap her mind around. "Mama, please don't. It's best just to leave well enough alone. Trust me, it will be a better party for him if I'm not there."

"Will you think about it?" The hope in her mother's voice tugged at her.

"I already did."

"Okay." She sounded so defeated, and Hunter couldn't help but hate herself a little bit for it.

"I'll see what I can do about July Fourth, though."

"See that you do. I'll talk to you soon. Make sure you're eating. Read a good book. And find someone to fall in love with."

Hunter smiled in recognition of the advice. The same three sentences her mother always left her with. One and two were easy enough. But three was a little lofty. She smiled internally at the pun. Love was overrated. She watched how it controlled people, dulled them in a way she wasn't at all keen on. But for her mother's benefit, she swallowed the opinion. "On it. As always. I'll call soon, Mama. I promise. I love you."

"I love you too, Hunter."

They ended the call and Hunter snagged a Twizzler from her desk drawer, checking number one off her mother's list.

❖

Friday night at a club in Chelsea, and Sam felt a little underdressed. When Libby had informed her of their destination that night, she'd honestly been a little tentative. Outside of Showplace, the nightspot she and her own friends frequented, she didn't get out to many clubs. Loud music and wild dancing wasn't really her scene. She'd always been more of a coffee and quiet conversation kind of girl.

But she was excited for tonight, as it was a celebratory occasion for her very deserving girlfriend, whom she was beyond proud of. So she could suck up the intimidation. Cut loose a little if that was the kind of evening Libby had in mind. She'd even brought her daisies and presented them to her when she'd arrived at Libby's apartment earlier in the evening.

Upon seeing them, Libby's eyes had widened and she'd covered her mouth. "Samantha Ennis, you're the sweetest, most thoughtful girlfriend ever. This makes me feel so special." Libby's blue eyes sparkled and Sam's knees went all soft and weak. The reward had been a kiss that had made the purchase all the more worth it. Moments later, Libby's best friend, Tanya, had arrived with an entourage made up of both men and women, most of whom Sam only knew peripherally. Beautiful and sophisticated, these people.

"Samantha, you're here!" Smooches.

"Is this *the* Samantha? Libby's mentioned you several times." Smooches.

"Look at you. You're just what Libby described. Adorable." Smooches.

"That's a darling dress on you." Smooches.

Sam grinned and laughed and smooched more than she'd ever smooched. Turned out she was a world-class smoocher. But in shocking news, she kinda liked it, the attention from these people who looked like they'd leapt off the pages of a trendy magazine. So for the next hour, she small-talked and laughed and sipped the Pinot Grigio that seemed to flow faster by the minute.

"You having a good time?" Libby asked her as the group poured onto the street. Sam estimated that they would need roughly four cabs to get to Splash, the club Tanya had selected for their outing. Always calculating, it seemed.

She turned to Libby. "I am. I haven't spent a lot of time with your friends. It's like this window into your world."

"And what do you think so far?"

She stared up at Libby, her heart squeezing that it mattered. "I think they seem about as awesome as you are. I like your world. It's fancy."

"Now I have to kiss you."

Sam glanced skyward. "My life is so hard."

After a little on-the-curb lip action, Samantha glanced over her shoulder to see that no one was actually taking the necessary steps to hail the cabs they needed. She was going to have to take matters into her own hands and organize this thing. Beautiful or not, these people needed someone like her if they had any hope of getting anywhere.

An hour later, and Sam looked on as throngs of twenty- to thirty-somethings jumped around the crowded dance floor at Splash. From the DJ stand on an elevated stage, a woman with green hair and giant headphones held court, blasting the place with a hypnotic beat that never seemed to end. Bangle bracelets, bare shoulders, and midriffs abounded. In contrast, her outfit was now noticeably bland. She'd worn a simple, sleeveless peach cocktail dress with what she now realized had a boring neckline. At home, she'd thought she looked pretty, somewhat chic. Here, her look could best be described as "on the steps of the convent." Mental note: she would need to invest in some edgier clothes. Maybe Hunter could help.

"You gonna dance?" Tanya shouted in her ear. They'd spent a handful of evenings with Tanya and she seemed fun enough. She was some sort of massage therapist, from what Sam understood. She also had killer moves, and they were right there on display as she spoke to Sam, sashaying easily to the music. Sam had no idea how to make her hips work that way.

"I think I'll work up to it," she told Tanya. A lie. She wasn't going to work up to anything. How was Sam going to explain that she was the world's worst dancer? It was one thing to dance with her closest friends at Showplace, where she could make fun of herself and cut loose and have a goofy time doing it. It was quite another to advertise her lack of any coordination in front of *People*'s 50 Most Beautiful People. "I'm probably going to kick back for a while. Hang out by the bar. You guys go ahead," she said to Tanya and Libby.

"But I want to dance with you tonight," Libby purred in her ear. Okay, that was hard to resist, especially when her stomach went all flip-floppy like that, but Samantha reminded herself of the facts. They'd been a full-fledged couple for only two and a half months now, and that could be completely undone if Libby saw her dance. It was that tragic a display.

"I'll dance with you," Tanya said to Libby.

Bless that girl. Bless her. "Perfect. You two dance. I'll order us more drinks," Sam said.

Libby seemed to warm to the idea, if her cozy proximity was any indication. "You sure you don't mind? I don't want to leave you by yourself. How about I stay with you?"

"Pshhh. Of course not. Join your friends. I'll be over here. You know, holding up the bar." Samantha made a ridiculous bar-holding gesture that she quickly regretted. From her facial expression, Libby seemed to think it was cute, so there was that.

An hour and a half later, bar holding had lost its appeal. While Sam looked on, Libby and her friends danced, laughed, danced some more, and once in a while returned to Sam's neck of the woods for a quick drink before tearing up the dance floor once again. These people could seriously party.

But the smile she kept on her face out of peripheral enjoyment was fading. By standing on the sidelines, she was missing out on the fun. Once again, she was on the outside looking in. Story of her adolescence.

Time for Plan B. She decided to pep talk herself. What would Suze Orman say? She would tell her to get her ass on the dance floor and live a little, that's what. And maybe take out an IRA.

"I'll have whatever he's having," she shouted to the bartender, pointing at the frat guy next to her downing a shot of purplish liquid. Purple meant grape, right? She loved grape. She tossed the drink back and oh my God, it burned like crazypants on its way down. *Not grape. Not grape. Not grape.* How did people do this? Good God. Didn't matter. She'd done it.

Relying on her newfound liquid courage, Samantha headed onto the dance floor and joined the group.

"Sam's here," one of the guys yelled, prompting the whole group to loudly cheer as they bumped and grinded and worked the dance floor like it was their job. The song was fast paced and loud, but Sam didn't care. She joined in, tossing her hands in the air and moving her hips subtly. Then Libby's hands were on her, and they were dancing together under the colorful strobe lights. And what could be better? The more she danced, the more her inhibitions floated away on the wings of a nice purple drink sent from the magical land of Deceptively Fruity Alcohol. She might or might not have been on beat, but the subtlety fell from her movements and she danced for all she was worth. She stepped on a toe here or there, but no one seemed to care. They were all out there together having the best time. They sang to the music at the top of their lungs and let the pulsing bass wash over them completely. All that mattered was the here and now.

And she was part of it.

She was present.

The night had just turned fun.

As the group cheered her on, she moved from person to person, dancing, laughing, and feeling like she owned the night. After what seemed like forever, she danced her way back to Libby, taking her hand and pulling her into the corner.

"I love that you're having a good time," Libby said in her ear above the pulse of the music.

The word *love*, while not the operative word in the sentence, snagged Sam's attention. Because she *was* falling in love with this woman and all that she brought to Sam's life. She wasn't ready to say it to Libby yet. There'd be time soon enough. Maybe over a quiet dinner next week. Some romantic lighting. Champagne. And the three words. *I love you.* Perfection.

"I *am* having a good time," she told Libby. "The best, actually. This was a good idea."

Libby kissed her then and she sank into it. "And you're not still upset about the film festival?"

At the mention, her spirits dipped, but only a tad, as she thought about Brooklyn, Hunter, and Mallory watching one of her favorite flicks without her just across town. "I wish we could have done both, but you make sacrifices when you're in a relationship."

Libby looked thoughtful, distant even. "You do, don't you?"

"Enough with the philosophical talk. Let's dance like crazy people."

Libby laughed. "Party-time Samantha is cute. I hope I get to see more of her. Let's get back to it."

And they did. They danced well into the morning hours, inhibitions thrown to the wind. It was a rarity for Sam. And you know what? It was one of the best nights she could remember having. She'd let go and it had paid off. Plus, she had Libby by her side. What more could a girl ask for?

❖

Please no hangover, were the first words that drifted into the forefront of Samantha's mind when her eyes fluttered open on Saturday morning. She took stock. No pounding headache, her stomach felt okay, and whoa, even sitting up was a total success. The eight glasses of water she'd consumed before bed had clearly done the trick. She owed Google a thank-you note and a fruit basket.

A quick clock check—quarter to nine. Excellent.

She'd come back to the loft the night prior because today was phase one of moving day for Brooklyn, and as sad as that made her, there was no way Brooklyn was going to be capable of organizing this move on her own. Awesome as her friend was, structure was not part of her vocabulary. For the past five years, the loft had easily been divided with Samantha's neat and orderly room to the right of the living space, and Brooklyn's cluttered chaos to the left.

She brushed her teeth, washed her face, and flipped on the radio, spending the next few minutes quickly unloading the dishwasher as she kept time to the music. Routine was everything. She lived and died by it. As Katy Perry roared from the speakers in the corner of the room, Sam bopped along. She was still riding the high of the fantastic night prior. Proud of herself for getting out of her comfort zone, she looked forward to telling Brooklyn all about it.

Sam did a quick mental calculation. She'd have time to shower, finish unloading the dishwasher, and down a quick breakfast before Brooklyn would be back from her morning run with Mallory. They could start sorting through her things then and have decent progress by midafternoon.

"Taking calls now from our lovelorn line," the morning show DJ announced as Sam turned the knob for the shower. "We have Tricia on the line. What's amiss in your love life, Tricia? Doctor Loooove is in the studio waiting to make it all better."

Samantha rolled her eyes and headed into her bedroom to select an outfit.

"Yes. Hi. I'm pretty sure I'm in love but can't seem to tell the person." Whoa. Sam paused, jeans draped across her arm. The voice was strikingly familiar. But there was no way. Was there?

"Do you think he feels the same way?" Doctor Love asked in a voice that was so low it was borderline ridiculous.

"It's a she, actually. I'm in love with a girl. And yes, I tend to think she's in love with me too." Well, holy Rachel Maddow, she was right. It was Libby calling in to a radio station and professing love, no less! The smile arrived on her face instantly and her cheeks felt joyfully hot. She grabbed her phone and fired off a quick text to Brooklyn to tune into the show. Libby wouldn't want them to know it was her, obviously, or she wouldn't have used a fake name, but this was too crazy a development not to share. How often did people talk about you on the radio?

Doctor Love grabbed the reins and Sam now held on to the bathroom sink. "I'd say pick a night this week, take your sweetheart somewhere romantic, and over candlelight and rose petals, tell her how you feel." *Yes, that'd be perfect. Let's do that. Bring on the rose petals.* Doctor Love was such an intuitive guy. She caught her face in the mirror; the smile was unmistakable. It was possible she was blushing.

"But the problem is that it's not my girlfriend I'm talking about. I'm in love with my best friend. What's worse is that I have a very kind and thoughtful girlfriend who's everything I should *technically* want."

"But she just doesn't do it for you the same way?"

A pause. "No." Sam blinked and watched the smile fade in front of her. Her heart clenched. She stared down at the sink. "She's perfect in every other way, there's just not the same spark. I don't want to hurt her, but my feelings for Tan—my best friend seem to be growing each day."

"Well, that's certainly trickier," Doctor Love said. "I think you have to tell the dishrag girlfriend to hit the road so you can explore the tasty cake you have waiting for you behind door number two. Life is too short to waste on the generic."

Libby sighed. "You might be right."

"Doctor Love is always right. Our next caller is Ron..." The words faded to the background. Time felt off, as if it were slow and fast at the same time. Samantha walked to the kitchen, though she wasn't sure why. Her legs felt shaky and the word *dishrag* had positioned itself in the forefront of her mind. Absently, she heard the water still running in the shower she'd yet to take. Didn't matter. Libby didn't love her. She kept her around because she was sweet and nice.

A dependable dishrag.

God, how had she not seen it?

Libby was supposed to be the one. She was the girl who made Samantha blush when she walked in a room. Kissing her was like floating through air, detached from everything else on the planet. She'd seen her future with Libby, two kids, and a dog. It was years down the road, but she had hopes it would happen. The shock that the happily every after was never going to play out was just a little too much to take in. She covered her mouth and a rare bout of tears hit. Slow at first before full on. They rolled down her cheeks in liquid hot waves. The loft door slid open with lightning speed and Brooklyn, clad in workout clothes, rushed to Sam wordlessly and wrapped her arms around her.

As they stood there in the kitchen, Samantha was flooded with a cold rush of emotion: anger, heartbreak, and the kingpin of them all: embarrassment. She almost had to laugh if she weren't already crying. Of course a girl like Libby wasn't *in love* with her. That didn't happen. How had she convinced herself that it had? The homecoming queen didn't fall in love with the mathlete.

Brooklyn released her and grabbed a napkin from the counter to dry Sam's tears. "I ran four blocks from the gym as soon as I heard. She's not worth it, Sam. Seriously, she's not. Who calls into a radio station for relationship advice anyway?"

Sam didn't answer. She couldn't. She didn't know what to say. All of her life, she'd dreamed of being special to somebody. Falling in love like in the books. The whole package. At long last, she thought she was on her way to that.

She raised her gaze to Brooklyn. "I thought she was saying she was in love with *me*, Brooks. That she was just figuring out how to tell me."

"She's a fool. And she doesn't deserve you."

Sam shook her head. "They're just three words. How do they have the power to hurt so much when they don't belong to you?"

"I'm so sorry, Sammie." The look on Brooklyn's face just about did her in. Sympathy she didn't want. It just made her feel all the more pitiful.

She gestured limply in the direction of the bathroom, the tears all but gone, replaced with a numbness she found strangely comforting, if not a little ominous. There was a tidal wave of emotion waiting to crash down on her, and she wanted to be alone when it hit. "I better jump in the shower before the hot water is gone completely." She didn't wait for a response.

"Hold on, Sam. Please?"

She paused at the entryway to the bathroom. "Yeah?"

"I'll be out here when you're done. We can talk. Eat chocolate peanut butter ice cream."

"It's nine a.m."

"All the more reason to do it."

Sam offered a halfhearted smile. It was the best she could do given the circumstances. Brooklyn was there for her and would help her work through what she now realized had to be the end of her relationship—a thought that was still too new for her mind to fully process.

As the still-hot water fell in cascades across her skin, she closed her eyes and let the tears run down her face, the emotion shaking her entire body. She stood like that until the water ran cold. The world felt different as she looked back over things with new eyes. Last night, Libby had smiled and laughed with her, but she'd also kept one eye on Tanya, wherever she was in the room. Samantha thought it was a best friend thing, but the exchanged looks, the close dancing, the quiet laughter just between the two of them…It all took on new meaning now, and she felt sick to her stomach.

She didn't bother blow-drying her hair, as it no longer seemed to matter. After she found her threadbare comfy jeans and white T-shirt, she and Brooklyn snuggled into opposite ends of the couch and watched a little *I Love Lucy*. It was understood that in light of the morning's events, phase one of packing was pushed to the back burner. They'd get to it eventually.

"I was born in the wrong decade," Sam finally said, after episode number five. "That's my problem. I'm not edgy enough for this period in history."

"Oh, please. You're edgy. Trust me. No one picks up my quips faster than you. Plus, I think they frowned more on lesbians in the sixties. Bisexuals, too, so you'd be screwed. Better off here."

Sam sat up. "It would mean I'd have to stick with men. Maybe that would solve my problem. Men are less complicated. There's something to be said for that."

Brooklyn rolled her eyes. "Don't let stupid Libby Weatherup of the ridiculously perfect cheekbones ruin you for lesbians everywhere. You happen to like women. A lot."

"I hate it when you make valid points."

"Then you must always hate me." Brooklyn smiled at herself and

Sam tossed a playful pillow her way. It was true that Sam had many positive experiences with men under her belt, and she was capable of finding them infinitely attractive under the right circumstances. But when it came to the physical alone, there was something about women she couldn't quite turn away from.

At least not entirely.

"If we're being honest," Brooklyn said, hugging the pillow, "I didn't think Libby was right for you. I never bought her wide-eyed, look-at-me-I'm-gorgeous routine because there's not much beyond it."

Sam's phone buzzed from where it rested on the coffee table. She checked the screen. It was a text from Libby.

Late lunch today?

She shook her head. "I don't think I can do this. What am I supposed to say?" She showed the text to Brooklyn, who turned fully to Samantha on the couch.

"Look at me."

"Looking."

Brooklyn spoke in a calm, even tone. "You go meet her and tell her to hit the road."

"I don't know if I can do that. This is Libby."

Brooklyn studied her as if mulling over her options. "So you're saying you want to stay in this relationship?"

Oh no. Here came the tears again. She took a deep breath to stave them off. "No. I'm not sure I could do that either knowing how she…" The emotion overcame her and the words died in her throat. "She doesn't want to be with me, Brooks. I'm not who she wants."

"I think you know what you have to do here. I'll have ice cream reinforcements waiting when you return."

❖

They'd agreed to meet at Ground Support, the little café that seemed to be their spot. At least the place had really good cheeseburgers. She tried to focus on that, the cheeseburger upside, which one should never overlook. The afternoon was full of sunshine and promise, and those conditions only seemed to mock Samantha all the more as she walked the three sun-kissed blocks to the café.

Twenty minutes later, Libby gestured in a circle with her fork. She looked fresh-faced and beautiful, just to make this suck all the more. "The Manolos were huge sellers this year, and I called that one at the first of the season. Jennifer in corporate wasn't at all convinced, but the order we placed was bigger because of my recommendation, and now I look like the hero. It was a really good week. But enough about work. How was your morning?"

Samantha stared blandly at Libby and played the question back. Ah, yes. Her morning. Here went nothing. "Not the best, actually."

"I'm sorry. Hangover from last night? You were adorable on the dance floor, by the way. Everyone thought so. It was so much fun to see you cut loose that way."

"Please don't call me adorable. I'm tired of being adorable." She seemed to be thinking out loud now. Fabulous.

Libby paused and a look of concern crossed her face. "Of course, honey bear."

The term of endearment that used to light Samantha up from the inside out now felt like a farce. Like the knife from that morning was now being twisted. She used the way she was feeling to force the necessary words from her mouth. It didn't mean she liked the taste of them. "Libby, I don't think we should see each other anymore."

Libby set her iced tea down slowly. And damn it, those turquoise blue eyes shone brightly in question. "You don't? Why?"

"I heard you on the radio this morning. As Tricia." She felt nauseous.

"On the radio?" Libby parroted back slowly. But her whole demeanor changed in the course of fifteen seconds, and that said everything.

Sam pressed on. "Yeah. So I'm not sure there's much left to say."

"Oh." A long, very telling pause. "I didn't plan for this to happen," Libby said, but the sparkle was gone completely from those eyes. She took a minute before finding her words. "The feelings I have for Tanya, I wanted them to go away, Sam. I hoped they would."

For whatever reason, maybe because her own feelings for Libby were still quite real, she felt bad for her. Didn't mean her heart hadn't been ripped out and stepped on. Violently. Publically. In a scenario she wished to God was not now part of her history. "I guess you can't control who you fall in love with."

"No. I guess not."

Another silence.

"I think the world of you, Sam."

She nodded. "Thanks."

Libby's face was earnest as she sat forward in her chair, trying to explain further. "No, really. I was thinking about this the other day. You're like my favorite pair of shoes, you know that? The comfortable ones that are worn and easy on your feet after a long day of work. You know they're going to be there for you when that day is over. The shoes you look forward to putting on after hours in killer heels. I love that about you."

Sam took a minute with the analogy. Was Libby *actually* comparing her to an old, worn-out pair of shoes? As in the kind you don't wear out around people? Had that really just happened? She shook her head in mystification. "So if we're keeping track, first I'm a dishrag, and now I'm a worn-out pair of shoes?" The beady-eyed waiter raised his eyebrows as he refilled Sam's water glass.

Libby's eyes widened and she placed her hand on her heart. "No! God, that doesn't sound how I meant it at all. You're not a dishrag. I never used that term. And the shoe thing, that was a *compliment*. I love my old shoes. Truly." Sam laughed out loud because she didn't know what else to do and there was no way she was going to let Libby see her cry.

"I wish you well, Libby. With Tanya, or wherever it is life takes you. But if there were an award for bad breakup speeches, I think you'd have a legitimate shot."

She watched her girlfriend's—correction, ex-girlfriend's—face fall further. Such a bad situation all around. "So that's it?" Libby asked.

God, she wished it weren't. But she couldn't undo what she'd heard. And how would she not think about it every time she looked at Libby? "I guess it has to be."

"Yeah." They stared at each other for a moment and it was enough for Sam to feel her heart breaking in two.

This was supposed to have been it.

Her own happily ever after.

Right here.

Libby picked up her hair and dropped it. "We'll still be friends, though, right?"

Friends. The word felt lethal. Samantha didn't know if that would ever be something she could manage, but she lied all the same. Pride was suddenly all she had left, and she was clinging to it with all her might. "Sure. It's not like we hate each other."

Libby broke into a wide smile. A relieved smile, if Samantha had to guess, and that stung all the more. "I'm so glad." She reached for the check. "And I'm getting this."

Sam didn't argue. After ruining her life, it was the least Libby could do.

CHAPTER THREE

There were boxes strewn across every available surface in the loft. The place kind of looked like a box convention, as far as Samantha was concerned, and they seemed to be multiplying and making little box children.

It had been quite a Monday, with the Savvy team knocking off at lunch to lend a hand in the moving process. Jessica had a late-afternoon meeting at work but would join them shortly, having agreed to bring in dinner for the group. The mission du jour was to pack Brooklyn's belongings and have everything ready for the movers to transport the following day.

So far so good, if she did say so herself. The workload was massive, and that was helpful in a way. It kept Sam from thinking too much about the state of her world. You know, the breakup that stripped her raw and the fact that her best friend was deserting her. *Bitter, party of one?*

On the flip side, Sam was grateful that Hunter and Mallory had agreed to help out, but then again, of course they would. That was what friends did for one another. Throughout the course of the afternoon, she and Mallory had traded off as project manager, as Mallory was best at wrangling the herd and Samantha was empress of organization. But the sheer volume of it all was overwhelming, as Brooklyn had a *ton of stuff*.

"Okay, Brooks, I think it's time we face facts here," Sam said, examining the contents of one of the few boxes Brooklyn had managed to pack on her own.

Brooklyn peered over Samantha's shoulder into the box. "What are we facing, exactly?"

"You're a bit of a hoarder. And I only threw in the words 'a bit' to soften the blow because there's really no 'a bit' about it. You need some sort of program with steps."

Brooklyn gasped. "I am not a hoarder."

Mallory looked across at them from the box she was packing and raised an eyebrow at Sam. "You got this?"

"I do."

"Excellent. I'm here if you need me."

Sam pressed on. "You have, let's see, seven circle brushes in this box. Two of which are missing most of their bristles. Now let's think about this. Is it necessary that all seven circle brushes, which happen to fulfill the exact same function in your life, make this move with you to Jessica's place?"

Brooklyn stared at the brushes resolutely. "Yes."

Samantha took this in. "Why?'

"Because I need them all. They're my brushes. You're my bitches and they're my brushes. Just how things are."

"Ha ha. That's good, bitches and brushes. I see what you did there, but let's stay on track, shall we? If you think about it, you don't need them all," Sam said as gently as she could. "You really just need one circle brush."

"Lose five of the brushes, Brooks," Hunter said from across the room.

Brooklyn turned to Hunter, wounded. "Et tu, Brute?"

"I have to raise my hand on this as well," Mallory said. "Overkill on the hairbrushes."

"When was the last time you used this one?" Sam asked Brooklyn, holding up the biggest offender. Old and battered. It'd been to hair war and lost.

Brooklyn was unconvinced. "It doesn't matter. It's going."

"And look over here. There are…" Sam paused to count. "Twelve pairs of manicuring scissors in here. *Twelve*. We could write a Christmas carol and give each their own verse."

Brooklyn shrugged. "Manicuring scissors are important. I take care of my nails." She held up her hand. "Look, neatly trimmed." Sam sighed and ushered Brooklyn to the sofa. She understood that Brooklyn's compulsion to hold on to everything she came in contact with probably came from her years growing up in foster homes where she had very little that was hers alone, but enough was enough.

"Wouldn't it be nice to work toward a fresh start when you and Jessica move in together? Lose some of the extra baggage, and that way you can get new stuff. Together stuff. Together stuff is crazy romantic."

Brooklyn thought on this and smiled dreamily. "Together stuff sounds nice." And it did. In fact, Sam loved the idea. Not so long ago she thought she'd be investing in together stuff in the not-so-distant future herself. That is, until Libby tore out her heart and stomped on it.

"See? There's an upside to streamlining."

Brooklyn offered a halfhearted nod that said she was trying. "Maybe I could get behind streamlining."

As Hunter looked on, she admired Samantha's ability to reason with Brooklyn. She was a good friend and easily the sweetest one of their group, if not on the planet. But she'd dimmed noticeably once the conversation shifted to relationships. Given what that stupid ex-girlfriend of hers had done two days prior, she couldn't exactly blame her. She decided to help the anti-hoarding cause. "So maybe a compromise?"

"A compromise could work," Samantha said, sending Hunter a grateful look.

"Two brushes and four pairs of manicuring scissors?" Brooklyn said.

Sam sighed. "Fine. I can agree to that. Progress is progress." As Brooklyn headed back to work, Samantha leaned in next to Hunter's ear. "If I find thirty-eight staplers in her desk drawer later, some of those puppies are gonna mysteriously go missing. Stapler heaven needs to prep for a few more stapler angels."

"I have your stapler back," Hunter whispered.

"That's why you win the award for best new roommate."

The loft door slid open and Jessica Lennox strode into the room with two piping-hot pizzas in hand from John's in the Village. And that was good, because Hunter was starving. And who didn't love John's Pizzeria? She'd gone out with the hostess there once.

It wasn't just the pizza that was hot.

"You're here. Hi, baby," Brooklyn said and greeted her girlfriend promptly with a hello kiss. Hunter had to admit, they were a good-looking couple and really seemed to click. Given, this kind of thing—settling down—was a mysterious quandary she didn't really understand. But she had to admire the forever quality other people seemed so fond of. Speaking of which, she should really give that yoga instructor a call.

"Busy day at the office, Jess?" Hunter asked, snagging a slice of pepperoni and raising an eyebrow at the love of Brooklyn's life. "You're a rock star for bringing us the pies." Packing was quickly moved to the back burner in favor of the newly arrived dinner. Her friends moved about the kitchen, passing around plates, napkins, and beverages.

"Hired a new account executive," Jessica said, shrugging out of her tailored suit jacket and letting her hair down from the twist she'd secured it in. She had a way of transforming herself from all business to laid-back Jessica in just a few simple moves.

"Uh-oh," Mallory said, her eyebrow raised. "Sounds like more competition for us to blow through."

"Humor from the peanut gallery over here. You're very funny," Jessica said and playfully tossed a breadstick in Mallory's direction for emphasis, which of course she caught. She was Mal.

It hadn't been easy when Brooklyn started dating their biggest competitor, but over time, they'd found a way to make it all work. Humor helped. The key seemed to be not to take any of it too seriously, and to know when to leave work at work. It had been a learning curve, but they'd fallen into a livable rhythm. Plus, it made Brooklyn the happiest she'd ever been. Well worth it.

"So I hear you're moving in tomorrow," Jessica said to Hunter. "Need any help?"

"You're going to move me, Jess?" Hunter asked, batting her eyelashes. "I'm honored."

Brooklyn handed Hunter a soda. "Don't flirt with my girlfriend."

Jessica laughed. "No, I will not be moving you. But I'll send over a few guys as soon as they finish delivering to our place."

"Our place," Brooklyn repeated reverently. "I like the ring that has. Speaking of, there's going to be significantly less to deliver once Samantha is done with me," she said in her most pathetic voice.

Jessica mouthed the words *thank you* to Sam. "Are you sure you don't want to move in, too?"

"Tempting. But I have a new charge." Sam slid an arm around

Hunter's waist. "And from what I already know of her, she's a handful."

Hunter shook her head and offered her best smile to the group. "You understand that her life will never be the same."

That elicited laughter. She checked her watch. Still time to call the yoga instructor. The night was young.

❖

It was close to midnight when Samantha and Brooklyn decided to watch one more episode of *I Love Lucy*. Everyone had cleared out hours ago and left them on their own. It felt like the old days again, even though it was the last night they'd be roommates. The end of an era, and it weighed heavily on Samantha's heart. She decided not to point that out to Brooklyn. Too emotional. Sam was the type who snuck out the back door to avoid saying a difficult good-bye.

Brooklyn, however, must have had other ideas and steered them into the skid. "It's our last marathon, Sammie."

"No, it's not," Sam said, brushing off the comment. "We have a million more of these things ahead of us."

"Not as roommates." Brooklyn turned to her, horror stricken, as a new realization seemed to hit. "You're not going to be my roommate anymore."

Sam nodded sadly. "I know. But I'm not going anywhere. And this is the right move for you. You're in love. You're doing the grown-up thing."

"But maybe I don't want to grow up." Brooklyn resembled a terrified child.

"Yes, you do."

There were tears in Brooklyn's eyes. "I'm going to miss you, Sam. I'm going to miss…this." She gestured between them and the room. Samantha understood the all-encompassing gesture and knew that it included the last seven years and all they'd been through together. And the tears that Samantha swore she'd avoid at all costs were now fresh in her eyes. Damn it.

"I'm going to miss you, too, Brooks."

Brooklyn reached for her and she leaned into the hug. They were both crying and laughing at themselves at the same time. "It's stupid,"

Brooklyn said. "I'm going to see you at work every day."

"Definitely. And we're going to go out just as much as we always do."

Brooklyn squeezed her tighter. "Of course we are, so stop crying."

"*You* stop crying." Which only made them laugh again.

They turned finally to Lucy and watched one last time as she managed to get herself into one goofy predicament after another. They laughed and shared a bag of microwave popcorn before Brooklyn called Jessica and headed off to bed.

Sitting there alone in the living room, Sam had no one to call.

She wondered what Libby was doing. If she'd professed all to Tanya since the breakup. If they were snuggled up somewhere, enamored of each other. Frolicking on an island in Jamaica. And then she pushed those thoughts from her head because they didn't do anyone any good.

She climbed into bed and pulled her duvet around her for comfort. Her world felt wildly out of kilter for a number of reasons. Her relationship was over. Her roommate was leaving, and a new chapter of her life seemed like it was about to begin. She stared at the darkened walls of her room, terrified for what was to come. *You're going to be all right*, she told herself. *You're going to be all right.*

She would, wouldn't she? Because honestly, it didn't feel that way.

❖

Hunter sat atop the kitchen counter with Elvis asleep on the floor next to her as the movers carried in the last box. It had been a seamless process, getting her stuff from her studio to the loft. She owed Jessica big-time for the moving guys she'd sent over. Apparently she'd called in a favor and didn't mind sharing the wealth with Hunter. All she asked was that they were tipped generously, and that she could do.

"Where would you like this last one?" the six-foot-three, broad-shouldered one asked. He seemed like the type of guy most straight women drooled over. She had to give him credit, he was in shape.

Hunter gestured to Brooklyn's room—correction, *her* room— and handed off an envelope containing some cash for him and his two buddies, who must have already headed down to the truck.

Mover guy wiped his forehead and smiled once he returned. "Thanks for this," he said, holding up the envelope.

"No problem. Can I get you guys a couple of waters for the road?" she asked.

"That'd be awesome." He followed her behind the bar that separated the kitchen from the living room, but honestly, the loft was just one big open space with the two bedrooms shooting off in either direction.

Sam smiled at her knowingly from the sofa as Hunter handed off the waters.

"I didn't catch your first name," mover guy said to Hunter.

"'Cuz I didn't offer it. But it's Hunter."

"Jonathan. Here's my card if you ever need anything." She accepted the offering, wondering what exactly he hoped she might need. But he seemed like a genuine enough guy, and who could fault him for being a little friendly. "My number's on the bottom corner. Call it for…whatever reason."

"A ride to the airport for my six a.m. flight?"

He laughed. "Um, sure."

"Awesome." She studied him in all seriousness. "Bail money?"

"Why not?"

"Advice on what to get my girlfriend for Valentine's Day?"

A pause. "Oh." And now they were on the same page.

"So not that last one, then?" Hunter winked at him. It was her way of letting him know she was just being playful. *No hard feelings, buddy.* "Thanks for the help today."

"No problem. You guys have a great afternoon." He hesitated. "And sorry about the, um…"

She shrugged. "Why? I thought it was fun."

Jonathan nodded, attempted a smile but was out the door rather fast. She hoped she hadn't embarrassed him, but then again, he'd live. She turned to Sam, who regarded her with a twinkle in her eye.

"What?" Hunter asked.

Samantha rounded the counter and poked Hunter in the ribs as she passed, snagging a water of her own. "You have to stop that. The carnage is piling up."

"Stop what?"

"The breaking of hearts. It's inhumane."

"I would never break anyone's heart. I love hearts. Especially girl hearts. And other aspects of the anatomy."

"Don't you ever get tired of it?"

"What?"

"The dance. The flirting. The banter. You're very good at it. I mean, I've been blown away at your skill level on more than one occasion, but I imagine it's exhausting having all those girls, and okay, guys, too, figuring out what they can get from you."

"Uh-uh. I'm a giver." She threw a playful smile that she punctuated with a raised eyebrow. "And now I'm *your* giving roommate. Surreal, huh?"

Samantha laughed. "I'm happy you were able to move in. It saved me, you know."

"Yeah, but aren't you just a little terrified right now of what the next year of your life, at the very least, is going to be like?"

Samantha held her ground. "No way. You just moved in with about seven boxes. That's about fifty-eight fewer than Brooklyn. I'm thinking you're low maintenance, which I kind of don't get because you have so many clothes it's ridiculous."

"Correction. I wear a lot of different outfits. But I donate the old ones every six months or so. I like to keep things fresh and travel light."

"Kind of how you manage your women."

Hunter laughed. "Touché."

"At least you're self-aware. And the clothes thing, who knew there was something I didn't know about you after all these years?"

"I'm willing to bet there are a few more tidbits left to learn. I have layers, Samantha Ennis. I'm a complex girl."

Sam shrugged. "Well then, this could get interesting." She reached down to pet Elvis, who sighed and licked her hand sleepily. "I've never lived with a dog before. Anything I should know?"

"Nah. Elvis is chill. That's why we get along so well. I take him out a handful of times a day. He loves to chase balls in the park and would probably like you to pet him now and again. Now you know everything."

Sam looked from her to Elvis. "He's never far from you, is he?"

Hunter shook her head. "I think it goes back to his shelter days. He likes to stay close by, know he's safe."

"That's sweet." Sam shook herself out of it. "I have a ton of work to make up after the last two days of rotating roommates. So I'm going to head downstairs."

Hunter eased back onto the counter. "Could have called that one. You have your serious numbers ponytail happening. And in about two point eight seconds, I'm expecting serious numbers glasses to appear." It was how you knew Samantha was heading into the zone. She got her academic look on. The duality was fun.

Without missing a beat, Sam popped the glasses on her face. "And now we go to number-crunching war on that new spa chain's budget. What are they called again?"

Hunter thought for a sec, biting her bottom lip. "Serenity."

Sam was struck. Hunter had a lot of sexy going on. Maybe she should take notes now that she was single.

"I need to do more things like that," Sam said, thinking out loud.

Hunter stared at her. "Like what? Hitting up spas? They're our clients now. I have a feeling you could score some free passes pretty easily."

Sam waved a hand in front of her own face in attempt to erase the confusion. "Not the spa, the lip-biting thing you just did. It was a good move. I need more moves. Part of my problem, maybe."

Hunter's eyes took on understanding. And oh, there it was again. Sympathy. Sam hated that. "She made a huge mistake, you know," Hunter said. "She'll figure that out at some point."

Samantha took a deep breath and decided to go with honesty. Hunter was the kind of friend you could level with, for good or bad— one of the many things that was great about her. "Maybe. Maybe not. I'm not exactly exciting or edgy or ridiculously beautiful. So if you think about it, of course she fell for someone like Tanya over me."

Hunter stared at Sam, her expression carefully blank. "You're a smart girl, Sam, but that's one of the more stupid things you've said in life. Do you know that I had a mad crush on you at NYU? Freshman Psychology."

Okay, there was no way that was true. "Please. That is a total lie to make me feel better. You were constantly flirting with the blond girl who must have bought stock in midriffs. I watched it play out daily."

"Correction. Midriff blondie flirted with me. I was just being nice."

"No."

"Yes. I've never told anyone about this." And that was when Sam saw it. The touch of red that colored Hunter's cheeks and hinted at sincerity. She looked vulnerable even, which was so not Hunter's style.

"Are you serious right now?"

Hunter nodded. "I mean, it's ridiculous to think about now, but I used to drag my feet after class because you took forever to pack your neat little backpack and I desperately wanted to talk to you." Hunter's gaze fell to the countertop and she traced the pattern of the granite with the side of her thumb. "We became friends not long after, and the rest is history. But you had firm hold of my attention for maybe—"

"Two weeks?"

"About a year."

Sam blinked. She took a step back, pointing at Hunter. "You're funny. You're very funny, and I get that you're trying to do something nice for me. Bolster my confidence after a catastrophic breakup or whatever, but really, it's okay." She touched her glasses because she didn't know what else to do.

Hunter straightened. "That. That little glasses thing you just did is a move, by the way. A total move. And it used to drive me crazy. Believe me or don't, it's your call. But I wanted to sleep with you. It happened. It's a fact. You've always been a head turner, and you need to recognize that—my only point in telling this story."

Samantha was staring at her for a beat longer than normal, and for whatever reason, Hunter felt incredibly exposed after what she'd revealed. A new feeling for her. It was a schoolgirl crush, what she'd felt for Samantha back in the day, one she hadn't ever planned on mentioning to anyone, much less Sam herself—especially now that they were all as close as they were. But that longing had been real, and if it helped Samantha to know about it, well, she was willing to feel a little stupid in the process.

A grin took over Sam's face and she leaned her hip against the counter. "Wait. So you're not wanting to rip my clothes off anymore?"

"Doesn't mean some other poor sap isn't pining away for you right this very minute. Or won't be before the day is out."

"Huh." Sam picked up her attaché. "If nothing else, it's nice to imagine." Her eyes softened and her voice took on sincerity. "Thanks, by the way. You didn't have to say all of that. But just…thanks." Hunter nodded. "Will I see you down at Savvy soon?"

"Right behind you, after I organize a bit. I have to get used to this thirty-second commute."

Sam quirked her head. "And I have to get used to a roommate who organizes. Mind-blowing concept." And then she was gone.

Hunter headed to her bedroom with Elvis right behind her. Her goal was to at least start the process of putting her room together. But as she laid the contents of the first box across the dresser Brooklyn had left her, the recent conversation clung to her. It had her in a new headspace entirely. She hadn't thought about those old feelings in such a long time, and doing so now took her back there, in a sense. It was a point in her history when she was excited for the next day, for what life had to offer, for a variety of reasons. It was nice feeling that way about someone, even if it had been temporary. Full-on crushes like that one just didn't happen to her anymore.

She'd grown up. And that was a good thing.

❖

There's a dog staring at me.

While Sam should have been nerding out and tearing through this month's edition of *Money Magazine*, that was all she seemed able to concentrate on: the dog sitting on the floor next to the couch. Staring at her.

As she was lying on her stomach, the way she always did when she read, Elvis was at her eye line, innocently looking on. Blinking periodically. Probably wondering what she was up to and why she wasn't staring back. Or more importantly, why she was home alone on a Saturday night reading a magazine. "Because I'm just that sought after," she said knowingly to Elvis.

It had been two weeks since Hunter moved in, and so far, so good. Well, mostly. If you didn't count the fact that the mail was never where it was supposed to be on the counter, or that she put the big knives in the regular silverware drawer, or that she came in at all hours and shut the door loudly. Hunter also had her own schedule, or maybe a better way to describe it was a lack of one. It had been difficult for Samantha, who thrived on routine and predictability, to figure out when Hunter might want to shower, which seemed to happen at all sorts of random times of day, or what nights she'd likely be home versus going out. Okay, so not that big a deal in the scheme of things, except the randomness of it all drove her a little over-the-top-crazy-frustrated. Hunter hadn't killed a small child or anything, but everyone had limits.

And she never in a million years would have imagined it, but Sam missed the stuff, Brooklyn's stuff, that she was used to scooping up and tossing in her room: the clothes that lived in a pile on the floor just beyond Brooklyn's door, the towel she would often pick up from the countertop in the bathroom because Brooklyn wasn't so great at remembering to do so herself. There were also no half-empty glasses of water on the end table for Samantha to carry to the sink. It was irritating. Where were the water glasses? With Hunter, who the hell knew what to expect?

Plus, Hunter was a lot more streamlined. The bedroom barely resembled Brooklyn's chaos personified. A couple of well-placed pieces of art—one of them metal interestingly enough—and her guitar in the corner. The floor was clear of debris, the surfaces devoid of any clutter. And all of the furniture was visible. Visible!

Not to mention, Hunter wasn't there a whole lot—pretty much the perfect roommate except that she wasn't. Samantha couldn't even tell someone how many days it had been since she'd watched an episode of *Lucy*. She stared at the dark television screen and shook her head in remorse.

Sam tried her magazine again, going at it with fresh eyes.

No go. Why?

There's a dog staring at me.

She sighed. Samantha wasn't averse to dogs. In fact, she thought they were adorable, though she'd never really spent time with one on such a consistent basis. She'd always liked Elvis, though, and did what she could to help out with him. But this particular dog, it turned out, stared a lot. At first, she thought there might be a reason. She'd taken him out, checked his food and water bowls, but all was well. Maybe this was just what he did.

It was disarming.

Not sure what else to do, she met Elvis's big brown eyes and smiled. "Hey there, buddy. El. Do people call you El? I might." He cocked his head in question. She pressed on. "I'm sure Hunter will be back later. No worries. It's dark out, which means she's on a *date*. Do you know what a hot girl is? She's probably with one right now." Elvis whined softly at the attention she offered him and his little tail beat back and forth like a windshield wiper of joy. Sam smiled. She had to admit, the blue bandana Hunter tied around his neck made him a dapper little guy. His coat was mostly white with accents of brown and black here and there. While he clearly had some terrier in him, he resembled a corgi more with his stocky body and short little legs. Hunter had already added a photo of Elvis wearing sunglasses to the refrigerator door.

Okay, you can do this. She gave her head a little shake and attempted to refocus on the article about the best apps for taming your bills. She loved taming bills. And apps. A perfect combo.

But five minutes later, when she'd read the first paragraph eighteen times without retaining what she'd read, she flipped the magazine closed. "You win," she told Elvis as she sat up. His response was to leap onto the couch next to her, tail thwacking away. "Better view?" she asked him.

She grabbed her phone from the coffee table and checked the clock. It was a quarter to eleven. Libby would probably be out on the town. Or, you know, maybe she was at home. Thoughts of Libby were pretty rampant still. Totally normal, she told herself. It would get easier, except it hadn't yet. She stood and paced the length of the loft. Elvis followed the action like a tennis match.

"A text can't hurt, right?" Elvis only stared back at her, but his answer was clear. Of course it was all right, was what he was surely saying. Impulsively, she typed two words. *Hey, you.* But that was stupid, so she erased them. Maybe this was better: *I thought I'd give this friends thing a try. How's life?* Beyond pathetic. She decided to go with a basic *Happy Saturday* and see what it got her. Before she could hit Send, the loft door slid open and her roommate sauntered in, fresh from a real Saturday night.

"Hey."

"Hey," Sam answered back.

Hunter paused. "Why are you looking at me like that?"

"Like what?"

"Wide-eyed and guilt-ridden. Like you just ate the last chocolate chip cookie."

Samantha shrugged. "I didn't eat any cookies."

Hunter strolled farther into the room, investigator mode in full effect, and gestured to the phone in Sam's hand. "Who are you texting?"

"No one." Sam decided to lose the evidence. She set the phone gingerly on the arm of the couch and stepped away from it, but she already felt it: the shame. *Oh, the shame.*

"No one?" In a lightning-quick move, Hunter lunged for the phone, causing Samantha to lunge, too, but damn it all, Hunter was taller and had longer arms. She snatched the phone easily and strode to the kitchen, holding it in the air and studying the screen.

Sam blew out a breath, her hands on her hips. "It was a moment of weakness."

"Clearly." Hunter turned back to her. "Good thing I came home, saved you from yourself."

"I guess. Yeah."

Hunter shrugged out of her dark red suede jacket that only she could pull off. "You would have regretted that text tomorrow, Sam. Never make any relationship-oriented decisions after nine p.m. That's just basic."

"Basic, huh? What happens after nine?"

"Everyone gets super dramatic and sex fuels everything."

Sam thought this over as her life's history came into sharp focus. "You know, you might be onto something there."

"Trust me. I know stuff. Especially about sex." Hunter sank into the sofa and gestured to the phone with her head. "And I'm holding on to this for a little while longer. I refuse to let you text that woman. Let her ride off into the sunset with Tasha."

"Tanya."

"Tanya. Whatever. I don't care what her name is. And those two can talk about shoes all day and bore each other, rather than us. See how that works out?"

"I'd rather not talk about shoes. I guess that's a silver lining."

"Of course it is. Bam."

Samantha laughed and sat on the arm of the sofa. "Why are

you home so early, anyway? The night is still young." Hunter was not exactly the come-home-early type. Whenever the girls went out together, Hunter outlasted them all.

She shrugged, nonchalant. "No idea. I was bored. Wondered what was going on here."

"You were bored?!"

She blew out a breath. "Yeah. I don't know. No worries, just an off night. I'll be in full fun mode tomorrow." She released the hair that she had pinned back on one side, and it cascaded down her left shoulder.

Sam took in the visual. "This is kind of a momentous occasion. You home early. I'd take your photo, but you stole my phone."

"It is kind of odd, isn't it?" Hunter had a faraway look in her eye that moved Samantha out of the teasing zone and into be-a-friend territory.

"It's okay. We all have off nights. Wanna watch *Lucy*?" Sam offered. It was the best she had.

Hunter hesitated. "I'm not really into *Lucy*. That's bad, right? I lose roommate points."

"It's a little criminal. How about I turn it on and you can watch or not?"

"I can agree to this."

Samantha popped in a DVD and Hunter kicked off her shoes, tucking her feet beneath her. Two weeks in the loft, and it was really starting to feel like it was home, like it was her place. Given, the roommate thing was still a bit dicey. Samantha seemed to want everything done a certain way, her way. And Hunter couldn't help it— she wanted to play with that a little, test her boundaries. She didn't thrive on structure, or shower schedules, for that matter, so she'd taken to jumping in there whenever she felt like it. Sam would live.

"So, who is her friend?" she finally asked, out of *I Love Lucy* confusion.

Samantha gaped at her like Elvis did when he realized the ball was still in her hand. She pointed to the screen in slow mystification. "That's Ethel, her best friend in life. She's married to Fred."

Hunter nodded and they watched a bit more. "Ethel's an enabler," she told Sam finally.

"Excuse me?"

"Lucy gets these harebrained ideas, and instead of telling her what a crazy person she's being, Ethel just does the ridiculous stuff along with her. And I think this Ethel person knows better. Thereby she's what you would call an enabler."

Samantha's mouth fell open and Hunter watched her attempt to recover. "They're *friends*."

"They should just tell that Ricky guy what happened, though he's kind of an ass, admittedly. And why can't she be in that damn show anyway?" Why she was getting worked up over *I Love Lucy*? She had no idea. But there was something oddly domestic about the whole experience: sitting on a couch, in her apartment, watching a TV show with her roommate, who just also happened to be one of her best friends. It was...kinda fun. Even the debate part.

Samantha had on her patience-face when she turned to her, the one she reserved for the elderly she volunteered with once a week. "Because if they told Ricky, there wouldn't be anything left to the plot. If she was allowed to be in the show all the time, she would have no goal to work toward."

"But she's not that great a singer. Maybe she should work toward something else."

That did it. Patience-face was gone and replaced with outright exasperation. "No more *Lucy* for you! Executive decision." With one flick of the remote, Sam turned the television off, bringing them to silence. Samantha was cute when she was angry. People didn't generally like to be told they were cute in moments like these, so she kept that tidbit to herself, but it was there, the cuteness.

"Seems a little extreme," Hunter said.

"I'm not sure you're ready for *Lucy*."

Hunter tried desperately to hold back the smile tugging at her lips because it was clear Samantha was taking this very seriously. "I'll take your word for it. I'll try harder next time." But she was laughing now, because she couldn't help it.

Sam threw a pillow at her. "Look at you. No, you won't."

"Probably not. No."

Sam sighed. "You are more than a little frustrating. Has anyone ever told you that? And I've had enough of your antics for tonight. I'm going to bed. Can I have my phone?"

"If you promise to be a strong person and not text the shoe girl."

"I promise. Just a momentary lapse in judgment." A pause. "Thanks for being there."

Hunter handed Samantha the phone. "Happy to help. Night, Sam."

"Night."

"Maybe tomorrow we could go grape stomping," she called after her.

Sam didn't turn around, but Hunter faintly heard the words "shut up" just before the door closed, which made her smile.

Living here was fun.

CHAPTER FOUR

Tuesday brought with it Savvy's weekly staff meeting, a time set aside for the group to gather around the office's kitchen table and, over a working lunch, discuss where they were on various projects.

Sam loved staff meeting Tuesdays. It was her chance to get a bird's-eye view of where Savvy needed her most and always sent her back to her desk with a new burst of motivation. Plus, today they'd brought in sandwiches from Bo Peep's a block down. She'd lay her life on the line for their turkey bacon guacamole.

Mallory waited until everyone had settled into lunch a bit before taking out the official agenda. Mallory was famous for her agendas, and Sam had no complaint. The agenda kept them on track, and she bowed down to it.

"Okay, let's go ahead and get started," Mallory said, bringing Brooklyn and Hunter's argument about who made the best pickle in Manhattan to a brief hiatus. "Last week was a little crazy with the time we lost on apartment musical chairs, but we're rebounding really well, which is great. I've been meeting with Serenity regarding their various spa locations. They seem eager to work with us, but I think I need to meet with them one more time to go over final details and get an official agreement in place, really understand what they need from us. They could definitely use a stronger online presence, and that's where you come in," she said, gesturing to Hunter.

"I checked out their website. Not a lot there. I already have ideas, just waiting for the word 'go' before I start anything too time consuming. We have the second round of the Foster print ads approaching deadline, and I didn't want to lose momentum."

"No, I think that's the right call. As for Serenity, they're not nationwide but they have some pretty popular locations in New York. They're worth our time. Sam, how's the budget for them coming?"

Samantha flipped through her notes. "I've worked up some sample possibilities, but I gotta be honest, what they're asking for and what they are willing to spend seem to be two different realities."

"Maybe you should take the meeting with me," Mallory said.

"Fun times," Brooklyn mused.

Mallory swiveled to Brooklyn. "Whatcha got for me, Brooks? What can I take them?"

Brooklyn sighed. It was her job to construct an idea they could pitch, and though Sam knew she was struggling with Serenity, she also knew she rarely came up short. "The problem is, there aren't a million directions you can go with this one. They're interested in a straightforward commercial spot, as humor and a serenity spa don't really jibe. So, I'm thinking more a day in the life of a New York businesswoman. She's pounding the pavement to work in sneakers, but we see her slip into serious heels as she arrives at the office. A series of quick shots follow and show our girl being slammed with calls, appointments, and a barrage of people who need things. But at the end of it all, we crossfade to her at Serenity. Gentle hands descend and slowly massage away the day's tension as a flute of champagne is placed at her side—a complete contrast to where she's been. It's as if she's entered a whole separate world. We watch a slow smile take shape on her face. She's at peace. Total serenity."

Sam blew out a breath. "I need a massage."

"I'd like to head there now," Hunter deadpanned.

Mallory lifted her head from the notes she'd taken and smiled. "Sounds like it worked on these guys." She rubbed the back of her own neck. "And me, too, now that you mention it. Write it up. I'll take it to Serenity later this week and maybe make an appointment while I'm there."

Brooklyn fell dramatically back in her chair. "You like it? For real?"

Hunter snagged a salt and vinegar chip from Samantha's plate. "No. We hate it and just like to screw with you."

Samantha elbowed Hunter and stole one of her jalapeño chips in retaliation before refocusing on Brooklyn. "We love it."

Brooklyn beamed. "I'd like to thank Jesus and Red Bull."

Sam raised her Diet Coke in solidarity. "They both give you wings."

"I like what you did there, Sammie," Brooklyn said, tapping the Styrofoam cups together.

"Thanks. I'm the funny one in the apartment now, so I gotta step up my game."

Hunter glared. "Excuse me. I'm funny."

Brooklyn put her thumb and forefinger very close together in response. Hunter stared back at her, looking like an adorably confused puppy.

"You win stylish, though," Brooklyn assured her.

"You do," Mallory said all businesslike, without looking up from her notebook.

"I can be stylish and funny," Hunter mumbled into her Dr Pepper.

The meeting continued, and they moved on to other clients, strategizing over problem-child accounts and how to keep their big fish, like Foster Foods, happy and impressed. The campaign they rolled out for Foster's new line of summer drinks had proved to be a slam-dunk success when the commercial and print ads went live two months prior. While they were flying high on the good faith that campaign afforded them with Foster, it was important they not drop the ball while basking in the success.

Six hours later, Samantha was still at the office plugging numbers into a spreadsheet. It was one of those days where her brain was starting to feel fuzzy, and she was having trouble making out the numbers on the screen despite her incessant blinking. Mallory and Hunter were gone for the day, and Brooklyn seemed to be packing up at her desk.

"Headed home soon?" she asked Sam, coming around to her desk.

"Yeah. The stupid Serenity people want some kind of numbers magic. I don't think it's doable."

"Then we tell them no."

"Yeah, not sure Mal's of the same opinion."

"She will be. You gotta stick up for what you know. She trusts you. We all do."

Samantha rubbed the back of her aching neck. "Yeah, you're right. Just hard sometimes. Hey, I was hoping you would have time to grab some dinner. Want to?"

Brooklyn winced. "I'd love to, you know that, but I promised Jess I'd be home. She's cooking, and that could go a lot of ways."

Sam forced an understanding smile and tried to hide her disappointment. Ever since Brooklyn moved out, they'd seen each other in the course of business, and as always, joked around throughout the day. But it wasn't the same. She missed her friend. She missed their long talks. Throwback Movie Wednesday. *Lucy* marathons.

As if she were reading Sam's thoughts, Brooklyn perched on the edge of Samantha's desk. "I do miss getting to talk with you, about life, about everything. Just us. We should make a point to get together more, just the two of us. Catch up on the little things."

Samantha nodded. "I'd like that." And she would. She hadn't been in the best headspace since the breakup, and the distance she'd felt from Brooklyn only added to that.

"Perfect. We'll do it. How are things going at the loft with Hunter?"

"Great. Good. Okay. Sometimes not."

The office was empty but Brooklyn lowered her voice to a whisper anyway. "What? Does she bring girls home or something?"

"Actually, no. I'm starting to think we give her a harder time than she deserves on that front."

"Please. She's a player, and she loves it."

"Maybe. But I think it might be more show than we realized."

"I'd be shocked, but stranger things have happened." Sam nodded and Brooklyn regarded her, looking at her sidewise in contemplation. "What's with the look? There's something bothering you about Hunter, isn't there?"

Sam blew out a breath, giving into herself. "It's stupid, but there are little things that are probably normal when you first start living with someone."

"Like?"

"She puts the big knives in the silverware drawer." Samantha held out a hand in emphatic punctuation.

Brooklyn's eyes widened. "Uh-oh. I did that once. Never again."

"Yeah, and she doesn't really subscribe to any kind of schedule, which is harder for me because—"

"You're a robot when it comes to your routine."

"Right."

"And when it's disrupted, you—"

"Die inside."

Brooklyn laughed. "A little dramatic, but yeah. You do. It's rough for little Samantha to roll with the punches."

"Yes, it is." Sam ran a frustrated hand through her hair. "Thank you for getting that. It's been a little touch and go. Sage advice?"

"Teach her where the knives go before you use one of them on her." Brooklyn patted her head. "Night, Sammie-Sam."

❖

It was just past ten on Saturday morning when Hunter hit the sidewalk after her morning yoga class. April hadn't taught it—a damn shame. But she'd attended anyway, needing a bit of re-centering. Her body now felt sated and alive, and with the day stretched out luxuriously in front of her, she was up for anything. She almost felt like jogging home, but c'mon—*let's not get too crazy*.

The morning was a beautiful one and as she turned the corner onto their block, the aroma of coffee from the cart on the corner wafted past and had her full attention. She stopped and bought a cup for herself and one for Sam, picking up a couple of doughnuts as a bonus. A chocolate and a glazed. Yoga earned you doughnuts, and your roommate by proxy. Everyone knew this rule.

When Hunter slid open the door to the loft, she was met with music, which was cool with her. The fast-paced sounds of Usher breaking it down matched her mood perfectly. As she made her way into the apartment, she paused, watching as Sam sashayed to the downbeat and returned two coffee cups from the dishwasher to the cabinet above the sink. Samantha only wore a T-shirt, light blue. It covered her ass and the tip-tops of her thighs, but that coverage was undone each time she went up on her toes to reach the much taller cabinet. Hunter's lips parted as she took in the visual. Her legs, while not especially long, were firm and smooth looking, and Hunter had a flash of her own hands running up their length. Sam's auburn hair was down this morning and curly in an untamed kind of way, which only added to the alluring image. Hunter was perpetually intrigued by how some moments, Sam's hair appeared brown, and in other moments, red.

Today was a slightly red day, and the haphazard waves fanned out in a million different directions. Translation: sexy. Was it wrong that her mouth was now dry?

Right then, Samantha turned and danced back to the dishwasher, stopping abruptly when her eyes met Hunter's.

"Hi." She laughed, her hand flying to her forehead at having been caught. "How long have you been standing there watching my *So You Think You Can Dance* impersonation?"

Hunter opened her mouth to answer, but her mind wasn't working. It was stuck on the expanse of creamy skin and the wonderfully curvaceous body in front of her. She'd always found Samantha attractive. Hell, she'd even admitted so a few weeks prior. But this scenario was taking that opinion to new and challenging heights. The girl was flat-out hot in her present state. And this mind-warp thing was new, because since when did her mind not work properly? She was the one with the smooth moves in life, and this inability to behave like a normal human was an unforeseen obstacle. "Oh. Um. Just a sec or two."

"Lucky for you it was only that long."

Or not, Hunter supplied internally. Oh, hey, her brain was back.

"Who are those for?" Samantha asked.

She stared down at the two cups of coffee in her hand and held one blindly out to Samantha. Hunter's cheeks seemed to be giving off massive amounts of heat—probably from yoga. Definitely not from checking out her best friend's awesome ass. Yeah, that was a total lie.

"For me?" Sam asked.

"Yep. Thought you might not have had your coffee yet. And there are doughnuts in the bag."

"What?" Sam's eyes widened in excitement and she snatched the bag, peering into it. "Way to bury the lead. No roommate has ever brought me doughnuts before."

"No big deal. Also, you forgot your pants."

Sam glanced down in nonchalance. "Yeah, I always unload the dishwasher before I shower. It's a thing I have, routine. On my way there now." She held up the coffee. "You're the best for this. I'll snag a doughnut after. Thank you."

"No problem," Hunter said as Samantha headed off in pursuit of her shower. As the music continued to play, she fell back on the sofa and stared at the ceiling. Okay, so *that* was kind of unexpected. And as hard as she tried, she wasn't able to shake the overt reaction she'd just had to her partially clothed, incredibly sexy roommate. Her heart thrummed away and her body felt warm. Okay, more than that, on fire. And this was apparently an every-morning occurrence in her apartment? How was she supposed to maneuver that exactly? Because she couldn't have those kinds of thoughts, not about Sam. There were a handful of women who were explicitly off-limits, and Samantha was one of them.

Maybe it was talking about her college crush on Sam that had prompted such a powerful surge of lust, just an aftershock of something that once was. She shook her head in mystification, because it sure felt like more than an aftershock.

Damn it.

Why couldn't anything be easy?

She looked at Elvis, who sighed and laid his chin on her foot in solidarity. "Did you see what I saw?" Elvis merely blinked back. "You're lucky you're just a dog." She shrugged. "Apparently, I am, too."

❖

Serenity Day Spa was kind of like a little slice of heaven on Earth. Samantha hadn't been excited about accompanying Mallory on the client visit, mainly because she hated to be the bearer of bad news, and the bottom line was that Serenity was going to have to cough up more cash if they wanted Savvy to be able to work for them effectively. Plus, she preferred to work behind the scenes and let Mallory handle the schmoozing.

"Look at this place," Mallory whispered. "Didn't I tell you?"

"I think the Dalai Lama might live here," Sam whispered back. "The girl version, though. Probably wears a bow." It was part of Serenity's platform, in fact, a spa for women only. And from everyone she'd seen entering and exiting the place, *beautiful* women only.

They were standing in what Samantha could only imagine was the lobby, but it was like no lobby she'd ever seen. The lighting was dim and the main wall held a rather realistic portrayal of a beachfront. Waves rolled in and then out again. Seagulls glided lazily overhead.

Sam glanced around to find the projector, but came up short. It was so lifelike, it was jarring. All around them were the calming sounds of water, an occasional bird chirp, wind rustling past. A person could get lost here.

Serenity, indeed.

A receptionist with flawless skin and a perfect blond bun approached. "Ms. Spencer. Ms. Ennis. Eleanor will be with you shortly. Please, won't you relax at our waiting station?"

A station? Well, okay. They could hang out at the station. She and Mallory took a seat on perhaps the most comfortable couch known to man as they waited for their meeting with the spa director. "What do you think this thing is made of?" Sam said, pushing down on the ultra-soft cushion. She could totally nap in this room. Would that be wrong?

"Five-hundred-dollar bills," Mallory said without blinking. "Look around. They have cash, Sam. We're not cutting them any financial breaks, agreed? We need to lock them in at budget number one or two."

"I don't really play hardball. That's your job. I'm the sweet one, remember? I like to make friends."

Mallory smiled. "Just follow my lead."

That's when yet another striking blonde approached. "Mallory, it's so good to see you. And you must be Samantha. A joy. I'm Eleanor." She held out her thin hand in greeting.

A joy? She'd accept joy. "It's nice to meet you, Eleanor. This is an amazing space you have."

"It's transformative for all of our clients. It's what Serenity does." In not-at-all shocking news, Eleanor had a calming voice.

"Of course. I've heard great things."

She smiled. "This way."

Eleanor led them down a long hallway with sounds of the ocean and distant wind chimes accompanying them the whole way. They entered a conference room where a series of water pitchers, each containing a different type of fruit, lined the center of the table. Eye catching, the little pops of color within each pitcher.

"I hope you don't mind, but I'd like my guest services navigator to sit in on our meeting."

"We don't mind at all," Mallory said as she pulled her laptop from her attaché.

Sam shrugged. "The more navigators, the better, I always say."
The levity was greeted with a serene smile from Eleanor. Maybe not the
place for whimsy after all. The door behind her opened, and yet another
tall, blond woman entered. Was height and hair color an employment
qualification at this place? Could she see the application? But Samantha
didn't get beyond the musing as the new blonde broke into a smile
when she saw Sam and, *oh my God—Tanya?*

Seriously, universe?

How was this fair?

"Samantha? Oh my goodness. How *are* you?" Tanya said, showing
off her flawless smile and perfectly tanned skin.

"Great. How are you, Tanya?" Her brain worked furiously to
understand the series of events. Tanya was here. At Serenity. Which she
guessed made sense as Tanya worked in massage therapy and—lucky
her—she'd apparently stumbled into the very spa Tanya worked for.
What a fantastic coincidence!

"Busy day," Tanya said, pulling up the chair next to Samantha.
"Our new memberships are keeping me on my toes. Lots of intakes to
navigate. What about you?"

"Oh, I'm having quite a day, too. Maybe a little less navigating on
my end, though. I could probably use some," Sam said quite honestly,
because running into the perfect-looking girl Libby left her for was her
nightmare scenario. Happy Monday to her. She owed the powers-that-
be a gift basket.

Mallory seemed to pick up on something and looked between
them before an element of understanding crossed her features. She
made brief eye contact with Sam and offered a confident smile. That
helped, because though she felt the need to hyperventilate and run from
the room, Mallory had her. And when Mallory was in control, all was
well with the world.

"Shall we get started?" Mallory asked.

And they were off.

Mallory ran through a series of print, Internet, and TV options
including Brooklyn's commercial spot concept. Samantha listened,
admiring Mallory's charisma, her polish, as she delivered the very
detailed pitch. There was a reason she landed them account after
account. When she finished, Eleanor raised a sculpted eyebrow.

"I like it. I think we might want to incorporate a few more of the Serenity principles, however. There are ten, you know. Each one very important to Serenity and what we stand for on the planet."

"I didn't. I'd love a list," Mallory answered.

"I'll make sure our receptionist gets those for you."

"Excellent. I'll now pass the proverbial baton to Samantha, who will go over some of the financials we should agree upon before we sign."

Samantha sat up a little straighter in her chair.

Oh, that was her.

Right.

She opened her leather-bound folder and pulled out the first budget. The one that afforded them the funds they needed to do a bang-up job, with a touch of wiggle room for error. No way Serenity would agree to hand over the amount of cash she was about to ask them for. They'd shown themselves to be rather protective of their funds in prior meetings, but this big number would be a jumping-off point for negotiations. She had a second and third budget prepared, in which they'd cut Savvy's fee beyond what she felt was fair and gone with a smaller budget for the TV spot.

After handing a copy to everyone, Samantha began to explain the need for each line item and the cost associated with it. She was already picking up hints of disdain from Eleanor: a well-placed sigh, rubbing the back of her neck, and let's not forget the appearance of a crease between her eyes that, earlier, Samantha wouldn't have guessed possible before it appeared. Did serene people crease?

When she finished, Eleanor didn't hesitate. "I'm not sure this is a figure we can commit to at this point. It may be a tad ambitious. What else can you do?"

Sam paused. Totally predictable. "I understand. Let's look at some other options." Tanya was staring at her with a mixture of regret and sympathy. Oh dear Lord. She didn't need this woman to feel sorry for her. She was fine, damn it. *Fine.*

"Wait," Tanya said. "Eleanor, Samantha knows what she's doing. And I, for one, trust Savvy's expertise. I think ambitious might be the way to go."

"You do?" For whatever reason, Eleanor looked conflicted, as if Tanya's opinion carried weight. And hey, maybe it did. Samantha didn't really have an organizational chart for attractive blondes at a spa.

"I do," Tanya said. "I say we give Savvy everything they need to take this place to the next level."

Eleanor seemed to mull this over. "I suppose I made you guest services director for a reason." She turned to Mallory. "Let's put it in writing."

Well, that was a fast turnaround. Was this actually happening? They were going to pay Savvy their full rate because Tanya felt bad about stealing Sam's girlfriend? Somehow the victory felt less than sweet.

Mallory produced the necessary paperwork. "Just need a few more minutes of your time and we can begin strategically placing Serenity on the lips of every woman in New York City."

"That's what I'm banking on," Eleanor said smoothly. Ah, the robot-like calm had returned.

Tanya stood. "Eleanor, while you and Mallory sort out the details, how about I take Samantha on a tour? Show her around?"

Sam balked. Alone time with Tanya was so not necessary. "Oh. No. I'm sure you have things to do. You just said it was a busy day."

"I think it's important for our advertising agency to know what we're all about," Tanya said, blinking back at her with a quiet intensity. She wasn't getting out of this.

"Perfect," she squeaked. Mallory stared at her helplessly. It would be bad form to refuse.

They started in the secondary waiting area. Excuse her, secondary waiting *station*. Soft music flowed and the aroma of oranges hung in the air. Again there were pitchers of fruit water available in the corner.

"This is where our journeywomen begin their experience," Tanya said, walking into the room.

"Oh, you call them journeywomen?"

"We do. How about a glass of lemon water?"

"Nah. I'm good," Sam said, feigning intense interest in the room and its décor. Spending time with Tanya wasn't wildly uncomfortable at all. Nope. She squinted. Was that Gwyneth Paltrow on the wall?

"Have you recognized water as a necessary part of your existence, Sam?"

Okay, how does one answer that, exactly? "Well, I need it to live. So I'm going to go with yes." How had she not realized Tanya was a bit of a fruit loop when she'd spent time with her previously? Apparently, context was everything.

Tanya poured her a glass of water anyway and extended it to her. "It's more than that. Water is fundamentally transforming. It cleanses and purifies from the inside out. It can heal and nourish. I have a feeling you need more of it in your life."

"More water?" Sam took the glass she'd already declined. "Who knew?"

"It's true. Once you embrace water, you'll harness your glow. That's what's missing, Sam. Your glow."

"Missing?" Tanya thought she was missing something? Well, join the club.

Tanya sighed and met her eyes. "I feel horrible about how things went down with Libby. Don't get me wrong, I fully believe that we're meant to be together, in life and celestially, but I feel badly that your feelings might have been bulldozed in the process. I want to find a way to make it right."

"I'm fine, Tanya. I'm glad you guys are happy." Not exactly the truth, but there was no way she was letting Tanya know how devastating the whole scenario was for her. How she still felt it on a daily basis: the rejection, the humiliation, the sinking feeling that she'd be alone forever.

Tanya placed a surprised hand on her heart. "Really? I'm so glad to hear that. Libby will be, too. You know, I've always thought you were this awesome girl who could really pop given the right assistance."

Sam stared at her. "What do you mean?"

"I can help you." Tanya beamed. "Pop." The accompanying hand gesture caused Sam to jump. "You know what? I'm going to set you up with Serenity's all-encompassing Journeywoman Membership—on the house, of course. And before you know it, you'll have to beat 'em off with a stick." Just then, yet another tall blond person entered the room. Tanya turned. "Naomi, don't you think Samantha could be a knockout? We just need to find her glow."

"And pop," Sam supplied quietly.

Naomi-of-the-Glamazons strode toward her with the wide stride of an Olympic gymnast and looked down at Samantha as if she were an insect under examination. "Definitely." She placed a hand on Samantha's cheek. "I see such potential in you. Have you found your way to water?"

Sam held up her glass weakly and gestured with it toward Tanya. "We're working on the water thing."

"What about a series of facials?" Tanya asked Naomi.

"Would definitely tighten up those pores."

Oh, snap. They did not. Samantha placed a hand over her face. "Thanks. But I think I'll be fine."

Naomi nodded at Tanya as if Sam hadn't spoken. She was here, wasn't she, in the actual room? She glanced around to be sure. "And maybe a spray tan," Naomi added. "You're exceptionally pale. We offer twice-a-month spray tans with all of our journeywomen memberships."

"Which she now has. She's a journeywoman. A full one," Tanya said with reverence and a triumphant smile.

"I feel we also may need to work on integration," Naomi said.

Sam looked from Naomi to Tanya. "What does that mean?"

"It's the search for self." Well, at least they were speaking to her again. "The relationship between mind, body, spirit, and environment. You seem to need it, and we can help with that." Naomi pulled a multitude of brochures from her burgundy coat pocket and handed them to Samantha.

Suddenly feeling like a glowless klutz with Grand Canyon pores, Samantha decided it was time to get the hell out of there. She handed the water back to Tanya, forcing a smile, because her mother brought her up right. "I appreciate it. I do. The advice. The uh…transformative water et al. But I'm not feeling very well, so maybe we could postpone the rest of the tour?"

Tanya's eyes widened. "Of course. And I'll set that membership up for you right away. You'll be on your journey in no time."

"I'd better pack. Thanks. It was nice meeting you," Sam told Naomi as she headed blindly for the door. She'd walked into Serenity with a shred of self-worth and walked out feeling wildly inadequate yet again, as if all the progress she'd made over the last three weeks had been wiped clean.

CHAPTER FIVE

Hunter loved her guitar. She just never quite came up with enough time to play it. But when she did, it was an easy and welcome place to get lost after a long day at work. As far as guitar playing went, she had potential; at least that's what her instructor once told her at the lessons her mom agreed to pay for when she was a kid. But as with a lot of things, she'd lost focus when puberty hit and pretty girls demanded to be stared at, attended to. That was also around the time when she'd gotten a lot of attention for her keen compositional eye in art class. As a result, the guitar fell by the wayside.

She lamented that now, but had done her best to self-teach along the way.

Alone in her room, she strummed away at her own adaptation of "Blackbird," loving the melody and adding her own classical guitar flavor to the chorus. It filled her up, playing music, though she'd never been a performer or played in a band. She played for herself, and that was enough. She lost herself in the outro and closed her eyes as the last note lingered.

"That was beautiful," Sam said from the doorway.

Hunter looked up abruptly and smiled, shaking her head, her face now heated. "I had no idea you were home. God. Now who's the embarrassed one?"

"Maybe it's our thing, showing up unexpectedly." Sam, still dressed from her meeting with Serenity, leaned her head against the doorjamb. "And don't be embarrassed, please. I've never heard you play before. I knew you could, but I'd yet to experience it in person until now. I wonder how we've missed that step after knowing each other for—what? Almost ten years?"

"It's not something I show to people. Ever. It's just a hobby for me around the house. Helps me unwind, drift away from the daily grind."

Samantha nodded thoughtfully. "I love that song you just played. 'Blackbird.' The lyrics have always haunted me. I don't know what Paul McCartney was trying to say with them, but to me that song has always been about being on the outside looking in, and the painful distance that comes with it." The way Samantha said the words struck something in the center of Hunter's chest, and she didn't like it.

"You've felt that way before?"

Sam smiled, but there was sadness in her eyes. "I'm sure we all have at one point or another, but yeah. I have. In high school, I was salutatorian, and though I had a few friends, I was never a part of the In Crowd. Never invited to the cool parties, you know? I secretly wanted to be. I'd fantasize about it all the time."

While the memory sounded like a horrible one, Hunter couldn't help but feel something else was going on. Samantha was missing her normal upbeat, fun energy. "Did something happen today? Mal said the Serenity meeting went great."

Sam straightened. "Not my favorite day, no. But we sealed the deal on the account, and that's something."

Hunter breezed past the work talk, because in the scheme of life, it didn't matter. "Tell me what happened. You seem off-center."

"You know what? Let's skip it. I'm in need of unattractive, comfortable clothes and some self-pity." She pushed off the doorjamb and headed to the living room, but Hunter wasn't done. She set her guitar down and followed right behind Samantha.

"If I were Brooklyn you'd tell me."

Samantha grabbed some eggs and bacon from the fridge and tossed them onto the island. "Nope. And you're just as much my friend as Brooklyn is."

"But you confide in her."

Sam blew out a breath. "Yeah, I do. But she's not around so much these days, so…"

"Give her time. Being in a serious relationship is new for her. She'll find the balance soon. In the meantime, I happen to care about you a lot, and I'm incredibly interested in your day. And I'm really sexy, so there's that."

Samantha laughed at Hunter's playful bragging. It was a specialty of hers. "So you're saying you want to put on comfy pajama pants and watch *Lucy* with me for hours and love it?"

Hunter winced. Okay, so maybe she wasn't the perfect Brooklyn stand-in. "I could try. I would do that for you."

Sam shook her head and cracked the eggs. "You're sweet, but it's not necessary. You just be you, who I happen to like—most of the time anyway. And of course you're sexy, who can argue with that? It's not even fair to the rest of us. Want bacon and eggs? Or do you have a date?"

"I'd sell you my mother for bacon and eggs."

"Done," Sam said, pointing the spatula at Hunter. "I adore your mom. She calls me *Mino'aka*. I have no idea what it means, but I stand by it."

"It means beautiful smile in Hawaiian."

And God, was it true.

Sam was still wearing heels and a pencil skirt that showed off her legs. She'd lost her suit jacket, but her white button-up shirt was now rolled up at the sleeves. Her hair was in a professional-looking ponytail, and Hunter would have no problem freeing it from the rubber band and running her hands through—*whoa.*

Major friend infraction. *Stop right there. Do not pass Go.*

"It means beautiful, huh?" The smile was gone from Samantha's face as she cracked the eggs, lost in thought.

Hunter forced herself to breathe. A deep, cleansing breath that would center her and get her back on track, keep her present in the conversation. "Yeah, definitely means beautiful."

"You really hit the jackpot with your mom. Maybe it's to compensate for your dad and all his issues."

"I can't argue with that. It's a valid theory I've also subscribed to myself on many occasions." Hunter slid into one of the stools at the counter and watched as Sam went about making them dinner. Her goal was to focus on the preparation, but she was wildly infatuated with the quick, methodical movements Sam used to prepare the meal. The little flicks of her wrist were so spot-on and sexy that Hunter's stomach flip-flopped, her skin tingled, and she was right back to square one: lusting after the unavailable. She gave her head a little shake and focused on what Sam needed. "How about a trade-off? You tell me about your day and I do something for you? I'll unload the dishwasher for the rest of the week." Two birds with one stone, that deal.

"I like unloading the dishwasher. It's—"

"Part of your routine. I know." A crash and burn, which meant more of the sexy T-shirt. She thought for a moment, drawing upon her tried-and-true skill set. "How about this? I'll make you your very own Samantha Ennis website all about old movies and TV shows and numbers and fluid sexuality and a great big heart around the state of Pennsylvania." Okay, so she was being ridiculous, but Sam seemed to need a little levity. And while she humored Hunter with a smile, it was brief. Samantha stared at her, a new sincerity in her eyes.

"Play for me."

"What do you mean?"

"I'll tell you about my day if you agree to play your guitar for me. One song."

Okay, that wasn't really something Hunter was prepared to do. She didn't play for other people. It just…felt weird. Playing music was personal.

"I take it that's a no," Sam said to her lack of response. She shifted her energy to flipping the bacon. And there was that defeated look again.

"You know what?" Hunter couldn't believe she was agreeing to this. "Okay."

Sam whirled back around and raised a hopeful eyebrow. "Okay?"

"Yeah, I'll play for you. But first, you change clothes while I finish dinner. Then, while we eat, you tell me about your day."

"I think we have a deal."

With platefuls of scrambled eggs, bacon, and biscuits from the can, Samantha, now clad in jeans and a blue hoodie, told Hunter about running into Tanya so unexpectedly and the events that followed. Sam shook her head and studied the table. "I walked out of there feeling about two feet tall. And I know I shouldn't have let any of it get to me, but it did. Women like that have a way of making me feel like less of a person, and lately that sentiment seems to have hit an all-time high."

Hunter pushed her plate away. "You mean since the breakup?"

"Yeah. I mean, I've always had some stupid insecurities, but Libby did a number on me."

"It would have done a number on anyone to essentially be dumped on a live radio show. It was unfair and childish. But let me ask you this: If I were telling you this same story, that some woman who wore a glorified smock and worked at a spa told me that I need more restorative water in my life to increase my glow, what would your response be?"

Sam took a moment with that and flipped perspectives. The answer came to her easily. "That she was a crazy lunatic and that you're awesome."

"And if I continued on and told you that the Earth"—she consulted the brochure on the table and read from it—"was as a part of you, and aligning yourself with its gravitational pull was tantamount to your physical well-being?"

"I'd tell you that you were a new age freak and ask what you did with my best friend Hunter."

Hunter raised a shoulder. "Yet you listened to them. And they're fucking crazy."

Samantha laughed at that last part. "Fucking crazy, huh? Well, when you put it that way."

"There's no other way to put it. Crazy spa bitches. That's what we should call them from now on. CSBs."

Samantha was laughing full on now. "I can totally get behind that."

"We should swap all the water in their pitchers with Diet Coke and see what happens. Spa Armageddon. Attack of the CSBs. Blondes Who Kill for Water."

With tears in her eyes from laughing, Sam held up a hand. "You have to stop now. My stomach hurts."

"Fine. But can I say one last thing on the topic?"

Samantha took a fortifying breath to regain composure and blew it out. "You can."

"I've never known anyone with more of a glow around them than you, Sam. You light up rooms when you walk into them. It's kind of amazing to see it happen."

Sam paused the clearing of the plates, because it was obvious Hunter wasn't joking anymore. What she said came from a sincere place, and that meant a great deal to Sam. Who would have thought she could feel so much lighter with just that one comment from Hunter? "Thank you." She glanced at the ground and then back up. "You're a good friend, you know that?"

Hunter met her eyes. "I'm just telling you what I see every day. You're the real deal is all. And I can't say that about a lot of people."

"Well, I can say it about you," Samantha said. "You're probably the most genuine person I know."

"Thanks." Hunter smiled and in that moment, Samantha felt something important pass between them. It was a weighted exchange that Sam wasn't so sure she wanted to move out of. It felt comfortable, and yet so very not, at the exact same time. Was that possible?

Hunter's long, dark hair was down tonight. She seemed to wear it down around the house more, something Sam had noticed since they'd moved in together. The edgy hairstyles seemed to be more indicative of her outside persona. But there was a softness to the way the first strand fell just shy of her eye. They were staring at each other, and Sam realized neither one of them had said anything for a while.

"Time to play something," she said finally, moving them past it.

Hunter took a deep breath. "This is terrifying for me. You should know that."

Samantha couldn't remember a time when Hunter had seemed afraid of anything—or at least admitted to it. "Terrifying is okay once in a while. Now give me my money's worth or I'm calling my lawyer. We have a contract."

"Aggressive, but okay." Hunter shook her head, smiling, but dutifully retrieved her guitar. Without another word, she took a seat on the footstool across from the couch where Samantha sat with her legs tucked beneath her. After a brief moment to orient her fingers to the strings, Hunter began to play, quietly at first. Sam easily recognized the song, "House of the Rising Sun." It was one of her favorites, but then Hunter knew that.

As Sam listened, she slipped easily into the melody and even closed her eyes to soak it in, let it wash over her.

And then something amazing happened.

Something that hadn't been part of the deal.

Hunter began to sing.

Samantha was struck, her brain on pause and her face warm because the voice that came from Hunter, though not very big, was clear and pure and bluesy and awesome. She felt her lips part in utter shock at Hunter's raw ability. How was this possible? As the song continued, Hunter gradually gave more of herself over to it. She didn't just sing the song, she seemed to feel it. The emotion was raw and the music soulful. Samantha experienced each note right down to her core, and though she'd closed her eyes on the first few chords of the song, there was no way she could do that now, because the woman in front of her was stunning. More than that. And don't get her wrong, she'd always thought Hunter stunning, but when she sang, there was a whole new layer to the stunning. Jaw-dropping stunning. She was looking at Sam now as she sang, and Sam held that gaze, transfixed. Had she ever been transfixed before? She wasn't sure.

After three verses, Hunter brought the song to a close. The last strum of her guitar held on before the vibration of sound faded altogether. Hunter set her guitar next to her. Silence enveloped the room. She dipped her head and looked up at Sam, her eyes wide, as if she were suddenly exposed. But the trepidation shifted to concern once she took in the expression on Sam's face. "Why are you crying?"

Samantha hadn't realized she was. But an effective blink told her there were, in fact, tears threatening to spill from her eyes. She blinked back against them. "I guess I didn't know what else to do. Hunter...I had no idea." She lifted her hand in explanation, but let it drop when the right descriptive words weren't there. Instead, she said what was in her heart. "That was beautiful. And I'm honored that you played for me." It was clear to Sam that Hunter wasn't entirely comfortable with what she'd just shared. She looked nervous, vulnerable—two things Samantha hadn't realized Hunter capable of until now. There was a lot to this woman that she was only just beginning to realize.

"You don't have to say that."

"You're right. I don't. It just so happens to be true. You're so talented. I can't believe you hide it away."

"Technically," she said, gesturing to Sam, "I don't hide it away anymore. I've shared it with you." A smile touched her lips as she looked earnestly at Samantha. "I'm glad I did."

With that, a jolt of something powerful hit Samantha square in the chest. Something she couldn't name. But it came from the depths of the deep brown eyes she stared into, and it rocked her. She stood only because she didn't know what else to do. "I think I'm going to do some reading," she told Hunter quietly. Hunter nodded, seemingly at a loss for words as well.

Once she'd closed the door to her room, Samantha stood there with her hand against it, wondering what the hell had just happened. Was she suddenly into *Hunter* now? That was an outrageous and stupid concept all at the same time, one she immediately brushed away. A total rebound reflex, she told herself. That was all this was. And since rebound feelings weren't real, she thereby had nothing to feel ashamed of.

She caught sight of her own reflection in the wall mirror. The girl staring back at her didn't look especially sure of herself. She wasn't glamorous or tall. But Hunter's words echoed back to her, and she smiled, because maybe Hunter was right. Sam looked again, just to be sure, and there it was.

Her glow.

❖

"Wait. So the big knives can't go in the regular silverware drawer is what you're saying?" Hunter was trying to take it all in. "What does it matter?"

"Trust me. It matters," Brooklyn said, accepting Elvis's leash so Hunter could tie her shoe. It was their weekly morning walk through Central Park, something Hunter looked forward to exponentially. When she'd first adopted Elvis, Hunter made it a point to take him for some extra recreation once a week in Central Park in addition to his daily walks through the neighborhood. Somewhere along the way, Brooklyn took to tagging along, and now it was their standing date.

She and Brooklyn used the time to touch base with each other, offer advice, or just enjoy the serenity of the sights and sounds of the park waking up in the morning. Joggers, cyclists, bird watchers, and street vendors galore—they were all there. The city of New York stretched languidly from a good night's sleep and went about its day all around them.

Elvis loved the park and whined his enthusiasm as they inched closer to the lawn, where he knew his dreams would come true and they'd play a game of fetch with his tennis ball—what the little guy lived for. To say he pranced his way there would be an understatement. Elvis the Clydesdale was an accurate description.

Brooklyn glanced at Hunter as they walked, dodging a school tour. "To you and me, knife placement sounds minor in the scheme of things. And it is. To Samantha, it's her universe wrapped up in a nice little neat and orderly kitchen package."

Hunter smiled. "It's shockingly true. The little things matter to Sam in a huge way. I've always known that about her, but I think I'm now beginning to understand the true magnitude of that statement."

Brooklyn deadpanned, "You have no idea. It's endearing in some ways, but let me just say again: *you have no idea.*"

"I think I might have to move everything around just to mess with her a little." She grinned at the thought. Samantha getting all worked up and sexy-angry, using her authoritative accountant voice.

Brooklyn placed a hand on Hunter's forearm and regarded her with concern. "You're a braver woman than me."

Elvis stopped to greet a pretty lady walking by and Hunter nodded at him in approval. A dog after her own heart. Strangely, she didn't check out the woman herself. Just not really in that mindset today. The weather was gorgeous, the birds chirped, and even the tourists seemed to move at an appropriate pace on the sidewalks.

"Oh, and the mail's a big thing," said Brooklyn. "I always picked it up for us and dropped it smack in the middle of the counter."

Hunter laughed. "So anywhere on the counter's not enough? Needs to be the center, because otherwise, people may die? The world hangs in the balance of the mail's placement?"

Brooklyn held up a hand. "You're preaching to the choir, Billy Graham. I get it."

"Fine. Middle of the counter is where the mail shall land. No mail has ever been so centered as the mail I plan to deliver. What else has she said? This is helpful stuff."

Brooklyn stopped their progress just inside the park and turned to Hunter. "For the record, I'm only divulging what would otherwise be confidential friend details because I feel guilty for moving out and want this roommate thing to work out for you guys. Plus, it would ruin the Savvy vibe if you guys wound up hating each other."

Hunter took a minute with that. "We're not going to hate each other. That could never happen."

"I don't know. I heard TV time was a bust."

"Yeah, I don't really get *I Love Lucy.* And TV time is fun to an extent, but there's so much out there to do in the world. Plus, this Lucy chick is completely—"

"Before you voice anything about Lucy that you can't take back, let's just say that you're off the hook in the TV time department. I'd be jealous if Sam replaced me anyway."

"Not possible. She misses you, Brooks. I know you're caught up in the new living situation and the wonder that is Jessica Lennox, and rightfully so, but Sam's had a rough go of it lately."

Brooklyn sobered. "I know. I've been meaning to set aside some us time. I miss her, too."

"So stop talking about it and just do it. Lemonade?" Hunter asked, as they passed a street vendor just inside the park.

"Does Justin Bieber look like a chick?"

Hunter nodded. "Lemonade it is."

With a couple of cool drinks in hand, they made their way to the lawn. Elvis yipped and leapt vertically a few times in celebration of what was about to happen. She handed the beat-up tennis ball to Brooklyn. "Want to do the honors?"

"Excuse me, Elvis-the-dog? Is this what you're after? Elvis-the-dog wants me to throw it?"

Hunter smiled. "I think he likes it when you call him Elvis-the-dog."

"Well, it's his name."

At just the sight of his ball, Elvis came undone. Turning in a half dozen frenzied circles, he shrieked loudly and wagged his tail for all he was worth. When Brooklyn didn't immediately throw it, he used his two front paws to bounce off her chest. A process he repeated until she held up her hands. Of course one of them contained the ball, so he about lost it all over again. "All right. All right. And…go!" Like a rocket, Elvis tore off after the ball as if his life and those of his loved ones depended on its prompt retrieval. Brooklyn tilted her head. "I think he's getting faster."

Hunter had to agree. "I will enter him in the dog Olympics."

"He'd win," Brooklyn said.

Hunter waved her hand. "All the trophies."

"He'd be in the Dog Hall of Fame for decorated dog Olympians."

"He'd need a parade."

"Mal could organize it." Brooklyn sipped her lemonade. "So

what's new with you, my ultra-hip friend? Some girl named Cindy asked about you at Showplace the other night. I pled ignorance as to your whereabouts."

Hunter shrugged and slipped on her shades. "Haven't been out much lately."

"Oh no. What will happen to the lesbian population of New York? Who will collect numbers and flutter hearts in your place? Service the girls who need"—she coughed purposefully—"servicing?"

Hunter shoved Brooklyn playfully in response to the overt teasing. "I'm sure they'll survive. And they can service themselves. You know, you imagine I sleep with way more women than I actually do. Flirt, yes. Sex, only occasionally. There's a difference."

"Who knew?" But she dropped the smile, and Hunter understood that Brooklyn did, in fact, know.

"I've been staying home more. I kinda like it."

Brooklyn stared in mystification. "Someone broke Hunter. You're saying you've outgrown New York City? I don't want to burst your bubble, pal, but from here, there's no place more exciting. You could try Jersey, but…it's *Jersey*."

"I love New York. That's not it."

Brooklyn studied her. "Maybe it's your wild-child ways that you're outgrowing. Is that even possible?"

It was an interesting hypothesis, but one Hunter quickly discarded. "Let's not jump to crazy conclusions." And then, before thinking better of it, she asked Brooklyn the question that had been on her mind all week, the question she hadn't exactly planned on asking anyone: "Have you ever been into someone physically that you really shouldn't be into?" Elvis had returned and, after waiting patiently, nudged the ball to Hunter, placing a paw on her knee for maximum customer service. "Here you go, pal. Make me proud." She threw it for him again, and with a yelp, he was off.

"Falling for someone off-limits?" Brooklyn raised her hand and glanced around. "Um, story of the last year of my life. Where have you been?"

"Right. Not my brightest question. What did you do?"

"I fell madly in love despite my vehement protestation and moved in with her. Now we wake up together every morning and it's the most wonderful thing that's ever happened to me."

"While I'm happy for you, that's not really an option for me, and lusting after her is not something I plan to embrace. Wouldn't be a good idea. She's not the kind of girl you just hook up with." She left out the part that she'd already moved in with Samantha. Elvis had returned and now tossed the ball for himself into the air. Hunter looked on but was acutely aware of Brooklyn's eyes on her. "What?" she finally asked, turning.

Brooklyn shook her head, a smile across her face. "Since when have you ever been opposed to lusting after someone? *Since when? This is getting so good.*" She glanced around the park. "Where is the hidden camera?"

"You're funny. But I'm asking you for some actual advice." And you know what? Maybe she'd said too much already. But the situation with Sam had been on her mind a lot of late, and she was about tapped out of ideas. They'd run into each other the morning before, both on their way to the shower. She should have paid more attention to the time, but she'd overslept and found herself face-to-face with Sam in the hallway. Sam, wearing nothing but a towel. A towel that offered an awesome glimpse of the tops of breasts and bare shoulders and soft skin. Life, in that moment, became too complicated for her to live it.

She blew out a breath in defeat that was not at all lost on Brooklyn, who readjusted to face her more fully.

"Who is it? The off-limits object of your lust-filled daydreams?"

"You're enjoying this way too much, Brooks."

"I am. I'm reveling. Doesn't mean you get a free pass. Who is she?" Brooklyn threw the ball for Elvis, whose tongue was now hanging sideways out of his mouth from his glory-filled exertion. But he refused to give in and headed out in search of the offending tennis ball.

Realizing there was no way she could escape this conversation, which she was at fault for starting, Hunter had to think fast. "My yoga instructor."

Brooklyn thought on this and a lazy smile took shape. "Some people are really into the whole teacher-student thing."

She wasn't opposed to the dynamic. It did sound kinda sexy. Then she remembered to play her part. "Not me. I need yoga to be an escape. I don't want to ruin that. Yoga matters, Brooklyn. Big-time."

"I can see that. You're hardcore."

It was a total lie and she felt horrible about it, but there was no way she was telling Brooklyn that it was Sam going through her mind each day, and her smile, and the way her hair landed just so when she tossed it, and the look she got on her face when she was contemplative. God, she loved that look. Not to mention the sexy accountant glasses that came and went and left Hunter in a perpetual state of wonder.

"I'll need a name."

"What? Oh, um, April."

"April is a very sexy name."

Hunter rolled her eyes. "Doesn't matter. When you have an existing relationship with someone, especially an important one, it's a bad idea to bring romance into the picture and risk the really good thing you have."

Brooklyn eyed her skeptically. "So…yoga, and its place in your life, constitutes an important relationship?"

She was going with it. "Yep. Yoga saves lives. You're not paying attention."

"If you say so."

"Are you with me right now?"

Brooklyn nodded. "So with you." A pause. "Wait, so you're talking *romance* and not just lust? You have legitimate feelings for yoga queen?"

Hunter hesitated at the question. But no. Uh-uh. She refused to consider that option. There had been a time when she'd had a few butterflies for Samantha, yes, but she was long past them. It was an immature reaction to a minor crush. "No, this is physical attraction. Purely. I mean, I think she's great, don't get me wrong, but the problem is that I want to make out with her for an hour. And I can't think that way about her. Not this girl."

"I don't know. There seems to be more to this than maybe you're admitting, even to yourself. I think you're feeling a little out of your depth with this woman, and that says something. Don't put limits on your feelings, Hunter Blair. I'm in a relationship, so I'm suddenly quite wise."

Hunter laughed. "The wisest, clearly. And I am not out of my depth."

"Or course not. Not you." Brooklyn leaned back onto her elbows. "So this April is—"

"Hunter? Hey. I thought that was you!" Hunter turned at the sound of her name and—oh, sweet Mary in heaven. Seriously? Was this really happening to her right now? April stood just a few feet away wearing, wouldn't you know it, yoga crop pants and a snug hot pink workout top.

"Hey, April," she said, standing.

Worst timing ever.

Brooklyn was up and next to her in 2.3 seconds, smiling like she'd just won the coincidence lottery. "April. Wow. Hi, I'm Brooklyn." The two shook hands. "Hunter speaks extra highly of your class. It's nice to put a face to the name." At that, Hunter cut Brooklyn a warning glance.

Too late. In response to Brooklyn's words, April's smile turned into a beam, and beaming was *so* not part of the plan. Except maybe it should be. Maybe April was the perfect distraction, or even the cure-all, for her lusting-after-the-roommate dilemma.

"It's nice to meet you, too. I was going through a little pre-class workout before heading to work. Helps get my head in the game. Plus, outside stretching is so peaceful."

"I've found that, too," Brooklyn said with a straight face. "The stretching. Of the outdoor variety. It's awesome. All the leaves. Nature rocks." Brooklyn held up a fist in solidarity and Hunter shook her head. Brooklyn had never stretched outdoors in her life.

"Will I talk to you later?" April asked.

Spontaneously embracing her new plan, Hunter slid April her best smile. "Definitely. I'll text you tonight. See what you're up to."

April jogged backward a few feet, causing her hair to bounce, along with other admirable parts of her body. It should have affected Hunter, the bouncing. It really should have. A quick check-in with herself, and…nothing.

A really hot girl was bouncing, and nothing!

Not cool at all.

Unacceptable.

"Perfect. Nice to meet you, Brooklyn." And with that she was on her way. Hunter stared after her just in time for a punch in the arm from Brooklyn. "Yoga queen is super hot. And completely ripped—you left that part out. Did you see the abs? I'd buy them dinner, so I vote yes. Fall madly in love with her, please, and have tiny, flexible yoga babies. They can Tree Pose in height order. Think of the Christmas card potential."

"You don't get a vote."

"Pshhh. I do, too," Brooklyn said. "I won most valuable voter in high school."

"You did not. That's not even a thing."

"It is. I promise. I rock at it. Voting and such."

Hunter laughed and slung her arm around Brooklyn as they made their way out of the park. There really was no one like her. "Come on, trouble. I better take this dog home so he can sleep for a few hundred years."

"I like my new nickname. Trouble. I sound dangerous."

Hunter grinned. "And you are. I've seen you behind the wheel."

"Aw, thanks for noticing."

Bouncing failure or not, at least Hunter had a plan. She needed a little distraction and she'd get it. It would just take more concentration. She'd hope to gain some insight from her walk with Brooklyn, and she had. She was Hunter Blair. And per usual, she was calm, cool, and in control.

CHAPTER SIX

D ating was a bitch.

There was a reason Samantha had enjoyed being free of it for a while, in the cushioned existence of a relationship. She hated the vulnerability of it all, the great unknown. But after some careful thought, maybe rebound mode wasn't such a bad place to be. If nothing else, it was a distraction from some of the more difficult feelings associated with the loss of Libby in her life. Maybe she should take that rebound ball and run with it. So after unloading the dishwasher, showering, and getting ready for the day, she sat with a cup of coffee and studied her laptop.

Bachelor number one was kind of cute, in a bookish way. Samantha had to tilt her head to the side in response to the bow tie he wore in the photo, however. She squinted at the computer screen in contemplation. She wasn't sure she was a bow tie kind of girl. Reaching for her coffee, she scrolled to option two. A bachelorette this time. This one looked serious, and so did the hateful glare she sported. It said something about a person who glared at the camera and then selected it as their profile photo, didn't it? *Yeah, it says serial killer.* Next.

PairUp.com, the dating site Savvy represented, kept Sam occupied for the next half hour. She'd added her profile a few days before on a whim and already received a handful of hits, or "smiles," as they were called, from interested parties.

It had been a month since her unceremonious dumping on regional radio, but Samantha decided to take life by the horns. Plus, there had been that notable reaction she'd had to Hunter a few nights back, and it was imperative that she find another place to rebound.

The memory of Hunter that night had stuck with her. It had been something, taking in that raw emotion in her eyes, the way her mouth formed the lyrics to the song. It had seemed…sexy. But then, *of course* it was sexy. It was Hunter. And she was so not willing to be one of the millions of people who lusted after Hunter. Head heartbreaker in charge of all things charming—nuh-uh. And even if she was okay with that setup, there was no way she was risking the friendship just to let off a little steam. Even thinking about what she'd felt that night had her annoyed all over again. Damn it all. She took a cleansing breath to remedy that situation and refocused on the screen and her potential rebound-dating pool.

Fortunately, by informing PairUp of her bisexual status, she seemed to have upped her number of smiles substantially. Once in a while there were perks to the fact that her attraction was specific to the individual and not simply their gender. She'd grown comfortable with her sexuality over the years, even if the rest of the world gave her a hard time for it. She was to the point where she was tired of apologizing to people on both sides of the fence. So kill her.

"Who's that?" Hunter asked, passing behind Samantha on her way to the kitchen. She and Elvis had returned not long ago from their walk with Brooklyn. She'd say she was jealous of her friends' routine outing, but she'd been born with a keen aversion to exercise and anything that resembled it. And let's be honest, that park was endless.

She glanced at Hunter. "That is Howard J. from the Lower East Side."

Hunter made her way over and dipped her head over Sam's shoulder to see the screen better. And if Samantha wasn't acutely aware of Hunter's proximity, her stomach made sure with the flip-flop thing it just did. *No, no, no. No flip-flopping.* "And why is he smiling at you on your laptop?"

"A smile is when someone on PairUp wants to get to know you, take the next step. I think Howard J. wants to chat me up."

"Or something like that." Hunter straightened. "How come he's smiling at *you*? You're online dating now?"

Samantha took a deep breath and sat back in her chair. "It's come to this. After my most recent catastrophe, I thought maybe I should try something new. Maybe if I go on a date, it will take my mind off Libby and what could have been."

Hunter narrowed her gaze at the screen. "And you're into Howard J.?"

"I don't know yet," Sam said defensively. "Maybe. He seems like a normal guy. Software developer is kind of a vague job description, but you never know."

"What if the J stands for Johnson? You don't want to date a guy named Howard Johnson, do you? Mr. and Mrs. Howard Johnson. Think of your children. Don't put them through that."

"I'll have you know that I don't care about such trivialities."

"Big word. I bet Howard will like it. I bet Howard will eat up the word 'triviality' and the way you pronounce it. Say it again."

Samantha stared at her, her mouth agape. "You are a mean and hateful girl."

Hunter smiled sweetly. "But you love it when I tease you. Remember when you poured coffee on your pancakes instead of syrup at that restaurant on Fourth? And then ate them anyway because you're too nice to ask for new pancakes?"

"No. I don't remember that."

"You do, too. I brought you maple coffee to work every day for a week."

Samantha shook her head nostalgically. "You went to a lot of effort on that one."

"I did. And you laughed secretly. I know it. Just like you're laughing inside now. Just look. The edge of your mouth is pulling and you want to smile so badly, it's killing you."

Damn it. Hunter was annoying when she was right. Unable to stand it anymore, Sam gave into it, breaking into the smile she could no longer hold back. "Fine. I think you're funny. Once in a very great while."

"Then it's doubly tragic that I have to leave you alone with Howard now. A hot shower beckons." She pulled off her shirt as she walked, wearing just a black sports bra underneath. Samantha stared after her and the expanse of olive skin now in plain view. With Hunter's glorious curves highlighted for her to see, Sam's mouth went dry in reflex. God, that woman had a fantastic body. She should have become a Victoria's Secret model after college. *Who needs graphic art? Think of the money she'd have made.*

Samantha rolled her eyes at how generic those thoughts made her seem, especially when there was so much more to her friend than just that.

The shower turned on then and Samantha switched her mind off. *Not gonna think about your friend naked in the shower. Not going to happen.*

"All right, Howard J. Where were we?"

❖

Hunter blinked against the darkness all around her.

She was disoriented as she glanced around at what she now remembered was her new bedroom. Sam and Brooklyn's Soho loft. Right. The clock next to her broadcast 3:16 in bright green numbers. She felt Elvis, warm at her feet, just as a clap of thunder hit so loud she shot into a seated position, her hand clutching her chest instinctually to brace against the scare. Elvis raised his head in question, never one to worry much in the midst of a storm.

She blew out a slow breath.

The thunder had woken her, she now realized, as the ghost-like sound of heavy wind vibrated against her window. Her throat was dry. She turned to the glass of water she kept by her bed, but found it empty just as another clap of thunder hit. With a deep sigh, she raked all ten fingers into her hair and headed through the dark apartment. Still not fully awake, she walked with eyes half open in search of cool water. It wasn't until she neared the kitchen that she registered the glow of a dim light. Blinking to allow her eyes to adjust, she realized it was the refrigerator light. Standing there, in pajama pants and red cami top, was Samantha. Her hair cascaded past her shoulders in lackadaisical waves. She looked like an angel right there in that kitchen.

Sam turned at the sound of her approaching. "Couldn't sleep," she said in explanation, gesturing to the juice in her hand. "White grape juice."

Hunter didn't say anything. Instead, she filled a glass of her own from the faucet and drank generously before turning back to Sam, whose eyes were luminous tonight. The green popped brightly in the slash of moonlight. Sam tilted her head and studied Hunter. She had the most awesome lips. "Storm wake you, too? Loud."

"Yeah," Hunter managed to say, still transfixed by how beautiful

Samantha looked. There seemed to be less air in the room, and she wondered distantly if the two things were related. She was also still wondering about Sam's mouth. What it would feel like against hers, opening beneath it? What it would taste like? Maybe residual sleep had dulled her restraint, but she had to find out the answer to that question. In that moment, she couldn't have stopped herself from kissing Sam any more than she could have stopped herself from breathing. As she stepped into Samantha's space and dipped her head, Sam searched her face curiously.

"Hunter, are you okay? What are you—"

But that was all Samantha managed to get out before Hunter's lips were on hers, seeking out what she'd so desperately craved for weeks now. Startled at first, Sam seemed to brace against the kiss and placed one hand on Hunter's chest, pushing her backward. But it was only a second or two before the push disintegrated. Sam softened and met her there, giving herself over to the kiss in the most unexpectedly wonderful way. That hand on Hunter's chest slipped up and around until it landed on the nape of Hunter's neck and pulled her in. As Sam's mouth moved against hers, her lips parting to receive her, a tidal wave of need crushed Hunter's senses. She moved her hands to Samantha's face, holding her in place where she kissed her hungrily, slowly.

And God, it was good.

Better than she would have even guessed. It was like no other kiss really and she couldn't get enough.

The room around them lit up with a flash of lightning. A shock of thunder followed, but Hunter didn't care. She was exactly where she had to be.

Sam went up on her toes for better access, and in the process her breasts brushed against Hunter's, sending her entire body to places hot and deep before it tightened with an aching arousal. She didn't want to stop. She didn't want to return to reality. But it was too much, the physical pull. Heat licked through her like an untamed wildfire and she had to take back control.

Slowing the kiss, she ran her tongue across the bottom of Samantha's lip, tasting the wonderful sweetness of the grape juice long forgotten. Finally, she pulled her mouth away entirely and instead caressed Samantha's cheek with her thumb, now acutely aware of all the things Sam made her want to do. "God, Sam," she managed before taking a step back. Samantha stared at her in wonder, probably searching for some sort of explanation. But without another word, she removed herself from the situation before she took actions she couldn't erase. She would pay for that kiss later. Of that, she was sure. But it wasn't like there had been any way around it. She needed that kiss as much as her body needed the water she'd set out to retrieve. So for tonight, she'd revel in the tantalizing exchange she'd shared with Sam in the kitchen. Dream about it. The world and its consequences could wait until morning.

Samantha stood in the kitchen watching as Hunter disappeared behind the door to her bedroom, her mind struggling to catch up with the series of events that had her lips swollen and her body lit up like a Christmas tree.

In her kitchen.

In the middle of the night.

Repeat.

She'd just made out with *Hunter Blair* in her very own kitchen.

As her breathing returned to normal, she touched her still-sensitive lips and stared blindly at the rain pelting the nearby window, but it offered no answers. And how could it? What had just happened was crazy.

Her grape juice, still half-full, sat on the counter's edge. She abandoned it and walked slowly back to her bedroom, her heart beating a fast-paced rhythm in her chest, her world wildly off-kilter.

Sleep didn't come easy. She lay there examining the encounter from every possible angle, struggling to make sense of what had been easily the most unexpected and hottest exchange of her life. To say her mind didn't eventually shift to the kiss itself would be inaccurate, because Sam relived every second of that, too. She shifted uncomfortably as her body responded to memory. The softness of Hunter's lips when they'd pressed to hers, coupled with the command of that mouth not long after. She could still feel its effects on every inch of her. Torturously awesome and horrifically wrong, all wrapped up in the same event.

She blew out a breath and stared at the ceiling.

It was going to be a long night.

❖

When Samantha arrived at the Savvy loft the next day, Mallory looked like she was ready to kick a baby penguin. "Morning," she muttered to Sam and dropped a file folder onto her desk with a thud. Well, wasn't that the most cheerful greeting ever?

"Morning, Mal," she said tentatively. "Do you need any coffee? You look like you need coffee." She was willing to make a Starbucks run if it would help Mallory not kill someone.

"Nope. I'll get some soon. Check your email."

"Will do."

Samantha glanced at her watch. Just past eight and no one else was in yet, which made sense, as she was fifteen minutes ahead of her own schedule. Possibly on purpose. She'd woken herself early that morning, gotten ready, and left the apartment without encountering... well, anyone. Avoidance was a lame solution, but it was all she had in her arsenal after the kitchen kissing. And God, she needed to talk about it with someone, but Brooklyn was the person she talked about those things with, and there was no way she could tell Brooklyn about the random kitchen kissing, or about the way her stomach tugged pleasantly every time she thought about kitchen kissing. This really shouldn't be happening.

Sam switched on her computer monitor and saw immediately that Mallory had sent an email to all three of them with instructions to pause all work for Foster Foods. Whoa. In other words, their biggest project. This didn't bode well. She peered around her monitor and stole another glance at Mallory, their fearless leader, who in this moment sighed deeply and shuffled a few dozen sheets of paper around. *Still in penguin-kicking mode,* Samantha decided. Something was most definitely up.

"Coffee delivery girl," Brooklyn practically sang as she slid open the door. "I'm here to make morning dreams come true via caffeine."

"The coffee fairy didn't forget us, Mal," Samantha said as Brooklyn deposited a plain latte on her desk.

"Yay," Mallory deadpanned.

"Morning, Sammie-Sam." Brooklyn kissed her cheek with a smack.

"And she's in a good mood. Again."

Brooklyn inhaled and smiled. "That I am. Because I had a fantastic night." Translation: She got laid and was all sparkly because of it. It had been a constant sparkle ever since she and Jessica had entered official couplehood back in December. It was cute at first. Not so much anymore. But maybe she was just in a bad place.

"Almond latte for Mallory," Brooklyn said, delivering the drink. "With your name spelled correctly. I didn't even have to tell them."

"Aw, thanks," Mallory said without taking her eyes off her screen. Brooklyn turned to Samantha with a raised eyebrow, to which Sam could only shrug back. Brooklyn pressed on. "A café mocha for me, and an Americano," she stared at Hunter's empty desk, "with absolutely no home. Your roommate's missing. What gives? Did you murder her over mail placement?"

"Absolutely no murdering." Sam glanced behind her, feigning nonchalance as if she hadn't noticed Hunter's absence at all, when in reality she was acutely aware. "Huh. That is interesting. Probably on her way down."

"Probably," Brooklyn said, dropping off said Americano on Hunter's desk anyway.

"Check your email," Sam whispered.

It wasn't long before she heard a murmured "What the…" from Brooklyn's desk. "Mal, are you planning to elaborate on this email?"

Mallory swiveled around to face Brooklyn. "Just waiting till we're all here, and then I'll go over what I know."

"Go get her," Brooklyn said, addressing Sam. "Drag her out of bed if you have to. I don't care if she was out late."

Okay, the concept of walking into Hunter's bedroom and throwing the covers off her barely dressed body didn't sound like a wise idea at all. Not good for the whole avoidance tactic. Nope. The kitchen kissing had trumped any kind of expectation of rational, mature behavior. This was the panic zone, where it was every girl for herself. "She'll be here soon. It's just now eight-twenty. Relax, coffee fairy."

"I'm texting her." Brooklyn fell back into her chair dramatically and the office once again lapsed into silence. Samantha busied herself in deposit slips, Mallory tick-tacked away on her keyboard, and Brooklyn stared at the wall, which meant she was doing that creative thing. At long last, the door slid open and Hunter made her way in.

Brooklyn stood. "Finally. Can we discuss this now?" she asked Mallory.

"What are we discussing?" Hunter asked easily. "Morning, guys." Her hair was in a low ponytail and she sported an army green button-up that she'd left untucked atop black leggings and lace-up boots. She looked fresh and chipper, as if she'd just had the most restful sleep of her entire life, which just irked Samantha further, as she'd clocked *maybe* forty-five fitful minutes.

"We're discussing why we're halting all work on the Foster account," Mallory said, already heading into the kitchen where they could meet around the table.

"Well, that's news," Hunter said, dropping off her stuff and picking up the Americano. She held it up in Brooklyn's direction questioningly.

"You're welcome," Brooklyn said sweetly, heading to the table before stopping and regarding Sam curiously. "You're in my seat. Why are you in my seat? This is strange. You like everything to be exactly the same."

The reason for the seat switch was that her own seat was across from Hunter and the concept of staring across the table at her during the meeting, or the opposite, forcing herself to look away, was too daunting to deal with and too difficult a problem for this morning. But she wasn't about to explain that to the room. Instead she shrugged. "I'm trying something new. Spontaneity."

Her friends exchanged looks. Hunter sent her a small smile and shrugged in a way that seemed to say, "Good morning. Last night was no big deal." But that wasn't a sentiment she shared. Because while she wanted the world to go back to normal, desperately she did, one cannot simply unkiss her best friend. And as her thoughts began to take off on a panic-laced tangent, Mallory's words roped her back into the here and now.

"Foster Foods filed Chapter Eleven late yesterday."

Samantha ran that sentence back through her brain one more time. It still didn't add up. "I'm sorry. What did you say?"

"No fucking way," Hunter said, leaning back in her chair. "So they're done. Gone?"

Brooklyn placed a hand over her mouth in devastation. Mallory held up one finger. "Not exactly. Apparently some really bad business moves have dropped them on their ass financially, but Royce Foster isn't going down that easily. They're working on restructuring their debt."

"What does that mean for us?" Brooklyn asked with the hopeful eyes reminiscent of a Disney princess.

"It means…we're on hold. We may lose their business altogether, and if so, that means we need to replace it. It means I need to hustle. Brooklyn and Hunter need to dazzle on the creative so much that our current clients can't get enough of us, and Sam needs to make some money magic happen so we can stay in the loft despite the crazy rent hike. That might mean a whole new monthly budget. Starting from scratch."

But the larger problem settled over Samantha and she met Mallory's gaze grimly. "We're not getting paid on those outstanding invoices, are we?"

The subtle shake of Mallory's head caused Sam to inhale at what a blow that would be. They'd been floating Foster's bill for several months now on good faith, thinking they'd just gotten caught up in the paper clog of a large corporation's accounting department. But she'd been counting on that money. The four of them spent the majority of their time working on Foster projects. And now with the rent so much higher, she didn't know how in the world they were going to have done all of that work for free.

"This is bad," Sam said to Mallory, and then proceeded to explain to the others the outstanding invoices, the true state of things.

"How is that possible?" Brooklyn asked, infuriated. "We did that work. We deserve to be paid."

"It's possible we still might be," Mallory said. "But it probably won't be for a while."

"So you're saying we need to step it up a little to split the difference?" Brooklyn asked.

"That's what I'm saying."

Brooklyn sighed. "Okay, but can I just say that this sucks? I think we're going to need afternoon Pinkberry to survive this. The S'mores kind. I nominate Hunter to go get them midafternoon. The counter girls love her and then we get extra toppings."

"I second this idea. That's why we keep you," Mal said to Brooklyn.

"Just earning my keep, boss."

Hunter stood and gave a nod and easy smile. "I accept my mission."

See, that right there annoyed Sam. The cavalier attitude. The mission to make girls swoon. It was whatever. Samantha resisted a visible eye roll but she definitely participated in one internally. As Brooklyn and Mallory headed back to their desks to work on the accounts still in play, Hunter lingered in the kitchen with Samantha a moment longer.

"Maybe we could talk later about last night?"

Samantha felt her cheeks redden, suddenly on the spot. "Um, sure. Of course. If you want to."

"I do."

Samantha stole a sideways glance across the office and dropped her voice further. "But not here. I don't want to involve…"

Hunter's eyes widened instantly. "No. Definitely not. We can talk tonight. Just us."

"Perfect. I'll be home."

Hunter nodded. "And I'll be home, too."

"Great. Both home. So we can talk."

"And we will," Hunter said.

"See you then."

Hunter hesitated. "I mean, I'll see you around the office first. And I'll be getting you Pinkberry later, so…"

"Right," Sam said, jumping in. "We'll both be around, probably." God, this was the most awkward ever. Sam hated it.

"But…tonight is best. Yeah."

Hunter turned on her heel and headed back to her desk, cursing herself and her inability to speak to Samantha like a functioning human. Maybe it was because Sam was in her relaxed mode today. She wore a navy blue skirt and red short-sleeved knit top with her hair down and luxurious. She looked great, and thereby Hunter was apparently relegated to sixteen years old and tongue-tied. But damn it, she wasn't even like that when she *was* sixteen. Where the hell were her moves? She'd been a stammering, staring idiot.

Four hours later, she put herself to the test at Pinkberry.

"Hunter, right?" The girl behind the counter grinned widely. It was the same girl from last time. Blond, shoulder-length hair, with a stud through the top of her ear and a smiley face tattooed on her right wrist.

"That's right. And you're Kayla." Hunter was great with names. It was a skill she'd picked up early in her flirting career. This seemed to make the girl infinitely happy.

"How is your day today?" Kayla asked.

"I've had better, but it's starting to look up about now."

"Oh, yeah?"

She inclined her head, employing the head tilt/direct eye contact combo that always seemed to elicit a blush. "Definitely." Wait for it. One, two, three, and full-on blush. Perfect. She could feel her confidence crawling its way back to her.

"So what can I put together to make your day even better?" Kayla asked.

"Three medium S'mores for my friends and a Watermelon Cooler for me. Light and refreshing on a warmer day, you know?"

Kayla stared at her for a moment before snapping to attention. "Right. Yes. I definitely know." She wiped her forehead. "It is warm in here, isn't it?"

"I meant outside."

Kayla looked stricken. "Of course."

"But I'm starting to feel the heat you mentioned."

A second blush. Perfect. Kayla gave her head a little shake. "I'll get your order ready."

"Thanks, Kayla. You're my favorite. Oh, and my friends wouldn't mind extra chocolate chips. I mean, if you have any to spare."

"Anytime, Hunter. Just ask for me next time. I'll get you set right up."

As Hunter walked from Spring Street back to the loft with the bag containing four small frozen yogurts, she did so with a confident stride. It turned out she wasn't broken after all. She just seemed to lose her power around one particular person. Not a major crisis. Just something she would work on.

❖

"All I'm saying is that you don't *have* to follow me into every room. You probably have stuff to do."

Elvis stared up at Samantha in response, his stubby little tail thwacking back and forth. "Listen, you're very handsome. I concede this. But I already scratched your ears and your stomach and tossed that fake newspaper for you like eight times since I've been home from work, and it was kind of a hard day. We lost a major client, Elvis. You feel me? So what more can I do for you?"

Elvis upped the ante and now it appeared that his entire body wagged.

"Yes, you're adorable and I really, really like you, but I don't know how to help you further. Your mom should be home soon." She turned and walked through the door to her bedroom, Elvis still at her heels. This dog came with a lot of pressure. He had apparently developed some sort of affinity for her, and his attention, while complimentary, was not something she was used to. She didn't know quite what he needed, but she was tempted to offer him a cocktail. Lord knows she could use one.

As Elvis looked on from the spot he favored on her bed, she changed from her work attire into her denim capris and a heathered pink T-shirt, and scrunched up her toes in celebration of no work shoes. She then went about making some pasta and pesto sauce in the kitchen, the same kitchen she'd had her world rocked in just hours prior. She tried not to dwell on the world rocking.

Mid-stir, the door slid open and Hunter strolled in, her messenger bag diagonal across her body. "Hey," she said to Samantha.

"Hi. Want some pasta?"

"I definitely do. That smells amazing. What is it?" Hunter bent down to greet Elvis, kissing his face, and slid her bag off her shoulder. "Solve all of the world's problems today, Elvis? You're helping Samantha cook, I bet. You excel at cooking."

"He's okay. Honestly, he could do a little more stirring and a little less staring." She inclined her head to the pot. "And that is pesto sauce. Ennis specialty. My mom passed it down." Okay, good. This was feeling fairly normal, and she so needed normal right now.

"Anything I can do to help?"

"Grab some plates."

Hunter did as she was told and set the table for them both. "So that was crazy today. The Foster deal."

Samantha shook her head. "I just wish we'd had more warning. I would have been more conservative with last month's receivables, you know?"

Hunter shook her head. "I don't know how you do it."

"Do what?"

"Money magic. My mind just doesn't work that way."

Sam set the bowl of pasta on the table next to the salad she'd thrown together. "But mine does. Keeps things interesting." She shrugged. "I like the black and white of it. The structure. It's something I can control."

"You like to be in control of things, that's for sure."

"What? And you don't?"

Hunter leaned back in her chair. "I think we can both agree that I'm a little more go with the flow."

"That's true. You do your laundry on whatever day of the week you want. It's barbaric."

"Yeah, well, don't tell anyone."

Samantha sat a bit taller. "Sunday is for washing clothes. It's the perfect day for it."

"Of course it is. And on the seventh day, God did laundry. Everyone knows this."

Sam laughed. "You're teasing me again."

"I have to. You know this."

"That part's true."

As they settled into dinner, Sam was smiling because things seemed to be falling back into place. She and Hunter had reclaimed their easy rhythm, and it felt so comfortable that Sam relaxed for the first time in sixteen hours. Plus she'd poured them each a glass of Merlot, so that helped. And God, the sauce had turned out great. She should open a sauce shop. Sam's Sauce. She'd rock sauce sales.

As they ate, Hunter glanced over at her thoughtfully. "I dare you to change it up."

Samantha raised a curious eyebrow. "You dare me to change what up?"

"Do your laundry on Thursday this week."

"You mean take a walk on the wild side with you?"

"You might like it, Sam." Hunter smiled and Samantha felt it right in the center of her stomach.

"Maybe. But I also happen to like my life as it is. My routine helps me stay focused. Keeps my life together."

Hunter stared back at her in challenge and Sam made note of the fact that Hunter's eyes were probably her most expressive feature. Big and the softest brown imaginable. She also had the most elegant neck, slender and smooth, leading down her body to curves that could not be ignored. As tough as Hunter seemed, as cool and charming as she often was, there was something innately soft and feminine about her that Samantha loved. Hunter came with a lot of layers.

"Is that a no to the laundry challenge?"

Oh.

Right.

There had been a conversation in progress.

"Fine. I'll swap up my laundry day, but what do I get in return?"

Hunter stared back at her knowingly, a small smile playing on her lips. And just like that, Samantha felt the color enter her cheeks at the unspoken insinuation. Her world skidded wildly off center once again. Damn it.

"We should probably talk about last night," Hunter said. The teasing smile faded from her lips, the deal temporarily forgotten in favor of the larger issue.

"Okay." That was about all Samantha could manage. The room now felt small and she wasn't quite sure what to do with herself, with her hands, so she began to straighten up, clearing things from the table and setting them across the island to wash.

"It was bad of me. Kissing you like that."

Sam stopped what she was doing and turned to listen.

"I was half-asleep and…well, I hope that you'll accept my apology."

It wasn't exactly an explanation, and as much as Sam wanted to move forward from this, she needed one. "What made you do it?"

Sam watched Hunter take a deep breath before meeting her eyes with reluctance. "Because in that moment, I couldn't imagine not doing it. You were so beautiful standing there, the moonlight playing in your hair. Stunning. So I…acted."

Samantha's lips formed a tiny "oh," but no sound escaped them. She couldn't remember the last time someone had called her stunning. It hadn't been what she'd expected to hear and that stripped her momentarily of her trajectory.

Hunter continued. "I didn't tell you that to make you uncomfortable. But you did ask."

"No, I did. I just…" Finally, Sam found her footing and said what her mind was thinking. "Really? You thought that about me?"

Hunter nodded, knowing full well it was a bold move, the honesty, but when asked the question, she couldn't quite bring herself to sidestep the truth. Because it wasn't some girl from a bar asking, it was Samantha. Samantha, who knew her better than most people on the planet. As Sam stared at her, Hunter felt a prickle of heat in her cheeks.

Sam glanced at the wall in mystification before shaking her head and meeting Hunter's gaze. "I thought you'd maybe been sleepwalking."

"I was awake." And then because they were being so honest, Hunter took it one step further. "What made you kiss me back?"

At the question, Sam resembled a terrified puppy. Just as Hunter opened her mouth to let her off the hook, she got her answer.

"Well, you happen to be a really good kisser."

Hunter laughed. She hadn't seen that one coming. "Yeah, well, right back at you."

Samantha walked around the island toward Hunter. "It can't happen again. You know that, right? It would ruin everything that's important."

Hunter placed her hand over her heart. "I do, and it won't. It was a moment in time. Our moment." And then she grinned. "We'll always have the kitchen, Sam."

Samantha tossed a dish towel at her playfully and then covered her eyes with one hand. "I cannot believe you just said that to me."

"I'll never look at white grape juice the same way again."

Sam gasped. "You have to stop or I will be forced to kill you. This is embarrassing enough." But she was laughing and that was good.

"You can't kill me. You adore me."

Samantha stopped her advancement, her expression now sincere. "Now that part is true. You know that right?"

"I do." A pause. "Leave the dishes for me. You made our dinner. I'll clean up."

"Roommate points. You sure?"

"Yep." Hunter glanced at the sink. "I'm an amazing dishwasher. Prepare to be impressed."

"I can hardly wait. While you do that, I'm off to Queens."

Hunter smiled at Sam's once-a-week volunteer gig at the retirement community. "Say hi to Mr. Earnhardt for me. And see if you can snag his lasagna recipe."

"He swears he's taking it to his grave, but I'll see if I can't sweet-talk him."

"I have faith in you."

Hunter put on the Eagles and went to work scrubbing the pots and plates they'd used for dinner. She was pleased with the kiss debriefing and felt they'd both handled the delicate situation quite well. They'd even laughed about it, which was just absolute bonus.

Her phone buzzed in her pocket and she automatically assumed it was April. They had plans to get together at nine just after April's final class. She'd thought about canceling, but the distraction was much needed. But instead of April's face smiling up at her from the screen, she saw her mother's instead.

"Hi, Mama."

"Hello, angel girl. Are you eating?"

"Right now? No. We just finished dinner. Why?"

"No, in general. You look too thin on the Facebook thing. It concerns me."

Hunter smiled. Her mother was new to social media but was definitely making up for lost time. "I haven't lost any weight, Mama. I promise. What photo are you looking at?"

"I don't know. You were tagged by a girl named Stacey who has her arms around your waist. I hit 'like,' but I didn't really like it at all."

"She's just a girl from a club I was at, Mama. I don't really know her that well."

"She wants to know you, that's for sure. If you don't know her, don't let her up against you like that, *nani kaikamahine*. Everyone on the Faceplace is going to think she's your girlfriend. My mah-jongg group will see and think there's a wedding."

Hunter smiled. "You're right. I'm sorry." She knew when to pick her battles. Her mother was the sweetest person on planet Earth, but she came with a rock-solid set of morals and values that she expected her children to adhere to as well. And while Hunter did her best, she sometimes felt there was an unavoidable generation gap. Plus, her mother had never lived in New York City.

"I'm calling about your father's birthday this weekend. It's going to be more of a celebration than I originally thought. We're having a party for him at the NCO club on base. All of our friends are coming."

"Oh yeah?" She didn't see why this had to involve her just because the location had changed.

"It would mean a lot to the family if you came. There will be pictures, and every time I look at them, my middle baby will be missing."

Hunter dropped her head back and stared at the ceiling. Not this again. If she knew him, her father would actually prefer it if she didn't show up. It would be the best birthday present she could possibly give him. Why put herself through that and spend a weekend angry and resentful all over again? "He doesn't need me or want me there, Mama. We both know this. If anything, it would just cause problems. He'll make some sort of passive-aggressive comment. I'll take offense and fire back. Nothing good ever comes from us being in the same room. You'd have photos of angry people."

"That's not true. I still hold out hope that you and your father will see eye to eye someday. Underneath it all, he's a good man. He just has trouble communicating sometimes."

And accepting his children as they are, Hunter wanted to supply. But her mother was caught in the middle, and that couldn't be an easy place to reside. She should cut her some slack. "I don't think it's going to work out this time. Plus, last-minute flights are hard to snag. I'll come on a different weekend. How about next week?" She knew her mother was craving a visit, and if she dangled an impending trip in front of her, it might get her off the hook.

Her mom paused in defeat, not taking the bait. "It matters to me that you're there. I want all three of my children present together when our friends and family come out to celebrate. You're coming. You'll find a reasonable flight. I'm your mama, and that's what I say."

What could she do here? Feeling as though her hands were tied and wanting to do whatever she could for her mother, she blew out a breath. "Fine. I'll be there."

"I love you, Hunter. Be good."

"I love you, too, Mama. I will."

Chapter Seven

Sam arrived at the Balmy Days Senior Center ten minutes late. She'd hopped the L train to Queens, but due to maintenance on the track, they'd been delayed and forced to transfer at the last minute. When she'd arrived, she was met by the usual suspects, all concerned she wasn't going to make it for their scheduled scrapbooking class.

Samantha had begun volunteering at the retirement home three years prior, and since that time, had developed a steady following of residents who looked forward to their time together. While she tried to work up a variety of activities for them to participate in during her time with them, scrapbooking quickly emerged as their clear favorite. If there was one thing elderly people seemed to like to do, it was reminisce about the past, and organizing their old photos seemed to serve that purpose nicely.

"Sorry I'm late, everybody," Sam said, sliding her bag off her shoulder. "Subway trouble."

Mr. Turner nodded gruffly, but unfolded his arms. That was a start.

Mrs. Linehart clapped. "Well, at least we can get started now."

"Thank God you're all right," Mrs. Swientek said, patting her shoulder. The others headed off to the recreation room, ready to get moving.

An hour later, with remnants of a glue stick all over her fingers, she moved about the room helping each resident as best she could. She looked forward to the time she spent at the senior center and loved her little group, even if they did bicker with each other incessantly over who was dating whom, or what the cafeteria should really look into serving. But one thing was clear: They all seemed to adore Sam—even

Mr. Turner, who'd rather eat paper than admit it. Regardless of his stern demeanor, he showed up voluntarily each week, and quietly assembled his own scrapbook of mementos from his life.

"Samantha dear, do you have any glitter? I'd like to add some glitter to my single girl page. Make me a little bit of a rock star."

"Sure, Mrs. Guaducci. What color would you like?" Mrs. Guaducci had recently added a pink streak to her white updo, in response to Mrs. Potter asking Mr. Glenville to sit with her in the dining hall. It was all a very big deal and still a bit touchy.

"Well, since I'm going for more of a hussy vibe with this page, to accentuate my swinging single years, what would you recommend?"

Swallowing her smile, Samantha selected a deep purple and handed it off.

"Samantha, dear, have I ever showed you a photo of my sweet Martha and me on our honeymoon?" Mr. Earnhardt asked.

"I don't think so, Mr. Earnhardt." She crossed the distance to his workstation and stared at the black-and-white photo of the young, happy couple standing next to a sand castle on the beach. Mr. Earnhardt had lost her five years ago to cancer. "Oh my. She's beautiful."

Mr. Earnhardt beamed at her words and looked back at the photo. "She was the prettiest girl in all of time. I think I'm going to give this photo its own page. Spotlight it some."

Samantha smiled. "That sounds like the perfect idea to me. How about some beach die cuts? I have some in my supply bin."

"It would be nice if you had one of the sun shining brightly."

"I'll see what I can come up with."

The two-hour session seemed to fly by, but by the end of it, each of the residents had made much progress on their project. As Sam packed up all of the scrapbooking paraphernalia, her most dedicated gang of troublemakers hung close.

"When are we going to get to meet your girlfriend, Sam? You told us you'd bring her with you one day soon."

Samantha hesitated, closing her eyes briefly at the still-painful Libby reminder. "I did say that. But unfortunately, she's not my girlfriend anymore. We broke up."

"Tramp," sweet Mrs. Swientek shot. Sam's eyebrows rose in response to the otherwise grandmotherly woman. "You're better off without her, then. Burn her stuff."

"Oh, wow. Thanks, but it's not her fault. It just wasn't meant to be."

"You'll find someone better," Mr. Earnhardt said.

Sam sighed and fastened the lid on the box of supplies she stored in the closet. "Maybe someday."

"Well, if she can't visit, maybe you could bring back those friends you work with sometime. They were very nice girls."

Samantha smiled. The residents craved visitors, and she did what she could to bring folks in to see them. Mallory, Brooklyn, and Hunter had been great about stopping in every now and then, sitting in on her classes and helping as best they could.

"Now that is a definite possibility."

"I like the blond one. She's the most fun," Mrs. Guaducci said.

Mr. Glenville raised a finger. "I think the dark-haired, exotic one should come back."

Mrs. Guaducci scoffed and muttered under her breath. "Babelicious."

"Excuse me?" Sam said, looking in question from Mrs. Guaducci to the others. "What does 'babelicious' mean?"

"It's what these men call your friend. Downright disturbing if you ask me," she grumbled. "Bunch of old men chasing after a girl her age."

"We're not chasing after her," Mr. Earnhardt corrected. "That would be impolite. We just like it when she's here. And we can see her."

Sam couldn't hold back the smile. "You call Hunter babelicious?"

Mr. Glenville shrugged sheepishly.

Sam laughed. "I'll have to remember that one."

❖

"Can I order you another?" Hunter asked April, gesturing to her dwindling glass of Merlot. Not feeling wine herself, she'd gone with a vodka tonic and could already feel the day slide off her. She was relaxed, at ease with April, and feeling like herself again. It had been a good idea, this little late-night get-together.

They'd met at a tiny little French bistro in the Meatpacking District, not too far from the gym where April had just finished with work. They were the only table in the place, but then again it was after ten on a weeknight.

"Oh, no thanks," April said, holding up the glass. "One is my limit during the week. Trying to stay on the fitness train as best I can. I'm happy you called. I don't know if I said that already, but it's true."

Hunter smiled. April had a tendency to repeat things. It was kind of endearing. "Me too. I needed to get out tonight. This is perfect."

April tilted her head to the side and studied her. "So what's your story?"

"My story? Well, I work in advertising. Graphic art, more specifically. Recently moved from just down the street here to Soho. It's an artist's loft, so I can live and work in the same building due to zoning allowances. I have a dog, I'm into yoga, and work with my three best friends."

"And date a lot of girls along the way."

"Who told you that?"

"Just a hunch. You're way smooth."

"Thank you for catching that."

It was light, their banter. They'd settled further into the place and traded stories about their days. April was funny and good looking and seemed to have a head on her shoulders. But she was nervous, that much Hunter picked up on. Luckily, she knew how to help. She dipped her head and met April's eyes. "You're very pretty, you know that?" It wasn't a lie.

April's gaze fell to the table before it bounced back up. "Thank you, but you don't have to say that."

"I don't. And wouldn't, in fact, except that you are."

April placed her elbows on the table and leaned her chin on her hands. "This is our third encounter, you know."

Hunter hadn't been counting. She sipped her drink casually. "Is it?"

"Mmm-hmm. Class, the park, and now drinks."

"Three's a good number."

April glanced at the bartender and offered him a head nod. Hunter saw where this was going. "I live just around the corner. Do you want to walk me to my door?"

"I was just about to offer." They were definitely on the same page.

Twenty minutes later and Hunter was taking in the small but cozy one-bedroom apartment April had off Twenty-first. It seemed they'd been practically neighbors until Hunter moved to the loft. The compact living room was simple, a no-frills kind of place. Comfy beige sofa, red chenille blanket, some rather awesome art above the small dining table. "Is that one of Jon Allen's?" she asked, admiring the wall-mounted metal sculpture.

"It is. An original I was lucky enough to snag before he blew up. Right place, right time kind of thing."

"I don't know anyone who knows Allen's work. Your cool points just increased exponentially."

"I live for cool points," April said in her ear from behind. "And now you do know someone familiar with Allen."

"That makes you awesome. You realize this."

"I'll have to find a way to live up to awesome. Oh, hey, I have an idea." Her arms slid around Hunter's waist and she pressed her body to Hunter's tightly. Hunter turned and traced the outline of April's cheek with one finger. She'd always been one for a little buildup before going in for more. April not so much, apparently. She caught Hunter's mouth and kissed her hungrily, no preamble needed. Well, to each her own. April's hands were on Hunter's waist and moving up her rib cage, clearly on a mission. Hunter smiled into the kiss at April's tenacity. It had been a while since Hunter had had sex. Well, a while for her anyway. She was ready to put an end to that streak.

She took control, moving them down the hall to where she imagined she'd find the bedroom, all the while checking in with herself, taking stock. Okay, so she wasn't exactly on fire, but maybe she just needed time. April halted their progress and without breaking the kiss, backed Hunter up against the wall just outside of the bedroom with a thud. It should have been hot, except it wasn't. It had been a little painful.

"God, you're beautiful," April murmured against her skin, as she transitioned her attention from Hunter's lips to her neck, placing hot kisses there as her hands wandered lower. Hunter exhaled slowly and gave her head a little shake in an effort to focus on the action, lose herself in the sensations that should be overtaking her body soon.

Yep.

Any second now.

But nope.

Not a go.

Maybe if she closed her eyes, stopped trying so hard. April slipped her hands underneath the back of Hunter's shirt and cascaded fingers across her skin at the small of her back. But the contact had little effect on her. In fact, she felt altogether removed from the encounter. She just couldn't seem to get there. Never one to give up, she reached down and brought April's lips back up to hers and reversed their positions in a move that should make the difference. She liked being in charge, so why not capitalize on that? As she kissed April, she used every technique in her arsenal, and it seemed to be working…on April, who let out a quiet murmur of appreciation. Hunter smiled at the encouragement, but with her eyes still closed, another image slipped into the mix. It was Sam sitting at her desk. Serious money glasses on, ponytail in place, smiling at her, those green eyes dancing.

And that was it.

Fuck. She blinked to clear her head, released April, and took a step back.

April touched her lips at the loss and studied her curiously. "You okay? You look a little pale." Hunter didn't answer right off, unsure of what had just happened. Why she was so totally thrown. Her mind and body were refusing to engage when there was a gorgeous woman, who she liked very much, ready to rip her clothes off.

"I'm sorry. I don't know why, but my head is in a weird space tonight."

April looked sympathetic. "Yeah? Well, I think I can help. Maybe you just need to relax." She stepped into Hunter's space and kissed her jaw. "Take a break from the rest of the world."

Yes. God, that was exactly what she needed. April was right. And she wanted this to happen. She did. Her refocused lips were on April's and they were back in business. But no sooner had she congratulated herself than she flashed on Sam laughing as she had earlier that night at dinner.

Yeah, this wasn't going to happen.

She pulled her lips from April's and placed a soft kiss on her forehead. "I'm sorry. Please don't hate me, but I think I'm going to have to take a rain check on tonight." The look of rejection on April's face caused her stomach to drop. "It has nothing to do with you. You're the coolest, sexiest girl I've met in a long time. I mean that. I'm just not feeling great."

April nodded and offered a halfhearted smile. "It's okay. I

understand." And then changed modes, eager to help. "Can I get you an aspirin or some water? Do you want to sit down?"

Hunter straightened the items of clothing that had been unstraightened in their make out session. "No. You've been more than great. I think I should just head home. I'll be fine." Hunter made a move for the door, eager for fresh air, anything to help her rebound emotionally, but turned back at the last minute. "April?"

"Yeah?"

"You're great. I just want you to know that."

April blew out a breath and smiled genuinely. "Thank you."

As Hunter waited for the train, the series of events played again in her mind, and the more she went over them, the angrier she became. It wasn't cool how she'd walked out on April, and it wasn't okay the way she'd let herself be so overtly affected by Samantha. And what the hell *was* that anyway? Since when had one woman been able to influence her time with another? By the time she arrived back at the loft, her coping skills were at an all-time low, and she felt like she was in a fucking tailspin.

"Hey, you're home," Sam said from the living room chair. She was watching some sort of show from the 1960s, which was such typical Sam behavior. With a flick of the remote, Sam turned off the TV and centered her attention on Hunter. "How was your night?"

Her smile was bright and friendly, which Hunter, given her evening, found selfishly annoying. She wasn't in the mood for chitchat. Not with anyone and especially not Sam. "Fine."

"Oh. Well, good, I guess. Mine was fun. My gang at the senior center was so sweet tonight, Hunter. Mr. Earnhardt started working on a scrapbook page for his honeymoon. You should have seen how he lit up when he talked about his wife."

"Sounds awesome." It was all Hunter could give because the obstacle to her evening was sitting on the couch looking rather beautiful and unaffected. And whether any of that was Samantha's fault or not, Hunter was beyond frustrated. And done with it.

Sam sat forward. "Want some ice cream? I bought coffee flavored at the deli on the way home. I remembered it's one we both liked."

Oh, how wonderful. She'd been extra thoughtful, too. Hunter's anger only escalated. This girl was too much. "Nope. I'm not hungry."

"Another night, then." Hunter made a beeline for her bedroom, but

Samantha was still talking. "You know what else was funny tonight? You have to hear this. Apparently some of the guys at the center came up with a nickname for—"

"Can you stop?" Hunter whirled around, making no attempt to mask her anger. "I'm not in the mood. I don't want to hear about your good-hearted volunteer job right now. I just can't."

Sam shifted. "Whoa. What's with the attitude?"

"I don't have an attitude," she said louder than was probably warranted. "I just can't listen to you do the adorable thing tonight, okay? The adorable thing causes problems, and while we're at it, no more of the sexy thing either. That means sexy glasses are off the table." Hunter slammed her door before opening it one last time. "And I'll unload the dishwasher from now on, got it? Because it's not fair!"

Samantha stared at her wide eyed and held up her palms. "Be my guest, crazytown. Just remember when you're unloading that the big knives go—"

"I know where the damn big knives go. God. I'm tired of the big knives." And with that, she slammed the door again, leaving Samantha wondering what the hell had just happened. Moments later, the door flew open again and Hunter stalked to the bathroom. "And if it's okay with you, I'm going to take a shower. At *night*. Which is totally off schedule. Outrageous, right? I hope you'll find a way to live."

Bang went the bathroom door. Sam jumped as it echoed through the loft.

Okay, so Hunter angry was a new experience for Samantha. In fact, she'd never known a more laid-back, easygoing person in her life. But something had Hunter's ire up in a big way, and she hadn't a clue what it was. What she was aware of, however, was how unexpectedly hot it was. Angry Hunter was a whole new kind of intriguing that she felt the effects of, well…all over. She heard the water flash on and, once again, pushed herself not to imagine Hunter in the shower, standing under its stream, the water rolling down her skin. Hot, wet, and soapy. God, there was a time not so long ago when showers were merely a method to get clean. Could she go back to that, please? Trade in the lust-induced visions, which were now even more blatant following the amazing kitchen kissing. It was as if the night before had unleashed a whole new kind of longing. Damn rebound mode. She couldn't wait for it to pass.

Raising her hands in the air and dropping them helplessly, she decided to escape the situation to her room and busy herself with getting ready for bed. But her skin was extra sensitive as she slipped into a T-shirt, the weight of it noticeable as she slid beneath the cool covers. It wasn't long before she heard the shower switch off. She knew from experience that in a few moments, Hunter would travel from the bathroom to her bedroom wrapped in a towel. She also knew that if she timed her totally necessary trip to the kitchen for a glass of water just right, she'd steal a glimpse. She threw the covers off and walked confidently to the kitchen. Because water had restorative powers and she should be drinking more of it.

Everyone knew that. *Everyone.*

CHAPTER EIGHT

The office clock read 5:53 when Samantha checked it Wednesday evening. Somehow, between her call with Serenity to finalize a payment schedule and her creation of a new Excel spreadsheet for their account, Brooklyn had left for the day. This meant she was probably headed home to change into comfortable clothes for Throwback Movie Wednesday and Samantha needed to step it up if she wanted to be ready in time.

They'd selected *Boeing Boeing* with Tony Curtis, which had Sam excited because she'd never seen it. After tying up some final loose ends at Savvy, she headed upstairs and went about prepping for the film. Comfy clothes, check. Diet soda, poured. Popcorn, popped. Wine, open and breathing, for post-popcorn consumption. She cued up the DVD and checked the clock on the microwave. Only a couple of minutes after seven, so technically Brooklyn wasn't late yet when you took into consideration that Brooklyn operated on an entirely different time system.

Hunter's bedroom door was closed. She'd beat Samantha out of the office, but Sam could hear the faint sound of a guitar, which meant Hunter was definitely in there and probably lost in her own world. Earlier that morning, she'd stopped by Sam's desk and quietly apologized for her outburst the evening prior, citing a bad night. Sam accepted, and they'd moved into awkward overly polite territory, which fell away by lunchtime when Hunter stole three French fries off her plate as she passed, prompting Samantha to throw a wadded-up piece of paper at her retreating form, earning them each an admonishing look from Mallory, who was on the phone with a potential client.

At 7:36, Samantha's allowance for Brooklyn-time was slipping. She checked her phone and stole a bite of popcorn in the process. No messages. She fired off a text.

On your way?

Time ticked by, but no response came in.

"Hey," Hunter said an hour later as she passed by the couch. Sam lay on her back staring up at the industrial rafters across the ceiling. "What happened to the movie?"

"You ask an excellent question."

Hunter paused, peering down at her. "Oh no. Brooklyn canceled?"

"No. That would have required some sort of communication. That would have been the thoughtful thing to do," Sam answered resolutely. "We made plans for Throwback Movie Wednesday over the weekend. She was the one who brought it up and now she's flaked out on me. I can only *assume* that's what happened, however. Either that or she's been put in jail for reckless driving."

"That second part is a definite possibility." Hunter perched on the arm of the couch. "I'm sorry, Sam. Want me to watch it with you?"

"Negative."

Hunter didn't exactly know what to do here. She was pretty sure Brooklyn hadn't meant to stand Sam up, but at the same time she was angry at Brooklyn for allowing this to happen, especially after she'd just vowed to fix her friendship with Sam, who now looked like a dejected little puppy. She had an idea. "You know we're gonna need our own traditions, don't you?"

Sam shifted her gaze to Hunter, a modicum of interest taking shape on her face. "What do you mean?"

"Well, you and Brooklyn had your whatever-day-of-the-week movie nights, that I can never keep straight, and your Lucy-the-troublemaker marathons. We probably need to step up our roommate relationship if we have any chance of competing."

A small smile tugged at the corner of Samantha's mouth. Jackpot. "Yeah? What about Dishwasher Fridays?"

"You think you're funny." The green eyes danced and Hunter shook her head. "How do you feel about jigsaw puzzles?"

Sam seemed to think on this. "I did those little square ones as a kid."

"No, amateur. I mean, the real ones. The five-thousand-piece monsters that take over the kitchen table for a week or two."

Sam sat up. "Do you have one of these puzzles to contribute to the cause?"

"More than one. And three of them, I've yet to work."

"And you want us to do one?" Sam looked hopeful.

"I think it could be fun. Want me to get it?"

"Well, that depends. Can we drink wine while we work it?"

"Oh, I think we have to drink wine while we work it. I mean, if you want to do it right."

"And I do." Samantha scurried up from the couch and went about clearing off the kitchen table. Hunter warmed at Sam's sudden excitement and retrieved a box from the top of her closet. "I've been holding on to this one for a special occasion, and I'm feeling like this is kind of the night for it."

"Because I'm in rebound mode, and now my friend has neglected me, too, and you feel bad?"

"And now we have to hit pause."

"Why are we pausing?"

"Because there's something you need to recognize. This is not a pity move, Ennis. I've never worked a puzzle with anyone. I'm pretty proprietary about my puzzles, and I'm only agreeing to work this one with you because I want to. Is that understood?"

A smile grew on Sam's face and her voice was quiet when she answered. "Understood."

"Great." She turned the box around. "We'll be working on *Rue Paris* by the artist D. Davidson."

Samantha took the box from Hunter and studied the image on the front. "It's so beautiful. God, I want to go to Paris." Hunter peered over her shoulder. It was a favorite piece of hers and one of the reasons she'd held the puzzle back for a special occasion. The artwork depicted a Parisian street just after a rain shower. There was a bicyclist on his way somewhere, two old-fashioned cars parked on the curb, and an expanse of gorgeous French buildings complete with window box flowers of all different colors. At the end of the street, the Eiffel Tower could be seen peeking out from behind a building. But probably Hunter's favorite part was the two-story street lanterns that brought the whole scene together. It was a breathtaking painting.

"All right," she said to Sam. "There'll be time for us to get more acquainted with the image as we go. First, let's get some basics out of the way." Hunter went on to explain to Sam the best strategy for effective puzzle assembly. Creating the outline of the puzzle first, color sorting, and section assembly—all the things that would see them through. "So let's find our corner pieces and get started."

Hunter put on some Beatles music, and the two went to work in companionable silence, grooving to the music here and there. As she worked, Hunter stole occasional glances at Sam, who had a tendency to chew the inside of her cheek when she concentrated, making it hard for Hunter to turn away. But somehow she did. She also worked extra hard at ignoring the way Sam's slim-fitting green T-shirt hugged her curves and dipped a tad in the front. That part was hard, because the skin there was smooth and probably soft, but she refocused because the mission in front of them was an important one and worthy of her attention. It wasn't long before Hunter's experience showed and her section took noticeable shape over Sam's.

As the music transitioned to "Eleanor Rigby," Samantha surveyed the workspace and straightened with a sigh. "This isn't at all fair. You're a visual person. It's what you do for a living. I'm cerebral."

"We need cerebral on jigsaw puzzles. Trust me. And we're not in competition, champ. We're on the same team."

Sam brightened. It was cute. Really cute. "You're right. I forgot that part. More wine?"

Hunter glanced at her mostly full glass. "I'm good." The outline of the puzzle was close to assembled, and they'd been at it for just over an hour. Sam came around the island with a refreshed glass of Pinot Grigio and studied their progress.

"So once our frame is in place, what's next?"

"How about you start work on the café tables at the bottom left and I'll start assembling the top of the apartment building at the top right?"

"I think that's an excellent decision."

"Well, your faith in me speaks volumes." Hunter's phone buzzed from its spot on the counter. She ignored it, focusing on gathering pieces of the brown building and green shutters. Samantha glanced down at it.

"Someone named 'Misty from Club' wants to know what you're up to."

Hunter continued to sort pieces. "Does she?"

"Shall I tell her you're assembling Paris and to try back later? Or do you want to take a few minutes and talk to her?"

"I find that if I'm busy, it's best to just not answer."

Samantha tilted her head as she came back around to her side of the puzzle. She seemed thoughtful as she began to sort pieces of her own. "So you name them after what? Where you met them?"

It was embarrassing, Sam seeing that text and the label it that came in with. She straightened, feeling the need to explain. "It was something I started doing when I was younger. I exchanged numbers with more girls than I should have—"

"Because you never want to hurt anyone's feelings. I've met you. You've always been that way and then you wind up with more women following you around than you know what to do with. You should be more up front if you're not interested."

Hunter shrugged. "I just don't like upsetting anyone. But then the girls who asked for my number would inevitably call, and I'd have no clue who they were. Hence, labeling the number in advance."

"Hence, indeed." Sam passed her a look. "Your feelings matter, too, you know."

"Yeah, well, I'm a work in progress, what can I say? Pass me that piece with a sliver of green on the side."

Sam handed her the puzzle piece. "I'm terrified of what the readout says when I call you."

Hunter laughed. "My lips are sealed."

"Favorite roommate?" Sam asked.

"Again, I simply can't say."

"I could just call it right now, you know."

Hunter grinned. "But that would ruin the fun."

They went back to work. Hunter enjoyed working alongside Samantha, watching her get frustrated when she couldn't find the piece she needed and then celebrate when she finally did. And Sam was a toucher; always had been. It spoke to her warmth. Every so often, she'd place a hand on Hunter's back as they talked, or she'd trail her fingers briefly across Hunter's forearm when she made a point. She probably didn't notice it herself, but it was thrilling. Hunter studied Sam as she concentrated. She'd pulled her hair back halfway through the night to keep it from getting in the way of her work, leaving her slender neck visible. It looked...edible.

"Why do you think my chair doesn't resemble the painting on the cover of the box?"

Hunter glanced at her work. "Hmm. Because the leg is wrong. You've jammed the leg from one of the other tables onto this one. Geez, you were determined to make that work, weren't you?"

Sam laughed helplessly. "I figured it was close enough."

Hunter stared at her. "Shock! Horror! What if Pinkberry put the toppings on someone else's yogurt because it was *close enough* to yours?"

"Now you're just being dramatic. Look at you. You have dramatic face."

Totally true, so she milked it even more. "Poor little puzzle piece didn't deserve to be manhandled."

Sam pointed at her. "You're a mean person, preying upon my well-known tendency to assign feelings to inanimate objects."

"I think you broke its little heart," Hunter said, staring sadly at the puzzle piece. But they were both laughing now, and Sam playfully nudged Hunter's shoulder with her own.

"This is fun, you torturing me, me learning how to properly work a puzzle." Sam turned more fully to Hunter as her laughter melted into a sincere smile. "You're fun. This, I have to admit, was a genius idea."

"I think so, too."

"Can you imagine if I'd just advertised blindly for a new roommate? There'd be no sought-after lesbian or her staring-obsessed dog living in my loft with me. And I'd never have gotten to work this really awesome puzzle."

"And I'd still be thinking of unloading the dishwasher as just a mundane activity."

"Or that," Sam said, finding Hunter's eyes.

Because of puzzle-assembling necessity, they were standing rather close to each other. Extra close, Hunter noted. And Samantha's gaze had dropped to her mouth, where it now lingered. God, Hunter wanted to reach out and touch her cheek, pull her in. She felt that tug all over. To act, to take what she craved. The moment had shifted from playful, and now the air around them felt quite heavy, electric even.

"How are we right back here?" Samantha asked quietly. But she hadn't exactly moved away. If anything, she felt closer.

"I don't know," Hunter murmured. "There's this thing that…"

"That what?"

"That makes me want to be near you, to touch you, to kiss you like I did the other night. Bottom line, I think I'm really attracted to you." She wasn't sure why she was showing her cards, maybe because she'd tried the aversion tactics and they hadn't worked. However, there was one thing she knew for certain. Ever since she'd confessed her long-ago feelings for Sam, it was as if she'd unlatched some sort of Pandora's box of thoughts and events that she could no more undo than she could step away from Sam right now. But the one thing that had her on hyperalert, that snagged her attention above all else, was that Samantha was looking at her with the exact same longing.

"Me, too," Sam said, just barely above a whisper. "And I don't even know when that happened. I think maybe I'm in rebound mode."

Hunter assessed the situation, never taking her eyes off Sam. "So. Two people who are attracted to each other. A lot."

"It's probably something we should deal with," Sam said.

"There are a lot of ways to do that."

"Some more tempting than others."

"Mmm-hmm." Hunter touched the very cheek she'd thought of touching just moments before. Samantha's skin was soft, warm, and those green eyes with the gold flecks held steady to hers. What was so wrong with two consenting adults…consenting? Her heart was beating out of her chest as she remembered the way Sam's mouth had felt, slanted over hers, all hungry and amazing. For the first time, she wasn't sure what move to make. She didn't have to decide. Samantha, in an unexpected turn, went up on her toes and slowly slid her hands against Hunter's cheeks and then into her hair as she brought her lips to just within millimeters of Hunter's. But then she paused there, face-to-face, in a delay that was so purposeful it was intoxicating.

"What are you up to right now?" Hunter asked.

"No good," Sam answered. There was no denying who was in control of this exchange. Finally, Sam inclined her head and pressed her lips to Hunter's in a move that had Hunter dizzy and breathless and wanting so much more. The door to the loft slid open behind them and without hesitation Sam pulled her lips from Hunter and transitioned the kiss into a hug with lightning-fast agility, just in time for Brooklyn to fly into the space.

"You are amazing," Sam said loudly as she squeezed Hunter to her, clearly in play-it-off, we're-just-two-friends-minding-our-own-business mode. "Who knew you were so good at puzzles?" Hunter plastered a smile on her face, but no cognizant thought seemed to come. They turned to Brooklyn, Samantha looking about as casual as casual could be and Hunter struggling desperately to keep up. *Try to be a person*, she told herself. *Try to be a person.*

"Sammie," Brooklyn said, her eyes wide with regret. "I am so sorry. Exponentially. You have no idea."

"It's fine," Samantha answered quickly, but there was a distance in her voice as she went back to assembling her outdoor café. "We were just working a puzzle."

"It's not fine," Brooklyn said, tears now brimming. "I'm this horrible friend who thought today was Tuesday and when I saw your text and remembered it wasn't, I just grabbed my bag and raced back. But it's too late. The night's ruined." She dropped onto the couch and the tears fell uninhibited.

Samantha didn't know what to do here.

She looked to Hunter, who shrugged worriedly back at her. True, Sam's feelings had been hurt at being stood up, but Brooklyn wasn't a crier, and the fact that she now sat on the couch in shambles was a red flag if Samantha had ever seen one. Pushing her own feelings aside, she moved to the couch and sat, putting her arm around her friend. "Brooks, really it's okay. You forgot. It happens."

Hunter sat in the chair next to the couch and placed a hand on Brooklyn's knee. "Is something else going on?"

Brooklyn wiped the tears from her eyes but more just fell in their place. "I'm just screwing everything up. I've been a horrible friend to you. I can't seem to think of Jessica's place as ours. I don't know my away around the Village well enough, and the Foster account was my baby. That loss is on me. No one else." She took a shuddering breath, seeking a composure that didn't come. "I'm screwing everything up."

Sam opened her mouth to speak, to tell Brooklyn not to worry, but Hunter beat her to the punch. "Are you ready to hear the truth?"

Brooklyn blinked back at her, sobering. "Yeah."

"Your world feels upside down right now and you feel a little out of control. Am I close?"

"Uh-huh." Brooklyn had the adorable child thing down pat.

"And that makes perfect sense because you took a big leap moving in with Jess. Does she make you happy?"

The smile was on Brooklyn's face instantaneously. "You have no idea."

"Then it's time for you to make the Village your bitch. Learn its nooks and crannies. Find a favorite coffee spot. Pinpoint the best bench to sit and stare. Because you love to brainstorm."

This seemed to pump Brooklyn up in a way Samantha wouldn't have predicted. "I can do that."

But Hunter wasn't done. "Foster made poor business decisions. They're a multimillion-dollar company, and that Royce guy with the plastic hair could have bet it all away at the racetrack, for all we know. You did not single-handedly take down Foster Foods. You're not that powerful, are you?"

"No. I mean, it would be awesome if I were. But I'm not." Brooklyn seemed to sit a little taller.

"So, the loss of the account was out of your hands. We wowed them every step of the way. *You* wowed them. And if they bounce back, you'll wow them again. If not, you'll work your magic on the accounts Mal is going to land to replace them." Brooklyn nodded five or six times, taking it all in. Her resolve seemed much stronger, and Sam passed Hunter an appreciative smile.

"I'm really sorry about tonight, Sam. I really miss you and was looking forward to it. I've just been so stressed that I got my days jumbled."

"Don't fucking let it happen again," Samantha said harshly. Brooklyn's eyes went wide and Sam smiled. "Kidding. Was just trying the Hunter approach, but I'll stick with what I'm good at. Now hug me like you love me, 'cuz you do."

Brooklyn threw her arms around Sam. "I do love you. More than the moon and covered bridges and root beer and fast cars."

"That's a lot," Samantha said, squeezing her back.

"And maybe we can do Throwback Movie Wednesday on Make-Up Thursday?"

Sam lit up. "I like Make-Up Thursday. It's new."

Hunter looked on. "Perfect." Friend fest was clearly in full effect. "You guys are quirky and weird again. Excellent. Wine, Brooks?"

Brooklyn stood. "Better not. I need to get into the office early tomorrow. I'll let you two get back to whatever it was you were doing." At that, Samantha's gaze brushed Hunter's, and a surge of heat raced through her at the memory of where they'd left off. With a quick final hug to both, a decidedly much happier Brooklyn headed home for the night.

As the loft door thudded closed, silence reigned.

Not really sure what to do with herself, Samantha took to straightening up the place. "It's getting late," she said. It was really just something to say. She wasn't tired, and in fact would probably read for another hour or so before bed. *Bridget Jones's Diary* was on tap. She loved an underdog. And luckily, the mood from earlier had been broken. The courage she'd found to initiate that kiss had been crazily out of character for her. She'd been reckless and blamed the wine. She should stick to a zero to one glass limit on weeknights from here forward. Zero was probably in her best interest these days.

"I'll help." Hunter grabbed her own glass and the bowl of popcorn from the coffee table. They met at the kitchen sink, reaching across each other to deposit the dishes. Their shoulders touched, and that was really all it took for Samantha. She stole a sideways glance at Hunter, who really was just so beautiful.

"Hey," Hunter said.

"Hey, yourself. Pass me that glass?"

Hunter did as she was asked. "So…"

"Well, don't hog all of the words."

Hunter grinned into the sink. "I guess I don't know exactly what to say, which is odd."

"I guess that makes two of us."

The first time they'd kissed, she'd been so caught off guard that she'd felt her way through it blindly, only relishing the exchange in the moments after. The replay. This second time, she'd known enough to appreciate what was happening, but it had been so damn short-lived with Brooklyn's interruption.

And now what? *Now you ignore that tingly feeling in the pit of your stomach and the obvious urges elsewhere. You also ignore your*

*preoccupation with Hunter's awesomely full lips, and you go to bed.
Put some distance between the two of you. Now.* "I'm exhausted."

"Yeah, me, too." Hunter leaned against the counter. "We should probably get some sleep."

"Right." Sam gestured to the puzzle. "But we're going to finish this, right? We have to."

Hunter smiled at her. "Of course. It's a puzzle rule. Once you start, you have to finish."

"All right, roommate, I'm holding you to it. Because tonight, well…it was much needed. It made me want to have more nights like this one."

Hunter held her gaze and Sam felt the sincerity pass between them. "Me, too."

She needed to walk away now. It was important that she walk away. "Well, good night."

"'Night, Sam."

Once she was safely tucked away in her room, she blew out a breath. Crisis averted, at least temporarily. But she'd stirred the pot. She'd initiated the kiss that had her knees going weak. And thank God Brooklyn had interrupted. Where would it have led otherwise? Her lips on Hunter's. Their bodies pressed together. Her hands wandering underneath Hunter's shirt, exploring the breasts that—God, she was doing it all over again.

Samantha looked at her reflection in the mirror. "You," she said to herself, "are an idiot." God, why did life have to be so complicated? But it had been a good move, sidestepping whatever was bubbling between her and Hunter, even though she was super tempted to just give herself over to it. Live a little.

She needed to think it through from a few different directions and then come up with a plan that would help them push past this little blip in their relationship so life could be normal again. Because the tension that seemed to have taken up residence between them was not of the friend variety. She had a couple of options: run with the newfound chemistry or fight it. And choice two simply had to be the way to go, because Hunter was one person she simply could not get involved with. Excellent decision. Go her!

But her victory celebration was cut short by the knock on her door. She dropped her head in defeat, and pep-talked herself the short distance it took to open it. But as soon as she did, all bets were off. Hunter stood there, her gaze purposeful, her lips parted slightly, and Sam knew she was in trouble. Hunter, who was usually cool and calm, was seemingly on a mission, and it was sexy as hell. Sam was pretty sure Hunter had a few complicated ideas of her own. Without a word spoken, they moved to each other and met in a kiss that couldn't be described as sweet or tender or slow.

No, this was primal and fast and unbridled, a clash of lips and tongues, and it was way past good.

Hunter kissed her with abandon—hard, thorough, aggressive. And she gave back just as much, surprising even herself. But kissing this woman was like a newly discovered drug. Sam felt alive in a way she hadn't in so long.

Sam backed them farther into the room, her need shooting up exponentially with each step she took. Hunter's hands were on her now, and that was excellent because she craved that. First they moved to Sam's waist, then her rib cage. They covered her breasts, and Sam moaned into the kiss as a sharp bolt of heat shot quickly from her center downward. She pushed her tongue into Hunter's mouth and explored, the taste of her making Sam forget all the reasons this was a bad idea. Had this off-the-charts sizzle been between them this whole time? As they sat together in the Savvy offices all these years, they'd been capable of this?

Amazing.

Clothes were coming off, she realized absently.

She was undressing Hunter, breaking the kiss only to navigate pulling the shirt over Hunter's head. And there, standing in front of her in just a black bra and panties, was the Victoria's Secret body that should have come with a warning label, because the slender lines that melted to sexy curves were doing a number on Sam's ability to think clearly. But there was no time for that anyway. Samantha wanted to feel that body against hers. She found Hunter's mouth again and steered them toward her bed on a mission. She would deal with the ramifications later.

They landed on the soft duvet, which evened out their height difference nicely. Hunter was on top and moving against her subtly, kissing Samantha's neck with skilled precision. Their pace was fast and purposeful. As intoxicating as this whole experience was, Sam knew she wasn't going to last much longer as she met each movement of Hunter's hips, straining already for sweet release. She was on fire, the aching between her legs insistent. As if reading her mind, Hunter made quick work of the T-shirt Sam wore and undid the clasp of her bra with one hand. Impressive, the real-life version of herself thought. But the sex vixen in her didn't dwell, and pushed her hands into Hunter's hair, thick and glorious.

Hunter's head dipped to Samantha's breast and caught a nipple, swirling her tongue against it, taking it fully in her mouth. Samantha almost came undone then and there, pushing harder against Hunter's knee, the throbbing now too much to withstand. Without shifting attention from her breasts, Hunter reached into Sam's pants and stroked her softly on the outside of her underwear. "More," Sam breathed. She was dying, simply dying. Taking matters into her own hands, she grabbed the sides of Hunter's panties and pushed them down as much as her position would allow her. She needed to feel Hunter against her before this was over. Fully. Understanding her intention, Hunter kicked off the underwear, tossed her bra onto the floor, and then removed the last of Sam's clothing in rapid succession. She settled back on top of Samantha. As she pressed against her, skin on skin, Sam's mind went white. Reaching a hand between them, Hunter slipped inside her and with her thumb offered Samantha attention where she needed it most. With purposeful movement of her hips, cradled between Sam's open thighs, Hunter pushed against her hand slowly, driving Sam utterly wild. She turned her head against the pillow as the pressure built inside her steadily until she was sure it couldn't possibly climb any higher. And then she did. Thrust upon thrust sent her to new and unexplored heights she couldn't quite perceive. Finally, in a burst of pleasure, she came hard and fast, uncontrollably flying. She clutched Hunter and rode out the blissful waves that took her over completely. The expanse of pleasure that crashed into her was shocking.

Hunter generally took her time with sex; she liked the unravel. But something about her desire for Samantha had superseded that preference, and she couldn't have slowed her pace if she'd tried. Watching Sam during that last moment of release had Hunter more turned on than she'd probably been in her entire life. And what was even more shocking was that, without having been touched much herself yet, she was only moments behind Samantha. She looked down at Sam, whose lips were still parted, whose breathing was still heavy, whose hips still moved against Hunter's in a rhythmic dance. Samantha was still coming down herself, but she met Hunter's eyes and seemed to know. She reached between their bodies then, and with only a couple of firm strokes, sent Hunter tumbling over the edge after her. Sam clung to her tightly, rocking her through it. God, the sensations tore through her hard and fast, like no other time she could remember. She felt that pleasure well into her fingertips, her toes, all over. She eased onto the bed next to Samantha and stared up at the ceiling, attempting to breathe, as Sam brought her back down from the last remaining sensations gently, with her hand, placing small kisses on the underside of her jaw.

A moment passed, and Hunter's sensibilities drifted back to her.

Sam turned her head on the pillow and faced her. "We're going to hell, you know this."

Hunter laughed quietly, still on a euphoric high. "We are not. We're adults. We're allowed to do that if we want."

"Adults who are going to hell." She covered her eyes with both hands.

Hunter's gaze traveled the expanse of Samantha's body, on display for her now and everything she imagined it would be. And, okay, more. She really couldn't get enough of Sam's breasts. She stared at them now, tracing a nipple with her index finger, causing Sam to inhale sharply.

"You're good at this, you know that?" Sam said, her eyes still closed.

"At this specifically?" She traced the underside of the curve and leaned down, pulling a nipple into her mouth.

Sam sucked in a breath. "At sex. God, okay, specifically this, too. You have to stop now."

Hunter propped her head up on her elbow and looked down at Samantha, grinning. "If that's what you want."

Sam covered her eyes with both hands. "I don't know what I want. I can't believe I just had sex with you. That wasn't supposed to happen. As in ever."

Hunter sobered, understanding the importance of the line they'd crossed but trying to help Sam through it. "I know. But there are worse things. Floods. Hurricanes. Republicans. Plus, you have to admit, this was really good. I'm still feeling it."

Sam stole a peek at her. "It was, wasn't it? Wasn't just me?"

Hunter shook her head slowly. "No way."

"Hot or not, I think we broke some kind of cosmic friend rule."

"That part's possible. But sex is part of life. We just have to handle ourselves as such. So we're physically into each other. There don't have to be strings. Ramifications."

Sam pushed herself up onto her elbow. "Are you proposing a friends-with-benefits arrangement?"

Was she? "Maybe, given our recent struggles, that's not such a horrible idea."

Samantha stared at the ceiling and Hunter wondered if she'd just said the completely wrong thing. "Well, I *am* in rebound mode."

"You are. And I'm not going to complicate your life. You can rebound with me all you want. Plus, we genuinely like each other."

Samantha stared off. "Could be a win-win."

"You see who you want to see. I'll see who I want to see. And if this happens again. Not a big deal. No drama."

Slipping under the sheet, Samantha blew out a breath. "Okay, no drama. I can do that."

"And we're not the first two people on the planet who've slept together."

Samantha laughed. "No?"

"Nope." Hunter sat up. "But I get why you're freaking out. Big knives are in the towel drawer."

Sam passed her a look. "Decode, please?"

"I'm naked in your bed right now, which is not one of my roles in your life. Thereby, I'm not in my proper place. Like the big knives. It's okay. It's just how you work. I'm learning this more and more."

"I guess there's truth in that."

Hunter kissed Sam's cheek and lingered a second, enjoying the scent of Sam's sweet-smelling shampoo. "I'll head back to my drawer now. The world will keep turning. I promise. Sweet dreams." She gathered her various clothing items and without putting them on walked slowly back to her room, feeling Samantha's eyes on her the entire time.

If she'd peeked into Pandora's box with that college confession some weeks back, then she'd just blown the whole damn lid off the thing with that little escapade. But maybe this arrangement with Sam was just what she needed to kick her back into business-as-usual mode. The itch wasn't going away. And now she'd scratched it. Problem solved.

As she climbed into her own bed, a chill moved through her. Much the way it had shortly before the Midnight Chocolate that brought her to the loft in the first place. She pulled the covers tighter around her body and sighed against her pillow. Something important was working its way to her.

CHAPTER NINE

H unter checked her watch. Late.
    She stood on the white steps in front of the NCO club on Wright-Patterson Air Force Base. It was a quarter to eight and her father's birthday party had started at six. Her flight had been delayed an hour, and the gate guard was newly on duty and had trouble locating the guest list for the party. Without a military ID, she'd been sent to the visitor's center to fill out the necessary paperwork. So much for making a good impression.

    She made her way into the lobby of the club and could tell from the direction of the music that they'd selected the Daedalian Room for the party. She looked around at the brown tile, the black-and-white photos on the wall of some of the famous squadrons from years gone by, the shadow boxes that commemorated so many of the pilots who'd come before her father. He'd once been a member of the Air Mobility Command Unit, but Hunter couldn't tell you much about what that was. He'd never really talked about it with her. God, it was surreal to be back on base, though. The same club in which her family'd had breakfast once a month for most of her life. Her mother's idea. Her father, meanwhile, had spent much of his spare time in the bar straight ahead of her. He wasn't an alcoholic. In fact, he never had more than a couple drinks at one time. No, it was more about dodging as much time with his kids as he possibly could. Sometimes she wondered why he'd even agreed to have them.

    "There you are!" Hunter turned and smiled at her older sister, Claire, who was picturesque in a white dress. Her dark hair was touched with blond highlights and swept into an overly fancy twist. And just like that, Hunter felt underdressed in her black pants and sleeveless dark green sheath.

"Hiya, Claire. Sorry I'm late. The flight."

"Mama's been worried sick. She thought you'd changed your mind. Give me a hug, and then come and say hello to everyone." Claire paused. "Oh. You wore pants. Well, you look nice anyway. It won't matter."

"Thanks, I think." The hug was quick but it was enough for a potent hit of her sister's Chanel perfume. A trademark. Claire had fully assumed her position as Debutante Barbie—that much was true. Hunter followed her sister into the ballroom, scanning the faces from the perimeter. "Where's Kevin?" she asked, excited to see her little brother. The kid used to follow her around incessantly, her consummate shadow. The larger age gap made her extra protective of him. While Hunter was only three years younger than Claire, her brother was twelve years her junior and had been a bit of a surprise to her parents. But as a result, they'd avoided the typical sibling bickering, and instead Kevin had developed sort of a hero worship for Hunter. But she adored him right back. He was kind, and funny, and come on, just adorable. He'd turned sixteen this year, and a shot of guilt hit as she remembered she'd not been there to celebrate the occasion. She really needed to be around more for him.

"You're here!" Hunter turned at the exuberant sound of her mother's voice and folded herself into the open arms she saw waiting for her just a few feet away. Her mother was quite a bit shorter than she was, but won the award for the best hugs on the planet. She savored the safety she felt when enveloped in one.

"Hi, Mama. I promised you I'd be here, didn't I?"

"You did, and you're here. How was the flight? Did they serve a meal?"

"It was fine, and no. They don't really do that anymore."

Her mother shook her head. "That's horrible. Someone should write a letter." She'd released Hunter from the hug, but still had a firm hold on her arm. That was the thing about her mom, once she got Hunter home, it was like she couldn't stop touching her to make sure she was really there. Hunter complained about it as a formality, but deep down it made her happy. "Let's go say hello to your father. I think the crowds make him uncomfortable."

Yeah, well, what didn't?

Her mother led the way through the throngs of party guests, stopping to point out Hunter's arrival to all they passed. Friends and neighbors of her parents gushed about how grown up she now was and exaggerated about how pretty she'd turned out. She smiled and hugged and said the appropriate thank-yous, all the while dreading the moment that was fast approaching. To distract herself, she took in the colorful decorations, birthday-themed mostly, but with the ever-present Hawaiian luau accents on the side. Clearly, her mother and Claire had raided some contrasting aisles at Party City—pretty typical of any Blair gathering.

As they approached her father at the front of the room, he was talking to a man Hunter vaguely recognized as a former serviceman— one of his cronies from the good old days. He'd aged, her father. That was the thing that jumped out at her most. The hair that on her visit just last year had been salt-and-pepper was now entirely white. The lines impressed upon his face had deepened as well. It was a startling realization when your parents aged. Her father turned in their direction, and after only a minor pause, went back to his conversation. *Nice.* Inside, she laughed wryly. How very Richard Blair of him.

"Rich, say hello to Hunter. She flew in for your birthday."

For her mother's benefit, she played the part. "Happy birthday, Dad."

"Thank you, Hunter. You look well. I'm glad you made the trip." Also for her mother's part. The crony, whoever he was, grinned warmly in her direction.

"I remember when you came up to here," he said, indicating a spot close to his hip. The man opened his arms and pulled Hunter into a full-on embrace. "It's so good to see you, sweetheart." She accepted the warm hug, noting the irony. This stranger was overjoyed to see her, while her own father could barely be bothered to glance in her direction. He stood there, clearly uncomfortable and unsure what to do about it as the man released her. Hell, it was his birthday. Why not throw the old guy a bone and let him off the hook?

"I'm going to go find Kevin," she told the men, slipping away effectively with her mother at her side. Once they were a safe distance away, her mom squeezed her arm. "You did good, Hunter. It was the right thing to do to come to the party, and he will remember this. That you were here."

"Look, Mama, I came for you. Because I love you and it's what *you* wanted. You've been both mother and father to me for a while now. Let's be real about that." The smile that had been on her mother's lips just moments before had dimmed noticeably, and Hunter was sorry to have been the cause. "But I don't want to concentrate on any of that. I'm here now, and I want to spend time with you and Claire and Kevin."

Her mother nodded, and it seemed like something else was on her mind. "About your brother…"

"What about him?"

"He's had a rough time lately. I was hoping your visit might help to cheer him up."

"Cheer who up?" Claire asked. "Mama, the McElroys are leaving and want to say good-bye."

"On my way," her mother said. "Will you find Kevin so Hunter can say hello?" she asked Claire. At the mention of their brother's name, Claire sighed audibly. "He's out back. He pulled off his tie and tossed it in the Dumpster."

Seemed a little extreme. "How do I get there?" Hunter asked. Claire pointed at an unmarked door at the back of the room.

"Maybe you'll have some luck. I'm done trying for tonight. Have you seen Chip? I want to slow dance." Hunter pointed across the room at her rather preppy brother-in-law. "There's that handsome guy. Remind me to tell you later some tricks I learned."

Hunter blinked at her sister. "Tricks?"

"In the bedroom, silly. Good stuff, too. We use props now. It's revived us in a big way."

Hunter was instantly uncomfortable at the thought of her sister and Chip going at it, but did her best to push aside the upsetting visuals in favor of sisterly support. "Can't wait," she said, forcing a smile. Claire winked and took off in search of said husband as Hunter tried to erase that conversation from her brain forever and always. Claire had always been a bit of an over-sharer.

Hunter followed Claire's directions to the back of the club. She couldn't wait to see the little rugrat, knock him in the head, and work their secret handshake. Smiling, she pushed through the door to the outside and found herself on the loading dock where three boys stood together in conglomeration. Dark hair, dark clothes, and yep, that was eyeliner. Goth kids, perfect. "Hey, guys. Have you seen Kevin?"

The three regarded her with what could best be described as bored tolerance. "What?" the one in the middle asked, totally uninterested in the question. He had his hair spiked, his eyebrow pierced, and dark makeup that made him look a little bit like the undead, but that was her brother all right. Good God. What had happened to that happy-go-lucky smiler she'd seen just under a year ago?

"Hey, Kevin," she said smiling. "You're not even going to hug me? It's been forever."

"My sister," he said with mild annoyance to his friends. "Text me."

The other two scary kids mumbled some sort of assent and took off into the night. Kevin turned to face her before his eyes settled on the ground. "Hey." He was much taller now and his voice was an entire octave lower. It was more than a little shocking. He made no move to hug her, so she completed the distance herself and wrapped her arms around him in what had to be the most awkward hug in history. He was easily her height and probably not done growing.

"I can't believe how much older you look." Usually, this would be the point where Kevin would grin in triumph as he was always trying to impress her. Except for now, when he couldn't care less.

"Yeah, well, time is real."

Time is real? Interesting. He was fixated on the door behind her and she understood that he was counting the seconds until she'd leave him alone. Hunter remembered what Claire had said. She'd given up on him. She remembered her mother's imploring look *to talk to Kevin*. Clearly, there had been some changes in her brother over the course of the last year, and they weren't all physical. Some were to be expected. Teenagers acted out. Hell, she did. But this was something else entirely. The kid looked like he hated the world. She wasn't about to give up, though. "So when did you start wearing eyeliner?"

"When did you?"

Fair enough question despite the fact that his face gave off a lot of scorn. "Fifteen or so, I guess. I didn't mean that as judgment. Just curious."

"Cool." He looked away.

"How's school going?"

"Fine."

"You still playing soccer?" She was grappling here. One-word answers seemed to be Kevin's new thing.

"Nope." Okay, no soccer? Now that really was a red flag. Soccer was Kevin's entire life. He played it incessantly. Had posters on his wall of his favorite players. It was rare you saw the kid without a soccer ball under his arm.

"What do you mean you're not playing soccer? Why did you quit?"

He shook his head in disgust, which just upset her further.

"Okay, what's with the look? I'm struggling to understand what's going on with you, kid, but you're not giving me much."

"Doesn't matter." He walked past her for the door.

"Well, it does to me."

He shrugged. "That's gotta suck." It was the last thing he said to her as the door closed and he disappeared into the club.

Hunter was thrown. She didn't know who that chip-on-his-shoulder, hate-the-world teenager was, but it certainly wasn't the younger brother she knew and loved. She shook her head and stared out at the Ohio night sky. She should have been here more. Screw her father and the way he made her feel. Why did she let that dictate the relationship she had with the rest of her family? Her brother was a mess. Her sister had washed her hands of it. And her mother, bless her, was doing everything in her power to hold them all together. And what had she done? Ignored them for the past year? Only visited a handful of times since college? Hunter knew with painstaking clarity how selfish she had been, and she hated herself for it.

With renewed determination, she found her sister inside the club. "How long has he been like this?"

Claire looked suddenly tired and uncomfortable. She'd never done well with conflict and preferred to think the world was a happy, shiny place for all to live. "The black clothes hit about six months ago and the attitude was shortly behind them."

"Do you think it's just a passing fixation or is it worse? Is he into drugs?"

Claire shrugged. "It's not like he'd tell me. I offered to take him for ice cream to talk, but he pretty much ignored me."

"Ice cream, Claire? Are you kidding me? Have you seen the kid?"

Claire's shoulders sagged. "What? I was trying to help."

And she was. She was simply ill-equipped. "What does Mom say?"

"She's concerned, but she's letting Dad handle it."

Had Hunter heard that correctly? "I'm sorry. Dad? Since when has Dad ever handled anything?"

Claire glanced quickly around to see who might have overheard. "First of all, keep your voice down. Second of all, he's really been trying lately. And Kevin responds to him. Well, as much as Kevin can respond to anyone."

She had to laugh, because really? "Somehow I just can't imagine that happening."

"He's not *all* bad, Hunter. No one is all one thing. Maybe it's because his health has not been so great, but I've noticed a big change in Dad. He's taken an interest in us, and I for one am not going to deny him because of the past. Life is too short. If he wants to turn over a new leaf, let him."

"Well, that's bullshit," Hunter said.

Claire studied her. "You really hate him, don't you?"

How was she supposed to answer that? "I'm not a fan. No."

"For Mom's sake, I hope you at least try." Claire headed off to the cake where the guests were preparing to sing "Happy Birthday" to the man of the hour. Hunter scanned the room for Kevin, but he was nowhere to be found.

The next morning when Hunter awoke, the smell of bacon and fresh coffee had her smiling before she even opened her eyes. She was home. Her mom was big on breakfast. What she hadn't planned on was the set table she encountered once she'd showered and come downstairs. "What's all this?" she asked.

Her mother smiled. "There's my girl." She came around the counter and placed a kiss on Hunter's cheeks. "I do think you're even more pretty than the last time you visited."

"Sweet of you to say, but the genes came from somewhere."

Her mother smiled at the thought and pointed her spatula at Hunter. "You're right. I'm pretty good-lookin' myself." She turned back to the sizzling bacon and flipped a strip. "I'm bringing sexy back."

Hunter laughed, nearly spilling the orange juice she poured. "I can't believe you just said that."

The back door opened and Claire entered with Chip and their four-year-old twins, Connor and Christopher. The little guys high-fived Hunter on their way into the living room where their "grandma toys" were stashed behind the couch, always waiting for their visits.

"Good morning, everyone!" Chip enthused. He tended to speak in exclamation points, which Hunter found amusing.

"Morning, Chip," Hunter answered. "Mom's cooking for us. Fancy breakfast time."

"I can hardly wait!" He stared off into the living room, his eyes wide. "Christopher, don't hit your brother with that lamp. That's what your grandmother uses to see." Oh, the joys of parenting.

Claire took the seat next to Hunter at the table and leaned in. "Last night was Star Wars role play," she whispered in her ear.

"What does that mean?" Hunter asked. Claire raised her eyebrows a couple of times pointedly until the meaning of the phrase came into focus. Hunter resisted a blatant face palm and instead nodded and smiled, now picturing her sister in Princess Leia mode against her will. "Sounds awesome."

"If you want the rules of role play, I have them. They're quite simple. Though you'll need to identify the aggressor. Last night, it was Chip. Tonight is my turn."

God save her from this conversation. "You know, I'm good on rules for now. But I'll certainly let you know if I change my mind."

Claire winked at her and went about helping their mother finish up breakfast while Hunter poured juice for the rest of the table. Fifteen minutes later, they were all gathered. Even Kevin, who begrudgingly emerged from his room, again wearing black jeans several sizes too large and a metal spiked wristband. He set to eating his eggs without so much as a glance at anyone else.

"Hunter, how are things at the Savvy agency these days?" her mother asked.

"Busy. We had a few projects shuffle, and I think we're just trying to keep up."

Her father looked up from his plate. "I read an article about the company online. A piece in *Time Out*."

Hold the phone. Her father had not only spoken directly to her, but shown enough interest as to Google her company? Had hell frozen over and she missed the memo? She didn't know what his angle was, but she really didn't care. "Yeah, we're doing well."

But apparently he wasn't done. "Do you foresee expansion into any kind of investor relations?"

"What the hell do you care?" Okay, it was harsh, but it was what came out.

All eyes swiveled to her, including the four-year-olds'. "Hunter," Claire said quietly.

"Sorry, was that too candid?"

Her father looked mildly uncomfortable. "It's okay. I was just curious about the business. But we can…talk about something else."

As the conversation picked up around them, it was clear that the others had shifted into overdrive to cover the less-than-successful exchange. Everyone was extra nice and polite, as if setting an example for what breakfast conversation *should* sound like. Hunter busied herself with her plate, feeling guilty for making the rest of the room uncomfortable. But not for how she'd addressed her father, the same man who told her she was an embarrassment when she'd taken her first girlfriend home—this after not having acknowledged her existence for years prior.

Her mother caught her eye as she ate and smiled. She had a way of doing that. Centering Hunter when she needed it. And it helped to pull her back into the fold of things. She watched her brother for a moment. "Plans today, Kevin?"

He looked up, seeming almost shocked to have been spoken to. "Don't know."

"I was going to head to the air show on base later," her father said to him. "You can go with me if you want."

Kevin nodded at his food. "Yeah. Cool. What time?"

"Couple of hours," her father said. "Hunter, any interest?"

She felt like she'd stepped into the Twilight Zone. She made sure to answer with civility she didn't actually feel this time. "No, I have a flight late this afternoon. I'll stay here with Mom. Catch up."

He nodded and went back to his food.

Strangest visit home ever.

Samantha shuffled through the puzzle pieces looking for the one that showed three-fourths of the blue window awning. It was Sunday afternoon. Hunter had gotten in from Ohio late the night before, and this was the first chance they'd had to talk about her trip. "So, do you think he was extending some sort of olive branch?"

Hunter handed her the piece she sought. "That's the thing, I have no idea. For my father, any kind of interest in my life is uncharted territory. But at this point, it's unwelcome."

Sam stopped her work on the puzzle and looked at Hunter. It was clear the trip had her in a weird place. "Maybe don't be so quick to say that."

Hunter balked. "Really? You know what he's like."

Sam shrugged. "Yeah, but people change. Maybe he's trying."

Hunter moved to the couch, clearly in contemplative mode. "Claire said his health hasn't been so great. And he looked older. Much."

"So maybe that's it. Maybe whatever is going on with him physically has him rethinking the way he's treated his kids all these years. I'm not saying that you should race into his proverbial open arms, but think about keeping your mind open for down the road."

Hunter met her eyes. "Not sure I can do that. But enough about him." She dropped her palms onto her knees with a slap. "What have I missed? How have you been? What have you worn?"

Samantha smiled at the questions, genuinely happy to have Hunter home. She'd been surprised at just how much she'd missed her while she'd been gone. The apartment felt lonely, but not just for anyone. She abandoned the puzzle and came to sit on the arm of the couch. "Well, Elvis and I entered into a bit of a crossword puzzle competition. He was woefully second place. But in better news, he won the sustained eye contact competition that followed, hands down."

Hunter leaned down and scratched Elvis under his chin. "She's telling lies about you. We both know you rock at crosswords." Elvis whined quietly in response. He'd stuck close to Sam while Hunter was away, even sleeping next to her bed. But it was obvious now, as he refused to leave Hunter's side, that he was thrilled she was home. Something they both agreed on. "Hey, are we okay?" Hunter asked.

Sam understood the implication. Hunter was asking about Sexgate, which was essentially the last time they'd seen each other. She felt a little unsteady with their arrangement, especially since it was atypical behavior for her. She was a romantic, after all, and sleeping with someone for the sake of anything other than actual emotion was outside her experience level. But then again, she was feeling ready to venture away from her norm. And this felt like taking life by the horns for once. Plus, Hunter was her friend, and she felt safe with her. "Yeah, I think we are."

"So did you think about me while I was gone?" Hunter teased. "Dream about me?" She raised an overly seductive eyebrow, which forced Samantha to throw a pillow at her, because she wasn't getting away with that.

"Just because I slept with you doesn't mean you can flirt with me."

"It doesn't?"

"Nope. Against the friends-with-benefits rules. We're friends right now. This is the friend part of our relationship."

"Well, that seems wildly unfun."

Sam pushed off the couch and went back to the puzzle. "Deal with it. And get back over here and help with this puzzle. My café is gaining on your building. You gotta keep up, slacker."

Hunter stood. "You are really, really bossy."

"And you love it."

Chapter Ten

So, Howard, what brought you to New York?" Sam sipped the champagne that Howard had insisted they order, enjoying the way the bubbles tickled her throat on the way down. Her spirits were high. It felt good being out on an actual date.

"Women," Howard said.

She choked a little on the champagne at his response. "I'm sorry. Did you say women?"

"Oh, yes," he said in his cute little Howard voice. Almost like a well-mannered cartoon character, sitting there with that red bow tie—the same one from his profile photo—and tan jacket. She wasn't judging him. It was a definite choice, that outfit, and he was owning it. "I heard that the women in the Big Apple are the prettiest women just about anywhere, so I moved my software company from Iowa to find out for myself." He certainly had a slow delivery style, as if each word carried special meaning for him.

"Oh, and how has that worked out?"

"Well, have you looked in the mirror lately?" He pulled his face back and shook his head. "My, you're stunning, Samantha. I'm so glad you opened up your heart to the world of online dating. There's so much for people like us to explore."

"Thank you. Um…it's a little new for me. I will admit to being nervous. I've never been on a blind date, much less an online one."

"But do you want to explore?" The waiter chose just that moment to deliver their meals, which bought her a moment to ponder how one should answer such a strange and vague question.

"Explore?"

"Our love connection."

"Oh, I think it might be a little premature for the word 'love,' don't you, Howard? Maybe we could just have this meal together and get to know one another a little."

"Well, that sounds just dandy. Everything you say is dandy." Wow, genuine enthusiasm. It was sweet. Not exactly sexy. At all. In any way, shape, or form. But he was an earnest little guy and that counted for something, right? She had him pegged at about five-three, with a slight comb-over. That part had not been well represented in his online photo.

"Do you enjoy NASCAR?" he asked, taking the tiniest bite of steak ever assembled.

Really, what was the point of a bite like that? She watched him chew the sliver daintily before reminding herself of the question. "As in racing? No. I've never really been into NASCAR."

"That's okay. I'll teach you. The cars, they go in a whirly circle and try to catch one another. It's like tag for cars. It'll be so much fun when we watch at my place on Sundays."

There would be no NASCAR watching.

Silent sigh.

And she didn't have the heart to point out that, in fact, NASCAR was nothing like tag. "I'm more of a book and movie kind of girl myself. Do you read much?" At this point, she was just trying to make conversation before exiting politely. Howard was not, as he would say, her love connection.

"I enjoy reading cookbooks."

"Oh, so you like to cook?" At last, an overlap. They could compare notes, recipes, or discuss their enjoyment of creating a new dish.

"No. I just like to read them."

Sam took a sec. "Oh."

Howard leaned forward, stealing a glance at a nearby table to make sure no one was listening. "How am I doing?" he whispered.

"What do you mean?" she whispered back.

"My neighbor, Sheila, says I'm worthy of a restraining order."

"Is that a statement or a goal?"

"I'll have to think on that." He sat back in his chair, pensive, leaving Samantha more mystified than ever.

She ate the remaining food on her plate, smiling politely at

Howard, who continued to cut his food into infant-sized portions before delicately placing each bite in his mouth with practiced care.

"When would you like to get together again?" Howard asked, taking out a pocket calendar.

Sam took a deep breath. "Here's the thing. I'm not thinking that's such a good idea."

"Is it the love connection?"

She made a point to look sorrowful. "It is, I'm afraid."

"The love connection is important. And if it's not there, you can't force it."

"You can't force it. Exactly."

Howard was gracious enough to pay the check and walked Samantha to the corner. "You're just a wonderful Big Apple girl. I can tell. Thank you for having dinner with me at this fine bistro down the block from us now."

Okay, he was back to being cute again. She wanted to straighten his tiny bow tie and pat his head. "I'm happy to have met you, Howard. I wish you well." She placed a kiss on his cheek.

"I wish you well, too, Samantha. In all of your life's pursuits. I hope you find your extra-special love connection." He placed something in her hand and walked away. She glanced down and found herself staring in mystification at a one-hundred-dollar bill.

"Howard, wait, no!" But he closed the door to an idling cab and was gone.

She looked down at the cash. Seriously?

❖

"How'd your hot date go?" Hunter asked from the couch when Samantha arrived home. She was tucked under a blanket with Elvis curled into the crook of her knee. Once he spotted Samantha, however, he jumped down from the couch and came to greet her, his entire body wagging like a tail.

"Hi, little El." She stooped down and scratched behind his ears, which seemed to make him smile his Elvis smile. She'd never met a dog who'd mastered the art of smiling the way he had. She straightened and stared at Hunter. "I might be a prostitute. You should know this. A dinner prostitute, but still a prostitute."

Hunter, who had the top of her hair pulled back in a clip today, studied her nonchalantly. "A dinner whore? Congratulations. I don't know many of those."

"You think I'm kidding. I'm not. The guy literally handed me a hundred bucks on the street and then took off." She held up the hundred as evidence.

"Whoa. Well, you are an excellent dinner companion."

Sam hung up her cardigan on the coat rack. "Right? Maybe I should add it to my résumé."

Hunter smiled. "Please list it as 'Dinner Whore.' I'm in favor of the term. It's growing on me, moment to moment."

Sam batted Hunter's feet out of the way and sat at the end of the couch. "You're on. DW for short." And then she caught a detail she'd missed when she first arrived.

Hunter eyed her. "What?"

"There's an actual book in your lap. Oh my word. You're all cozy and reading."

Hunter glanced down at the novel and shrugged. "It happens on occasion. I thought I'd see what the fuss is about. And then there's the fact that I do whatever I can to hear you say 'oh my word.' Say it again."

Samantha ignored the jab and lifted the spine of the book as she dipped her head. "*Pride and Prejudice*. One of my all-time favorites."

"I figured as much from the broken-in spine. I like this Elizabeth. She has a subtle humor about her. A cool chick. She makes jokes when she's nervous. You do that, too, by the way."

"Yeah, well, in a perfect world, I'd rather be like you. Composed and unaffected in those sort of moments."

"No way. That would be boring. The world needs a blushing Samantha Ennis who diverts with humor."

She smiled at Hunter. "I like that you're reading it. It will be fun to see the book through someone else's eyes. Yours especially. I happen to value your thoughts a great deal."

"That sounds like pressure. I hope I don't disappoint you." Hunter met her gaze and held on. "I'm sorry your night was cut short. I know you were hoping Howard J. would be the bow-tie-wearing man of your dreams."

"Le sigh. I was hoping, but I'll live," Sam said. "And never look at NASCAR the same way again, consequently. Or steak, for that matter."

"Care to explain?"

"I'm not sure I could find the words. It's safe to say that Howard and I are not a match. And it's now occurring to me that finding my match, if he or she is even out there, is a more difficult task than I had originally hoped. Is it horrible that, after everything, I still want that for myself? Someday, down the road, I want the romance novel."

Hunter studied her, the playful smile of earlier replaced with a sincere understanding. "And you deserve it."

Samantha adjusted her spot on the couch and brought her knees up to her chest. "Several years back, I made this list of everything I wanted in the perfect person for me. Kind, funny, successful, good-looking, wants to have kids, gets my quirks, a killer chef, well-read...I mean, the list went on and on." She covered her face with her hand as embarrassment struck. "I can't believe I just told you that. Miss Anti-Relationship. You must think I'm so naïve and pathetic."

"I don't think that. I'm happy you told me about your list. There's nothing wrong with having one."

Samantha dropped her gaze to the floor and examined the swirling patterns where the rug met the cement. "I think I'd settle for kind at this point. Funny couldn't hurt. But the full package is unrealistic. That list needs shortening, and I think it's time I acknowledge that." Hunter stared at her, and it was one of those rare moments where Sam didn't know what she was thinking. It was a faraway look that Hunter only got once in a while. "Hunter. You in there?"

Hunter took a breath and smiled. "Yeah, sorry. Right here."

She placed her hand on top of Hunter's and squeezed. "Thanks. You've been a great friend to me through all of this. Libby, Howard... us." She left it there, knowing that Hunter would fill in the gap, as saying "the night I ripped your clothes off" felt somehow outside the mood.

Hunter straightened. "You're one of the most important people on the planet to me, you know that?"

The words prompted a warmth to move through Samantha and brought a smile to her face. "I do. But it's nice to hear it. I can safely say the same right back to you."

There was a silence between them now as the comments hovered and settled, but not the uncomfortable kind. That was the thing: As different as they were, things were always easy between them. Samantha cherished that.

Finally, Hunter closed her book and turned to Sam. "I don't know if you're home for the night or not, but Mallory and I were planning a jaunt to Showplace in an hour. Brooklyn and Jess might join us later. It could cheer you up from your crash-and-burn date."

"A jaunt, huh?" she said, swatting Hunter's knee. "You're all Jane Austen over there. I love it."

"I may be a club kid, but I'm capable of high culture," Hunter said, looking adorably proud of herself.

Samantha had to smile, despite the surge of something powerful that pulsed through her in response to the display. Friend or not, Hunter had a way of doing that to her, and it would probably take some getting used to. Surely, any minute, her body would stop its thrumming. "It seems you are."

But it was only natural to see Hunter in a new light now, given recent events. Probably the perfect cure for it all was a night out with her friends. A little fun and distraction now that her social calendar was unexpectedly free. Samantha stood. "I should probably go stare at my wardrobe in confusion before pulling something off the hanger randomly and putting it on."

"You come up with the best plans."

"Yeah, well, steak with Howard and Showplace on a Friday night seem to call for different costumes."

"*Grey Gardens* shout-out."

Samantha turned back. "Whoa. How did you know that?"

Hunter shook her head and returned to her book. "I know a lot more than you give me credit for. You consistently underestimate me, Samantha Ennis. And I have lots more to surprise you with. Buckle up."

Sam headed off to her room, all the while turning that last sentence over in her head, because she was beginning to think Hunter was right. She did underestimate her.

They'd known each other forever, yet there seemed to be a lot more to Hunter than she'd ever realized, and for whatever reason, that knowledge zapped her with a surge of extra energy, an excitement, that carried her right into her bedroom, until a strange sight on the edge of her bed pulled her focus. She paused, studying the neat pile of envelopes. "Hunter?" she called out to the living room.

"Yep?"

"The mail is on the end of my bed."

"I know," Hunter called back. "It looks good there. It wanted to branch out."

Sam nodded in amusement. She understood the message and mentally accepted the challenge.

❖

Hunter was ready for a throwaway kind of night. One of those times that blended with a hundred other times just like it. And the fact that Showplace was wall-to-wall people when she and Sam arrived was awesome for her plan. "The more the merrier" had always been Hunter's go-to philosophy. Well, that, and a no-regrets kind of mantra. She'd stayed away from the party scene long enough, but her head was a mess, and she needed to remedy that.

Showplace was located just down the block from the loft. The casual bar turned nightclub on the weekends had easily developed over time into the foursome's favorite hangout. Monday through Thursday, it was the perfect place to gather and kick back over drinks and some good conversation. But once Friday night hit, a DJ set up shop and the space transformed. Hunter loved the dichotomy. While the place was out of the way enough that tourists weren't an issue, word of the bar's killer vibe had trickled out, and the crowds were slowly picking up.

While not exactly a gay bar by definition, it was safe to say that Showplace fell more and more that direction as time went on. The high ceilings of the converted warehouse gave the room a spacious feel, even though the place wasn't that large. The minimalistic décor coupled with the purple and blue light bulbs that hung from the rafters provided an industrial vibe reminiscent of the neighborhood that Hunter found rather chill. The front portion of the room was comprised of a dozen or so tall bistro tables with leather-backed chairs, all surrounding a central metallic bar.

She and Sam located Mallory easily enough at their standard table to the left of the bar, set back from the dance floor. Mallory sipped a martini, which she raised to them as they sat. "I got started early. That kind of week."

Samantha grimaced. "You really have been pulling the crazy hours. Serenity?"

Mallory nodded. "Those women are high maintenance. And they have a lot of opinions."

"About water?" Sam asked.

Mallory's eyes widened. "How did you know?"

"Been there. What else?"

"Twelve potential new client meetings since Wednesday. And I took Brooklyn with me on five. She really knows how to pull them in with her description of her ideas. She just lights up."

"She's great at making her excitement contagious," Hunter added. "It's the Brooklyn factor. Hard to resist." She pointed at Samantha. "Cucumber martini?"

Sam nodded and smiled. "Yes, please."

Hunter maneuvered her way to the bar, but the journey there was delayed by quite a few necessary hellos to various friends and acquaintances.

"Hunter's here," a voice called.

She nodded hello.

"Hey, Hunter!" From another side of the room.

She waved.

"Where have you been?" a random girl in front of her asked. "I've missed you."

"Just busy. You know how things can get."

It seemed as soon as she finished one exchange, there was someone else waiting to steal a kiss on the cheek or make her promise to dance with them later. She pressed forward just as another hand landed on her back.

"Hunter Blair, also known as missing in action?"

Stephanie. They'd hooked up once last year. It might have been twice. She was a fun girl. Short-cropped hair that she kept bleached blond and a few well-placed piercings—some less visible than others, if she remembered correctly.

Hunter grinned. "Not MIA. I've been around. You just haven't been looking hard enough. Good to see you, though. I dig the jacket."

It was something to say. She tended to compliment women whenever she could, an automatic pilot thing. She enjoyed making other people feel good.

"Can I just say," Stephanie said, moving her hands from Hunter's elbows up her shoulders, "that I have never seen you look more delectable."

"Delectable is quite a word, Steph."

"I know lots of big words, sweetie. I can say them for you later if you'd like."

"Wow. Now that's an offer. Let's just see how the night plays out. You never know." She continued on her path to the bar. She had no intention of starting anything with Stephanie, and she wondered why she'd engaged in the flirtatious exchange. Her conversation with Samantha a few days prior played back in her head. *Because you never want to hurt anyone's feelings. You should be more up front if you're not interested.* It seemed that advice wasn't exactly easy to implement.

She waited patiently at the bar, subtly moving her head in time to the music, until Hope, the bartender, caught her eye and smiled. Speaking of a lot of attention from girls, Hope always had her hands full with the groupies that flocked to Showplace just to sit at the bar and stare awestruck at her all night. She'd started work at Showplace about six months prior and was instantly the talk of the lesbian regulars. With medium-length blond hair (generally pulled back when she was working), soft brown eyes, and an easy smile, Hope garnered lots of attention. But she kept her head down, made the drinks, and collected her tips, preferring to stick to her job rather than chatting up girls. She and Hunter had struck up a friendship over the past few months and found that they had quite a few things in common.

"Hey," Hope said, resting her forearms on the bar in front of Hunter. "How's your night?"

"Just getting started," Hunter said, projecting her voice above the music. "How's yours?"

Hope glanced around. "It started picking up about eight and hasn't slowed down for a second. I'm going to sleep like a baby tonight. Won't make it home until probably three."

"But you've landed at least ten phone numbers already, if I had to guess."

Hope grinned, dropped a cherry on top of a beverage, and handed it across the bar to a waiting woman. "You know I don't pay attention to that kind of thing. I'm working. Six fifty," she said to the girl before turning her attention back to Hunter. "Hey, did you check out that band in the East Village? I wanted to hear what you thought before I ventured out."

"No. I skipped it. But if you decide to catch a set sometime, let me know. I'll tag along."

"You're on. Now what can I get for you?"

"I need a cucumber martini and a bourbon and Coke."

"Coming up." When Hope returned with a tray with three drinks instead of two, Hunter raised a questioning eyebrow. Hope shrugged. "Mallory's drink looks a little low."

Hunter stared at Hope, enjoying this. "But you don't pay attention to that kind of thing. You're working."

"Spotting a customer in need of a drink is part of that job." She winked at Hunter. "And I'm excellent at my job."

It wasn't the first time that Hope had sent Mallory a drink. And it probably wouldn't be the last. "Well, thanks." She slid Hope some cash for hers and Sam's cocktails and made her way back to the table.

"A refresher for you," she said to Mallory, placing the drink in front of her. "On the house. You're officially a stud, by the way. Mad props."

"Oh no. This is from the bartender, isn't it?" Mallory eyed the drink critically. "I don't know how I feel about stud status."

Hunter stared at her. "Don't overthink it. Hard for you, I know, but you'll manage. Enjoy your drink and wave to Hope. It's what you do." She shifted her focus. "And a cucumber martini for Sam." She placed the glass in front of Samantha.

"Thank you." Samantha smiled widely in appreciation and Hunter couldn't seem to look away. She radiated tonight. She'd complained about her inability to put an outfit together, but there was something so simplistic about her look, a casual solid green sundress with a silver necklace that brought out her eyes and easily made her the most attractive woman in the room. Her hair was down and she must not have blow-dried it that day, as it fell in subtle waves that clung just past her shoulders, shiny and soft like some kind of shampoo commercial. Hunter remembered the way it had cascaded softly through her fingers when they'd kissed in the entryway of Samantha's room. How sweet it had smelled when she buried her face in it in Sam's bed. A tingle moved through her at the very vivid sensation.

"Hunter?" she heard Brooklyn say. And then there were hands on her shoulders from behind. "Hey. You in there?"

"Yeah, totally. Sorry." She turned and focused her attention on the newly arrived Brooklyn, breaking into a smile at the addition to their table. "You guys made it." She'd seen Brooklyn earlier that day, but she pulled Jessica in for a quick hug.

"Thanks for the invite," Jessica said as Hunter released her. "We had dinner at home first. But it's nice to get out."

"There might have also been a quickie," she heard Brooklyn whisper to Samantha as she assumed the seat next to her. *Ah, yes, young love. What must that be like?* She chose not to dwell, downing half of her drink instead. She had a lot of feelings swirling and because she didn't quite know what the hell they were or meant, she opted instead for a bit of unbridled distraction.

"I need to dance," she said to everyone and to no one. Without waiting for a response, she made her way to the dance floor and let the music take her far from life's complications. The floor was crowded, but that almost made it easier to lose herself among the masses. The beat was fast and she lifted her hands and tossed back her head. The prickle from the alcohol snuck into her system, loosening her limbs and dulling her senses just enough. A girl turned into her and they danced together. She slid one of her arms around the girl's waist. She'd seen her before. They'd chatted over drinks sometime back. They danced closer with each rhythmic pulse. Hypnotic really, the sensation of pressing against a virtual stranger to a monotonous beat.

"Well, Hunter's in game mode tonight," Mallory said, smiling from their table, her eyes on the dance floor. But Samantha didn't need the update. She'd seen for herself. As Brooklyn recounted her most recent run-in with a traffic cop, Samantha perfected the art of divided attention. Though she threw in the occasional *no way*, *wow*, or *nice* in response to Brooklyn's story, her true focus remained about a hundred feet away, where Hunter danced in a rather sexy manner with some club kid who looked like she wanted to devour Hunter right then and there. It wasn't long before the random girl's arms moved up Hunter's body to around her neck in a display so overt that Samantha rolled her eyes.

"What's with the face? You don't agree?" Brooklyn asked.

Busted. She had no idea what Brooklyn had just said, but she could totally play this off. "No, you're right."

Brooklyn seemed satisfied. "I just think that as long as I'm not putting anyone in danger, what does it matter if I push the bounds of a yellow light?" Brooklyn continued her story, but not far away, the brunette pressed her body to Hunter's just as that Stephanie girl joined them on the dance floor. She watched as Hunter turned to Stephanie and the two moved like they were born to dance with one another. Hunter tossed her hair. Stephanie smiled, entranced by the visual, and matched her step for step.

For whatever reason, it angered Samantha.

All of it.

And the fact that she was angry just made her that much more angry in some sort of exponential anger scenario that royally sucked. Because what did she have to be angry about, really? Those women were not good enough for Hunter, true. But if Hunter enjoyed that kind of thing, who was she to care? Just because she'd been with Hunter once did not give her the right to dictate who she danced with.

And she was so not jealous right now anyway.

Because what the hell? She was not that girl. She just wasn't.

The music was pounding way too loud.

There were too many people.

And if that Stephanie chick danced any closer to Hunter, they'd be the same person.

"Sam, did you hear me?" Brooklyn asked.

She turned to Brooklyn, the words flying out of her mouth before she had time to censor them. "You want to know what I heard? You're a menace behind the wheel of a car. You always have been. But you know what? I think you kind of like it. And that's what I heard."

While Brooklyn's mouth formed a tiny "oh," Mallory studied Sam with concerned interest, always the voice of reason. "Sam, everything all right with you tonight?"

"Me? Fine. Never been better. Why do you ask?" She had no idea why she was yelling but had no ability not to.

Brooklyn raised her hand as if called on in class. "Because your eyes are flashing scary."

"And then there is the fact that your eyebrows are kind of drawn down into a hostile little line," Mallory added, moving her hand in a circle.

Samantha balked. "I do not have hostile eyebrows."

"They're a tad hostile," Jessica said calmly. "Not to interrupt the banter."

"Hey, you guys," a random girl said, leaning on their table. She was maybe twenty-two at most and a little too perky for Sam's liking. "Don't mean to bother, but is Hunter here tonight? One of my friends was just curious."

Brooklyn opened her mouth to speak, but Sam was on it. "She's right over there. Tell your friend the line starts to the left. There'll be a survey after."

Once the girl moved on, Brooklyn slid Sam's martini a little closer to her. "Have a drink, Sammie."

"You know what? Best idea of the night." She picked up the martini and downed the sucker. But she knew where there were more and headed off on a mission to locate one.

❖

When the music changed, Hunter was ready for a break. The dance floor was hot, both literally and figuratively, and she needed a moment to catch her breath. She spotted Samantha at the bar, and though she was technically the reason Hunter had attempted to distract herself, she just couldn't seem to stay away. A glutton for punishment, clearly.

"Hey," she said, sliding in next to Sam. "Number two for you already. You're cutting loose tonight."

"Something like that," Sam murmured without giving Hunter so much as a sideways glance.

Hunter nodded her head in time to the music. "This place is crazy tonight. More people than usual. I think our secret is out."

"Seems like it." Still no eye contact, and either Sam was participating in a "scarcity of words" contest or she didn't want to talk to Hunter.

"What's going on?" she asked.

"Nothing."

Another short answer. Okay, so did this mean they were in some sort of argument she hadn't been informed of? "Hey, why aren't you looking at me?"

Samantha turned fully then, and Hunter had the answer to her question, as Sam looked anything but friendly. "Better?" she asked coolly, as her eyes settled on Hunter's. Hope presented Samantha with her drink and a moment later she was gone, leaving Hunter standing there, wondering what the hell she had done to deserve that arctic blast.

When she arrived back at the table, there was yet another new arrival. Jessica's right-hand man, Bentley, stood next to Brooklyn. She'd only spent a limited amount of time with the guy, but they'd quickly bonded. He was laid back and fun. Someone she could mess with at will. Him being a bit of a ladies' man himself, they seemed to recognize the common ground in each other.

Jessica looked between them. "Hunter, you remember Bentley, yes?"

"Of course. Hey there, Bent. Your Mets are looking like a band of sixth graders lately."

He grinned and raced around the table, wrapping his giant arms around her in a playful chokehold from behind. "My favorite rascal is here," he said, kissing the side of her head several times. "And my Mets will run your Reds all over the field."

He released her and she stumbled forward before reversing direction and punching him in the arm hard for the physical harassment. She got him good, too, the wily bastard.

"Ow. Stop beating me up. I'm fragile," he said.

"Please. As for my Reds, I guess we'll just have to wait and see," she said, dusting her hands together.

The fast-paced music shifted behind them to a slower, more melodic tune. To keep the scene vibrant, they didn't play a lot of slow songs at Showplace on weekends, with the exception of one or two well-placed crowd favorites throughout the night. If she had a crystal ball, she'd expect Stephanie to approach her any moment, but she had other ideas. She met Sam's eyes across the table and inclined her head subtly in the direction of the dance floor. She wanted to fix whatever was off, and she wanted to do it now. Holding Samantha as they moved slowly to the music was just an extra-added benefit that she didn't allow herself to dwell on.

But Samantha's gaze glided to Bentley, who shrugged at Hunter.

"She promised her first dance to me." He offered Samantha his hand and she accepted. Hunter watched them take their place among the dozen other swaying couples. But it was the moment when Samantha looked up at Bentley and smiled that Hunter felt her stomach clench in the most uncomfortable manner.

"You okay?" Jessica asked, placing a hand on Hunter's thigh. "You aren't looking so good."

"Maybe drink some water," Mallory offered, mistaking her demeanor for too much to drink. But that was good. Let them think that, because if the world knew how she was really feeling, like she didn't even recognize herself, well, things would certainly get a lot more complicated.

Hunter was feeling something she didn't understand, that she couldn't quite name, and it was freaking her the hell out. She'd been lusting after Samantha for weeks. But was this more than just lust? And as if in reflex, she panicked, because that's not how she operated. "I have to go," she announced to the table. Brooklyn and Jessica exchanged glances.

"I'll walk halfway with you," Brooklyn said, pushing back from the table. "Make sure you're all right."

Hunter didn't so much as pause. "Do what you want, but I'm fine." Just before pushing the door open, she stole one last look at the dance floor. At Samantha swaying sweetly with Bentley, smiling up at him. Jealousy was unattractive, a trait she'd always prided herself on never having to deal with. She was the exception to most any rule, damn it.

Not anymore, apparently.

Because the healthy dose of envy she'd just been doused with served as a sobering reminder that maybe she'd given herself too much credit. New verdict: Jealousy sucked.

"You want to talk about it?" Brooklyn asked as they walked the darkened street, dodging passersby. Hunter folded her arms across her body, partly to brace against the chill and partly in self-protection mode. She wasn't in a good place.

"Not really."

"This isn't you drinking too much. I've met drunk Hunter many times, and she's a happy drunk. Something else is going on with you and it has been for a while now." And then Brooklyn stopped dead in her tracks, forcing Hunter to pause and look back at her.

"What? Are you coming or not?"

Brooklyn's mouth fell open. "You've totally fallen for her, haven't you?"

Hunter felt the blood drain from her face and she grappled for the words that would best explain what she couldn't even explain to herself. She wasn't falling for Sam. She didn't do love. But there *was* a depth of emotion there that she couldn't quite pinpoint. How could she explain to Brooklyn that there was something pure and wonderful about Samantha, unlike any other girl? That she was kind and funny and quirky and so beyond beautiful that it wasn't fair? That when she stared up at Hunter with those fathomless green eyes, Hunter ran out of air? But instead of sharing those things, all she could manage to say was, "No, that'd be crazy."

"But you have feelings for her," Brooklyn countered.

Hunter dropped her head back and looked up at the sky. "I don't know. Maybe a little."

The corners of Brooklyn's mouth turned up in happy excitement as she skipped the rest of the distance between them. Was Brooklyn happy about this? Because honestly, Hunter wasn't sure she would be. It complicated so much.

Brooklyn snatched up Hunter's hand and squeezed it against hers. "So are you guys going to live together and get married and have little yoga babies? Family Tree Poses for the win!"

She blinked at Brooklyn, trying to decode the sentence before understanding zapped her. She'd told Brooklyn about April in the park, and the misinformation had carried through to this very moment. Damn it. As she stood there on the corner of Spring and Broadway, she recognized that the crossroads in front of her literally mirrored the decision she faced about what to tell Brooklyn. But why ruin the chemistry of the group for something that wasn't going to go anywhere anyway? That couldn't go anywhere. She and Sam were hook-up buddies. That was it. The people Samantha dated were nothing like Hunter.

So what would be the point in confessing her feelings to Brooklyn? Just because it would help to talk out her situation with someone? Not a good enough reason. Hunter took a cleansing breath. "Yoga babies might be a little far off." She swallowed the truth and felt heavier for it.

Brooklyn pulled her into a hug and held on. "I know you are probably freaking out over this. I did the exact same thing. Just don't run from your feelings. Promise me? Give them a chance."

"I promise." Hunter returned the hug, knowing that was an agreement she wouldn't be able to keep.

❖

Sam was feeling a little bit tipsy when she and Mallory walked home from Showplace that night. The sky was clear, and there was a night chill that had Samantha wishing she'd brought a sweater. It was just after midnight, and despite her best efforts to turn the evening around, the images of Hunter dancing with that Stephanie girl hung on like the plague, making everything that followed taste bitter and unhappy.

Mallory nudged Sam's shoulder with her own as they walked. "Something's going on in that analytical brain of yours."

She fired a glance at Mallory as they split the sidewalk to leave room for a gaggle of teenagers to pass. "What makes you say that?"

"You're uptight, argumentative, and quiet. Which is the way you get when column A doesn't match column B. I'm expecting you to go home and put on your glasses and serious ponytail while you work out the life details."

"The serious ponytail definitely helps me focus. It might be coming out later. The glasses are just for, you know, vision."

Mallory chuckled quietly. "Okay. So what gives? Is it Bentley? You two looked really good together out there. I counted three dances. Are you interested?"

"Not really," Samantha offered a small smile at the memory. "He gave me his number, though. He wants a proper date. And I have to admit, it was nice to be noticed that way. You know, really *noticed*."

"Why do you say it like that? You're a very noticeable girl, Samantha. You don't give yourself enough credit. And I think you should call him. Bentley, I mean. Don't let the whole Libby scenario take you down. You're a romantic, and I've always loved that about you."

"Thanks." Sam nodded, considering Mallory's words. "I'll think about it." But Sam knew she wouldn't be calling Bentley. There hadn't been that draw she felt with Libby or the spark she felt with—nope. Not going there.

"But my advice is don't stress about it. Start off casual. Low pressure. You're just coming off a big heartbreak and you need to allow room for yourself to live a little, to—"

"I slept with Hunter."

Holy Hillary Clinton!

Had she just said that?

She hadn't intended to confess to Mallory, but the words apparently had a mind of their own.

Mallory stopped in her tracks on the sidewalk and tilted her head to the side in confusion before giving her head a little shake and smiling. "I'm sorry. I think I hallucinated for a second. It happens. I'm not even going to repeat what I thought you said. Could you run that by me again?"

There was no turning back now, and the rogue words tumbled out of her mouth without preamble. She blamed the alcohol. Or maybe just her stupid subconscious. "I slept with Hunter. I did. We had sex. And it was good. Astronomically good."

Mallory didn't say anything. Her lips parted slightly, but that was the only indication that she'd taken in any sort of information.

"Mallory. Talk back now. Your turn."

She shook her head slowly. "Can't. Still processing."

Samantha shook Mallory's arm a bit. "It's not the end of the world, right? I mean, friends sleep together sometimes. Right? I mean, *right?*"

"You and *Hunter* were together?"

"Yes."

"On purpose?"

Sam stared at her. "Well, we didn't just accidentally bump into each other, if that's what you're asking!"

"Oh, God."

"I know. I've been 'oh, godding,' too. Take a minute and do some. I'm trying to be mature about this and move on from the godding, so I'm not gonna join in. It's kind of my lot in life, maturity, and yours, too, by the way. So where are the mature words of wisdom, Mal? Because I'm counting on them."

"This is bad." Mallory took a deep breath. "We should sit because I don't know what else to do with myself."

Samantha scanned the street, craning her neck around the random guy dressed as the Green Lantern. She shook her head. This city on Friday night. "There's a bench outside the coffee shop a block up. Do you want some coffee?"

"If it comes with a bench, I do."

"The bench is part of the agreement."

Mallory took a deep breath. "Great. Take me to it."

Ten short minutes later, and Samantha presented Mallory with a hot cup of coffee and held on to one for herself. She blew into the cup, watching as the steam rose and disappeared into the air around them. She took comfort in the cozy visual and warmed her hands on the toasty cardboard. Finally, she stole a look at Mallory. "Listen, I'm sorry I sprang that on you back there. The thing is, you've always been someone that I admire, Mal, who has a head on her shoulders. I guess I really needed your input on this. Whether I knew it or not."

"Is it serious between you?"

Sam shook her head. "Pshhh. No. I was attracted to her. That part is true. Hell, *everyone* is attracted to her."

Mallory turned on the bench to face Sam. "But you're not everyone. You don't just jump into bed with people because you think they're hot. So it makes me wonder if there's something more to this."

This was a valid point. "Well, she's my *friend*, too. And I care about her a lot. And maybe I'm a little bit in rebound mode. And she was there for me."

"Oh, I bet she was." And then a thought seemed to occur to Mallory and she straightened. "Was *that* your issue tonight? It was, wasn't it? It wasn't Bentley that had you all worked up, it was Hunter."

Samantha covered her face with her hands. "I don't know what happened there. She was dancing with those girls, but she always dances with those girls. Yet somehow…"

"You were jealous," Mallory supplied. "Because there's this whole new dynamic between you now. You can't just sleep with someone in a vacuum, Sam. There are repercussions in life."

"There doesn't have to be with this."

Mallory held up a finger. "Unless you actually have real feelings for her."

Samantha sent her the same look she would have if she'd just announced Apple was selling at four dollars a share. Because it was so not the case. "No, Mal. You're not listening. It's lust. I'm lusting after one of my best friends on the planet and I should probably find a way to stop doing that. I need therapy."

Mallory stared at the sky. "And now I do, too. This is big! Do you know how big this is?"

Sam held up a hand. "You're kind of shouting. And yes, I know how big this is."

Mallory set her coffee cup down next to her. "Well, I'd be lying if I said it doesn't freak me the hell out in regard to Savvy. The four of us have this perfect little balance in place. I don't want to upset that and see it all fall apart because you two can't keep your libidos in check. It's too important, Sam."

"I won't let it come to that. It will not upset the balance. I'll make sure of it."

"You have to make sure this never happens again. It's too important."

Samantha took in the words. Mallory was right. It wasn't fair to just consider her and Hunter's take on the situation; Savvy had to come first. "It won't happen again."

"Good. The two of you are going to be alone in the office a lot this next week. You going to be able to handle this?"

"Of course. Who do you think I am?"

"I'm not sure I know right now."

When Sam arrived home that night, Hunter was once again on the couch reading her book. She knew Hunter'd left Showplace ahead of her, but she'd been fairly confident that she'd headed off to a second location. She'd been in party mode, and that usually, in Sam's experience, meant late nights.

"What are you doing here?"

Hunter looked up from her spot on the couch. She was wearing black cotton short-shorts and a red tank top. The fact that there was so much skin on display just served to annoy Samantha that much further. Because seriously, she was over all the Hunter thoughts and anything that prompted them. Done.

Hunter shrugged and returned her attention to the book. "I live here."

The apartment was chilly, both literally and figuratively, and as Sam was already cold from the night air, she moved to adjust the thermostat. "I just figured you'd be out with one of your many groupies. You know, bumping and grinding until the wee hours of the morning at some new club."

"As you can see, you were wrong." Hunter glanced up this time, but it was barely a flick. For whatever reason, the lack of engagement was beyond frustrating and only propelled Samantha further.

"You know, we probably need a system for when you bring one of them back here, some way that I know to stay clear of your room. Because, Jesus, can you imagine? A scarf on your door would work. It's ridiculously clichéd, but probably necessary now that we live together."

"Yeah, I'm not into systems."

Samantha shrugged in a patronizing manner as she faced Hunter, her annoyance at the situation flaring. "What's it like to just pick one out at the end of the night? Is there any sort of criteria or just eenie meenie miney moe when the clubs close?" Her tone wasn't the nicest. In fact, she did nothing to hide her judgment. Her anger had spread out and sprouted wings, and there was apparently no holding it back.

"Are you kidding me with this?" Hunter stared at her, eyes blazing. Oh, she had her attention now. "I've lived here for over a month. Have I once brought a girl home with me?"

"I don't monitor your every movement."

"Are you sure about that?" She glanced at the thermostat on the wall. "And did you just make it warmer in here? I'm tired of being hot at night. Can you turn it back?"

"My bad," Samantha said, returning to the thermostat. "I forgot how *hot* you were. And how important it is that you're treated as such. I mean, right? That's what's important to you."

Hunter closed the book and leaned forward. "What is your deal right now? Something you want to discuss, Sam? Or are you just trying a new personality? Quite frankly, I'm not a fan."

"No, I'm good." She headed for her bedroom as if it were the most casual thing in the world. Outside, a siren blared past the building, and inside felt just as chaotic. Everything in Sam's world was off, askew. She hated it.

"Yeah, you looked like it by the end of the night. Glad it's all working out for you."

She turned back. "Meaning?"

Hunter lifted a shoulder. "You looked pretty content with Bentley is all. Maybe he does it for you more than any of the women I danced with ever could."

Sam took a minute with the comment and to be sure she understood its implication. The end result stung. "Yes, I did enjoy dancing with Bentley. And that's all it was, a dance. But the fact that you just made some sort of veiled dig at my sexuality is not only juvenile but offensive as hell."

Hunter closed her eyes in disappointment at herself. Samantha was right. What she'd just said was horrible. It was one of those fights that took over until it felt like the fight was having you. "Sam, wait."

"No." Sam shook her head. "Please don't assume you know anything about what it's like to be me—to feel slighted on a daily basis by either the straight or gay community, depending on the day. So, no, I'm not going to wait. I'm ready for tonight to be over. Enjoy your book."

Hunter sat there on the couch stunned as the door slammed shut. She had no idea what had just happened, how their interaction had spiraled so far out of control. The comment she'd made was totally out of bounds, and the recriminations were already swirling to the point that she felt sick to her stomach.

She'd acted out, attempting to strike back at someone she cared about because she was jealous. When in fact, it wasn't even representative of how she felt about Samantha's sexuality at all. It was the low-hanging fruit, and she was embarrassed that she'd gone there. The night's events and her own realizations had her already in a bad place, and Samantha's antagonistic comments had just piled on to the point that she was feeling aggressive and a little out of control.

And did Samantha really think she slept around? She was a flirt, that much was true, who wasn't opposed to after hours activity here and there, when it seemed appropriate. She was still in her twenties and wanted to enjoy them. But she had standards.

She reached for Elvis and stroked his head, but the rest of her felt numb. She hated the way she looked through Samantha's eyes.

Wild.

Careless.

Unworthy.

And it resonated.

CHAPTER ELEVEN

"Thank you so much for agreeing to have lunch with me," Tanya said, sipping from her water glass. It was Tuesday afternoon, and though Sam had come up with every excuse to not have lunch with this woman, her hand was forced when Tanya finally copied Mallory on the request for a budget consultation. Shrewd, very shrewd.

Tanya had selected a rather upscale restaurant on the Upper West Side, the kind of place with white tablecloths, multiple forks, and women eating from large bowls of lettuce alongside Chardonnay.

"No problem," Sam said. "You mentioned the budget, so I've brought with me some of the details we initially decided upon." She reached for her leather-bound portfolio until Tanya placed her hand on her wrist, stopping her progress.

"Can we get to that later, perhaps?"

"Oh. Sure. You'd rather eat first?"

"If that's okay. I thought we could talk a little." Right on cue, the rather pretentious-looking waiter stopped by to take their order. While Samantha was dying for a cheeseburger, she followed Tanya's lead and ordered the spinach salad, dressing on the side. Yay.

"So how have you been?" Tanya asked, eyes wide, enthusiasm oozing from every perfect pore.

"I've been fine. How about you?"

"Not so great, actually," she said, her voice cracking. Oh, and there were tears. Not tears, please. Lunch sans tears was what she signed up for.

Obligatorily, she followed up. "Tanya, are you okay? Why are you crying?"

"It's Libby," she practically sobbed. "She's not happy. I can tell. She thinks I'm flighty or too new age or whatever."

"No? Really?" Shock! Disbelief! Was it bad that she wasn't completely torn up about this? Because she actually full-on agreed with Libby. But what really came out of Sam's mouth was, "I'm so sorry."

"Thanks, Sam. I invited you here because I was hoping you had some girl-to-girl advice."

Oh no. This wasn't happening to her. Wasn't there some sort of get-out-of-jail-free card for comforting your ex-girlfriend's new love interest? Surely she should be spared, under some kind of fine print. "I don't know that I'm the one to come to for words of wisdom when it comes to Libby. You know how things ended for us."

"But she just thinks so highly of you, Sam. It's always 'Samantha says you have to find a goal for yourself and stick to it. Samantha is so levelheaded and has a handle on life.' Sometimes I think she wishes I were more like you."

Interesting tidbit that she had to admit she enjoyed a little. "I'm sure that's not true. You guys are just figuring each other out, probably. Do you want to look at the budget?"

But it was as if Tanya hadn't heard her. "We are figuring each other out. And don't get me wrong, the sex is amazing. Mind-blowing even. That part we've got down." Okay, low blow. Sam glanced around in desperation. Maybe she should order one of those salad-Chardonnays. "But I feel this distance growing between us outside the bedroom, and I don't know what to do. I want to be her spirit animal, the lime to her water, but I'm failing."

Samantha sighed, hating the fruit/water analogy and wishing she wasn't having this conversation. She closed her eyes and forced herself to answer. "Have you talked to her about it?"

"No. I'm terrified of what she'll say. What if I'm right and she thinks we're a mistake? What if it's really you who she wants?" Okay, that was interesting information. Was it possible Libby saw things differently now? Samantha wasn't sure how she felt about that, but she filed it away for examination later.

"As much as you may not want to, Tanya, I think communication is the way to go on this one. Avoiding the topic doesn't make it any less real. And you might be surprised. This whole thing could potentially be all in your head."

Tanya seemed to like this and sat a little taller in her chair as the salads (dressing on the side) were delivered. "You really are smart, Sam. I'm glad I called you. I'll talk to her tonight."

"That's me," Samantha said, turning to her salad. "Good old dependable Sam."

"Should I talk to her before sex or after?"

Ahhhhh! "I'll let you decide."

Tanya leaned forward, full of new scary energy. "And now that I have you here, let's talk about chasing down that glow. I have a lot of ideas."

"Fabulous," she enthused dryly, understanding now that the budget had nothing whatsoever to do with the meeting. Samantha checked her watch and did a mad salad-to-exit calculation. It was time to get the hell back to Soho, because life was simply too short to spend on salad-time-with-Tanya.

But an hour later, as she stood on the crowded F train on the way back to work, her mind was still very much on the lunch from hell. What if what Tanya said was true? What if Libby did miss her? She might have a second shot. She hesitated at the prospect. There was a lot of water under that bridge. But then again, this was Libby she was talking about. Libby, who ticked all the boxes.

As she walked the short distance from the train to the loft, there was an extra spring in her step and a slight smile on her face. Life was full of endless possibilities.

❖

Hunter stared at the blond woman wrapped in a towel, her head tossed back in surrender as she enjoyed a luxurious mineral bath. Damn, she was tired of looking at this woman, and she ran her mouse across the model's face several times in angry protest.

She'd been working on the print ad for Serenity for hours but kept hitting the proverbial creative wall at every step. The image of the woman Serenity had supplied them with mocked her with all the relaxation and beauty and stupid luxurious blond hair piled on top of her head. Unable to stand the frustration a minute more, she shut her laptop with a noticeable thud.

Across the Savvy loft, Samantha jumped at the sound, turned, and regarded her calmly. "Problem, Hunter?"

They were alone in the office. And, outside of the occasional polite work exchange or apartment pleasantry, they hadn't fully engaged in any meaningful conversation since the war that was Friday night. To say things felt awkward was an understatement.

But with Brooklyn and Mallory out on a client meeting, she and Sam were left to hold down the fort. It wasn't all that unusual, as both of their jobs were mainly office based, though they were on their own more often now with the loss of the Foster account. Hunter pushed up from her desk and moved to the really uncomfortable couch that Mallory insisted looked awesome in the space. Hunter had a love-hate with this couch. It did look great. That part was true. It also was hella-hard to sit on. "The Serenity ad. I can't get it right and I'm sick of the stupid model mocking me."

Samantha took off the serious numbers glasses and rubbed her temple. "I'm sorry. The ad mocks you?"

"The woman in it does, yeah. She knows I'm struggling to get the opacity on the top layer perfect, and when I can't, she just looks all peaceful to contrast how angry I feel. It's her game. She's mocking me and I'm breaking up with her."

"Hmm. I had no idea stills of models could be so judgmental. Can I see?"

"The ad?" Hunter sighed, trudged over to her laptop, and joined Samantha at her desk. "Take a look. It's my best work ever in life," she said blandly, resting her chin in her hand in defeat.

Samantha studied the layout briefly before taking in air. "No way."

"You're that impressed?"

Samantha pointed at the screen and stared at Hunter, eyes wide. "She's everywhere. It's Tanya."

"Tanya. And that would be?"

"Love of Libby's life. Ruiner of happiness. Crazy representative of water and all things from the Earth." Sam sighed and sat back in her chair. "No wonder she was mocking you. You're lucky she doesn't reach through that screen and devastate everything that makes you happy, because that would be a typical Tanya move." And then she threw her head into her hands and downshifted. "That was mean. Tanya's never been anything but nice to me. Creepy spa nice and annoying as hell, but still nice. I'm a mean person." She lifted her head. "I didn't used to be, but I am now. I don't know why you talk to me." She dropped her head on the desk with a bang.

Hunter took in the dramatic display with a quiet smile and placed a hand on Sam's back. "Hey, accountant person. You're not mean. You're one of the nicest people I know. There is actually no better person than you. So knock it off."

"Really?" Sam squeaked from the doldrums of the desk. She lifted her head again and the bright green eyes sparkled at Hunter. "Because you didn't think so on Friday night. And we haven't really spoken more than a handful of words since."

Hunter shrugged a shoulder. "I know. I was in a bad place on Friday and acted like an asshole. The thing that I said, I didn't mean, and you should know that if I could take back that whole interaction, I would."

"Me, too. That was a horrible fight, and I take a lot of responsibility."

Hunter appreciated that. "But I took it where it didn't need to go. And I would like to apologize."

"No, I'm sorry. I was so out of line it was crazy. I don't want to fight with you. I happen to like you. A lot."

Hunter reclined in her chair and grinned. "Oh yeah? What about me?"

Samantha blew out a breath. But she was smiling, and that was everything, because Hunter had missed that smile. It had a way of turning around her entire day. "We're really doing this?"

"Oh, I think we have to."

But then Sam did something Hunter wasn't expecting. She took her hand, prompting the smile to fall from Hunter's face as the moment shifted into something new, uncharted.

"You, Hunter Blair, are valuable to me. You are talented and beautiful, but more than that, you're thoughtful. You look out for me. And when I'm around you, I feel challenged in the most unexpected of ways."

They hit her hard, those words. Coming from Samantha, they carried a lot of weight. She and Samantha were staring at each other now and Samantha's gaze dropped to her mouth. And God, that move affected Hunter. She had never wanted to kiss someone so badly in her life, and the knowledge that Sam was struggling too only doubled her desire. The air was thick around them and the sound seemed to fade from the room. Whatever was bubbling between them seemed to gain momentum by the hour. And the fight only seemed to have tossed gasoline on the fire. There was now a hunger in Sam's eyes that had Hunter captivated and aching to touch her. Intimately. She reached out and cradled Samantha's cheek, her skin soft and warm to the touch. At the contact, Samantha took a quick breath and hesitated a beat before backing out of the touch altogether.

"We should probably eat something," she said quietly, but her eyes hadn't once departed from Hunter's lips. "I'll pick us up something from, um, Lulu's." She blinked purposefully, grabbed some cash from her purse, and was gone, just like that.

Alone in the office, Hunter knew they were in sync. Maybe more than they had ever been. The question was whether to do anything further about it. She stared in frustration at the ceiling, wondering what she'd done to deserve this level of temptation surrounding the one girl she couldn't have. Damn the universe and all of its complexities. She opened the laptop and stared at the model. "What?" she asked the screen, and shook her head. Spa bitches.

❖

Twenty-five minutes later, Samantha made her way up the sidewalk, carrying a bag with their usual lunch fare: a turkey club for her and pastrami on rye for Hunter, homemade chips and two pickles on the side.

Luckily, her heart rate seemed to have returned to normal from the unexpected exchange at the office. She wasn't sure how they'd gotten to snap-crackle-pop status so quickly, but they had. One minute they'd been talking about Tanya, and two seconds later, the temperature in the room had risen twenty degrees and Samantha was having all sorts of… intense cravings.

She stole a chip from the bag as she turned the corner into the lobby of their building. There was purpose to her stride, as the world that had felt so wildly backward since her fight with Hunter was on its way to righting itself. Sure, there were still problems—she was already contemplating strategies to best keep herself from imagining Hunter naked for the rest of the afternoon. But anything was better than the not talking, even—Good God, what was *that*? Something small and furry interrupted her train of thought and darted across the lobby, prompting Samantha to freeze and crush the bag of food against her chest in defense. Moving like an NFL ball carrier in overtime, she hightailed it back to the street to spare her life and assess the situation.

Tiny rodent monster in the lobby.

Tiny rodent monster in the lobby.

It was the only sentence that would come. She didn't do rodents. Ever. In fact, they were high on the list of greatest fears. And this one had a long tail, which made her cringe all over at just the idea.

After several cleansing breaths, Sam gathered enough courage to peer into the small lobby through the glass for any sign of Sly, their doorman. Sly would know what to do about the tiny rodent monster. He knew what to do about everything. But damn it all, there was no sign of Sly anywhere. Probably on his lunch break, which didn't seem fair. Doormen didn't need lunch when there were battles to fight. She took another look through the glass to pinpoint the TRM's location. Gasp. But in even more frightening news, it was missing.

"It could be anywhere!" she shouted to the street, prompting a glance or two from passing pedestrians. "Okay. So what am I supposed to do here?" She studied the elevator. Probably ten steps away once she entered the building. But there was always the risk that the elevator wouldn't arrive right off and she'd be stuck with the tiny rodent monster in a small space. What if it got near her? What *then*?

But she didn't have a lot of choice. There was lunch and work and life to attend to. And she couldn't let a little rodent monster crisis get in the way of that.

She rolled her shoulders.

She could be a badass against a little mouse. Hell, she rode the subway! She sagged in defeat at a new realization. This was New York City. Who was she kidding? TRM was likely a rat, and that meant she would die if there were contact. Not of disease, but of abject horror, and that was all people would talk about.

Samantha Ennis died via rat horror.

She shook herself out of the ever-spiraling *what-if* scenario. Any more thought on the topic would be detrimental to the goal. So she cleared her mind, threw open the door, and scurried the ten paces to the elevator bay. Mashing the Up button eighteen thousand times in succession didn't seem to produce the elevator nearly as fast as she'd hoped. This was bad. *Come on. Come on. Come on.* And right on cue, there was the theme music from *Halloween* playing in her head. Excellent. Through it all, her eyes flew from one corner of the lobby to the other for any sort of furry movement. When she saw none, she shifted her focus briefly to the number readout above the bay and watched as the elevator descended from eight, seven, six, five, but then out of the corner of her eye was the slightest bit of rodent monster movement and oh, Warren Buffet, it was against the wall and sniffing its way in her direction! Was it a mouse or a rat? She didn't know, but it had tiny little claws that made very faint clicking noises on the tile. A sound that would surely haunt her dreams for life.

She tried to move, but her body was in charge and clearly on some sort of lunch break, probably with Sly. With every ounce of strength she had, she managed to run. It's possible she also screamed and tossed lunch in the air over her shoulder. She only knew that part in retrospect, ascertained from the safety of the sidewalk.

Finally, in desperation and fear for her life, she pulled her phone out of her back pocket and called Hunter upstairs.

She answered on the second ring. "Did you get lost?"

"Something horrible has happened."

Hunter's voice switched quickly to concern. "Okay. What's wrong? Where are you?"

"Outside the building. There's a giant rat. A rodent monster in the lobby. I'm not making this up. It won't let me get to the elevator. It hates me. I hate it back."

A pause. "A rodent monster?"

"I think you're focusing on the wrong thing here."

"What do you mean it 'won't let you'?"

Sam paused and leveled with Hunter. "I can't walk past it, Hunter. I just can't. Do you think you could—?"

"On my way."

She'd meant it, too, as three short minutes later, the elevator doors opened and Hunter strode into the lobby, cool as a cucumber, wearing her baby blue camo pants and her black V-neck. Hunter excelled at filling out that neckline. She tossed a glance at the monster, which appeared very interested in their discarded lunch, smiled to herself, and made her way outside.

"That's your rodent monster?"

Samantha balked. "Um, yeah. Did you see that thing?"

"It's a medium-sized mouse at best. And it's probably just as terrified of you."

"It's a rat. And it's evil."

"It's a mouse, and it probably wandered in when someone held the door open for too long. It happens. Not a big deal. Shall I walk you in?"

"I don't think I can do that," Sam said.

"So you plan to live out here?"

Samantha considered this. "What if you got rid of it?"

"I don't mind the mouse, but I'd rather not handle it personally if at all possible. I do have standards. Sly will deal with it when he gets back."

"I guess I'll just have to wait, then."

Hunter shook her head in what seemed to be mild annoyance, and without another word, lifted Samantha into her arms and carried her through the lobby. "You're kind of being a baby about this. You get that, right?"

But Samantha was lost in the fact that Hunter's arms were around her and she was able to inhale what seemed to be the aroma of fresh cotton and peaches. Would it be wrong of her to bury her face in Hunter's neck? Because really, that was all she wanted to do. Absently, she realized Hunter had said something. "Hmm?"

They stepped onto the elevator and Hunter met her eyes. The smaller space seemed more intimate, and with their faces only an inch or two apart, Hunter lowered her voice. "I said you're being a little bit of a baby. That mouse is probably hurt that you ran from him. He just wanted to get to know you better. His heart is broken. A mousy ache."

"A mousy ache," Sam said back, not fully taking in the conversation. She shook her head, refocusing. "That's a thing?"

"It is now." Hunter had the longest eyelashes. And the softest brown eyes. So big and expressive. It wasn't fair how easy it was to lose yourself in eyes like those. It occurred to her then that there had been a terrifying mouse incident just minutes before. Seemed a distant memory now. Hunter was still holding her in the elevator, she realized, and though she'd miss the contact very much, she should probably cut her a break. After she took just a moment to savor the feeling, that is, because it really was everything.

"You can put me down now," Sam said. "Thank you for your help."

Hunter held her gaze as the car ascended slowly. Her facial expression was resolute. "Not yet," she said quietly.

Samantha's eyes found the panel of buttons on the wall. And that was when she realized that they weren't on their way to the office. Hunter had pushed the button for the eleventh floor. Their apartment. Her stomach flip-flopped at the probable implication; her mouth went dry at the thought. She licked her lips, a nervous gesture, and turned back to Hunter, intent on pointing out the less-than-wise detour, but Hunter's mouth was on hers before she could react. And it turned out that was totally okay, because Hunter kissed like heaven on Earth. Samantha was shocked at the strength of that kiss, how fast her body responded, convincing her easily that the eleventh floor was maybe the best idea ever.

Her body now pulsed with a kind of electricity she never knew it could possess. It drove her crazy, so to compensate she pushed her tongue into Hunter's mouth, exploring, tasting, savoring. God, it felt so right to finally give in to what had her preoccupied for days. To just say *to hell with it* and follow her primal instincts. And God, was this instinct worth the wait.

The elevator dinged and Hunter didn't hesitate.

She carried Samantha into the apartment and deposited her quickly on the counter. Her eyes were focused, determined. She was on a mission as she pulled the black V-neck over her head, revealing a purple satin bra beneath. Sam stared in awe at the picturesque visual, the generous tops of breasts peeking out from the fabric. Hunter stepped out of her pants and stood succulently before Sam in matching lingerie. Without pause, she found Sam's mouth once again and kissed her with an abandon that was quite simply contagious. Samantha's hands pushed against that bra, her thumbs circling her nipples through the thin material. It was the hottest thing Samantha had ever experienced, this unexpected twist in her day. They'd been hard at work at the office just an hour before, and now look at them. She didn't do things like this. This so wasn't part of the routine.

Hunter's hands were on the move, unbuttoning Sam's shirt, her hands instantly inside it. Sam arched into the touch, pushing her breasts into Hunter's eager hands and closing her eyes at the sensation. She didn't have matching lingerie. Would that be a problem? Unimportant details, she thought as she pulled Hunter's bottom lip into her mouth in a move that had Hunter responding with a quiet moan. She smiled into the kiss. It turned out she was actually good at this.

Sam's shirt was off.

Her bra, too.

And she was on the kitchen counter—*the kitchen counter, people. C'mon.*

Hunter pulled back and stared at Sam, her chest rising and falling with labored breath. Watching Hunter try to maintain control when she was normally so confident was more than a turn-on. Because *she* had done that. She had affected Hunter that way. It was an empowering feeling, and Sam loved it. Placing her hands on either side of Hunter's face, she brought her back down for a searing kiss that, simply put, rocked her socks off.

"I want you," Hunter whispered against her mouth. "Now."

But for Sam, wanting was off the table. This was more. This was need. She nodded, meeting Hunter's darkened eyes. And that seemed to be all Hunter required as she lifted Sam from where she sat on the counter and carried her back to Hunter's bedroom.

Hunter was on top and Sam reveled against the feel of Hunter's weight lightly pressing her into the mattress, her warm skin flush against Sam's. They kissed in a hot tangle of lips and tongues until Samantha thought she might explode. But there was something she had to have first.

She reversed their positions and smiled at Hunter's surprised expression. But Samantha was on a mission and could not be deterred. It was unlike her to take such control in the bedroom, but she was finding it liberating. Like a drug. Removing the last of Hunter's clothing was fun, but discovering what lay underneath the fabric was the real reward. She studied the now naked body beneath her, curious about all the ways to make Hunter feel, something she desperately needed to do. She skimmed a hand from Hunter's neck down her breast to her stomach, encouraged as Hunter sucked in a breath. She took her time, kissing, touching, and experimenting. She made careful note of what Hunter responded to. Her neck was sensitive. Her breasts even more so. She wondered about the insides of her thighs and moved lower.

Hunter was feeling a lot of things. Number one was that she couldn't take much more of this languid exploration Sam seemed intent on. She was vibrating with desire and squirming beneath Sam's touch in an attempt at any kind of release. Samantha placed a slow kiss on the inside of her thigh that had her closing her eyes in surrender. "Sam," she managed to whisper. In fact, it was all she could manage. In answer, Samantha raised her head and moved upward for a kiss. It was slow, deep, and thorough. She brought her knee between Hunter's legs and applied direct pressure, wringing a gasp from Hunter as the kiss became rough and demanding.

"I've got you," Samantha said as she moved steadily down her body. She parted Hunter's thighs gently, her breath a soft caress. With the flat of her tongue, Sam licked the most tender part of Hunter, who was instantly hit with a jolt of something powerful. She squeezed the sheets in her hand, knotting them furiously. "God, Sam. Please."

As Samantha continued, Hunter turned her head against the pillow. It was too much, the onslaught of torturous sensation. Way too much. She was gone. Sam held her in place, moving her tongue in tantalizing circles as Hunter's body continued to climb, the pressure almost unbearable. She moved her hips helplessly against Sam's mouth, giving herself over fully. And then at one final swipe of Sam's tongue, she called out and arched against Sam's mouth. The pleasure came over her all at once, a tidal wave of sensation she was helpless beneath. She shuddered and held on because it was all she could do. It was amazing, the release. Heaven.

Hunter lost her bearings for a moment, unsure of where she was, who she was. But when they returned, Samantha was placing soft kisses to the underside of her breast and then peeked up at her with those perfect green eyes.

"You're beautiful," Samantha said quietly, shaking her head. She traced the curve of Hunter's cheek. The gesture caused Hunter's voice to catch in her throat when she attempted to answer. So instead, she smiled to let Sam know that she'd heard her, that it meant something. Cradling Sam's face, she placed a soft kiss on her lips and slid a hand between her legs. She closed her eyes against what she found there and stroked steadily, lost in how amazing Sam felt, how wet and ready she already was. Back and forth across her center. Slow and even. Samantha's lips parted in response to being touched. She closed her eyes in rapture as Hunter continued the movement. Back and forth. Teasing just enough. When Sam whimpered softly, she slipped inside, into warmth and wonder, all the while moving her thumb—more purposefully now—across that most sensitive spot. Samantha held on and moved against her in a sexy rhythm, her breath becoming more and more shallow with each second that ticked by. Hunter slid down the bed and pulled a nipple into her mouth, her fingers and lips working in tandem. Samantha squeezed her wrist in urgency, but Hunter couldn't be rushed. "Not yet," she murmured.

Hunter continued to massage and tease until even she couldn't stand it anymore. Knowing it wouldn't take much, she applied very firm pressure where she knew Samantha needed it most and held on as Sam clenched around her, moving wildly against her before reveling in the pause of release. But the shocking part was that Hunter was right behind her.

Again. Which never happened.

The unexpected orgasm shot through her as she pressed against Sam. She saw white as the blissful explosion rocked her body. She shook her head as she leveled out again. They were a force, she realized. The two of them, together like this.

Silence lingered as their breathing returned to normal. Once Hunter had recovered, she looked down at Sam. "Okay?" she asked.

Sam took a deep breath and nodded. "Still recovering." But there was a soft smile on display that helped to assure her. Hunter wrapped Sam up in her arms from behind and placed a kiss on her shoulder blade.

"We just did that a second time," Sam said.

"I don't think we had a choice. There's this thing between us. And it seemed to take up all the air in the room."

"And then there's the fact that we're really, really good at it."

"Right?" Hunter said. "Who knew? All this time."

Samantha turned over so they were lying face-to-face. She traced the outline of Hunter's breast with one finger. "It's kinda nice, having this option. Especially since I just feel, I don't know…so comfortable with you. Safe."

Hunter liked hearing that. "You feel safe with me?"

"I do. Like I can just be me."

"I feel the same way." It felt good, talking to Samantha like this. Candidly.

Sam turned onto her back. "We're totally going to hell now if we weren't before. And while I know this was theoretically a bad idea, it actually doesn't feel that way right now. A mirage?"

"A guilty pleasure," Hunter corrected.

"Well, there *was* a lot of pleasure," Sam said, looking skyward, all dreamy and cute. Then a thought seemed to occur to her. "We're supposed to be at work right now, remember?" The words spoke of obligation, but the mischievous look on Samantha's face overruled it.

Unable to stop herself, Hunter moved in and nibbled on Sam's neck. "But playing hooky is fun. And you happen to be really sexy right now. There seems to be no way to get enough of you. It's a problem."

"You've said that before." Sam wrapped her arms around Hunter's neck to better receive the attention. "You really think I'm sexy?"

"It's my number one thought in life right now."

"We never had lunch, you know."

Hunter pulled back. "No?"

"Nope. I left our sandwiches to the rodent in the lobby, remember? Sly is probably not our biggest fan right now as a result."

Hunter found she didn't really care. "He'll live. What do you want to eat?"

Samantha grinned. "I'll get it." But she didn't take the sheet with her when she got up. And she didn't even shrug into a T-shirt from Hunter's dresser. No, the woman who drove her wild walked, nude and confident, into the kitchen as Hunter looked on smiling. When she returned, she carried with her a package of olives, a box of crackers, and bag of tiny marshmallows.

Hunter studied the array. "And you somehow feel this is lunch?"

Samantha slid into bed next to her with her finds. "I always have weird cravings after sex. Can't help it. A fridge raid is a necessity." As Hunter regarded her, Samantha's eyes widened. "What? Stop staring at me in judgment." She shrugged. "Everyone has something."

It was a strange quirk, but at the same time, kind of endearing. "No judgment here. Pass me a marshmallow, weirdo." That earned her a marshmallow in the face.

They ate their eclectic lunch leisurely in bed, enjoying each other's company in a way that felt so natural it was shocking. Hunter stared at Samantha as a slow flutter moved through her. Because this felt different from any other sexual experience she'd had. She could lie here with Sam for hours. In fact, she wanted to. Maybe it was a testament to their friendship, but for Hunter it was beginning to feel like maybe it really was more. She hadn't been wrong about the direction of her feelings the other night at Showplace. It was terrifying, but at the same time, kind of exciting.

"We really should get back to the office," Sam said.

"We will." Hunter played absently with Sam's hair. God, she was feeling a lot of things and maybe she should just say them, be up front with Samantha and maybe even herself. Was it possible she was interested in something more with Sam? Was that absolutely insane? Because it felt like it might be. There was a lot on the line.

Savvy.

Their friendship.

But…and this was the big question: What if Samantha was feeling a little of what Hunter was?

Sam started to gather her clothes. As she buttoned her shirt, she turned to Hunter. "Will I see you downstairs?"

"Yes." A pause. She was vibrating with nervous energy at what she was about to say. She'd really never put herself out there to someone before. Where did one start? "Do you think maybe we should talk about it? Us?" She could feel her heart beating out of her chest, and she blinked in anticipation.

Sam looked caught. She opened her mouth and then closed it, her expression clouded as if she didn't know quite where to go with the question. Finally, she shrugged, relaxing into a smile. "What's to talk about? It's just sex."

And there you have it. "Right," Hunter said.

But then Sam's smile faltered. "You said so yourself a week ago."

Hunter nodded, solemn. Resolute. Clearly, she was on her own here. "No strings. That's the deal. Still is."

They stared at each other, and the silence was no longer the comfortable kind. Sam turned to go. "See you at work." And then, as if forgetting something, popped back around the corner. "You're the best. You know that, right?"

Hunter smiled. "Pshhh. You say that to all the girls." Laughing was easier than the alternative.

"Please. You're the one with the groupies."

She shrugged. "That's me." But even with Samantha smiling at her, teasing her, she was beginning to understand that what she really wanted was outside her reach. Alone in her room, she lay back and studied the patterns on the ceiling as one emotion after another took its turn with her. She looked over at the empty spot in the bed next to her, the one that mirrored the emptiness in her life. An emptiness she'd been quite comfortable with until now.

She'd never wanted to give herself over to someone that way.

And now she knew why.

Because the last thing she wanted was to feel *all this*.

CHAPTER TWELVE

Samantha had to hand it to Balmy Days. When the staff at the retirement community decorated, they *decorated*. Uncle Sam hats hung from the ceiling en masse. Red, white, and blue streamers crisscrossed the common room in a twisting, twirling parade of crepe paper overkill. Miniature American flags lined the wall, and if Samantha wasn't mistaken, there seemed to be an instrumental mash-up of "Yankee Doodle Dandy" and "You're a Grand Old Flag" piped in on the PA system.

The holiday weekend was still a few days away, and while she and her friends had plans to spend it in the Hamptons at a summer home owned by Mallory's family, they still had the rest of the week to get through. Sam wasn't about to check out early and miss scrapbooking class at the senior center. She'd even managed to wrangle the other Savvy girls into joining, per her class's request.

"Where do you want me, Chief?" Brooklyn asked, arriving ten minutes late and smiling warmly to make up for it.

"Mr. Turner has trouble with the scrapbooking scissors. See if he'll let you do some of his cutting for him." Then she lowered her voice. "He's a little grumpy, so don't take it personally."

"Grumpy old guy. Say no more. We're going to be best friends," Brooklyn whispered back before heading off in search of her charge.

Samantha surveyed the activity around her. Mallory had organized the women into a sort of circle and moved between them offering tips. "I find that if you lay out your page before pasting anything down, then you have the chance to make changes to the overall design. Planning is important."

"Yes, dear, but what conditioner do you use?" Mrs. Swientek asked. "Your hair is extra shiny."

Mallory smiled at the diversion. "I believe it's called Pureology."

"I'm going to tell the nurse's aide to order me some."

"It won't get you Harold's attention," Mrs. Guaducci muttered to her page.

"Guess we'll find out," Mrs. Swientek fired back. Mallory raised her eyebrows at Sam, who smiled and placed a reassuring hand on her back as she passed. "You're doing great, Mal. Keep tossing that shiny, shiny hair."

Across the room, as one could have imagined, Mr. Glenville hung on Hunter's every word, which was good because when it came to scrapbooking, the girl knew what she was doing. She had great ideas for complementary color schemes and shape arrangement. The pages coming together on that side of the room were next level. "Maybe you should be teaching the class," she said casually to Hunter, who had just finished explaining color theory to Mr. Glenville and Mr. Earnhardt, who were actually taking notes. She wore dark denim overalls with a sleeveless white shirt underneath. The half ponytail capped off her casual summer vibe. It was a really good look on her, and Samantha had more than noticed. Was it weird that she thought about Hunter that way? It seemed almost second nature, not something she could undo. A consequence of their arrangement, she guessed.

"We would never want to replace you, Sam," Mr. Glenville reassured her. "But maybe your nice friend could assist and come with you each week." He put his arm around Hunter, who met Sam's eyes, shrugged, and smiled widely.

"Well, I have a lot on my plate," she told Mr. Glenville, patting his hand. "But I'll be by every once in a while if it's okay with Samantha."

"And it is," Sam chimed in. "You're always welcome to help out. Lend your particular *skillset*." She winked at Hunter, who glared back playfully.

"So do you have a Facebook account?" she heard Mr. Glenville say as she drifted away. *Perfect.*

Next, she moved on to Brooklyn and gruff Mr. Turner, who

seemed to be engaged in some sort of heated debate. Not good at all. Seeing Samantha approach, Mr. Turner raised his hand and pointed at Brooklyn. "This blond girl thinks I need to put more photos on each page, and I think she needs to mind her own damn business."

Similarly, Brooklyn raised her hand. "I think Mr. Turner needs to suck it up and listen to my advice because one lonely photo in the center of the page is boring. There are lots of layouts to play with here, and he should explore them. Just my creative input." She crossed her arms and sat back in her chair.

Samantha shot Brooklyn a *what the hell* look. But, fine. She could solve this. "Mr. Turner, maybe you'd like to work with Hunter, and Brooklyn can help Mallory with the group she's—"

"No, no, no," Mr. Turner said in annoyance. "We're doing fine here. She's just spirited is all. I'm spirited, too."

"Yeah, leave us be, Sammie," Brooklyn said, smiling proudly. "We're the spirited table."

"Clearly." Understanding their unique camaraderie, Samantha smiled. "Then I'll let you two work."

It was turning into a great session. The residents had a palpable energy about them when new people came to visit. It warmed her heart to see them so reinvigorated, and she was grateful to her friends for doing her this favor. As they filed out at the end of the allotted class time, Brooklyn and Mallory went about helping Samantha with the cleanup. She gathered the glue sticks from the various tables and returned them to the large plastic bag, all the while keeping one eye on the front of the room. Hunter still sat quietly with Mr. Earnhardt as he took her through each page of his scrapbook and explained the significance of each memory he had shared with his late wife. Samantha looked on, struck by the way Hunter took the time to quietly ask him questions and compliment the work he'd put into each page. It was a heartwarming exchange.

"She's good with him," Mallory whispered to Sam.

Brooklyn nodded. "Hunter's a softy. Most people miss that about her."

Samantha's heart clenched in her chest. The scrapbook was important to Mr. Earnhardt, and Hunter understood that. She cared. The class was over and she surely had other places to be, but it was clear she was in no rush to clear out. This man had her undivided attention.

"What you don't realize," Mr. Earnhardt imparted to Hunter, "is that life is not as long as you once thought it would be. Time flies by and you have to devote those minutes to the precious cargo in your life."

"The precious cargo," Hunter said. There was something about Mr. Earnhardt and his approach to things that resonated with her. He was kind, yes, but it was more than that. He just seemed to get things, at least in retrospect, and she could learn something from the stories of his life.

Wise and gentle: that was the best way to describe him, and Hunter took his words to heart. You know, when you thought about it, he was right. It seemed like just yesterday she was starting her freshman year at NYU, and here she was all these years later, closing in on thirty. Where had the time gone? Outside of her career, what did she really have to show for it? What roots had she put down?

"Do you have any regrets?" she asked him as he closed the scrapbook.

"Oh, quite a few," he said, without preamble. "But the biggest would be not marrying my Martha sooner. Then we would have had more time together."

Hunter nodded. "And why didn't you?"

"Oh, I was stubborn and young. Kind of a horse's ass when it came to serious matters of the heart. Martha was right there in front of me the whole time. Just took my sweet time noticing."

Hunter nodded. "Thank you for sharing your stories with me."

He smiled then, his eyes crinkling at the sides. "I probably bored your socks off."

"Well, I'm not wearing socks, so we're good there."

Mr. Earnhardt laughed. "You're a pretty girl. Do you have a fella you go around with?"

"I do not. No fellas for me."

He took a minute and then, "Oh. Like Samantha. She used to have a *girlfriend*."

She smiled. "Yes, like that."

Mr. Earnhardt raised his eyebrows and tossed a glance Sam's way. "Are you two…?"

"No, sir. We're just friends."

He nodded and stood, pushing slowly off the chair, which took quite some effort. Hunter followed him up and held firmly to his upper arm to assist his progress. Once he was upright, he turned to her. "You might think twice about that. There's no sweeter girl than her."

Hunter's eyes settled on Sam automatically. She was laughing at something Brooklyn had said, and her eyes shone brightly the way only Sam's could. "Yeah," she said absently. "There's no one like her."

Hunter, Samantha, and Mallory split a cab back to Soho after seeing Brooklyn to the train. Hunter hopped in first, followed by Samantha in the middle and Mallory after her on the outside. The ride was a quiet one, as the day had been long. They each seemed lost in thought, taking in the darkened city streets as they flew past.

The cab's backseat failed to provide much room, which meant Sam pressed against her side with each bump and curve in the road. It wasn't a horrible sentence. And there was Sam's hand, sitting unobtrusively on the seat between them. It was an instinct to cover it with hers and intertwine their fingers. At the contact, Samantha turned to her, a look of question on her face. But it was the way she squeezed Hunter's hand in reply that caused her heart to beat faster. And it was the smile on Sam's lips that made the butterflies in Hunter's stomach zip and take flight. As darkness cloaked the cab, Mallory wouldn't see the contact.

No. This was just for them.

Midweek hit, and with it came big happenings. Samantha read her morning email with a mixture of shocked celebration. New in her inbox was a company-wide email from Mallory instructing them to pick up work on—wait for it—the Foster Foods account, sans a few of the smaller projects. "For real?" she asked Mallory, peering around her monitor to see her friend better. "They're back?"

"They're back," Mallory said, smiling. "I don't know all the details, but I got a call from Royce at the close of business yesterday. They're not a hundred percent out of the woods, but apparently some sort of infusion of cash has revived the corporation. Or at least the biggest parts of it."

Her mind hurried to catch up. "So this means, the past due invoices?"

"You should have payment today."

Oh, sweet Anderson Cooper. This was a fantastic turn of events. This meant she didn't have to lie awake at night, finding corners to cut and ways to trim the fat off the already bare-bones budget. But there was one catch. "What about all of the business we've brought in since then? Can we handle the new influx of work in the midst of a monster account like Foster?"

Mallory came around her desk, coffee in hand. "Well, that's what I've spent my morning trying to figure out. I think we can, but we're going to need all hands on deck."

Samantha interlaced her fingers and flexed outward. "I'm ready, Coach."

Famous last words.

By the close of business, Samantha felt like she'd been hit by a truck. Hours of data entry, a tedious trip to the bank that'd taken way too long, a conference call with their benefits provider, the processing of payroll, and the generation of fifteen million invoices had left her body tight and her mind hazy.

In the midst of it all, she was aware of Brooklyn and Hunter working on storyboards across the room while Mallory made client call after client call. Yes sir, the day had been a perfect example of the kind of hard work that had slowly made them one of the *Who's Who* firms in the advertising world.

"Hey."

Samantha blinked at her screen, mildly aware that someone was speaking to her. "Hmm?" she said absently.

"I said, hey."

Hunter.

Samantha swiveled in her chair, and as her eyes settled on the woman before her, the world seemed to spark into color again. She blew out a breath and smiled. "Hi, you."

Hunter smiled back. "You haven't moved from this chair in I don't know how many hours."

She blinked and checked the clock, surprised by how late it already was. "There was a lot to knock out."

"And now it's knocked. So let's go." Hunter inclined her head in the direction of the door. Samantha looked around, noticing for the first time that it was just the two of them left in the office. "Yep. You've even outlasted Mallory, which is tough to do."

"You must have, too."

Hunter laughed. "I went home two hours ago. I'm back now for you." She was right. Samantha vaguely remembered Hunter calling good-bye to her. And now she wore workout clothes. Sleek, form-fitting workout clothes. Sam swallowed.

"Where is it you want us to go exactly?"

"Yoga. You need to relax. And yoga is great for that. I think you'll like it."

Yeah, about as much as she'd like a hole in the head. No way, no how. "Have you lost your mind? I'm allergic to anything athletic. You know this about me. If you even talk about physical exertion in my presence, I need a nap."

"Come on. Give it a shot. For me?" Hunter purposefully batted those big brown eyes, which was so not fair. "I watched *Lucy* for you."

This was true. She sank in her chair. "I'm going to suck at it."

"And I'm going to help you. It could be a really nice distraction from the wild and crazy numbers party you got going over here."

She was actually considering it. Why was she suddenly tempted to do something so outside of her comfort zone? Because that was what Hunter brought out in her, she reminded herself. Hunter made the frightening seem safe. "Fine. But there will be no mocking."

Hunter held her hands up in defense. "Of course not."

But from the grin on her face, Sam couldn't tell if she meant it or not. And really, that was part of the fun. She poked Hunter in the ribs as she passed. "Give me fifteen minutes to change."

❖

Samantha eyed the clock. They'd been at this yoga thing for roughly forty-five minutes now, and while she had to admit there was a peaceful component to it all, her body simply did not bend the way the rest of these people's did. She watched as the man down the row brought his toes to the back of his shoulders while balancing on his stomach. His *stomach*. She was not born a human pretzel, and as much as she wanted to show balance and finesse and the ability to contort her body in the way her instructor, Carlos, thought she should be capable of, it just wasn't gonna happen, people.

She attempted the foot-to-shoulder. It wasn't pretty, and she ended up on her side staring up at Hunter's perfect foot form. "You doing okay?" Hunter asked quietly, careful not to disrupt the serenity of the room.

She smiled up from her position of failure and whispered back, "Totally. Just thought I'd try it a different way."

"And what way is that?"

"It's of the 'lie on your side peacefully' variety."

Hunter winked at her and went back into the workout.

But there was a rather nice perk to this whole experience. Hunter occupied the mat next to hers, and though the intent had been to help Samantha, a beginner, gain a better understanding of form, it also meant that she had an up close and personal view of Hunter in spandex moving in a variety of unique positions.

With each minute that ticked by, Samantha became an increasingly bigger fan of yoga. Not only that, but her body was responding more and more to the tantalizing visual, and for once, Samantha didn't fight against it. She steered into the skid and allowed herself to enjoy the slow burn that was happening within her. Stealing multiple stares, she let her eyes travel the length of Hunter's physique, up her legs to her absolutely perfect ass, across her back to her trim shoulders. And when the class moved into Up Dog, Samantha looked to her right and stole a glimpse of Hunter's really awesome cleavage, which led her up Hunter's neck to her eyes that were staring right back at her. *Damn it all.* Caught!

Hunter raised an amused eyebrow. "Enjoying yourself?" she whispered.

Sam shrugged sheepishly back. "Best view I've had in a long time."

And there was an energy bouncing between them now. It was sexual, yes, but it was also playful and fun. They exchanged flirtatious glances throughout the remainder of class, made very quiet comments to each other, and generally just had a good time. When Carlos ended the session with "Namaste," Sam was glad she'd come.

As the rest of the class filed out, friends waiting on friends, Hunter turned to her. "So what did you think?"

"Well, I suck at yoga as predicted—big-time, in fact. But I had fun with you."

"We were not model students today," Hunter said, stepping into Sam's space.

Oh, hello there. She relished the intimacy of their new dynamic, where it felt okay to be open with the things she was feeling. With Hunter, there was no pressure to impress. She didn't have to try. She could just be herself. Her eyes swept the space, taking inventory of just how alone they actually were. Carlos moved about, probably putting the room back in order, but his attention was elsewhere. "No, you're right. *We* were not model students today, but you were. You can Tree Pose with the best of them." She placed a hand on Hunter's stomach and the warmth coming through the thin, stretchy fabric of her workout top was a little intoxicating.

"You can do it, too. Let me help?"

Sam laughed. "You're gonna help me Tree Pose? Is that what's happening?"

"I am." Hunter came around behind her. "I'll spot you, and by the end of this lesson, you'll be a world class Tree Poser. People will line up for demonstrations."

"I had no idea you were capable of working miracles. Where do I sign up?"

"Right here," Hunter said in her ear. Her breath tickled and sent a shiver through Sam's body.

"You have a student with a high potential for Tree Pose failure, you know this?"

"You won't fail," Hunter said. "I've got you." God, that was true in more ways than one. "It's actually a very basic pose and perfect for beginners."

Sam shot Hunter a look over her shoulder. "Not helping."

Hunter grinned. "Sorry."

"All right. Now what do I do first?"

"First thing I want you to do is shift your weight from your right foot to your left foot and back again a few times."

Sam did as she was asked, repeating the action several times slowly. "How's this?"

"It looks great from back here."

"Don't sexualize me while I'm Tree Posing."

"Tall order," Hunter said. "Get it? Tall like trees."

Samantha shook her head. "That is sadly not funny. You're bad at jokes. You should probably accept that. But on the flip side, you have many other admirable qualities."

"There are some things I do *very* well." At the allusion, a shock of something powerful shot through Sam, and she felt her face heat. "But I'll try to be professional," Hunter amended.

"Do," Samantha said. Carlos glanced in their direction and smiled before leaving the classroom. "I take my education very seriously." She heard Hunter chuckle behind her. She was close but, God, Samantha wanted her closer.

"Okay. Now I want you to find a spot on the wall that can serve as your focal point. Don't take your eyes off it. Got it?"

Samantha tilted her head. "They need to change their wall calendar. Still says June."

"Concentrate, Ennis."

"My bad. Concentrating."

"Do you have a focal point?"

"I'm going with the mislabeled month."

"Of course you are. Now shift your weight onto your right foot, and while keeping it strong, lift your left."

Samantha did so, but after balancing for a few moments on one foot, she teetered, just in time to be steadied by two hands from behind. With Hunter's hands on her waist supporting her, she tried again. Knowing this time she wouldn't fall.

"Good," Hunter said. "Now place the sole of your left foot up against your inner thigh."

"My inner thigh?" Samantha said. "Yoga is full of sex talk. Now I see why you come here."

"Stop laughing," Hunter said. "You have to concentrate."

But it was too late. Sometimes when Samantha got a case of the giggles, there was nothing she could do to hold them back. "I'm sorry, I just…" But they were upon her again and she couldn't quite get the words out. She could be twelve years old some days, and this was apparently one of those days. She took a few deep, cleansing breaths.

Hunter waited patiently. "Better?"

She blew out a slow breath. "Totally. Now where were we? Oh yeah. Inner thigh." She fought the smile and instead backtracked to the part where she placed her left foot against her right thigh and this time with Hunter's hands there to steady her, she was home free. *Just look at June. Just look at June.* Finally, she felt Hunter's hands fall away from her waist and she stared at that calendar with all her might. And what do ya know? She was doing it! She was Tree Posing, world! And not falling on her face like a glowless klutz!

Hunter's voice floated to her from behind. "That's awesome, Sam. Hold focus. Now with your left hand, draw your knee back to open up your hips." That did it; not only did she break out into a full-on laugh, but she lost her balance in the process. It took her several moments before she could form actual words, as that was what gigglefests did to her.

"Open up my *hips*? Really?" she managed to say, tears brimming in her eyes from the hysterics. "That language can't be serious." She could tell in the midst of her immature laughter that Hunter was doing her best to stay above the joke, but losing the battle as she was grinning from ear to ear. She grabbed Sam's hands and attempted to get her attention in the midst of her lost composure.

"You have to be mature about this."

"*You* have to be mature about this and not say things like that." Samantha pushed back against Hunter's hands, and they entered into a bit of a wrestling contest, which was so ridiculous, it only added to how funny Samantha found all of this. "How can anyone be mature when you're talking about hips and inner thighs? I think you did it on purpose."

"I did not," Hunter said, earning the physical upper hand. "I was actually about to tell you to draw in your pelvis."

"Oh dear God," Sam collapsed backward in laughter onto the floor, taking Hunter down with her. She wiped the tears from her face. "My hips and pelvis don't like to take orders."

"Don't forget your inner thigh," Hunter said between giggles, sending them into more laughter.

"Or the—"

"Sam?" It took her a minute to realize that someone other than Hunter had said her name, because the world was just feeling too damn funny. But as she turned her head to look, her smile dimmed a bit and the world came to a screeching halt.

"Libby. Hey." She sat up and brushed the hair from her face, her right hand still holding fast to Hunter's wrist. "We were just—" But how exactly did you explain a bout of playful public wrestling brought on by yoga hotness? *Push forward. Push forward.* "What are you doing here?"

Libby gestured to the yoga mat under her arm and Tanya by her side. Samantha had somehow missed Tanya on her first glance. Perhaps that had been her subconscious sparing her the gut-wrenching reminder of their couplehood. "Just here for the next class. Hi, Hunter."

"Libby," she heard Hunter say.

Could this be more awkward? She opened her mouth to speak, as it kind of seemed like it was her turn, but quite honestly she had no idea where to go. Her brain seemed to have downshifted at the sight of Libby. In fact, she was vibrating with nerves with no real concept of how to navigate this unexpected encounter. This was the first time she'd laid eyes on Libby since the breakup at the café. Her hair was in an athletic-looking ponytail, but she seemed to have more highlights now, or maybe her hair was just streaked from the sun. Either way, it was pretty. Samantha pushed up from the ground and forced herself into action. *No more staring at the ex-girlfriend who dumped you and now stands alongside your taller, blonder replacement.* "Oh, well, it's a great class. One of the better ones, right?" she said to Hunter, who seemed to be busy gathering their stuff.

"The best," she tossed back.

It bothered Hunter, the way Samantha had about-faced the second her eyes had landed on Libby. The fun had all but left her demeanor and had been replaced with what could best be described as anxious vulnerability. She hated that Libby was still able to affect Sam that way. And don't even get her started on Libby, the stupid princess of a person, incapable of realizing what an amazing catch she'd had in Samantha. And now here she was with the new trophy girlfriend, that mocking model from the Serenity ad layout. As she zipped her gym bag, she decided to take action.

"We haven't met yet," she said to Tanya. "Hunter."

Tanya held her gaze and then her hand for a beat longer than necessary. Libby looked on with—was that annoyance? It was. Excellent. "Tanya. You work at Savvy as well, right?"

"I do," Hunter said, pulling her hand back and slipping her arm around Samantha's waist casually, if not a little possessively. Sam shot her a questioning look. "With this one. We spend a lot of time together."

Libby's eyes flicked to the motion, and her gaze shifted to Samantha's face and back to Hunter's as if trying to work a difficult and unpleasant puzzle. "You two seemed to be having a good time when we walked in." Libby attempted a smile, but it was weak at best. Awesome.

Sam looked up at Hunter. "Oh, Hunter was just giving me some instruction."

"Private instruction," Hunter added.

"And we got off on a tangent. Sometimes I have trouble focusing." Samantha looked up at Hunter, gratitude now apparent. Yep, they were on the same page. Although she'd have thought the temperature in the room dropped several degrees, from Libby's adjusted demeanor. Her cool stare could have frozen the Sahara.

Tanya pointed at Sam and then Hunter. "Oh, so the two of you are—"

"In that fun stage where everything is exciting and new." Hunter dropped her voice to a whisper. "When you just can't keep your hands off each other."

"Wow. You two make a gorgeous couple," Tanya said, beaming.

Sam smiled. "Thanks, but we're really more—"

"Don't be modest," she said, kissing Sam's temple. She turned back to Tanya. "But Samantha's the beautiful one. I'm very lucky she's in my life."

Tanya grinned as if she'd just been named spa queen of the Western world. "That is so sweet. And I might be overstepping my bounds here, but maybe we can all get together sometime. Grab dinner out." Hunter could feel Samantha's entire body tense at the suggestion, so she took the reins, steering them clear of assured catastrophe. "We're just kind of doing our own thing right now. Taking our time. But maybe someday."

"Perfect," Libby said quietly, her eyes still fixed on Sam, who did a great job of looking casual and laid back when Hunter knew she was feeling anything but. As men and women filed in all around them for the next class, Hunter grabbed her bag and handed Samantha hers. Time to hit the road. "I guess we should let you guys get ready for class," Hunter told them. "Have a great night." As they passed, Libby placed a hand on Samantha's arm, stopping her progress.

"It was really nice seeing you, Sam."

"Yeah. You, too." Her eyes lingered on Libby, and Hunter felt her stomach tighten in reflex, because there was clearly a depth to the feelings Sam carried for Libby. Maybe Hunter had purposefully chosen to ignore that fact, but it was hard to deny when they were clearly on display for her now. She couldn't fault Samantha for that. She'd never been anything but straightforward about what was happening between her and Hunter. No-strings-attached was the name of their game. Only, Hunter felt the strings quite forcefully in this moment, and they were tugging aggressively at her heart.

She and Samantha didn't speak as they made their way out of the gym. Sam had a faraway look in her eyes, and Hunter felt a bit like she'd been punched in the stomach. It was unrealistic to think that Samantha could be over Libby. After all, Sam saw her as the perfect girl, the one that got away, and maybe she always would. But seeing it play out up close and personal, especially after she'd just had the best time with Sam, well, it was a little hard to take.

As they crossed the street to the subway station, Sam stopped in the middle of the sidewalk. Clearly, the encounter had taken a toll. Hunter looked back at her. "Hey. Are you okay?"

Samantha nodded, but she was clearly emotional. It took her a moment to speak. "I just need to say thank you. What you did was… well, thank you."

Hunter walked back to Sam and pulled her by her hand under the awning of a store closed down for the night. "You don't have to thank me. It was a rough situation. But, hey, you survived. You sure you're okay?"

"Yeah. It was a lot easier because of you. You were there for me. Again. You always seem to be there for me." Samantha shook her head slowly, and tears crept into her eyes.

"And that's not gonna change." She took Samantha's hand in hers. "Come on. Let's get out of here."

The train ride home, while short in theory, felt like one of the longer rides of Samantha's life. She played back the events of the evening beginning with the end of her workday through the conversation she'd just had with Hunter on the sidewalk.

She was a little rocked by the whole thing.

Seeing Libby again—standing there with Tanya, no less—had been a surprise, but what had blindsided Samantha more was the gesture from Hunter, the way she'd been there for her, no questions asked. It hadn't been the first time either. And while she should be sitting here, traumatized by a post-breakup Libby run-in, she wasn't. She was fixated on Hunter and how much they'd laughed together at yoga. And how she went out of her way to cheer Sam up when she was down, how she brought out so much in Sam that even she didn't know she was capable of. And then there was the way they fit together so perfectly in the bedroom, hot and tender at the same time. Suddenly, everything Hunter barraged her at once, and it was as if someone had turned on a light in a dark room.

Maybe it had been Hunter all along. She just hadn't been willing to see it.

As they walked the remaining blocks home, her thoughts took a darker turn, because this wasn't a good thing, these feelings that blindsided her. Here she was, yet again, falling for a woman who didn't love her back. What the hell was wrong with her? This was heartbreak by design.

Hunter was attracted to her, that part was clear. But she didn't do relationships. She'd said as much for as long as Samantha had known her. Hunter hated the very idea of coupling up, and even if she didn't, it wasn't like anything real could come of what they had going. They couldn't jeopardize Savvy with complicated emotions. Mallory's words from the coffee shop rang loud and clear in her head, and Mallory was someone she knew she should listen to, someone who saw things for what they were.

When they reached the loft, Sam walked straight to the fridge without preamble, took out the coffee ice cream, and went to work on it. Because everyone knew, when you were in a difficult spot, coffee ice cream soothed your soul.

Hunter and Elvis watched her curiously, almost as if they were a little unsure how to proceed as she set about her task of hardcore avoidance by way of creamy snack. And that made sense, because she wasn't sure of anything right now herself either. The world looked rather new and problematic, and she had to find a way to gain traction.

"You gonna share some of that?" Hunter asked, watching her from one of the bar stools across the island. She was doing the adorable puppy-dog eyes, which no living human could resist. Samantha passed Hunter a small spoonful of ice cream and watched as she slid it into her mouth. God, that was an awesome visual. Hunter ran a tongue across her bottom lip, capturing the residual ice cream, and then came around the island to Sam. "I had fun with you today."

Samantha flashed to their after-class session and had to smile. "It was definitely memorable."

When Hunter's hands came to her waist, she inhaled, savoring the touch. She stared into those big brown eyes and lost herself. And when Hunter's thumbs moved across Sam's stomach, a prickle of heat started in her center and moved outward. God, she wanted to be kissed. It wasn't smart, but that didn't stop her from craving that closeness with the woman she'd begun to see in a new light. *Kiss me already.*

"Remember when you told me not to get attached?" Hunter asked.

"I do."

Hunter leaned and kissed her softly then, and Samantha melted into it. "That this was just sex?" Another kiss. She could do just this— kiss Hunter all night and never get bored.

"Yeah. I remember. Our deal."

Hunter pulled back enough to meet Sam's eyes. "That still true?"

Sam blinked, understanding for the first time that maybe Hunter didn't want it to be. She knew her feelings for Hunter were real. New and terrifying, but real all the same. She also understood that an *admission* of those feelings was something else entirely. And she didn't know if she could go there with Hunter, not after the way things had turned out with Libby. No, she should enjoy what it was they had and not be greedy. Keep her world balanced and even, where she was most comfortable.

Samantha slid her hands up Hunter's forearms, needing to feel the warmth of her skin beneath her fingertips. "Don't worry. Nothing's changed." She slipped her arms around Hunter's neck and went up on her tiptoes, capturing Hunter's mouth in a hungry kiss. Hunter reciprocated but something felt off, like Hunter's heart wasn't really in it. It was only a moment before she pulled back and stepped out of Samantha's touch entirely. Her eyes searched the room, the walls, the couch, as if she didn't quite know what to say.

"I'm sorry…I just—" Hunter sighed. "I can't do this. I thought I could, but I was wrong." The look of hurt in her eyes was unmistakable as she walked into her room, closing the door behind her.

Sam stood there in her kitchen, grappling to understand. She stared after Hunter, at the door that was closed to her now, as a tidal wave of regret overcame her. Her heart lodged in her throat. Had she actually just let Hunter walk out of there thinking it was just sex between them? She didn't know how long she stood there doing her best to work it all out in her head. How was it possible that one person could evoke so many emotions in her? Excitement? Definitely. Hunter had her doing things she never would have done on her own. She made life interesting. Lust? Double check. The urge to shake her sometimes? Big-time. Hunter could infuriate her like no one else. Happiness? She closed her eyes, and the answer was there. Yes. She was really starting to think so. Hunter made her happy. But that didn't necessarily outweigh the risk. She covered her mouth with her hand and stared at the ceiling, willing some sort of divine knowledge to strike her, to set her on a course for what she should do.

But she knew.

Beneath it all—the fear, the worry about upsetting the balance—she knew where she wanted to be. She turned off the kitchen light, locked the loft door, and walked the short distance to Hunter's bedroom. She didn't knock. She slipped into the darkened room, illuminated by slashes of moonlight from the window on the far wall. The bed dipped when she sat on it, and Hunter turned over and stared up at her. She'd been crying, Sam realized, and the knowledge shook her. She wasn't sure she'd ever seen Hunter cry—in fact, she knew she hadn't. She had always seemed so unaffected, so tough. But that so wasn't the case.

Without a word, she slipped into bed, pulled Hunter against her, and just held on. And it felt like they were the only two people in the universe. She stroked her hair and felt the warmth from her body, comforted just by the sound of her breathing.

Hunter turned in her arms finally, her gaze questioning. With her thumbs, Samantha wiped the remnants of tears from Hunter's cheeks. "It's not just sex," she whispered finally. "It's so much more than that."

Hunter stared at her. "The truth?"

Samantha nodded. "I shouldn't have said what I did in the kitchen. I was scared. This is not something I'd planned on."

"Me neither," Hunter said quietly. "But it's hard to turn away from it."

Samantha wrapped her arms around Hunter's waist, easing a hand under her shirt, to the small of her back and the warm skin there. "I don't know what's happening between us, but let's just take our time to figure it out together, okay? Because what I'm feeling right now is new and scary, and I don't want to rush to any conclusions."

Hunter touched her cheek. "I just need to know that I'm not in this alone."

"You're not."

"Because this," Hunter said, placing Samantha's hand over her heart, "is you."

The sentiment was overpowering. Something shifted in Samantha's chest and she was kissing Hunter, unable to hold back any longer. They'd kissed before, many times in fact, but never like this. It was the kind of kiss that communicated so much, that carried the kind of depth that Samantha would never really forget.

They made love that night. For the first time.

Slowly, tentatively.

Each touch carried more weight than ever before, each caress much more tender. When Samantha reached the point of release, it was thoughts of Hunter she clung to. And when they lay tired and sated in one another's arms, Samantha didn't move to her own room this time. Instead, they fell asleep together, wrapped around each other in the pale, moonlit room on the eleventh floor. The world was still out there, waiting for them with all of its complications. But inside, tucked away, the night was theirs.

And it was perfect.

CHAPTER THIRTEEN

Hunter awoke to the sound of running water and took a moment to figure out why she felt so damn good. She glanced around her bedroom at the clothes that had been taken off her last night. Instead of lying on the floor where she remembered them landing, they were now folded into a nice, neat little stack on top of her dresser. She smiled at the gesture she knew Samantha couldn't help herself from making.

Order came first.

She stretched. Her body felt loose and relaxed and sore in the most wonderful way. She glanced at the clock, which read 7:14, and knew that she had a few minutes to play with before getting ready for work. And damn it, she wanted to play.

The bathroom door wasn't locked and there was music playing from the shower radio. She pulled the shower curtain open enough to slip in behind Samantha, who turned to her in surprise. "Whoa. *Whoa.* You're in the shower with me."

"Is that okay? I can leave."

Sam smiled and grabbed her arm. "Don't you dare."

"Bossy. But okay."

The water ran down Samantha's shoulders as she looked up at Hunter. "It's strange. I've thought about you in this shower. A lot." Her eyes moved across Hunter's body in appreciation and her hands followed eagerly, settling on her now-wet skin. Totally okay with Hunter. "And now here you are. With me. Good morning, by the way," she whispered and went up on her tiptoes for a steamy kiss.

"*Best* morning," Hunter murmured against her mouth, arousal hitting her fast and hard. She increased their connection until it was an intense tangle of tongues that only served to awaken more in Hunter. "Turn around."

Samantha traced the outline of her jaw. "I'm going to be late for work."

Hunter shook her head. "I don't know how you'll keep your job."

"In this moment, I'm not sure I care." Her breathing was already quick, her eyes heavy with heat.

"So what are you waiting for?"

Samantha eyed her, but did as she was told.

Pooling her hands with the wonderfully fruity shower gel, Hunter went about lathering Samantha's body, relishing the soapy, slickness of her skin coupled with the hot water. It wasn't long before the steam in the room came from more than just the faucet, however, as Hunter's touches turned more intimate and Sam's labored breathing indicated the hoped-for response.

"You're good at this," Sam murmured, closing her eyes as Hunter covered her breasts with soap, massaging and lathering generously, moving her thumbs around Sam's nipples and then across them.

She didn't linger, though; she kept her hands moving, active, never stopping in one place too long. As her hands dipped between Samantha's legs, Sam braced herself against Hunter's shoulders. But again she moved on. Teasing at its finest.

"Okay, you're also a little cruel," Sam breathed, but she was smiling in spite of her condition. "Hand me the soap."

Sam paid Hunter back and then some, moving her hands across every inch of Hunter's body, taking away just as quickly as she gave, until Hunter was in a rather desperate state, turned on and throbbing, and needing so much more.

Samantha traced the very subtle curve of Hunter's hip with one hand, the outside curve of her breast with the other. "God, I love your body."

"Yeah?" Not the most articulate response, but it was all Hunter could really manage. Her brain was otherwise engaged with the beautiful woman in front of her and the magic she worked with her hands.

The water was close to cold, prompting them to to dry off, each still very aware of the other. "We have time left," Hunter pointed out, walking backward toward her bedroom.

Samantha grabbed her watch next to the sink and looked at Hunter sorrowfully. "We really don't. It's twenty to eight."

"Plenty of time."

Samantha smiled and looked skyward, blowing out a breath in defeat. "It's not like I can say no to you after that." She inclined her head in the direction of the shower.

"We should do that every morning." Hunter punctuated the comment with a raised eyebrow, walking backward to Samantha's bedroom.

"In there this time?" Sam asked.

Hunter shrugged. "I like to keep you guessing."

Samantha loved that about Hunter. She did keep her guessing, and life when you were with her was anything but predictable. Two months ago, she never would have guessed she was capable of rolling with those punches. These days, she found it thrilling.

Five minutes later, with Hunter inside her, Sam found those soft brown eyes and held on as she coaxed and teased and drove her into blissful oblivion. She lay there rocked, having come harder than she could ever remember. Their time in the shower had her primed and ready, and the payoff had been exponential. Foreplay was so underrated.

"Maybe we could just stay here all day," Hunter whispered into her ear as she brought her back down again. Samantha moved on top of Hunter and pushed a strand of wet hair behind her ear.

"And I thought Brooklyn was the idea girl. God, you feel good underneath me," Sam whispered.

Hunter grinned. "Don't get too comfortable there."

Samantha laughed quietly. "Such a top, always so stubborn. You're gonna have to learn to relinquish a little of that control, you know?" She rocked her hips slowly against Hunter, whose eyes closed and lips parted in response. Hunter swore quietly. "What?" Sam whispered sweetly. "That's good?" Sam pressed deeper, grinding against Hunter more firmly, enjoying the ride. She groaned softly herself at the feel of Hunter against her, so ready.

Hunter grasped the headboard. "I take it back. You can do this any time you want."

"I thought you might say that."

It wouldn't take much. Samantha could already tell, and that made her heart beat faster in response. She eased Hunter's thighs apart for better access and moved steadily against her, over and over again. Watching Hunter try to control herself was a huge turn on in itself. Finally, she reached between them, and with her hand, pressed firmly on the spot that would finish what she'd started. With a quiet cry, the climax washed over Hunter in a gorgeous display. She shimmered, Sam realized, looking on. Hunter actually shimmered, and she felt her heart clench at the visual. She crawled into the space next to Hunter, amazed at what they'd turned an otherwise mundane morning into. Given, they'd be a few minutes late to work, but that was one of the perks of owning your own business, right? New life lesson: Morning sex trumped punctuality. She should write that down. Maybe a refrigerator magnet.

She stared at Hunter on the pillow next to her, feelings circulating that she still couldn't quite pin down. Hunter, who was so many things to her, wrapped in one. "You're kind of amazing, you know that?"

Hunter kissed her neck. "Amazing enough to skip work altogether? Because that's what I vote for."

"Tempting, hot stuff. But on the plus side, you come to work with me. So there's that."

Hunter smiled lazily and pushed herself up onto her elbow. "Did you just call me hot stuff?"

Samantha felt the blush hit her cheeks. It did sound ridiculous now that she played it back. "Pshhh. No. I would never have done that."

"You did, too. You called me hot stuff, and now it's my name forever."

"It is not."

"I think you mean 'it is not, hot stuff.' I feel very 1970s and I'm keeping it."

Samantha shook her head. "You're crazy."

Hunter laughed. "Maybe. But if this is crazy, I want to always be crazy."

Sam ran a finger across Hunter's collarbone as the butterflies in her stomach fluttered furiously. "I feel a little crazy, too, when I'm with you. I like it. It's kind of surreal. I'm at home with you, and comfortable, and constantly turned on, and laughing all the time. It's…a lot."

"Yeah?" Hunter asked, her eyes dancing. God, Sam loved it when those eyes danced. Little was more appealing.

"Yeah. And I have to tell you, it's the best feeling. Being with you like this."

Hunter good and kissed Sam one last time before walking confidently back to her room to prep for work. Sam lingered in bed a few moments longer, reveling in the eventful morning, because it was quite possibly the best one she'd ever had.

❖

"Hey, Sammie," Brooklyn said, perched on the corner of her desk. "Mal just texted that she's on her way back from a consultation and wants to have a meeting. Do you have time?"

Samantha glanced at the clock. "Uh, yeah. I have a ton of little loose ends in the air, but I could sacrifice a half hour. Speaking of time, did you turn in the hours you spent on the Dawson umbrella thing? I need to bill them this week."

"I did." She surveyed Sam's desk and located a sheet of paper in her stacking trays. "Right here. See? You look a little tired."

She grinned. *Uh-huh. That's right I do.* And then sobered for Brooklyn's sake. "Just not a lot of sleep last night. Tossing and turning. So much of that." Not a lie. There had been some tossing. And definitely some turning. Mmm-hmm, the turning had been world class, in fact.

"Maybe you should knock off early today. You've been staying late quite a bit."

Samantha blew out a breath. "I wish I could, Brooks. It's all the administrative stuff lately with the new accounts. It generally always falls to me, in addition to the books and the invoices and the benefits red tape. There's just been a lot to juggle."

"What can we do to help?" Hunter asked, sitting on the arm of that hard couch. Sam turned to Hunter. As her eyes settled, she felt a rush of happiness so swift that she took a minute to answer the question.

"Um...just back me up when I say I need it. And run Mallory interference when she starts asking for projections before I've even had a chance to get started on them. She's been extra eager lately. I think she's feeling the pressure, too. We now have too much business, which is good and bad."

Brooklyn turned to Hunter. "We need a plan. I'll stage some sort of screaming distraction and you tackle Mal from the side."

Hunter nodded. "Tackle Mallory. Got it."

Sam swiveled in her chair and held up one finger. "Tackling could make her mad."

"Mad Mallory is not my favorite Mallory," Brooklyn said.

"I agree," Hunter added. "She gets very quiet and freakishly smart when she's mad, and it scares me."

Brooklyn pointed at Hunter in mystification. "Whoa. She's funny today."

"She is," Sam agreed, catching Hunter's eye in a private exchange.

Brooklyn turned to Hunter. "Why are you funny? Did you have a good night last night? And the insinuation that you're picking up on is there on purpose, so don't sidestep it."

Hunter smiled shyly, and it was adorable. Hunter Blair was actually shy. "I did. I had an amazing night last night. Off the charts."

"Alert! Usually you just shrug and say it was cool. I'll need details."

Hunter's eyes brushed Sam's again and widened briefly. "I cannot supply them. I don't kiss and tell." With that, she took off into the kitchen.

"Since when?" Brooklyn said, following after her.

Hunter refilled her coffee cup. "Since I don't know. Maybe I'm super mature now and want to give my after-hours activities the respect they deserve."

The loft door slid open and Mallory appeared, attaché in hand. "What after-hours activities? What have I missed?"

Sam looked on, not knowing quite what to do here. While it was kind of fun sharing this secret with Hunter for a little while, it also felt wrong to blatantly withhold information from their two best friends, the people they simply didn't keep things from.

"Hunter's sexy-time activities," Brooklyn told Mallory. "She had some kind of torrid night last night and won't dish a single detail, which is breaking some sort of sexy-detail code. There should be at least one sexy detail. I might have to picket the office in detail strike."

Mallory's gaze swiveled to Samantha in alarmed assumption. And she was pretty sure her own deer-in-headlights facial expression answered Mallory's question in spades. *Damn it. For the love of Jean Chatzky!* Okay, there were too many dynamics to keep straight here, and Sam wanted to hide under her desk like a dog in a thunderstorm.

Mallory saved the day and turned to Brooklyn. "As much as I want to help you in your Hunter shakedown, because let's face it, those are fun, I was hoping for everyone's input on a couple of things."

Samantha didn't hesitate to run in this new direction. Diversion was her friend. She was clinging to it with all she had. "Happy day! Kitchen meeting? I love kitchen meetings. Let's do snacks. More truffles came in the mail."

"Kitchen snacks it is," Mal echoed.

Coffee was poured, laptops retrieved, and Samantha set out a tin of MollyDollys, her favorite truffles in the entire world. The Savvy girls assembled around the rectangular kitchen table. Samantha returned to her customary spot, as there was no need to draw any more attention, and waited patiently for what Mallory had to say.

"First of all, ever since the Foster projects have returned, we've had a lot on our plate. The new accounts that were meant to replace the business need just as much attention, small or not."

"Agreed," Brooklyn said.

"But the workload is a bit unrealistic and I think we could benefit from a little extra help."

Sam sighed. "I get where you're coming from, but the last time we brought in a temp, it was disastrous. He stared at Brooklyn's boobs all day, and I swear to you he systematically stuffed half of our office supplies down his pants by the end of the first week."

"Sticky Eddie. No one's objectified me that way since," Brooklyn said with false nostalgia.

Mallory raised a finger. "Agreed that Eddie was sent from Satan, but he did fill in a gap and gave Samantha a break on some of the administrative stuff, which let her devote her time to what she's really good at. Managing our money."

Hunter nodded and snagged a truffle. "So what are you proposing?"

"What if we took on an intern?" Mallory asked. "Some enterprising young person who's trustworthy, smart, and looking to gain some experience?"

Well, that was an idea. Samantha turned it over in her head. "I'd be all for it. It'd require a little training, but I like the idea of taking on someone who could not only help us, but would be excited to be here. I could check with the local high schools and colleges."

Brooklyn sat forward as an idea seemed to take root. It was what made her awesome. "Hear me out. What would you guys think about offering the position to Ashton?" Jessica and Brooklyn's next-door neighbor, Ashton, had been through a rough time recently when her mother was admitted to rehab. In fact, she'd moved in with Jessica until her mom was deemed fit. But through it all, she'd shown herself to be a remarkably great kid.

"Do you think she'd be into it?" Sam asked.

"She's looking for a part-time job now that she's sixteen. What's great about it is that she doesn't need the money. Her mom's loaded, and Ashton has a sizable allowance, but she wants to get out there and work, gain some experience in the world for her college applications. She's enrolled in the co-op program this next year at her high school, so she'd receive course credit for the hours she pulls. She just needs a place that will sponsor her study."

Mallory smiled. "Personally, I think that sounds like a really great fit. You've said she's smart, right?"

"An A student."

"All in favor?" Mallory asked. Four hands shot into the air. "Perfect." She turned to Brooklyn. "Have a talk with her and see if she's interested."

"Will do."

"Next up, I'd like to experiment with using a newswire to reach more of the specific trade publications for Serenity. I took a conference call with Emory Owen, who owns Global News Wire, and she's put together some agency prices for us." She passed the breakdown of the agreement to Samantha. "If you all are in agreement, I'd like to run a press release with them on a local circuit and see what kind of attention we get."

Sam studied the numbers. "This seems doable. It's the kind of account that could get picked up for some feature stories."

"Especially if we frame it like the ad," Brooklyn added. "A day-in-the-life kind of thing. The New York woman and trends associated with her is a popular angle. That shoot is Thursday, by the way. So I'll be on location all day."

Mallory scribbled the information into her day planner, totally old school. "Got it down. So, is the newswire a go?"

"I think it's a great strategy for them," Brooklyn said.

"And the budget can withstand it, so I say go for it. Hunter?" Sam turned to her, in all-business mode, forcing back down again the little surge of energy she got when she looked at Hunter.

"Yeah, it's a go for me." Her eyes trailed over Sam briefly before shifting focus to Mallory. "I'll shoot you a photo to go with it."

"Which was going to be my next question," Mallory said in amusement.

Hunter shrugged. "I'm simply too good at my job. Some might even say I'm hot stuff."

Samantha bit the inside of her cheek to hold back the laughter.

Mallory closed her notebook. "And on that very strange note, I think we're finished, unless anyone else has something to discuss."

Brooklyn's gaze landed on Hunter. "Maybe we could close the meeting with a sexy story from last night." And just like that, Samantha and Mallory hightailed it from the table like the thing had just caught fire.

"Lots to do," Sam called over her shoulder.

"Need coffee," Mallory tossed out. "I'm gonna head to Starbucks. They love me over there. They yell my name like Norm on *Cheers*. Can I get anyone anything?"

"A reprieve from Brooklyn?" Hunter asked, kissing Brooklyn's cheek as she rounded the table to her desk.

Mallory smiled sweetly. "Tall order, but I'll ask around."

Brooklyn sank her chin into her hand, alone at the table. "Defeat at the battle of Hunter's Love Life. One for the history books."

"You can't win 'em all," Mallory said as she slid the door to the loft closed on her way out.

The office fell into quiet as the three of them went back to work. Hunter checked her email and, after a few quick exchanges with their candy store client, glanced at her phone, disheartened that she still had no response to her texts to Kevin. She'd call her mom later in the afternoon and check up on things back home. Her recent visit had weighed on her mind a lot lately and had her heart heavy. She needed to make it a habit to get home more. Once a month.

Just then her phone tickled her hand in vibration as a message came in. Samantha.

Dinner tomorrow?

She grinned and typed back. *You asking me on a date?*

I am. Will you, Hunter Blair, go out on a date with me tomorrow night? An official one.

Hunter took her time answering. But when she did, it was *I'm thinking about it.*

Across the room, Samantha glanced at the readout on her phone and swiveled around, her mouth open in exaggerated outrage. Adorable.

"Yes," Hunter mouthed and nodded, which prompted the smallest of smiles onto Sam's face. Hunter turned back to her laptop in a state of happy anticipation. Yep, she was a goner.

❖

Samantha checked her reflection in the mirror, turning to the side to give herself one final pass. She'd selected a yellow sundress for their night out and chose to go with her hair down, leaving it wavy enough to carry some body. Not too fancy, but at the same time, cute enough. At least, she hoped so.

As she applied a touch of that shimmery lip gloss, her stomach fluttered. How was it that she was actually nervous right now? This was Hunter she was talking about, who she'd known for years and who lived just across the living room. But it was the good kind of nervous, the excited kind that stemmed from looking forward to something.

When she made her way into the living room, she took note of the soft jazz that played from the speaker in the corner. She found Hunter there with her back turned, staring out the window. The sky was already dark and the lights from the city twinkled back at them. It was a dreamy visual: Hunter standing there in front of the New York City skyline.

Because she couldn't resist, she came up behind Hunter, slipped her arms around her waist, and held on for a moment, enjoying the music and the scenery. Finally, she offered her a tiny squeeze. "Ready to go?"

Hunter turned, and presented her with a small wrapped box. "For you."

"You got me a first-date gift?"

"Open it."

And of course she did, only to find herself holding what appeared to be the box for a miniature jigsaw puzzle with a series of square roots on the cover.

Hunter leaned in and pointed at the box. "Apparently you match the numbers with their square roots."

Samantha stared at the puzzle, floored. "You bought me a math gift?"

"Yes."

"Most people would have gone with flowers." Samantha shook her head in wonder. It was the most thoughtful gesture, a puzzle tailored to her. The gift had her feeling special, like some sort of schoolgirl on prom night. It was silly, but at the same time, wildly okay with her.

"Would you have rather had the flowers?"

"I would have rather had this any day of the week to flowers. You gave me square roots."

"I did."

And that was when she noticed Hunter's look. As in, really noticed her. A sleeveless white shell accentuated with a long silver necklace that caught the light and slender black pants. Her hair was pulled up on the sides, but flowed down around her shoulders. She was soft and sleek all in one.

"You're beautiful," she said to Hunter. "And you're my date."

Hunter grinned. "And where are you taking me?"

"To dinner at STK. And then wherever you want."

Hunter looked skyward in a picturesque display. "Oh, the possibilities."

The restaurant was located in the Meatpacking District, and because of its trendy reputation, was already bustling when they arrived just in advance of their eight p.m. reservation. Once they were shown to their table, Samantha knew she had made the right choice in requesting rooftop seating. The view of the city from their table was breathtaking, as was the outdoor space decorated with strings of small light bulbs that glowed dimly around them.

"How's the book?" Sam asked as the two glasses of wine they'd ordered were delivered to their table.

"You're not going to believe this, but I'm actually into it. Who'd have thought?"

"It's a classic for a reason, you know."

"I should listen to you more often maybe," Hunter said.

Sam held up a hand, pretending to look for her phone. "Wait. Can you say that again? I should probably get an audio recording or something."

"It's a self-destructing sentence by design, so no go."

"You're full of all sorts of hidden talents."

Hunter sat back in her chair and took a sip from her wineglass. "You don't even know how many yet. But there's time for me to show you." The blush was upon Sam instantly and the heat that comment inspired was not far behind. "This is a really good dress, by the way," Hunter said. "Really good."

Samantha glanced down at the yellow sundress. "It is?"

Hunter shook her head ever so slightly. "You have no idea."

Dinner arrived, and it was quite possibly some of the best food in the solar system. Truffle mac and cheese, garlic chicken kebabs, and the most refreshing pear salad. When they'd finished their meal, they walked the perimeter of the rooftop, enjoying the perfect evening temperature and the slight breeze that tickled their shoulders and lifted their hair. And that was kind of how Samantha felt in that moment: lifted up. The moon shone brightly in its near fullness, casting a pale glow over the city beneath them. Sam basked in how romantic it all felt, as though the night had been designed especially for them.

"We need a photo," she suggested.

Without missing a beat, Hunter produced her phone and framed them expertly with the lights of the restaurant accenting them beautifully. At the last second, Hunter kissed Sam's cheek, and the resulting image was quite frankly, stunning. Staring down at it, Sam felt a chill move through her at just how perfect they looked together, how right it all felt.

"So where to now?" she asked, Hunter's hand in hers. Samantha was all for letting Hunter choose, but she didn't want the night to end.

Hunter turned her head and regarded Sam out of the corner of her eye. "Wanna walk?"

"I would love to walk with you." It was Friday night, so each bar, restaurant, or club they passed was overflowing with patrons and music. It was a lively night on the streets of the Meatpacking District, and Hunter held firmly to Samantha's hand as they walked. The solidity of it was nice.

They paused in front of a club with a crazy techno beat blaring from inside. "You could dance on top of a bar," Hunter offered over the music. "That could be fun. You'd make a ton."

Sam glanced up at her. "Later."

They walked a bit more and paused in front of a bluesy-looking cocktail spot.

"Oh, a little dive bar. I love little dive bars. Wanna?" Hunter asked. The place looked like a mixture of a lot of things, which carried appeal.

"Sounds like something I can get behind." Samantha studied the sign. "And hey, it's open mic tonight. You know what that means?"

"Semi-depressing people are going to line up to feel like rock stars as we watch?"

Samantha swatted her arm. "Or we get to see the next Lady Gaga before she's Gaga. This is New York, Ms. Blair."

"You're adorable when you call me that. Kiss me." Hunter said, a smile taking over her whole face as she leaned in.

It was the easiest request in the world and Sam met her in the middle and fixed her mouth to Hunter's in a sizzling exchange that left her warm all over. "Shall we?"

They slipped into a small table set back from the stage and listened as a singer-songwriter emoted about his castrating ex-girlfriend and her cat, clearly a cathartic experience for the guy, if unfortunate for the audience. The next girl was actually really good, very new age but with a Joplin edge mixed in.

Feeling uncharacteristically bold, Samantha snuck a hand onto Hunter's leg under the table. "So are you going to serenade me next?" Sam said in her ear.

Hunter stared at her, eyes wide. "You realize my biggest fear in life is being onstage in any capacity, and that if I were to do that, I would probably combust on the spot."

"So a no on the serenade? My little heart is breaking."

"Don't say that. I don't want to hear you say that."

Sam shrugged. "Can't help it."

"Are you serious right now? Because you know I have a weak spot when it comes to you."

"So serious. Look." She wasn't at all, but pointed to her face anyway in the spirit of the fun little exchange they were having. But the fact that Hunter stood from the table and approached the gentleman just to the side of the stage had her floored. Whoa. Because wait a sec—there was no way Hunter would actually go through with this, and Sam had only been joking when she'd suggested it.

But a few moments later, when Hunter took the stage with a borrowed guitar, Sam found her heart in her throat with guilt, and terror on Hunter's behalf.

"I've never done this in public before," Hunter said into a microphone. "So I'm hoping you'll indulge me." The crowd at the bar offered an encouraging round of applause before Hunter continued. "There's a girl out there tonight who once told me she thought she'd been born into the wrong era. So for her, I'm going to sing a little Frank Sinatra."

Hunter turned to her guitar and played the first recognizable notes from "The Way You Look Tonight," and Sam felt her insides melt. Her rendition of one of the most romantic songs in history was simplistically beautiful. Hunter had slowed it down a tad and given the song unique touches here and there, but it was breathtaking. She spent most of it with her eyes on the guitar, but the few times she did glance up, she held Samantha's eyes as she sang. God, she was like the craziest summer storm. All wild and unpredictable, but also soothing and calm and tender. Samantha didn't think she'd ever get used to all the facets. When Hunter came to the last line of the song, the place erupted into applause and whistles and shouts. She was a hit.

"I can't believe you did that," Sam said, standing and holding her arms open for Hunter, who came easily into them at their table.

"I'm the one who can't believe I did that. I'm still shaking."

Samantha took Hunter's hands in hers and kissed them, holding them against her chest. "That was easily the coolest thing that anyone has ever done for me, and you were so good, Hunter. It was beautiful."

Hunter had never experienced this kind of nerve-induced euphoria. But for the first time ever, she'd felt enough courage to push herself up on that stage and knew exactly who that motivation had come from... and she was wearing the most picturesque yellow sundress.

A couple of patrons on the way out of the bar stopped to pat Hunter on the back and to tell her they'd enjoyed the song.

Seriously?

Was this happening?

She was still reeling from the experience when they spilled out onto the sidewalk. She felt like running, or dancing, or better yet…She turned to Sam. "We need ice cream."

"Ice cream is the perfect celebration of the magic that just happened back there! And I'm buying. It's the least I can do for my song. What made you think of that one?"

"You did. You make me think of a lot of things. Inspire them, actually," Hunter leaned in and stole a kiss.

Samantha shook her head, sobering a little. "Wow. You have a way of saying the most important things sometimes."

"It's all true."

Sam entwined her fingers with Hunter's in front of her. "No matter what happens to us over the next seventy years, I will always have tonight to think back on. Because it feels kind of perfect, standing under this lamppost with you." And then she smiled that most beautiful Samantha smile, the one that always caused Hunter's chest to tighten. "Tonight will always be ours."

Hunter glanced up at the lamppost, then back at the girl in the killer dress. "This is an important lamppost."

Samantha laughed. "The *most* important."

"I've never had a favorite lamppost before. I feel so grown up."

"You are." Samantha tugged Hunter's arm. "C'mon. Places to walk. Things to eat."

After obtaining their ice cream—toffee nut for Hunter and chocolate and peanut butter for Sam—they took the long way home, snagging an extra block here or there as they talked about anything and everything, not ready for it to be over just yet.

"So you actually hated high school," Hunter stated, struggling to understand. "You seem like the type who would have relished every moment of it. You're so spirited. Football games seem destined to be right up your alley."

"They would have been, but I was so removed from the social scene. So in a sense, I get why maybe your brother is going through some stuff. High school is a difficult time. It's hard to find your place."

Hunter nodded. "I sent him a couple of texts when I got home from Ohio. He only answered one of them and used as few letters as possible."

"Well, that's something. And don't stop. Keep reaching out to him even if he doesn't reach back."

It made sense, and she would take Sam's advice. "Can I tell you something?"

"Of course."

"There's a part of me that was, I don't know, happy that my dad showed interest in my life. And I'm so pissed off at myself for feeling that way. Because how weak is that?"

Samantha studied her as they walked. "It's not weak at all. He's your dad. No matter what's passed between the two of you, you'll always be family."

"I just wish he didn't have the power to get to me."

"I know, but you're a human being, Hunter, and you have feelings. What would be weak is if you didn't." It was an interesting take on the situation, and it came from an angle Hunter had never really examined. She wasn't quite sure what to do with that information, so she tucked it away for later. "Do you know what else is weak?" Sam asked.

"What is that?"

"When there's ice cream on your face."

Hunter balked. "There is not ice cream on my face."

"Um, there is, too." Sam laughed. "But because I'm benevolent and always looking to further the greater good, I'll take care of it for you." And with that, she went up onto her tiptoes and gently kissed the small amount of ice cream from the corner of Hunter's mouth, using her tongue ever so lightly to aid in her endeavor. Hunter took in the sweet scent of Sam's shampoo, the softness of her lips. Lust curled slowly in her abdomen, gaining power with each tenth of a second. It was time for talking to be over. "What's that look?" Sam asked her.

"I think it's time we go home. Now."

Something came into Samantha's eyes that told her she knew exactly where Hunter's mind had gone and that she was right there with her. The temperature on that street corner seemed to heat up then and there.

"Lead the way."

❖

That following Monday, Ashton arrived on the scene for her hour-long orientation at the Savvy office and brought with her the energy of a hundred eager squirrels. With her strawberry-blond hair woven into a complicated braid and about a million bracelets decorating her teenage arm, she carried a fresh-faced, youthful vibe. She'd been beyond excited for the opportunity to work at Savvy when Brooklyn had presented it, and since arriving in the office, had thanked each of them at least a half a dozen times. Her enthusiasm was palpable, and that was a good thing.

"And this is generally where Hunter works," Sam said to Ashton as they approached her desk. Hunter was sketching this morning, which was part of her brainstorming process when starting a new project. "But she sometimes prefers countertops and the arms of furniture, so just ignore her and let her do her Hunter thing. Like Brooklyn, she often stares into space. It just means she's creating."

"Cool," Ashton said, and accepted a high five from Hunter. "So you know Photoshop pretty well?"

"It's my life's work."

Ashton beamed like Hunter invented the sun. "Maybe you can show me a trick or two someday?"

"I mean, if you bring me coffee."

"I will totally do that," the kid said, smiling.

"She's kidding," Sam whispered, shooting Hunter a chastising look. "You don't have to bring us gifts. Cash is cool, though."

Hunter shook her head in amusement and turned back to her sketchpad as Sam continued the tour of the office. She was just about finished with the secondary shading when her phone buzzed from its spot on her desk. Aha, an incoming text from Mallory, who was offsite at a meeting with Serenity.

Lunch today?

Hunter smiled. It was a thing they did on occasion to check in with each other. While she valued the individual bond she had with each of her friends, the friendship she had with Mallory was exceptional for its sheer unlikelihood. The two of them couldn't be more different. Mallory, of the ultra-uptight, and Hunter, of the go-with-the-flow, balanced each other out surprisingly well. And their one-on-one time was never short of valuable. A good centering activity, which maybe she needed.

She ruminated on the events of her life. Things between her and Sam had picked up steam this past week and that had her feeling unsteady, almost as if she were standing atop a very tall pillar, perched to fall at any moment. And you know, maybe she could use a little Mallory balance in her life about now. She fired off a reply.

You're on. Mooncake's at noon.

❖

That afternoon, Samantha flipped her sunglasses onto her face from where they perched on her head. It was hot out. July had arrived and was making sure everyone knew it. She and Brooklyn sat at a table at Soho Square Park not far from the office. Hunter and Mallory were doing one of their monthly lunches, and that was good. It gave her and Brooklyn a chance to hang out. They picked up their favorite, cheeseburgers and fries, and watched as the world passed by them in the small park.

Samantha gestured with her chin to a guy whizzing past on Rollerblades. "You think he woke up and thought, 'totally wearing pink biker shorts today.'"

Brooklyn popped a fry and nodded. "Yep. And was thrilled with his declaration."

"He high-fived his mirror."

"And moonwalked away from it."

Sam shrugged. "Well, it's what you do in the morning."

"Objectively. I did it twice."

"How's your life, Brooklyn Campbell?" Samantha sat back and awaited her best friend's response. She'd had a lot of life changes lately: a fairly new relationship with Jessica, the move, and then there had been reconnecting with her birth family not quite a year ago. It'd be enough to rattle anyone.

"A little overwhelming, if I'm being honest."

"And I want you to be. Lying takes too much time." To better see Brooklyn's face, Sam took off the sunglasses she'd put on just moments ago, because this conversation was important. Brooklyn was important.

"But overwhelming in a good way," Brooklyn said. "I talk to Cynthia—sorry. I talk to *my mom* probably once a week. Still getting used to calling her that. It's nice, though. My sister is going to come to the city for the weekend at the end of the month. That should be fun. I need a list of things to do with teenagers."

"Pshhh. Just ask Ashton."

Brooklyn lit up. "Good point."

"And Jessica? How is she?"

The lazy smile that took over Brooklyn's face spoke volumes. "She's working way less. We're cooking together, sitting on the balcony over the Hudson when it gets dark and discussing our days. It's like we just fit. I can't explain it."

But Samantha could. "You're home now."

Brooklyn glanced down at the table. The emotion of that statement seemed to really resonate with her and she took a moment before answering. She'd spent most of her life without any sort of anchor or consistency. Because she'd been bounced around in the foster care system, she'd never really had a family. Her eyes glistened when she raised her gaze to Samantha. "I think that's it. I'm finally home."

Samantha nodded as a lump formed in her throat. She was happy for Brooklyn, who deserved someone every bit as special as Jessica had turned out to be. In the midst of it, she thought of her own set of circumstances. The heartbreak she'd experienced over Libby, and now these new feelings for Hunter—strong, but still very new and unclassified.

"What about you?"

Sam lifted a shoulder. "What about me?"

"I know the breakup was hard on you. In fact, I've never seen you more defeated. But you seem"—Brooklyn shook her head—"I don't know. Happy again. More than that. Am I wrong?"

A smile touched Sam's lips as she reflected on the reason. "You're not." She didn't have all the answers, but a part of her needed to share everything that had happened to her lately with Brooklyn, who was maybe the closest confidante she had. She wasn't the best at keeping secrets, but just who exactly were they keeping things from at this point? Hunter knew. Mallory knew, albeit on the down low. It was wrong to keep Brooklyn out of the loop, and not only that, but she also *wanted* to share this new part of her life with her best friend.

Done.

Decision made.

She opened her mouth to dive in.

"Have you seen her?" Brooklyn asked, cutting off Sam's progress.

It took Samantha a moment to follow the curve in the conversation. "Seen who?"

"Libby. Since the breakup."

The name still packed a punch, dimming her spirits a tad. Interesting how that worked, how Libby still affected her. "Actually, yeah. At yoga last week. She showed up with Tanya, out of nowhere. It was awkward, to say the least, but that's to be expected, I guess." She blew the hair off her face. "I survived, thanks to Hunter." A perfect segue.

Brooklyn tilted her head in confusion. "Back that train up. Stop one. You went to yoga? You hate athletics and anything masquerading as such."

"True fact. But my new roommate is extra persuasive."

And then a light bulb seemed to go off over Brooklyn's head and she smiled. "Gotcha. Stop two. Did you happen to encounter an instructor by the name of April?"

"Are we going to continue this train motif for the whole conversation?"

"I haven't decided. I like it. Answer the question."

"Um…no. I don't believe so. Who's April?"

"She's this girl Hunter's got it bad for. A yoga instructor. I probably shouldn't spread that around, but I don't think she'd mind me telling you or Mallory."

Interesting tidbit that had a few preliminary alarm bells going off in Samantha's head. Not a big deal, she cautioned herself. She played absently with her straw. "What do you mean she has it *bad* for her?"

Brooklyn sat up a little straighter in excitement. "I mean she's gone on the girl. We ran into her in the park, April. She seems awesome, and as you can expect from a girl Hunter's into, she's way hot. Then a couple of weeks later, the night we were at Showplace, she told me she's kinda sorta falling for her. In Hunter language, that's code for so much more. It's cute, watching her try to figure it out."

Samantha took a minute with this because that was just a couple of weeks back. Hunter didn't just fall for people. Or maybe she did. "Are you sure you understood all of that correctly?"

"Positive. She was all worked up about it, which is how I know this girl is something major to her."

"And her name was April?"

"April of yoga studio fame. Yeah."

The branches above them rustled and the tiny breeze felt good. It was something Sam noticed distantly, however, because she was still trying to make sense of what Brooklyn had just shared. Maybe Brooklyn had just misunderstood.

As they walked the few blocks back to the office, Samantha couldn't shake the conversation. Because what if she was the one who had gotten it wrong, not Brooklyn? Hunter was a self-admitted serial dater. She enjoyed the company of a variety of women. That was how she worked. Hell, maybe she told them all what she'd told Samantha. This week, Sam had her attention. A few weeks ago, April. Where would next week take her? God, the thought made her stomach turn with how dumb she'd potentially been. She couldn't go through this again. Uh-uh. She couldn't. She didn't want to fall in love with someone who didn't love her back. And she was falling.

She studied the nameless faces of the people they passed on the sidewalk, halves of couples, some married for years and years. Several passersby held hands, probably enjoying New York on holiday. Last Friday, she'd felt like one of them. Like she was worthy. Like she belonged. But, not so fast…

Always on the outside looking in, she reminded herself.

That's you.

She paused outside the elevator. Numb. Confused. Maybe even a little dizzy, hard to tell.

"Sammie? You okay?" Brooklyn asked. Concern crisscrossed her face.

But she wasn't. She wasn't okay at all, and maybe she just needed space. From the world. From life. From everything. "I'm not feeling so good all of a sudden. If it's okay with you, I think I'm going to head home for a bit. Lie down."

"Do you want me to come with you?"

She forced a reassuring smile, which wasn't easy. "No. I think I just need some time. Tell the others? Maybe put out a do not disturb call to give me time to bounce back."

Brooklyn nodded. "Of course." And then, "Sammie?"

"I'll be *fine*."

After all, lying was easier.

CHAPTER FOURTEEN

Hunter was preoccupied that afternoon at the office.

Sam hadn't answered her phone calls. Or her text messages. Hunter wanted to send another, or better yet, run upstairs and check on her personally. But she'd apparently sent implicit instructions for some alone time, which was a little unlike Sam.

She checked the clock: It was nearing five, which would be a totally rational time for her to arrive home from work. It was her apartment, after all. If she was just home a little earlier than usual, she could still honor the request without looking like she was overbearing. Which was what you should do with someone you were involved with, right? Give them space when they asked for it. She was so new at this but wanted to do it right.

She needed to proceed cautiously with Samantha. If anything, that was what she'd taken away from her lunch with Mallory. They'd met at Mooncake's and snagged the small yellow table by the window. The place was small but popular, and the counter guy waved at them upon entry. It was a neighborhood place, and one they frequented. Lunch had started off standard enough with Mallory ordering the garlic chicken breast and Hunter opting for the seared tuna salad, but midway through it took a turn.

"So this thing with your father, is it possible he's just having some regrets about the way he's behaved all these years?"

Hunter mixed around the contents of her salad as she ruminated on the question. "Maybe that's part of it. I can't say the reason really matters to me. It was just weird though, you know? Like I'd entered into the Twilight Zone. He was asking questions about my life, Mal. About Savvy." She shook her head. "It's whatever."

"Don't overthink it," Mallory said carefully. "I think a wait-and-see attitude might be called for here. It's a sensitive issue for you."

"Yeah, there seems to be a lot of that lately." She said it more to herself than to Mallory.

"Because you're still sleeping with Sam?" Mallory took a casual sip of her Diet Coke.

Hunter had seen surprised people choke on food in movies, but she didn't know it was anything more than a cliché until that moment. She'd reached instinctively for her water glass so she could clear her airway and, you know, continue to live on Earth.

"Better now?" Mallory asked, waiting patiently for her to compose herself.

"I don't know. Did I just save myself from choking only to have you kill me?"

Mallory sighed. "I'm not going to kill you, Hunter, but I do need to ask what you're doing. Because, seriously, *what are you doing right now?*"

"It's more complicated than just that."

"Complicated is exactly what it's going to be if you two destroy everything we've built because you can't keep your hands off each other. This thing could explode in your faces and I don't want to be in the middle, picking up the pieces of your friendship and our business."

"And you won't be." Hunter sat back in her chair with resignation. "So I'm going to suppose Sam told you?"

Mallory nodded. "That Friday night at Showplace. I think she was freaking out about it."

She laughed. "She wasn't the only one. Trust me."

Mallory stared at her. "She's vulnerable right now, Hunter. She's had a rough summer."

"And you think I'm taking advantage?"

Mallory's voice was quiet. "Are you?"

The question hurt. "God, Mal. I wouldn't do that. I care about her."

"And what happens when the thrill wears off and you wind up hating each other? Or someone's feelings suddenly kick in, and it's not so much fun anymore? You can sleep with any girl you want, Hunter, just don't pick them up at the office."

"Wow. That's classy, Mal, really."

"I'm just trying to be realistic."

"And it's not realistic to think that this could maybe turn into something real?"

Mallory shook her head. "See, that's where I'm coming up short. Can you honestly say that you could be happy tied down in a relationship? Locked into one girl? I've known you a long time, Hunter, and you've never once shown any interest in settling down. In fact, you've avoided it like the plague your entire life."

"People change. Listen, I don't entirely understand it either. I thought we'd eventually burn out, too, but it's the opposite. If anything, we burn brighter with every moment we spend together."

Mallory passed her a dubious look. "You know this is a horrible idea, Hunter. I know you do."

But she didn't know that. Not anymore, at least. She never in a million years thought she'd be the girl who'd want to couple up and play house like the rest of the world, but Samantha had taken everything she thought she knew and tossed it right up in the air. And now she found herself longing for much more than she'd ever planned on. Because she *wanted* to work puzzles with Samantha and slow dance with her at Showplace and take her to bed, where'd they'd make love and talk until the early hours of the morning. She wanted to always be the one to rescue her from mice and watch her dance each morning in the kitchen and curl up with her on the couch when she delved into another of her romance novels.

"I'm not willing to walk away from this, Mallory."

"Why? Manhattan is full of people. You can have your pick of women, Hunter. This doesn't make good sense."

She opened her mouth, praying that something brilliant would come out. Instead, she went with the truth. "Because I think I'm in love with her."

Well. That got her attention. Mallory sat back in her chair, absorbing the brunt of those words. "Please tell me you didn't just say that."

"Look, I get it's not the best scenario for Savvy. But that's only if something were to go wrong. But, Mallory, what if it were to go right?" Her hopes soared at the concept. "What if this turned out to be the best thing that's ever happened to us? How can that not be a good thing?"

Mallory covered her eyes. "I don't know what to say here." But then she shifted gears and straightened and pointed at Hunter. "Yes, I do. If you hurt her, I'm coming for you. You know that, right?"

"I do."

"And it doesn't mean I'm happy about any of this, but I'm trying, because I adore you."

"I get that."

Mallory shook her head and sighed. "Brooklyn falls for our biggest competitor and you fall for one of the three off-limits people on the planet."

Hunter raised a shoulder. "At least it's never boring around here."

Mallory laughed wryly. "What I wouldn't give for a little boring."

They paid the check and made their way onto the sidewalk. And that was when Mallory asked the million-dollar question. "Does she love you back?"

Hunter stared at her, ruminating on the series of events that had led them to this point. The laughter, the arguments, the sexual tension, Libby, all of it. "I don't know."

❖

Samantha checked the clock on the microwave. Close to five. She'd missed the whole rest of the workday holed up in the apartment. She flipped the page of the newest issue of *Money Market* that she'd found in the freezer along with the rest of yesterday's mail. Hunter was getting more creative. She'd smile if she weren't in the throes of a highly indulgent emotional meltdown.

Reading had a way of distracting her and was what she'd been doing on one of the bar stools at the island since she'd retreated home. She'd initially picked up with where she'd left off in *Bridget Jones,* but as she was now more pathetic than her protagonist, she'd had to push it aside. Numbers were a better fit. You could depend on them and they didn't change the game on you midway through, just as you started to understand it. Elvis changed positions at her feet from his stomach to his side.

"You have it made," she told him from atop her stool. "Hang out here and let people dote on you as they pass through. No need to feel ridiculous things, only to have your heart stepped on again and again." She turned the page aggressively. "No being jerked around for you.

Nope. I need your life." Another aggressive thwack of a page. "Oh, hey, you want to work a puzzle and then have the best sex of your life?" Turn and thwack. "Or better yet, let me mesmerize you with a song on my guitar. How about that?" Thwack. "No one says those things to you?" she asked Elvis, who had cocked his head at her in confusion. Thwack, thwack, thwack. "It's for the best. Trust me."

There was a soft knock at the door. Maybe Brooklyn or Mallory, who would have just let themselves in if she hadn't locked the door behind her. Or maybe Hunter was home early and trying to be sensitive to her request for privacy. They should probably have a conversation about what Brooklyn had shared that afternoon. She'd feel ridiculous asking about some other girl, but it was better to find out now, right? She didn't want to lie to herself about what was happening between them.

She slid open the loft door and blinked curiously at Libby, who smiled tentatively at her. *Really, universe? Really?*

"Hi, Samantha."

"Libby." She glanced down the hallway, attempting nonsensically to gain a clue as to why Libby was standing at her door. "This is a little unexpected."

"I should have called. Texted or something," she said absently. "I'm sorry for just showing up." She was nervous. Sam could tell because she had a habit of brushing the hair from her forehead, whether it was there or not. It was her giveaway, and Sam used to find it endearing. It still kind of was, she thought faintly.

"It's okay. What's up?"

Libby shifted her weight from one foot to the other. "Right. I'm sure you're wondering why I'm here. Do you mind if I come in?"

Samantha glanced behind her and hesitated. "Listen, Libby, it's kind of been a day for me."

"Then I'll say what I came to say and get out of your way. Two minutes?" Those big blue eyes held such hope. She couldn't say no.

"Of course."

Libby took a fortifying breath and her eyes settled on Sam's. Somehow when that happened, a calm seemed to come over her and she gathered confidence. "I guess I'm here because I miss you, Sam. A lot, actually. I think back on myself, to where my head was a few months ago when I called that stupid radio station, and I don't even recognize that person. I was confused and misguided. And I know now that my priorities were out of whack."

Samantha shook her head. "What does that mean?"

Libby stepped toward her, a quiet intensity now present in the way she spoke. "It means I made a mistake. A big one. And I'm here to fix it." Libby shook her head in appreciation. "God, just look at you. You're beautiful, Sam."

Samantha couldn't believe what she was hearing. When you were unceremoniously cast aside the way she had been, you fantasized about a moment like this. But it never materialized. Yet here it was. The girl she'd elevated above all other girls was admitting she'd been a fool to let Samantha go. It was hard to wrap her mind around.

"What about Tanya?"

"Tanya's great but she's not what I need. It's not the same with her."

Sam lifted a shoulder. "She's not as comfortable as those old shoes, huh?"

Libby winced at the reference. "You know that's not how I meant it."

"It's okay, Libby. Really."

"I know you have something going on with Hunter and I respect that, but this is us we're talking about. You and me. We're supposed to be together, Sam."

Just like that, Libby was kissing her.

And for whatever reason, Sam let her. She could have put a hand between them, put a stop to it. But she didn't. Maybe she was caught off guard, or maybe part of her wondered about Libby, if the feelings she'd experienced had been real and if they were still viable. Regardless of the reason, one thing was crystal clear: She took no enjoyment in the kiss. In fact, with Libby's lips pressed to hers, she felt nothing. She pulled away, prepared to explain to Libby how different things were for her now just in time to see Hunter watching them from the hallway, her face carefully blank as she took in the scene. And though Sam had felt nothing moments before, she was certainly feeling a lot of things now as she stared at Hunter. *No, no, no. This is bad.* Her breath caught because damn it, this was a train she didn't know how to unwreck.

"Hunter," Libby said, smoothing her lip gloss. "I'm sorry you had to see that."

Hunter shook her head once. "No, it was probably good that I did."

"There's an explanation for this," Samantha said. The words sounded so stupid coming out of her mouth, so mundane.

"Don't even worry about it," Hunter said. "I understand and I'll leave you to it." She smiled then, that whatever-goes Hunter smile, but it didn't reach her eyes. No, the eyes that once danced were closed off to her now, and the sting was palpable. Hunter headed off calmly down the hallway.

"Hunter, will you wait?" Samantha called after her. "Stay here and talk to me for a minute, please."

"We can talk later. You're busy. Clearly." But she didn't so much as look back when she said it.

It was a helpless feeling. She wanted to explain, but in the end, what would she really say? And would it matter? Well, that was stupid, because it did. No matter what ups and downs they'd gone through in the past couple of months, this was still Hunter, who she'd never want to hurt.

"Honey bear, she'll get over it," Libby said, stroking her arm. "Give her time."

Oh. Right. Libby was still here. "You should go," she said turning to her matter-of-factly.

"Yes, of course. I'll give you time to explain things to Hunter. So are we okay? How about dinner tomorrow? We can talk more about us, about getting back on track."

"There isn't an us, Libby," she said. God, it was so easy now. She had no interest in going back to Libby or to the kind of relationship that took so much out of her. Where she had to work to seem funny, or cute, or desirable. Her life with Libby had been exhausting, when she thought back on it, and the payoff hadn't been nearly enough. It was a farce, like playing dress up to seem more adult.

"But there could be," Libby said, offering a smile. "Over time, I could see myself falling in love with you."

Samantha shook her head. "While that sounds super promising, I'm sorry, but no. I'm afraid I'm not interested."

"Wow." Libby took a minute with the information, finally nodding a quiet acceptance. "I think the world of you, Sam. Maybe one day we can be friends for real this time."

"Why don't we play it by ear?"

Libby turned to go, but stopped when a thought seemed to occur to her. "It's Hunter, isn't it? Because you found her?"

"It's because I found me," Sam corrected her, understanding it for the first time herself.

She tried calling Hunter, but, not surprisingly, she wasn't able to reach her. So she waited, trying desperately not to remember the look in Hunter's eyes as she stood there in that hallway, the look that said Sam had disappointed her deeply. As she sat there, a hundred different scenarios and conversations played themselves out like some sort of theatre of the mind, all the different ways this could go.

Eventually, a text came in from Hunter asking her to feed Elvis, as she'd be out late. That was it? That was all she was getting? *Perfect.* She shook her head in frustration and stared at the readout on her phone.

She selfishly wondered who Hunter was with. And while she wanted so much to explain away the display with Libby, a part of her considered that this might be her get-out-of-jail-free card when it came to Hunter. She could walk away now. Put things back as they'd always been between them—no harm, no foul—and dodge the probable heartbreak she'd be slammed with if she let her feelings for Hunter grow. And they would *inevitably* grow. They already felt as big as this loft they shared.

Because Sam wasn't sure what else to do and sleep didn't really seem like an option, she located her copy of *Pride and Prejudice* on Hunter's bedside table and picked up from the spot Hunter had bookmarked. And while she waited on the couch, she read, losing herself in the story of two people kept apart by a series of misunderstandings. It was all so frustrating, really. If Elizabeth and Darcy could just find their way to an honest conversation, they could avoid so many of these obstacles to their being together. She had to admit, it struck a chord in her.

She needed to afford her relationship with Hunter that same attention. It was too important not to. So, damn it, she would sit here and she would wait for Hunter to come home from wherever the hell she'd run off to and they would sort this thing out like grown people. She'd stay strong in the midst of those dreamy eyes and soft lips and she'd keep her head about her even if they found themselves in close proximity. She closed her eyes momentarily in exhaustion and vowed that she'd explain to Hunter her concerns about April and the many women like her. Sam started to drift, and as she did so, she wondered if there'd be a time when she could lie close with Hunter again, talking quietly until they both fell asleep. And wouldn't it be great if she could, once again, kiss the lips that she always thought about kissing. As sleep finally claimed her, it did so as she imagined what it would be like to go on another date with Hunter. A real one, where they'd sit in a restaurant, just the two of them, talking and laughing for hours, the way they did, teasing each other before coming home and making love until…

When Samantha awoke on the couch the next morning, with Elvis curled into her side, a quick glance at Hunter's room told her she'd not come home at all. Her spirits sagged, but she was no less determined to figure this thing out.

❖

"Do you want to talk about it yet?" Mallory asked, as Hunter poured a cup of coffee for herself and slid the one she'd already poured to Mallory.

"Nope," she answered resolutely. She had to hand it to Mallory; the nicer loft certainly did come with some awesome water pressure in the shower. She wore a borrowed robe and, with her hair wet, helped herself to breakfast in Mallory's gorgeous fifteenth-floor kitchen. "But I do enjoy these croissants. I didn't know people kept croissants in their homes. I thought that was more of a restaurant/bakery scenario. Go you."

Mallory slid into her suit jacket, which had been resting on the settee. Yes, Mallory had a *settee*. "Yep. Me and my croissants, rockin' the world."

"I want to be just like you when I grow up."

Mallory shot her a look. "And you can start now. Dean and DeLuca sells fresh rolls. All kinds. The world's full of exciting discoveries, isn't it?"

"That it is," she marveled, tearing off a piece of the croissant and closing her eyes at how awesome it tasted. Bread was dependable and temporary. Thereby, she loved it.

Mallory came around the island and went about loading her electronics into her attaché. "This hyperbolic, I-don't-care-about-anything veneer is going to fade away at some point soon, right? I don't know what happened between the two of you, but it'd be nice if you found a way to acknowledge it. You didn't even want to go home last night, Hunter."

Her eyes met Mallory's, and she felt her resolve crumble a bit. It was best she not think about it. She'd rather not revisit that very raw and painful wash of emotion that had her walking the streets until late last night. But it had been when she'd finally settled in on Mallory's couch that the real torture had begun. Because, as she lay there in the dark, she thought of the heartbreak Samantha had gone through because of Libby and the heartache she was experiencing now because of Sam. She'd stayed away from relationships her whole life for a reason, and now she was acutely reminded of what a bad idea they really were. She'd left herself emotionally vulnerable to someone, and regardless of whether it had been intentional or not, she felt like her heart had just been ripped out. And as much as she vowed in this moment to never let herself be that kind of vulnerable again, she also mourned the loss of what they'd had. And for that, she ached as she lay there, at times unable to catch her breath, it hurt so much. Because what she'd found with Samantha was rare and it was wonderful and it wasn't something she ever wanted to give back. But at the same time, she knew she had to. Call her a coward, but she preferred realist.

Hunter stared at the counter as she considered what to say to Mallory, what sort of explanation to give. "You were right, is all. Sam and I were a bad idea from the start."

"Doesn't mean I want either one of you hurt." Mallory wrapped her arms around Hunter and held on. Tears threatened at the support she felt emanating from Mallory, her friend, but she pushed them back "You gonna be okay today?" Mal asked.

"Of course. Aren't I always?" Mallory passed her a dubious look and she relented. "Fine. Yes, I'll be okay. Just, maybe, give me some space at work. I plan to just zone when I get there. Get things done." But the truth was, she wasn't sure she'd be okay at all. This was all so new to her. The emotional equivalent of being hit by a truck. Why did people sign up for this again?

"And the two of you?"

"She and I are friends. We'll get past it." Hunter inclined her head to the door. "Speaking of which, I'm going to head downstairs and change clothes. I'll see you at the office in fifteen?"

"You will. I work there."

Hunter kissed her cheek. "I thought that was you. Thanks, Mal. For everything."

In reality, she'd purposefully waited this long to head downstairs knowing that Sam would already be up and gone for the day before Hunter arrived. It was childish, but it felt like a game of self-preservation at this point, so she could live with the stigma.

After selecting a pair of slim fitting jeans and royal blue graphic T-shirt, Hunter slipped into work, intent on keeping her head in the game and her feelings on the back burner. Time to get back to who she used to be.

She ran her palm across the stickers on her MacBook and, with a quick motion, had it opened and primed for her first project: a tweaking of the half-page ad she'd designed for Foster's extra crunch peanut butter. The rep had asked for a more vibrant orange, and a more vibrant orange he would get.

"Hey. I was worried about you. You never came home." Sam stood at her desk. The look on her face was so incredibly earnest, that Hunter had to remind herself of the facts and fight the urge to take that face in her hands. That's how fucked up her feelings were.

Instead she kept her eyes on her screen. "I slept at Mallory's. It was late. Didn't want to wake you."

Brooklyn swiveled in her chair. "Sam sleeps like the dead. Trust me. I've tested this theory. You'd have been fine."

Hunter opened her mouth to answer Brooklyn, but Samantha pressed on, undeterred by Brooklyn's presence. "You stayed out because you didn't want to talk about what happened." Completely true. She headed to the kitchen to refill her coffee and escape the line of questioning. Mallory looked at her curiously from where she worked at the kitchen table, but Samantha was on her heels. "And you still don't apparently, but I do. I want to talk about it."

"Another time," she said, turning to face Sam and dropping her tone.

"Why are you avoiding this?"

"Look, I don't want to do this here."

Sam looked at her in exasperation. "I'd rather not either, trust me. But this seems to be the only place I can. You don't answer your phone, you don't return text messages, and you haven't been home since yesterday. You haven't left me with a lot of options."

"Maybe you two could take a walk, get some coffee?" Mallory offered, sympathy written all across her face. Hunter didn't need sympathy right now. She needed to get back to work and not think about this.

"Nope. Not necessary. Everything is fine." She looked at Sam. "It's fine. I promise."

"What's going on?" Brooklyn asked, now coming around her desk. "You guys had an argument?"

Samantha turned to Brooklyn and rattled off the facts. "Hunter walked up and saw me kissing Libby. We haven't told you this, but we've been seeing each other. Kind of."

"You and Libby?"

"Me and Hunter." Samantha turned back to Hunter, clearly on some sort of communication mission she wasn't about to give up. So much for not letting things between them interfere with work.

In the midst of it all, Brooklyn tilted her head to the side as if Samantha had just explained that caterpillars were the source of all evil in the world. "I'm sorry. Did you just say that *you two* are dating?"

Hunter raised a finger because that wasn't exactly correct, now was it? "Sleeping together, more like," she corrected. "As in, past tense. So no worries, Brooks."

Samantha stepped to her, eyes flashing anger. "Stop it. Right now. I know you're hurt and I get that, but 'sleeping together, past tense' is a little crass. You have to agree."

"I don't have to agree to anything." Suddenly, Hunter was smiling through sarcasm. Not exactly behavior she felt proud of, but everything seemed wildly out of control, and feigning indifference seemed safe. "The love of your life has flitted back to you, Sam. You should be ecstatic, not worrying about me."

"Wait. So Libby wants you back now?" Mallory asked, coming around the table.

"Yes," Sam said to Mallory before turning back to Hunter. "And I'm not ecstatic at all."

"And why is that?" Hunter asked. She hated that she allowed

herself to go there, but a part of her had to know. "It's exactly what you wanted."

"Because you and I have things to sort out. I can't believe you're being so cavalier."

It was how she protected herself. It had worked her entire life until she'd let her guard down with Sam. She just wouldn't let herself get caught up this way again. That kind of thing wasn't for her. Hunter shook her head. "We don't have to sort anything out, Sam, we're okay. I promise. Friends. Business as usual. I want you to feel free to live your life and not worry about me."

"You got hurt yesterday. I get that, and I'm sorry. But that doesn't mean we shouldn't see what this is, take the risk. I'm willing to do that."

"Yeah, well, I'm not." She headed back to her desk.

"What about April?"

She shrugged and turned back, not following the logic. "What about April?"

"Brooklyn told me about your feelings for April, and maybe that's part of what messed with my head yesterday."

Hunter passed Brooklyn a look only to have her stare back in complete mortification, as if watching some sort of horrific tennis match. "I didn't know," she mouthed.

Hunter didn't feel the need for any sort of grandiose confession. "April is not a part of this. Trust me."

"Of course I trust you. I'm just trying to understand the complete turnaround because of a moment in time that didn't even matter."

Mallory faced Sam. "If I had to guess, I would imagine that April was code for another name." And then to Hunter, "Am I right?"

Hunter shrugged, refusing to commit. Her feelings at this point were hers to deal with. Why complicate things further? She was willing to—

"Oh my God, you were talking about Sam," Brooklyn said as much as to herself as to Hunter. She pinched her nose between her eyes and then turned to Mallory. "Wait a sec. Why aren't *you* surprised by any of this?"

Mallory, who looked about as uncomfortable with the question as Hunter had ever seen her. "Because I was aware of the situation," Mallory said delicately.

"That's just perfect," Brooklyn said, tossing a hand in the air. But it was clear that it was Samantha she felt most betrayed by. "You told Mallory and not me?"

Samantha seemed to soften. "You're not great at keeping secrets, Brooks, unless they're yours."

"That is wildly untrue," Brooklyn said, pointing at Sam. "Did I tell anyone when Mallory slept with that Lisa girl junior year? Or when Hunter was late with the menswear layout and I ran interference with the client so Mal wouldn't find out?" The three of them stared at her in shock. "Okay, maybe I see your point, but this is different. This is your life, Sam. I would have never betrayed a confidence."

Samantha closed her eyes. "I know. I'm sorry."

And as the two of them continued their back and forth, Hunter's phone buzzed in her pocket. Anything to escape the uncomfortable chaos around her, she checked the readout. Kevin. Without hesitation she answered the call. "Kev, hey."

His words came out in a rush; the panic in his voice was evident. "Claire said to call you. The ambulance just left and they said they're not getting a response. The sirens are on and they're hurrying. They think it was a massive heart attack or something. We're driving there now. We were shopping and it just happened."

"Okay, slow down for sec, okay?" She covered one ear and moved away from her friends as they quieted around her in response to her movement.

She could hear her sister's voice in the background, shrill and fast. "Hunter, you need to get here!"

Oh, Christ. She squatted onto her heels, as if doing that would somehow make her be able to understand better. A million thoughts raced across her mind in succession. This wasn't how it was supposed to go down at all. Her father was an asshole, but he'd been trying. There was supposed to be time for her to work through some things, right? What if she didn't get that chance? But now wasn't the time. She needed to focus. "What hospital are you going to?"

She heard Kevin consult with Claire. "Kettering Medical Center," he came back with.

"I'll be there as soon as I can get a flight. Okay, Kev? I'm on my way."

Claire was on the phone now. "Hunter, it didn't look good. I'm freaking out right now. I don't know what to do."

"Take some deep breaths, Claire. Dad's a stubborn guy. He's gonna fight hard."

"Hunter." A pause. "It's Mom. Mom's in the ambulance. Mom had the heart attack."

She replayed the words, and the world went white.

She swallowed as her arm and the phone returned to her side. Her friends were asking her questions, but she couldn't quite make sense of the words. It was like a tidal wave had hit and there was no way to get out from under it.

She needed to get to Ohio.

CHAPTER FIFTEEN

Hunter arrived at the hospital just before midnight and studied the signs to find the Intensive Care Unit, where her mom had been taken. Her sister and brother-in-law were in the waiting room looking haggard, older somehow, their faces pale and eyes red. She could see nurses move about the nurse's station through the window to their right like a swarm of very efficient bees. One looked up and laughed at something another had said. Just another day at work. The room smelled of disinfectant and coffee. All of these things hit her at once like some kind of sensory overload, forcing her to grab hold of a nearby chair for momentary support.

But she was here. Despite ticket confusion and delayed flights and annoying passengers who insisted on blocking the aisle once they'd landed, she'd arrived.

And she needed information.

"Hunter," Claire said, jumping out of the daze she seemed to have slipped into.

"Is she okay? Is she alive?" Hunter asked. The two most important questions. And then her sister's arms were around her, which made the tears she thought she had under control fall unencumbered down her face as terror licked up her spine. "Please answer me, Claire. God, please."

"She's alive, but barely. I don't know what to do. Dad's wandering around. Kevin's sitting on the curb, refusing to come in, and I feel so helpless. I'm glad you're here."

"What's the update on Mom?" she asked her sister. The rest could wait. She distantly registered her brother-in-law coming around and squeezing her hand.

Claire shook her head. "Her heart's not working on its own. There was apparently a lot of damage to it from the heart attack. Her blood isn't oxygenating properly. They have her on a ventilator and some other device. The doctor said a bunch of stuff I don't remember." She held her palm up helplessly to Chip for assistance. He jumped in.

"Dr. Bayliss, the cardiologist, feels there's real cause for concern, Hunter. She told us to gather family. So I think you should prepare yourself."

She closed her eyes. It wasn't what Hunter had been hoping for, and honestly it didn't feel real. Somehow she had to figure out a way to undo all of this. Her mom was the warmest, most caring individual in the entire world. Her biggest cheerleader, her safe place to fall. Always. She couldn't imagine a world without her, and it wasn't fair that any of them should have to. Everything felt upside down, like a garish carnival ride on repeat. Mentally shaking herself, she found her focus again. "Can I see her?"

Claire took her hand and led to the double swinging doors. "We're only allowed visitation for a few minutes each hour. I'll take you."

She paused, wiping the moisture from her face. Her throat burned. "Do you mind if I go by myself first?"

Her sister nodded, seeming to understand the need for privacy. "Yeah, of course. I'll wait here. Second room on the right."

As she made her way into the unit, she was surprised by how dim it was inside, how quiet. Nighttime was in full effect as nurses moved quietly about. She paused in the doorway to the room with her mother's name on the chart, terrified to go in. In the corner stood machines, beeping and whooshing in a symphony Hunter found foreign and horrific. But in the midst of it all lay this tiny little form, so helpless and still. And that was all that it took. She moved to her mom, her lifelong protector, as if attached to a magnet. A sob tore from her throat and she covered her mouth to muffle the sound. She took in her mother's battered body, covered by a brown blanket. So unlike herself. So still. Finally, catching her breath, she took her mother's hand, which seemed swollen and lifeless, into her own.

"Hi, Mama." She swallowed, tasting tears and not sure what else to say. "I see you went to a lot of trouble to get me here this time." The machine whooshed as Hunter gathered her thoughts, fighting the damn lump in her throat. "We need you to be strong for us, okay? Because we need you here, and that means that heart of yours has to start working on its own. Maybe you can give it a talking-to. Claire needs her shopping buddy, you hear me? And Kevin, he needs you more than ever, Mama. He's just a kid." Her voice broke with emotion. "And don't forget about me, okay? Who's gonna check up on me and make sure that I'm eating and not posting stupid photos to Facebook? That's your job and—" Hunter tried to form the words, but her voice gave out. The tears blinded her and she submitted to them, bowing her head, her resolve too weak to continue. Absently, she felt a hand on her shoulder, and the strength from that touch moved through her like a drug. She turned and met the eyes of her father. Hunter didn't question the impulse, but instead fell into his arms, where he held her tightly as she cried. The differences between them didn't matter in that moment. They were family and they both loved her mother. His arms felt solid and warm, and for a fleeting moment she remembered what it was like to have a dad.

"It's okay to be sad," he said finally. "She would say so."

She nodded into his chest. "She has to be okay."

He nodded, but didn't say anything. Perhaps the sadness had gotten ahold of him, too. They stayed like that, with his arms around her, standing over her mother's bed for several long moments. He released her finally and ran a hand across the back of her hair. She saw the tears on his cheeks now.

"You look so much like her, you know. Everyone always says so."

It was the highest form of compliment. She nodded, suddenly self-aware again and a little uncomfortable. She placed a kiss on her mother's cheek, dodging the breathing tube that kept her alive. "Get some good rest, Mama. We're all here. I love you." She lingered a moment, memorizing the image. Just in case.

Her father walked her back out to the waiting room with a hand on her back. He didn't say anything, but his quiet strength emanated, making all the difference. A parent was here. Not the one she was used to, not the one she wanted, but a parent all the same. And there was comfort in that. Once Hunter was returned to her sister, her father headed out again, back to wherever he'd been.

Claire shrugged and watched his departing form. "He's just been walking laps around the hospital all night. It's how he's coping."

Hunter nodded. "He likes to control things, and he can't do that with this. He's scared."

They settled in for what would prove to be a very long night. Chip was good about playing caretaker. He refilled their coffee cups and made sure they were comfortable. As much as she'd rolled her eyes at him in the past, he really was a good guy. Hunter spent the time staring at the wall, the clock, the torn-up magazines on the coffee table, and the forlorn faces of those around them, waiting for news of their own loved ones. It was a depressing place. She fired off a text message to her friends back in New York, updating them on what she'd learned. She didn't know how long she'd be in Ohio, but an encouraging text from Mallory put her concerns to rest. They'd take care of Savvy while she focused on her family. She'd yet to see Kevin, and as time went on, she started to wonder about his whereabouts. He shouldn't be alone.

She stood and ran a hand through her hair. God, her neck muscles pulled. "I'm gonna find Kev."

Claire adjusted her position in the uncomfortable plastic chairs. "He's outside. Chip checked on him not too long ago. Won't come in. They're so alike," she said, referencing Kevin and their father. "So stubborn."

Hunter nodded and headed for the door. "Thanks. I just want to make sure he's okay." Because for her, Kevin was still that smiley little kid who'd do anything for anyone, who was thrilled each time a new person walked in the door. And he probably needed someone about now, whether he'd admit to it or not. She found him not far from the ambulance bay of the emergency room, hunched over on a bench, slouch hat in place and ear buds implanted. His new lanky form was something she was still getting used to.

Hunter sat next to him on the bench, prompting him to turn. He pulled one of the ear buds out and stared at her. The eyeliner was gone and left staring back at her were the big brown eyes of her little brother. As much as she wanted to, she didn't hug him. She didn't think he'd want that.

"Hey," he said.

"Hi." They sat there together for a bit. Neither one, apparently, felt the need to say anything, and that was fine with her. Hunter needed Kevin to get that she was here. That was all. God, the kid must be petrified. She didn't know how he could be so calm, so still. Cars raced past on the distant freeway. An EMT smoked a cigarette. After about ten minutes or so, he turned to her.

"Is she going to die?" And just like that he was eight years old again, looking to his big sister for guidance. His face held such innocence, such fear. It tore at her.

"It looks like she might," Hunter said, feeling the need to be honest with him.

He nodded and faced the street. Work traffic seemed to be making an appearance as the purple light of dawn faded in gradually. "I'm sorry I've been an asshole," he said finally, taking off his hat and squeezing it. "I've been sitting here for hours thinking about how I could have made things easier on her, but I didn't. So stupid and wrapped up in my lame life, and now—"

"Hey," she said slinging an arm around him. "First of all, Mom doesn't think you're an asshole. She'd be pissed we were even using the word. So don't be an asshole and tell her."

The tiniest of smiles hit his face. Well, look at that, he did still have teeth. "Cool. I won't."

"I don't know what's gonna happen, kid, but we gotta stick together through this thing. And it sucks that you're sixteen and you hate the world, but can you push pause on that for now? Maybe put it on the to-do list for later?"

He nodded, leaning into her arm a tad. "I just need that not to be the way she saw me last, you know? Acting like that." There had been a lot of tears shed over the past twenty-four hours, but the ones that brimmed in her brother's eyes now stabbed her square in the chest.

"She knows who you are, Kevin. And so do I. Come inside and wait with us, okay? No more sitting out here beating yourself up."

He nodded and followed her back inside to join the rest of the family.

Waiting. Hoping. Making crazy deals with the universe.

And attempting to stay strong.

❖

It'd been a week since Hunter had left for Ohio. Sam hadn't experienced a single good night of sleep since. She went to work but spent most of the time wildly distracted and probably ineffective. She was worried about Hunter's mom, Hunter's family, and most importantly, Hunter herself.

Sam hadn't received much direct communication since Hunter had left so unexpectedly for Ohio, just a few texts here or there, checking in on Elvis and offering gratitude for Samantha looking after him. The interactions were polite and surface level, which left her feeling very much on the periphery, a difficult place to be. Most of the medical updates came through Mallory, which she had to admit stung a bit. Mrs. Blair had shown signs of improvement, but was still dependent upon the ventilator, something they were hoping to wean her off slowly over the next few days. Time would tell whether she would recover fully, but it was certainly better news than last week.

"You done for the day?" Brooklyn asked, wheeling up to Sam's desk in her desk chair and stopping abruptly. It was her thing lately, wheeling places. She always did have a fascination with things that moved fast.

Samantha glanced at the clock. It was after six and she wasn't accomplishing anything anymore. Honestly, her heart wasn't in it. She looked up at Brooklyn regretfully. "Put a fork in me."

Brooklyn tilted her head to the side. "Seems cruel. Wanna have dinner at our place instead? Ashton is coming over. Then she and Jessica will inevitably play some sort of shoot-'em-up video game, and we can sneak off to the balcony and stare at things and talk."

It sounded nice actually. She and Brooklyn probably needed to check in with each other. The bickering that had been abruptly interrupted when Hunter received the phone call about her mother had naturally fallen by the wayside as the friends pulled together in light of the tragedy. But it hadn't ever really been addressed, and it probably needed to be.

"I'd love that. What can I bring?"

"You have any of those truffles left?"

"Mmm-hmm. A new tin just arrived today. And Mal called the bakeshop that makes them to see about maybe representing them. Putting that place on the map. We could sell the hell outta those things, Brooks."

"Yeah, we could." Brooklyn stared off at the wall in response to the news, which meant she was already in creative mode.

"Slow down, sparky." Samantha laughed, grasping her forearm. "We haven't signed them yet. Save the juice until the ink is dry."

Brooklyn pointed at her head. "Just doing some preliminary truffle warm-ups, you know how it is. Truffle wind sprints, if you will. Seven thirty tonight?"

"Perfect."

Brooklyn wheeled herself over to Mallory, who was still going strong at her own desk, firing off emails and doing all the Mallory things that Sam couldn't even begin to understand. "Dinner tonight, Mal?" Brooklyn asked.

"Can't. I need to pull a late night. Get my notes going for a presentation tomorrow with those brake fluid guys. I know very little about brake fluid, but that will not be the case by morning."

"Roger that, boss. Hey, anything from Hunter this afternoon?"

Sam's fingers froze on the keyboard and her heart sped up as she peeked around her computer monitor, awaiting Mallory's answer.

"She's a little stressed," Mallory began. "Between her father and her brother, the house is pretty much trashed, and they're surviving on fast food, which they pick up on trips back and forth to the hospital. She's not willing to leave her mom for very long, and her sister has her hands full with the twins, so there's not a lot of time to attend to, well…life."

Brooklyn blew out a breath. "She's gotta be going out of her mind. How's her mom?"

"It looks like there are some encouraging signs. The concern over brain damage has passed, as she's semiconscious and will squeeze the doctor's hand on command. But they're keeping her somewhat sedated so her body can heal."

Samantha closed her eyes and sent up a silent prayer of gratitude to the universe. And then she couldn't hold back any longer. "How did she sound when you talked to her?"

Mallory turned to her, soft smile on her face. "Like Hunter. Ever the trouper. You know how she is."

She nodded, attempting a smile of her own before staring at her keyboard as the well of feelings struck again. The sadness over what Hunter was going through, the guilt surrounding how they'd left things between them, and the sharp need to be there for Hunter through this rough time in her life. She'd pretty much been stonewalled on that front. She'd called several times, left messages, but Hunter had yet to call her back.

"Give her time, Sam," Mallory said.

"Yeah. Yeah. Of course." She blinked back the embarrassing tears and pretended to focus on packing up. No big deal at all.

Two and half hours later, she sat on Brooklyn's balcony staring out at the vast Hudson River. It was peaceful and calming out there. She got why Brooklyn relished it so much.

They spent the better part of an hour sitting together as Samantha recounted the details of how things between her and Hunter had first started all the way through how they'd ended.

"I don't know how I missed it," Brooklyn said, looking mystified. "I'm usually more perceptive than that."

"You're very perceptive, but it's not like you would ever imagine something like this."

Brooklyn held up a finger. "That's not exactly true."

Sam stared at her. "Explain yourself."

"You guys have always had this hard-to-explain vibe, a fiery chemistry. Back in college, I kind of wondered if you two would ever…" She raised a punctuating eyebrow.

"Seriously?"

"It crossed my mind once or twice, yeah."

"Man. You were way ahead of me, that's for sure," Sam said, a little amazed. She turned to face Brooklyn more fully and softened her tone. "I know you were hurt that I didn't come to you right away and honestly, if I hadn't been so freaked out, I would have."

Brooklyn nodded and stared out at the water. "It's partially my fault. I was wrapped up in my own world, and I wasn't the most available friend. So we both carry some of the responsibility."

The night was fairly warm and Sam felt like she could sit out there with Brooklyn for hours. Next to her friend, she could let it all go. Be honest with herself and with Brooklyn. No matter how bad things seemed, there was comfort in that.

"I know you're sad," Brooklyn said, breaking the silence. "But she's coming back, you know."

Sam nodded. "But as what? Some distant roommate who comes

and goes and speaks to me in overly polite exchanges? God, I don't think I could take that, Brooks, not after everything. Not with the way I'm feeling."

Brooklyn's mouth fell open. "You're a little lovesick, aren't you?"

"That would be colossally stupid, which I'm trying harder this week not to be. Hunter's not being stupid. Why should I?"

"Because this isn't grade school. And it's not objectivity you're dealing with here. Column A does not have to equal column B in matters of love. In reality, you don't know how stupid Hunter is or isn't being. She puts on a lot of bravado when she's hurt. That's what you saw at the office that day before she left. She was in self-protection mode."

Samantha nodded and let the comment roll around a bit. "Maybe. But she's probably right to be. We should stop now before there's any more of the hurting. Think about it. Her: a well-known player around town. Me: a pathetic exaggerator of all things romance. All of us: trying to run a successful business in a cutthroat city. Doesn't that sound like a disastrous combination?"

"Not if you're in love. Be honest with yourself. I know firsthand what it's like to fall for the one person in life you shouldn't. Doesn't mean it can't work itself out and be the most awesome thing you've ever experienced. And if it's meant to be, the world will adjust. There's only one question: Are you in love with Hunter?"

God, that word carried so much power. She'd thought she'd been in love with Libby. Hell, she'd been days away from saying the words to her. How silly that seemed now, in comparison. How trivial. And Brooklyn was right—it was time to be honest with herself. She took a deep breath and decided to lay it all out there. "I don't know the exact moment it happened, and I thought you were supposed to." She glanced at Brooklyn. "In the novels, they always know. But it's here, Brooks. This overwhelming feeling of wanting to be around her all the time and take care of her and make out with her and go to sleep at the end of a day with her in my arms. And it's more powerful than anything I've ever known. I do love her, no matter how much I fight it. So, lovesick?" She blew out a breath. "Yeah, I'd say so."

A smile started small on Brooklyn's face and spread out. "I'm happy for you, Sammie. I'll admit, it was a shock at first, and it's still taking some getting used to, but Mallory and I have done some talking."

This was new information. She sat up a little straighter, her interest piqued. "You have? And what was the substance of those talks?"

Brooklyn lifted a shoulder. "If you and Hunter are meant to be, we'll make it work at Savvy. We don't want you to worry about that part. Some things are more important than business, and Mallory and I both feel strongly that you and Hunter fall into that category. We want you to be happy. That comes first."

Samantha smiled as sheer relief washed over her in big, warm waves. "Thank you. I don't know what else to say. It means a lot to hear you say that."

"And now you have, but there's still a larger issue." Brooklyn leaned forward, met Sam's gaze squarely, and held on. "You're in love, Sammie. Now what are you going to do about it?"

Samantha blinked back. Honestly, she didn't have a clue. "I guess now I have to figure that out."

❖

Scraps of paper littered the floor, glitter was strewn about every available surface, and Pitbull played from the speakers in the corner. Scrapbooking class was in rare form tonight and Sam's group of students was, too. Something must have been in the air.

Ms. Guaducci chair-danced as she addressed Mrs. Potter. "I'm just saying that if he wants to flirt with the cafeteria workers, well, that's his loss. I'm on the market and plan to wheel my chair past that newcomer's door a couple extra times on the way back to my room."

"How's your page coming?" Samantha asked.

"Better than her love life," Mrs. Potter said, angling her head at Ms. Guaducci. Ouch.

"That's okay," Mrs. Guaducci said, patting Sam's hand. "Men are pigs, sweetie. But we love 'em anyway."

"That we do," Sam said, playing along.

"Ms. Samantha, I believe I've finished my book." Mr. Earnhardt stood in front of her holding his scrapbook reverently in his hands. He beamed at her, and the warm smile melted her heart.

"Do you mind if I take a look?" she asked.

He handed the book over to her. "I'd be honored." As she flipped through the pages, the rest of her class slowly joined her, gathering in a huddle of solidarity to look over their friend's work. Samantha watched as Mr. Earnhardt's time with his late wife passed by in a succession of photos that told the story of their life together. Stunning, complete, and full of love. A lump formed in Sam's throat, not just because of the poignancy of the couple's snapshots, but because she wanted that. All of it. The life. The bond. The till-death-do-us-part. But what was shockingly clear to her now was that it wasn't just some generic dream anymore. She knew exactly who she wanted those things with.

"Why are you crying, dear?" Mrs. Swientek asked, and placed a hand on her back.

"It's nothing," Sam said, doing her best to downplay her emotion. "There's just been a lot going on lately, and Mr. Earnhardt's scrapbook is just so beautiful and touching. You did such a good job on it," she said to Mr. Earnhardt.

"Thank you," he said, taking back what seemed to be his new prized possession. "I bet you'll have one just as nice when you're our age."

But she wasn't sure of that at all, and the uncertainty must have shown on her face.

"Samantha, sweetheart, what's wrong?" Mrs. Guaducci asked. Maybe it was the stress of the week, or how much she truly missed Hunter, or even the beauty of the scrapbook she'd just experienced, or maybe it was a culmination of all of those things that prompted Samantha to burst into tears.

"Oh no," Mr. Earnhardt said, looking nervously at the faces of his friends. The men quickly sprang into action, moving about and shouting commands, quickly trying to fix the situation.

"Get some water!"

"Turn the music down!"

"Someone sit her down."

The women were different. They crowded around Sam and patted her shoulder, easing her into one of the glitter-covered chairs.

"It's okay, dear."

"You're with friends."

"Let it out."

She felt ridiculous for crying and even more so for doing it in front of her class, but they took care of her, those lovable folks, and fussed over her until the tears subsided.

"You feeling better now?" Mrs. Guaducci asked. "A good cry always makes me feel better."

Sam gulped in a breath and nodded. "I think so."

"Well, are you gonna tell us about it?" Mr. Turner asked, in exasperation. She knew that, with him, the exasperation was really just code for concern.

She glanced at the faces all around her, the whole gang blinking back at her expectantly. "Well," she began. "I guess seeing that wonderful scrapbook reminded me how much I'd like to have a life like Mr. Earnhardt's. Full and rich and filled with love."

Suddenly everyone was talking at once.

"You can have that."

"Just gotta fall in love and settle down."

"I got divorced three times and turned out all right."

"Can we turn Pitbull back on?"

But she noticed Mr. Earnhardt quietly trying to ask her something in the midst of the mayhem, so Samantha held up her hands to obtain everyone's attention. When the room fell back into silence, she turned to him. "What were you saying, Mr. Earnhardt?"

"Do you love somebody, Samantha?"

If it was possible, it seemed like everyone leaned in a little closer at the question, eagerly awaiting some sort of hint to the answer. And after Mr. Earnhardt had shared the details of his life with her, she felt like she owed him an answer.

"I do."

"It's babelicious, isn't it?" Mr. Glenville asked.

The ends of Samantha's mouth turned up at the nickname, and she felt the blush the second it touched her cheeks.

"It is!" Mr. Earnhardt shouted, and the two old men high-fived each other with a loud smack.

"And does she love you back?" Mr. Earnhardt asked.

"I think it's possible. But I don't know for sure."

"Then you have to find out," he said simply.

The others all chimed in, agreeing with him, murmuring and nodding.

"It's not a good time," Sam explained. "She has some things going on in her life. Her mother isn't well."

"Well, then you should be there for her," Mrs. Potter said.

"She needs you," said Mrs. Guaducci.

Mr. Earnhardt stared hard at her. "What are you waiting for?"

It was a valid question.

What am I waiting for?

CHAPTER SIXTEEN

How about another bite of Jell-O, Mama? For me? Just one." It was getting late in the day. Hunter could tell as she glimpsed the sun on its final descent through the blinds. She'd been at the hospital since the doors had opened at seven that morning, and they'd been at this Jell-O thing for a good portion of the afternoon.

"No," her mother said, shaking her head and turning away. "No more." Her spirits were low and Hunter understood that this whole ordeal had taken a heavy toll on her. While her mother was out of the woods for the most part, she wasn't bouncing back as fast as the doctors had hoped either. Her progress seemed to have plateaued.

"Okay. Maybe later, then." Hunter sighed and set the dish down in defeat. While the week had brought with it a medical status downgrade from critical to fair, it had also presented its share of challenges. After she'd been removed from the ventilator, her mom'd had trouble swallowing, which was a side effect of the intubation. Now she wasn't getting the nourishment she needed. Not only that, but she was less than thrilled with the oxygen mask the doctors required her to wear and wasn't so enthused about the laps around the unit the doctor had prescribed to get her up and moving again. In fact, she was irritable, argumentative, and downright unhelpful. It turned out that Hunter's warm and wonderful mother was quite possibly the worst patient in history.

"I know today is hard, but I need you to work on meeting me halfway. I'm going to let you rest, but we need to go for a walk in a little while."

"I hate it here," her mother said sadly.

It about broke Hunter's heart. "Then we have to do everything the doctor says so we can get you home."

"I'm supposed to be taking care of my family, not the other way around." Her voice was still raspy from the many days of intubation, and it seemed to take a lot of effort for her to explain herself.

Hunter was as gentle with her response as her frayed nerves would allow her to be. She was running on so little sleep, it was a wonder she could string a thought together. She also couldn't remember the last time she'd had a meal that hadn't come in a cardboard container. "No one loves to be in the hospital. And what we're trying to do is get you out. I love you, Mom, and I want to get you home."

Her mother raised her hands which was clearly a struggle in and of itself. "Then let's go."

"Not so fast there, superstar. One thing at a time. You think you can rest?"

She nodded, looking about as forlorn as Hunter had ever seen her.

"Claire is going to come sit with you in a bit, once the twins have had their dinner," Hunter said. "And I'll be back this evening to take you for that walk." She kissed her mother's cheek, which elicited a smile. As she turned to go, her mother grabbed her wrist.

"Thank you, Hunter. I love you."

The sentiment slammed her with a jolt of emotion, as Hunter recounted just how close they'd come to losing her. "I love you, too, Mama."

"Your father?"

"Doing laps. You know him. I'm sure he'll be by soon." It was the only thing that seemed to make him feel better. He was definitely an interesting guy. In the time that Hunter had been home, they'd talked only about her mother's progress. But to his credit, and this was hard for her to admit, he'd been there every step of the way, for Kevin, for Claire. Even for her. It mattered.

On the drive back to her parents' house, Hunter nearly fell asleep twice. She knew she should catch a few minutes of rest before going back to the hospital, but at the same time, there was laundry that needed to be done, dishes to be washed, and if they didn't do something about their nutritional situation, her mother wouldn't be the only one with heart problems. Her dad and brother were virtually no help around the house, as they depended so heavily on her mother, who'd always handled all things domestic.

So though her coping skills were at an all-time low, sleep would have to wait.

She took out her key as she made her way up the walk, but was surprised to find the door unlocked. A quick glance at the front yard, which contained Kevin's overturned bike, told her he was back earlier than expected from his junior-year orientation.

What she wasn't prepared for, however, were the mouthwatering aromas that accosted her senses upon entering the home. She froze in the entryway, closing her eyes in surrender, because, good God, it smelled wonderful in here. Only when she opened them again did she also marvel that, in a shocking turn of events, the place was gleaming.

"What in the world?" she asked Kevin, who was kneeling next to an end table with a dust rag and a bottle of Lemon Pledge. She scanned the space. Every surface shone brightly, the clutter that had piled up to embarrassing heights over the past few weeks was completely absent, and soft music soothed from the stereo system. It was like stumbling upon heaven on Earth.

Kevin shrugged and went back to work on the end table. "Don't look at me. All her doing, and she doesn't mess around." He inclined his head in the direction of the kitchen. While Hunter was curious as to how Claire had so effectively propelled Kevin into action, her venture into the kitchen, let's face it, was inspired by her appetite.

"Hey, the kid is working like a rock star out there and I need to know what you're making, when I can have some, and—" She stopped short.

Samantha closed the oven door and turned to Hunter. She seemed to consider the question as Hunter took a step backward in surprise, her mind scrambling to make sense of the visual. "A: He just needed a little direction," Sam said. "B: Roast beef, mashed potatoes, salad, and sourdough rolls. C: Give me about ten minutes, and then grab a plate."

"Hi," Hunter said. It was the only word she seemed to have access to, and the smile on her face was automatic and huge. Samantha was like some kind of beautiful mirage standing there in her mother's kitchen. And she was responsible for all of this?

"Hi," Sam said back quietly. God, she looked good, so much so that Hunter wondered if she was even real. But there she stood, fresh faced and together, in capris and green top—a reminder that the real world was still out there in the midst of her family's turmoil. "I hope it's okay that I'm here. I thought you could use a hand."

Hunter wanted to cry in relief, understanding that she wasn't on her own anymore, but there'd been so much crying lately.

"Oh, and before I forget, there's someone else who wants to say hi, too." She opened the kitchen door that led to the backyard and Elvis ran in, stopping at Hunter's feet and shrieking in excitement at his discovery of her.

Okay, too late now, the tears sprang into her eyes as she knelt down and buried her face in his fur. "Hey, buddy. Oh my God. I missed you so much." He fell into her lap and then flipped onto his back, wriggling frantically as she scratched his stomach, all the while continuing his shrieking celebration.

"He missed you, too," Samantha said. "Talked about you nightly, before and after staring time, of course."

"I can't believe you brought him," Hunter said, standing. "And I can't believe you're here. The house, dinner, it's all just..." Her exhaustion got the better of her and she was no match for the overwhelming emotion.

Sam didn't hesitate, and pulled Hunter to her, wrapping her arms around her and holding on as she cried. "Shh. Everything is going to be okay," Sam said. "Have you slept?"

Hunter wiped her eyes, smiling through the remaining tears at her ridiculous behavior. "No. Part of the problem here," she said, pointing at her face. "No coping skills."

"Okay," Sam said calmly. "Dinner first, followed by a nap. Go tell your brother to wash up, and I'll finish up in here. And take Elvis, he keeps giving me puppy eyes and that's wildly distracting. He's already had some roast beef scraps, haven't you, little El?"

Hunter did as she was told and in just a few short minutes enjoyed one of the best meals of her life. And though Kevin headed to his room with his plate, Sam ate with her, catching her up on all the latest happenings back home. The news, no matter how trivial, was a more than welcome distraction to the kinds of things she'd been dealing with. Never before had Brooklyn's office antics seemed more hilarious, or one of Mallory's pep talks more inspiring. Hunter couldn't help but notice that Sam never once touched on the issues that had been at play between them when she'd left. It was Samantha at her most thoughtful, making things as low stress for Hunter as possible. And while they steered clear of all romance-related discussion, damn it if her heart didn't clench with startling relief just to be in Sam's presence again. Talking to her, looking at her, all of it.

Sam tore off a tiny piece of bread from the roll on her plate and Hunter couldn't help but smile at the move. "What?" Sam asked. "Why are you looking at me like that?"

"Because no one on the planet eats bread the way you do. In tiny, tiny little pieces."

"And you happen to be up on the bread habits of the rest of the planet?"

"I am. And you win at bread."

Samantha paused and a small smile touched her lips. "So this is a compliment? You're giving me a bread eating compliment?"

"Well, let's not get carried away." That earned her a tear-off of bread in the face and that was okay, because this felt good. All of it.

"Tell me the latest about your mom," Sam said as their laughter receded.

Hunter blew out a breath and adjusted to the topic shift. "Well, she's depressed. She wants to go home, and honestly, it's getting in the way of her progress."

"Can I see her?"

The sentiment warmed Hunter. "I think she'd love to see you. You want to go back with me tonight?"

"I do."

Behind them, the front door opened and her father entered, regarding them tentatively from the entryway. He nodded once. "Hey, there."

"Richard, come over and eat something right this minute," Sam said. She really was taking charge, and it was kind of awesome.

He glanced at the kitchen and then over at them. "I think I'll grab a quick shower and then take you up on that. Kevin get you everything you need?"

Sam smiled. "He did."

Her father nodded a couple of times and headed off to his bedroom. "Smells great," he said absently over his shoulder.

Samantha turned to her. "He didn't know what to do with me

when I showed up on the doorstep and demanded entry. I kinda had to bully him to let me come in and help. How have things been with him?"

Hunter shook her head, not really sure where to start. "He's so bizarre, Sam. Honestly. It turns out he's quite capable of positive emotion. It just makes him wildly uncomfortable and then he has to leave the room quickly after."

"He's trying," Sam said. "Sounds like he's pushing himself outside of his comfort zone."

"Well, he loves Mom. That's for sure. Doesn't like leaving the hospital unless it's for a shower, like now, or a meal. But he'll be up there later tonight, walking the halls in some sort of self-imposed hallway therapy. It's how he copes."

Samantha nodded. "Everyone handles things differently, don't they?" She said the words pointedly and their meaning wasn't lost on Hunter. Sam brightened, switching gears. "Finished?"

"Yeah. I can't tell you how much I needed that. And hey, let me do the dishes. You've already taken over the world in the short time you've been here."

"What do you think I'm here for? To stare at your beautiful face? No way. Go take a nap so we can go soon."

"Bossy. At least let me clear the dishes."

"*Nap.*"

Hunter held up her hands. "Okay. Geez. No need to use your aggressive accountant voice." God, she'd missed their banter. And while she never would have asked Samantha for help and would have even refused her coming if she'd mentioned it, Hunter was beyond grateful to have her here now. Exactly the shot in the arm she needed to get through all this. And when she drifted off to a much-needed sleep, it was with a peaceful smile on her face.

Samantha fed Elvis a little bit more of the remaining roast beef and then used the time Hunter slept to put the kitchen back in order. She had been nervous jumping in the car and driving eight hours with a dog watching her every movement, but she felt reaffirmed that the trip had been a worthy one. The Blairs clearly needed an extra hand, and she could be that for Hunter and her family.

In fact, she was happy to be.

She and Hunter could press pause on their personal complications. Not that it was easy to be in the same room with her and behave as any ordinary friend would. Just seeing that smile again had her heart in overdrive. But there'd be a time down the road to sort all of that out, and Hunter just happened to be worth the wait.

"Hey," she said to Kevin as he snagged a soda from the fridge. "Your mom is feeling a little down. What can you do to cheer her up?"

He stared at her like she'd asked him to work a Navier-Stokes equation. "I don't know." He turned to go.

"Freeze. Yes, you do. Think harder and dry this." She handed him a skillet and a towel. He stared at it a moment but then slowly went to work. You just had to be extra direct with this kid. He was a good egg.

"I guess I could tell her about my day. I got the teacher she wanted me to get for history. She always says I don't tell her things."

Sam grinned and faced him. "Perfect. I think we just found your lead. See? She's gonna love that."

"Really?"

She tossed another dish towel at him playfully. "Really. You're going to make her very happy with the story of your day. Toss in little details. Women love that."

He nodded and went back to work drying the dishes she handed him, but if she wasn't mistaken, traces of a smile surfaced there. She liked this kid. He actually reminded her a lot of Hunter, which was a total bonus.

Once they'd finished, she stood with her hands on her hips and surveyed the state of things.

Dinner complete.

Dishes done.

And after checking in with Brooklyn to get the lowdown on anything pressing at the office, she checked the time. Hunter had been asleep for two hours, and as much as she wanted her to catch up on her rest, she also knew that it was important to Hunter to make it back to the hospital.

The door to the bedroom was cracked a bit when she knocked quietly. When Hunter didn't answer, she peeked her head around the corner. Out like a light with Elvis sleeping at her feet. As it should be.

"Hey, sleepyhead." Nothing. "Hunter?"

With still no response, Samantha came into the room and sat on the bed alongside Hunter. She paused for a moment before waking her, utterly entranced by the visual of the woman who slept so peacefully before her. God, she'd missed her. Awake, Hunter was beautiful, but asleep she was undeniably an angel. With her hair fanned out across the pillow, and her full lips pursed just slightly, Sam felt her heart flutter in appreciation. While she wanted nothing more than to snuggle in alongside the curve of Hunter's form, she fought the urge, knowing that things were different between them now. Tenuous. She was here as Hunter's friend and support system and should honor that.

Instead, she touched Hunter's cheek and with her thumb stroked gently. "Hey, you," she said softly. Hunter's eyes fluttered a moment and as she stared up at Sam, a smile took shape on her face in recognition. She covered Sam's hand with hers.

"Hi," she said softly.

"Hi." They stayed like that, staring at each other for several long moments, the connection between them alive and well.

"I wanted to let you sleep, but I know it's important to you to head back to the hospital."

Hunter blinked as if emerging from a wonderful dream into reality. The smile faltered and she withdrew her hand, seeming to remember herself and the facts in the scenario. She glanced at the clock and pushed herself into a seated position, facing Sam. "I can't remember the last time I slept so well."

Samantha ran a hand up and down her arm. "Yeah, well, you needed it."

"If you hadn't shown up here and worked your Snow White magic, I'd still be racing around trying to get stuff done and biting everyone's head off in the process. I don't know if I've said it enough, but thank you."

"You'd do it in a heartbeat for me," Sam said casually in an attempt to shift attention away from herself.

Hunter nodded, her expression sobering. "That's true. I would." The sincerity of the words stopped Sam short and reminded her just how much Hunter was able to affect her. Not trusting herself this close to Hunter, alone in her bedroom, Samantha decided to rescue them from the weighted moment.

"Shall we?"

"We shall."

A half hour later, Sam followed Hunter down the hospital hallway to her mother's room, noting the squeaky floor and clinical lighting. A lot of people didn't care for hospitals, but Sam had always found comfort in a building whose sole purpose was to take care of others. Hunter went in first to alert her mother of the new visitor while Sam waited in the hall, clutching the bouquet of tulips they'd stopped for at her request.

Moments later, Hunter popped around the corner, her voice low. "Okay, come on in. Try to be a little bit friendly."

Sam glared at her playful dig, but shifted to a warm smile as she rounded the corner into the room. Mrs. Blair was sitting up in bed, smoothing her hair. She beamed at Sam as she approached. "There's my favorite *Mino'aka!*"

Samantha moved quickly into her open arms and, following Hunter's instructions, hugged her delicately. "I'm so happy you're doing better. I had to drive all the way down here and see for myself."

"When Hunter said you were here, I felt so special," Mrs. Blair said.

"Well, you are. You're my second mom, you know. Who else sent me banana bread care packages at school?"

Mrs. Blair seemed to sit a little taller at that news. "I'll make you some more as soon as I'm home."

"Let's not rush things," Hunter said from the doorway.

"I can rush things if I want for my Samantha."

Sam passed Hunter a knowing look and placed her flowers next to the array already present. "Looks like you have a lot of admirers."

"I don't know where they all came from! But I bet you have some admirers of your own."

"Not as many as you would think," Sam said, smiling back.

"Fools, then."

Hunter looked on as the two continued their conversation, struck by the upshift in her mother's energy. Downright chipper, if she had to categorize her, and she couldn't wipe the smile off her own face if she tried. It was refreshing to see her mom acting like her old self again. Maybe this visit was just the motivation she needed. Later, it was Samantha who took her mother for a walk around the wing, and it happened without any coaxing at all. Just two friends, gabbing away as they strolled. Hunter shook her head in wonder. It was shaping up to be a good night indeed.

As they walked back to the car that night, her father and Kevin having arrived to take over, Hunter felt like some of her burden had been lifted. "You really went in there and made a huge difference, you know that?"

Samantha shrugged. "She just needed to see a less-familiar face is all."

"When does that less-familiar face have to head back?"

"Tomorrow."

Hunter felt the loss immediately.

"With the drive being so long, it was about all the time I could manage. We're kind of slammed at Savvy."

"My fault."

"Not at all. We've all pulled together. We have your back, you know, and Mal said you've done some work from afar."

She nodded. "A few things here and there on my laptop."

A pause. Hunter listened as the crickets sang to them from the nearby trees. She and Sam were talking about everything except what they should be talking about. Probably by design. They were so careful around each other now because there were bruises, and it was best to keep their fingers off them.

As they stood there in that parking lot, something shifted in Samantha's eyes. They were so luminous in the moonlight, so open to her yet so out of her reach at the same time. Such a big part of Hunter wanted to pull Sam to her, kiss her in the moonlight and never let her go. But the larger part held her back, terrified of what she'd be opening herself up to and what she'd be holding Sam back from.

It was Samantha who finally broke the silence. "You need to concentrate on your family right now, but when you get home, we need to have a talk. About everything."

Hunter studied the stars on the horizon as they formed a halo above Samantha's hair, which moved softly against the breeze. "I don't think I can be what you need me to be."

Samantha's gaze found hers. "Funny. Because I've yet to say what that is."

It was a fair enough assessment. For all Hunter knew, Sam wanted to tell her that she and Libby were giving it another shot and what she really needed from Hunter was understanding. The thought made her want to kick the loose gravel around her feet, but it wasn't like she'd been vocal about offering Sam an alternative.

God, life was tricky.

When Hunter arrived home from the hospital the next day, Samantha and Elvis were gone, headed back to New York as scheduled. *Pride and Prejudice* had been left on her bedside table and in the freezer she found more than a handful of homemade meals, labeled with precise reheating instructions.

And for whatever reason, she found the mail there, too.

She smiled to herself. Maybe people *could* change…

CHAPTER SEVENTEEN

As Hunter packed her suitcase, she watched as one back-to-school commercial after another rolled across the television screen. They were well into August, and that blew Hunter's mind. Seriously, where had the time gone? Autumn would soon roll in, followed quickly by the holiday season. Just thinking about New York at Christmas had Hunter energetic and ready to head home.

The time in Ohio had been full of ups and downs, but it had been an important trip and one that would forever change the way Hunter viewed the world. When she arrived, it had seemed almost certain that she would forever lose one of the most important people in her world, only to get the most wonderful, if not exhausting, reprieve. She'd listened in horror to the details of her sister's sex life, but it had brought them closer together in a very strange way. She'd opened a new line of communication with Kevin and even engaged in a couple of short but positive conversations with her dad, who in his own really odd way seemed to be trying.

But she missed her friends.

Her job.

Her dog.

It was time to, at long last, head home. In the back of her mind, there were questions about what she would find waiting for her, and she would deal with those questions in due time. It certainly wouldn't be easy.

She rolled her suitcase down the hall to the family's living room, where she found her parents, sitting together on the couch watching the Game Show Network.

"What is peanut butter," her mother called out to the television from where she sat beneath a snuggly blanket. She'd been home for a week, taking it fairly easy on the couch. Didn't mean she wasn't cooking in her short spurts of energy, no matter what they tried to do to stop her.

"What is Nutella," her father said calmly. Alex Trebek agreed with him. They'd been spending a lot of time together since the heart attack, her parents. She was pretty sure the experience had beyond terrified her father. And while he was a hugely stoic guy, his actions had spoken volumes about how much he loved his wife. He'd been there every step of the way, and she had to give him credit.

"All packed?" her mother asked. "Did you take the lasagna?"

"Mom, you can't take an entire lasagna on a plane."

"You could if you tried harder."

"I'm not packing a lasagna. I'm just not."

The crease between her mother's brow appeared, but it was more adorable than angry. "You'll break my heart, and it just mended."

Hunter smiled in spite of the lunacy and leaned down to hug her mom. "You keep the lasagna, crazy woman. And please stick to your doctor's instructions. Rest as much as possible. I'll be calling you every night, so have some good stories ready to tell me from your soap opera."

"It's a date. I'll miss you, but I'm ready for you to leave."

"What?"

Her mother pulled a face. "I'm kidding. It's what all the funny mamas say."

As Hunter stepped away from her mom, her father stood nearby and shifted from one foot to the other. And before she even knew what was happening, his arms moved toward her into—oh God, this was happening—an awkward and rather quickly executed hug. Floored. That's the best description, because she could count on one hand the number of times her father had hugged her. But maybe she should get the other hand ready, as things seemed to be on a new course lately at the Blair household.

"Bye, Dad," she said quietly.

"Need any money or anything?" he asked, still doing the shifting thing with his feet.

"I'm good."

Her mother pushed herself to the edge of the couch. "Promise me these things, *nani kaikamahine*." Hunter was ready to recite the list. She knew it well. "Make sure you eat. Read a good book. And tell that girl that you love her."

Hold up.

What was with number three?

"I'm sorry, tell *who* I love her?"

"You know *who*," her mother answered rather assertively. "Don't play that game with me, Hunter Jane."

"Samantha," her father tossed in and then looked poker-faced at the floor for his unsolicited participation.

"You think I'm in love with Sam?" she asked and glanced at her watch, cognizant of the limited amount of time she had to make it to the airport.

"I saw you when she was here, all bashful and starry-eyed. That's the look. You had the look. Didn't she have the look?" her mother asked her father, who nodded once and met Hunter's eyes briefly.

"She did."

Hunter sighed and relaxed her suitcase to an upright position, her exit delayed. "It's more complicated than that."

"Of course it's complicated or it wouldn't be love. Love is hard. It takes work. It's full of ups and downs. If you don't want to put in the work, then stick with that little dog of yours for the rest of your life. I'm sure you'll both be very happy."

Whoa. "That seems a little harsh."

Her mother raised an unapologetic shoulder. "I almost died. I have to tell it like it is."

"Give it a shot. She seemed like a nice girl," her father said.

Her mother pointed at him. "Do you think things are always easy with this one?"

"I actually don't, no."

"But I love him and he loves me and we work at it. Plus, he was very handsome in his uniform back in the day." And now they were staring at each other all gaga and clearly immersed in memories from a time before her. Tragedy had a way of bringing people together, and it certainly seemed to have done so for her parents.

"I will take your words into consideration," she told her mother. "How about that?"

"See that you do," her mother said, and began making a list with her fingers. "Tell that girl that you love her. Take the lasagna. And call when you're there. Got all that?"

"Your list is getting longer."

"I'm allowed. Be safe. We love you."

Hunter took one last look at her family home and her parents, who settled back onto the couch for Double Jeopardy. Understanding that all was well, she headed back out into the world.

❖

Sam sat with Mallory and Brooklyn at Showplace for a quick Friday afternoon cocktail because, let's be honest, it had been a week. When a four-person team is down a man, or in this case, a woman, for an entire month, everyone has to stretch a bit to make up the difference. And it was starting to take its toll. Ashton had filled in more administratively and picked up some data entry responsibility that allowed Samantha time to liaise with the graphic artist they'd contracted until Hunter returned. It'd taken a lot of direction from Sam to get exactly what they needed from the guy, which made them all appreciate how seamlessly Hunter understood their concepts and executed them effectively with her designs.

"Big plans this weekend, Brooks?" Sam asked.

"No plans at all," Brooklyn said, popping an olive. "Jess has promised to knock off work at a reasonable hour and spend tonight with me doing something very low-key. Or possibly sexy. Preferably both. That is, provided I don't die after the week from crazy and ridiculous land."

"That's not a real place," Mallory said, energy at half-mast.

"Is now. I invented it. Anyway," Brooklyn said, shifting her attention to Samantha, "if I don't come to work on Monday, you'll know what happened."

"Things should go back to normal soon," Sam pointed out. "So don't die yet."

"That it will," Brooklyn said meeting her eyes. "What time does she get in?"

"The text said close to midnight."

"You nervous to see her?" Mallory asked, pulled back into the conversation. It had been a couple of weeks since her trip to Ohio, but it felt like more time had passed than that, as each day dragged into the next.

Sam sat up a little straighter. "Nervous in a good way. I just want her around again, you know? We'll figure the rest out in time. And I don't want to ambush her with any sort of declaration, but I do know what I want. This time apart has only made me more certain of my feelings."

"And it's Hunter that you want? For good or for bad?" Mallory asked.

Samantha nodded, feeling vulnerable at the admission.

Seeming to get that, Mallory covered Samantha's hand with her own and proceeded gently. "And if she wants something different?"

Her biggest fear.

The thing that made her heart squeeze and fall in her chest.

"I have to be prepared for that. And if it happens, well, at least we're still friends and she'll be in my life in that capacity, right?" The thought nearly strangled her. She wasn't sure how she'd go back to thinking of Hunter as only her friend, but she'd cross that bridge when she came to it.

Brooklyn smiled. "It'll be good to see her face again. Elvis and I have missed her on our park trips."

"I think autumn is going to be a better time for all of us," Mallory said. And with that, she held up the company credit card. "And to kick it off, Savvy's getting this one. We earned it."

"Cheers to that," Brooklyn practically sang. The three of them raised and clinked their glasses in declaration of a much-needed upswing.

❖

When Samantha arrived back at the loft, Elvis was waiting by the door to greet her. Their new tradition. "I'm home! Our love fest can continue."

The two of them had developed a special kind of bond in the wake of Hunter's absence. They'd both missed her desperately and seemed to find solace in that mutual understanding. Plus, he was a pretty terrific dog, staring aside.

"Hi, little El." He wagged the entire back half of his body as if on speed and whined softly. When she produced a gourmet dog biscuit for him from the jar on the counter, the excitement level tripled and the I'm-about-to-lose-my-mind shrieking ensued. She'd passed a trendy dog bakery last week and couldn't exactly walk by without scoring a little homemade something for her main K9. Apparently, she'd become a dog person when no one was looking.

Elvis inhaled the cheese and bacon treat in two giant swallows. Sam concurrently perused the mail en route to her room to change from her less-than-comfortable work attire into something cozy. She was way more anxious about seeing Hunter than she'd let on to her friends. Hunter would arrive late that night, probably tired from the trip. They'd chat for a few minutes, maybe have some ice cream or a drink, depending on Hunter's mood. And from there they'd see. Maybe she'd reserve any sort of talk or confession until sometime over the weekend. Give Hunter a chance to catch her breath.

Electric bill, advertisement, cable bill, her cousin's wedding announcement, and a catalog for Hunter from some sort of art supply store. Nothing of consequence. She tossed the mail on the edge of her bed and turned to her closet ready to go to fashion war.

But something was amiss.

She turned back to the bed for a reexamination, inclining her head at the sight of a hardcover spiral notebook propped against her pillow.

Now, that wasn't there when I left this morning.

Retrieving the spiral curiously, she sat on her bed and ran her hand across the cover, which displayed a title written in beautiful black calligraphy: "Just Three Words." She opened the spiral and began to read, amazed by what she held in her hands. It was a third-person account that began ten years earlier. Psychology class. And it was Hunter's handwriting. She settled in, enraptured as a sentence led to a page, which led to more pages. It was their story in novel format, and Samantha took in every word. She couldn't have put it down if she tried. The book highlighted all of the memorable stops on their journey, hers and Hunter's. Their meeting, their friendship, Hunter moving in, the kitchen kissing, even the kiss with Libby in the hallway and how much it had shaken Hunter. Samantha wasn't sure how long she was sitting there, but in that moment, time seemed secondary. The last section, however, left her breathless and so she read it again to be sure she understood.

> *Samantha loved romance novels and, knowing this, Hunter left their story for her, the tale of how they met through the present day (skipping the boring stuff, of course). She only hoped that through these words, Samantha would forgive Hunter's inability as a writer, but see instead how deep her love really was. Because she was in love with Sam, desperately, and couldn't wait for the chance to say those three words to her in person. The words she'd never spoken to anyone in the past and hoped to never say to anyone else in the future.*
>
> *The story wasn't finished, however. There were many blank pages that Hunter hoped they'd fill in together as they continued to live out their own romance novel in real life. She'd wait for Samantha at their lamppost and count the seconds until they'd see each other again...hoping against hope that maybe, just maybe, Samantha felt the same...*

Samantha thumbed across the bundle of blank pages left in the spiral, just as the narrative said there would be. She couldn't stop her heart from beating out of her chest at the thought of all that lay ahead for them. Good God. She needed clothes! And cute ones. But mainly, she just needed Hunter there in front of her so she could kiss her, and touch her, and laugh with her. The sooner the better.

Switching into turbo drive, she took the E train to the Meat-packing District in what had to be the longest ride in the history of the MTA. Hopping off at her stop, she shouldered her way through the crowds of people out en masse tonight, free from the workweek and looking to let off a little steam. Night had fallen on New York, and the air around her felt warm from the last lingering days of summer. While aromas from the falafel cart on the corner made her stomach growl, she would not be deterred. As she turned onto the final street of her journey, she paused. Because there she was, just a few yards away, and the visual was like wonderful sunshine warming her skin. Hunter stood under the lamppost just as she had promised. And there had never been a more beautiful sight. The light from above reflected off her hair, offering a luminous glow. As she turned to Samantha, her gaze settled in recognition and she broke out in a slow smile.

Samantha had planned on words. She'd even thought through what they might be, but something took over and her arms were around Hunter's neck before she could speak them. For several long moments, they remained in that embrace, and with Hunter's arms around her again, she felt like everything aligned. That the world had righted itself again. God, she could live in this embrace, inhaling Hunter's scent, fresh cotton and peaches.

"I didn't know if you'd come," Hunter said, quietly nuzzling her hair.

"Like I'd miss this," she murmured back. "God, you feel good. Don't you ever leave again."

As Samantha pulled back, Hunter brushed a strand of hair from her forehead and straightened. A smile flashed briefly. "I'm nervous."

"You're never nervous," Sam said.

"Not true anymore. Look at my hand. It's shaking."

Samantha took that hand in hers. "Well, then hold mine because I'm not."

Hunter nodded and met her eyes seriously. "You're here, so you've seen the book."

"I have."

"And?" She blew out a measured breath and it was adorable.

Sam looked skyward to gather her thoughts. "And it was... everything. Reading it all together like that stole my breath. I loved it."

The smile started slow and spread as Hunter glanced at the ground and back up again. "I started writing it that second week in Ohio. At first, it was a release of sorts, to get it all out on paper as I sat in that hospital waiting room. But underneath it all, I knew it was more. As soon as I saw you again in Ohio, damn it, I understood where I was supposed to be. I just had to find the courage to get myself there."

"Where is that?" Samantha searched her eyes, needing to hear it from Hunter.

"With you. I was *always* meant to be with you, I think." She took a deep breath as if about to jump from a very tall cliff. "I love you, Sam, which is terrifying to say. But what's infinitely more terrifying is the thought of never kissing you again or holding you again, or not walking through this world with you." She lifted a shoulder. "You're it for me.

And if you tell me that you need time or that you're not sure, then you should know that I'm going to fight for you and do whatever it takes to win your heart. I'll give you as long as you need."

As Hunter stared down at Samantha, her heart hammered away in her chest. Sam hadn't stood her up, which had been her biggest fear, but she still didn't know entirely where Sam's head was. What if she acknowledged Hunter's feelings but wanted to protect their friendship? The thought just about crushed her.

But Samantha was smiling and there were tears in her eyes. She slipped a hand to the nape of Hunter's neck. "So you would fight for me, huh?"

Hunter met her gaze. "You have no idea."

"And those other girls in your phone?"

"Are completely uninteresting to me. Deleted."

Sam shook her head slowly. "You don't have to fight for me, Hunter. I'm yours. I've never felt more alive than when I'm with you. Or more safe. Or more whole." She paused, placed her hand on Hunter's cheek. "Or more loved. I'm so in love with you I can barely concentrate on forming these sentences right now."

And then they were kissing because there was no way not to be. Not when Samantha had just said the most important words in the world to her, making her heart fly. The ones she never imagined ever wanting to hear, and now couldn't live without. The words were hers now, and Sam was hers, and nothing had ever felt more right.

"It's not going to be easy," Sam said when they came up for air. A breeze kicked in and Hunter felt the cooler air caress her skin.

"I don't want easy. I want you." Hunter's eyes blurred but she blinked them clear again.

Samantha took Hunter's hand and brought it to her heart. The gesture was so simple, yet said so much. "Shall we?"

Hunter nodded. "Home, please."

The moon peeked out from the tops of the tall buildings as if to guide their way. Hand in hand, they walked back to their place, toward their future together.

"I think you took the U-Haul cliché to a whole new level."

"I'm an overachiever."

"In more ways than one." Sam cocked her head. "Speaking of which, which room are we sleeping in?"

"I'll sleep on the kitchen floor as long as you're there..."

Samantha turned to her, walking backward. "We could start there. But I don't know how much sleeping there'll be."

"All the more reason."

As they walked, something came over Hunter. A warm, tingly feeling accompanied by a striking burst of energy, that all-encompassing intuition that something important was upon her. Not on its way to her this time, but here.

She thought back fondly to that moment in her apartment a handful of months ago when she'd experienced something similar. She knew now that it was Sam who'd been about to change her life forever. She smiled up at the universe, a silent thanks.

Hunter glanced next to her at the girl from psychology class, the one who caused her heart to clench and at the same time was her very best friend. The depth of feeling there staggered her. This was a new page in the story of Samantha and Hunter, and she for one couldn't wait to see what was going to happen next.

EPILOGUE

The view from the Terrace Room of the River Café was breathtaking. Sam had to hand it to Serenity. They sure knew how to seek out the picturesque in life, and this little gem of a restaurant in Brooklyn Heights was no exception. The cocktail gathering was in full swing all around her that Thursday night in October. She smiled on as much of the Manhattan elite mingled and sipped champagne, all gathered for the unveiling of Serenity's new commercial spot, which would hit local stations the following Monday.

"What if no one claps?" Brooklyn whispered to Sam from their location in front of the window. "And I love this dress. Can I borrow?"

Samantha turned to her very nervous friend and smiled. "Look at me. You know it's a great spot. You know you're awesome. You do this every time."

"I do, don't I?" Brooklyn asked.

"Both you and Hunter put a lot of work into this one, and if I do say so myself, the ad rocks." She glanced down at her green and white striped dress, purchased special for the very important client occasion. She held up a finger. "And yes to the dress, provided you return it, which is something you struggle with."

"I'm working on return reform. I have daily affirmations." Brooklyn tossed a glance behind her. "Where's your alluring girlfriend?"

"Excellent question. She wanted to call home and check in on her mom before heading over. But she should be here shortly. And it's after business hours, so I can make eyes at her and hold her hand territorially without repercussion."

"You can. Not that you don't make eyes at the office. We're onto you both."

Sam gasped. "No way. We're super covert. The most professional of the professionals."

"You're allowed, you know." Sam turned as Mallory appeared alongside her. "To be yourselves at work. Brooks and I are well aware of your inability to conceal your all-encompassing love. In fact, we've formed a two-person support group to get us through it." Brooklyn and Mallory exchanged some sort of secret handshake.

"Ha ha," Sam said. "You're funny. But both Hunter and I think it's best to remain focused on our jobs when at work. We've only made out in the kitchen once, and you were both gone for the day."

"Who's making out in the kitchen? Hi, baby," Hunter said and kissed Sam. And there she was, her hair pulled back into a thick ponytail, a slight wave in its descent. Hunter was a sexy display in an off-white babydoll dress with a cropped black leather jacket on top. Short black motorcycle boots completed the ensemble. A work of art, really.

Brooklyn grinned. "That would be you, stud."

Hunter's mouth formed a guilty "oh" as she faced Brooklyn and Mallory. "Sorry about that."

Mallory shrugged. "It was after hours. Besides, there aren't rules. Let's just do good work, and so far, you've both hit it out of the park in that department. No complaints." Mallory continued speaking about some detail of the party, but Samantha's eyes were on Hunter, who smiled back at her, lingering. She loved their private exchanges. They'd perfected them at work. Well, apparently not a hundred percent, but they'd work on it.

The past two months had surpassed any and all of Samantha's expectations. She didn't know it was possible to feel so much for just one person. The sensation could best be described as overwhelming in the most wonderful way. They took Elvis for walks together and discussed their individual days. Hunter still smiled at the many women who lavished attention on her at Showplace, but made it clear that *she* only had eyes for Sam.

No one had ever made her feel more special.

"And if it isn't the women of the hour," Tanya said, strawberry champagne glass in hand. "The commercial is amazing. We can't wait to do more with you."

Mallory smiled graciously. "It's been a fantastic partnership for us, too, Tanya."

Tanya beamed and her eyes settled on Sam. "Wow. I don't think I've ever seen you look more radiant. You just seem…"

"Happy," Samantha supplied effortlessly as Hunter's hand scratched the small of her back in solidarity.

Tanya nodded and smiled at Hunter. "Exactly. You found your glow. And speaking of people in love, I want to introduce you to my girlfriend. Sweetheart?" She glanced behind her and motioned to an approaching woman.

"April," Hunter said, suppressing a grin.

April's eyes widened on approach. "Whoa, Hunter. Hi. It's fantastic to see you."

Hunter shook her head. "Small world."

"Not really," Tanya supplied happily. "April was the yoga instructor from class that day we ran into you two. Apparently, a little bit of your luck rubbed off on me." Tanya really did look happy.

"And Libby?" Brooklyn asked. Then she passed Sam a look. "Sorry. Just curious." Sam shrugged. Honestly, she didn't mind at all and wished Libby the best.

"She left me for a shoe designer, and it was the best thing that ever happened to me." She beamed at April, who seemed a bit gaga herself. "But she seems happy."

"I'm glad," Sam said before turning to Hunter. "The Way You Look Tonight" began from the live quartet across the room and the opening notes alone made Sam smile. "Wanna dance?" she asked Hunter, whose eyes sparkled at the question, because when did Hunter ever not want to dance?

"I do. If you'll excuse us," Hunter said to the group.

As Hunter's arms encircled her, Samantha relaxed into the warmth and wonder that always accompanied any kind of closeness between them. "You look amazing," Sam whispered.

"I was hoping you'd think so."

"As if there's ever any doubt. How's your mom?"

"Gaining strength. She's almost back to her old routine. She was at her mah-jongg group when I called, but my dad updated me on all the latest. Kevin has soccer tryouts tomorrow for spring. I'm so nervous you'd think I was him."

"Don't be nervous. He'll be great. And your dad?"

Hunter shook her head in wonder. "Apparently, learning to play golf, which is new."

"I'm glad you guys are getting chatty."

"I don't know if I'd go that far."

Sam thumbed the white fabric of Hunter's dress. "How long until I can take this off you?"

Hunter's eyes darkened with a mixture of lust and amusement. "Meet me outside in five minutes?"

Samantha sighed in defeat. "Somehow I think leaving the party before the main event is frowned upon. But later…"

"I'm at your mercy."

"And don't forget it."

Right on cue, Serenity's CEO, Eleanor, took to the microphone, welcoming the guests, who quieted from their chatter at the sound of her ultra-soothing voice. After a few kind words, which included a thank-you to Soho Savvy for a job well done, the large screen flickered and came alive with vibrant color and sound. The work-weary woman in the ad battled the subway, her job, and the fifty million demands on her plate before receiving the royal treatment at Serenity in the form of rehydration baths, massages, and body wraps. At long last, she was whole again and ready to face the big, bad world with gusto. With Brooklyn and Hunter's storyboards so captivatingly brought to life, even Samantha felt wowed.

Brooklyn and Mallory stood next to them. The room erupted into applause as the screen faded to black.

"To another home run," Mallory said quietly, lifting a glass to her colleagues.

Three glasses met hers in the center of their circle, a private tribute to the work they'd done in the midst of what had been a very trying quarter all around.

But it wasn't over, their journey.

There were many projects ahead of them, clients to tackle and goals to achieve. Sometimes it felt like there really was no stopping the four of them if they stuck together.

The foursome enjoyed themselves at the party for the better part of an hour, accepting congratulatory wishes and dancing up a storm with the Serenity girls—and even April. It was a celebratory night and everyone cut loose in response.

After losing sight of Hunter somewhere along the way, Samantha tried her phone to no avail. She walked among the dancers, the minglers, and tried the call again, still unable to find where Hunter had slipped off to. Just then, she caught sight of a familiar form on the outside terrace, alone and looking out over New York Harbor. She pushed open the door that led outside, pausing and taking in the image of her beautiful girlfriend, her forearms on the railing and the starry sky all around her. Hunter turned at the sound of Sam approaching and held up her phone.

"Hey, you. Just saw you called. But you found me," Hunter said. "Ready to get out of here?"

"Wait. What was that on your phone?" Samantha asked smiling and attempting to see the readout.

Hunter blushed and shook her head. "Nothing. I don't know at all what you're talking about. We should go."

"Yes, you do, babelicious," Sam teased, and Hunter laughed at the ridiculous nickname. Without delay, Samantha snatched the phone from Hunter's hand and pressed Call on her own phone. She stared down as the photo of them from their dinner at STK appeared, followed by the name Hunter had assigned her in her phone. The name was in sharp contrast to *girl from club* or *brunette from laundry mat*. The simple words touched her heart: *My love.*

"You make me happy," Sam said sincerely, meeting Hunter's gaze and handing back the phone.

"That's because I love you," Hunter said. God, those words never got old.

"I love you, too." Sam stepped into Hunter and inclined her head upward. "Let's get out of here. I want to be home with you."

Hunter tucked a strand of hair behind Sam's ear. "I was hoping you'd say that."

It was an interesting concept, home. The dictionary, she'd recently learned, defined it as a goal or endpoint. After saying good night to their friends and thanking Serenity, they left the party hand in hand as Samantha ruminated on its meaning. For as long as she could remember, she'd always been seeking something, some sort of unnamed affirmation, inclusion, or validation in life. But in the time that she'd been with Hunter, that seeking had ceased. Because she now had all of those things and more. She'd reached her own goal or endpoint, and she'd never felt more herself as a result.

She really was *home*.

"Ice cream?" Hunter asked as they walked.

"You should know that the answer to that question will always and forever be yes."

Hunter grinned. "This is why I keep you."

"Gasp. That's the only reason?" Sam asked, her mouth falling open.

Hunter shrugged. "Well, you're also good at math."

"Hey!" She nudged Hunter's shoulder in protest, which earned her a kiss. "A kiss and ice cream?" Sam asked. "This is shaping up to be a pretty great night."

Hunter turned to her with a noticeable glint in her eye, which shot Sam's temperature up several degrees. "Oh, it just gets better from here. Trust me."

About the Author

Melissa Brayden (melissabrayden.com) is the multi-award-winning author of five novels published with Bold Strokes Books and is currently hard at work on her sixth. Alongside her writing, she is in pursuit of her Master of Fine Arts in directing in San Antonio, Texas.

Melissa is married and working really hard at remembering to do the dishes. For personal enjoyment, she spends time with her Jack Russell terrier, Bailey, and checks out the NYC theater scene several times a year. She considers herself a reluctant patron of the treadmill, but enjoys hitting a tennis ball around in nice weather. Coffee is her very best friend.

Books Available From Bold Strokes Books

Love's Bounty by Yolanda Wallace. Lobster boat captain Jake Myers stopped living the day she cheated death, but meeting greenhorn Shy Silva stirs her back to life. (978-1-62639334-9)

Just Three Words by Melissa Brayden. Sometimes the one you want is the one you least suspect...Accountant Samantha Ennis has her ordered life disrupted when heartbreaker Hunter Blair moves into her trendy Soho loft. (978-1-62639-335-6)

Lay Down the Law by Carsen Taite. Attorney Peyton Davis returns to her Texas roots to take on big oil and the Mexican Mafia, but will her investigation thwart her chance at true love? (978-1-62639-336-3)

Playing in Shadow by Lesley Davis. Survivor's guilt threatens to keep Bryce trapped in her nightmare world unless Scarlet's love can pull her out of the darkness back into the light. (978-1-62639-337-0)

Soul Selecta by Gill McKnight. Soul mates are hell to work with. (978-1-62639-338-7)

The Revelation of Beatrice Darby by Jean Copeland. Adolescence is complicated, but Beatrice Darby is about to discover how impossible it can seem to a lesbian coming of age in conservative 1950s New England. (978-1-62639-339-4)

Twice Lucky by Mardi Alexander. For firefighter Mackenzie James and Dr. Sarah Macarthur, there's suddenly a whole lot more in life to understand, to consider, to risk...someone will need to fight for her life. (978-1-62639-325-7)

Shadow Hunt by L.L. Raand. With young to raise and her Pack under attack, Sylvan, Alpha of the wolf Weres, takes on her greatest challenge when she determines to uncover the faceless enemies known as the Shadow Lords. A Midnight Hunters novel. (978-1-62639-326-4)

Heart of the Game by Rachel Spangler. A baseball writer falls for a single mom, but can she ever love anything as much as she loves the game? (978-1-62639-327-1)

Getting Lost by Michelle Grubb. Twenty-eight days, thirteen European countries, a tour manager fighting attraction, and an accused murderer: Stella and Phoebe's journey of a lifetime begins here. (978-1-62639-328-8)

Prayer of the Handmaiden by Merry Shannon. Celibate priestess Kadrian must defend the kingdom of Ithyria from a dangerous enemy and ultimately choose between her duty to the Goddess and the love of her childhood sweetheart, Erinda. (978-1-62639-329-5)

The Witch of Stalingrad by Justine Saracen. A Soviet "night witch" pilot and American journalist meet on the Eastern Front in WWII and struggle through carnage, conflicting politics, and the deadly Russian winter. (978-1-62639-330-1)

Night Mare by Franci McMahon. On an innocent horse-buying trip, Jane Scott uncovers a horrifying element of the horse show world, thrusting her into a whirlwind of poisoned money. (978-1-62639-333-2E).

Pedal to the Metal by Jesse J. Thoma. When unreformed thief Dubs Williams is released from prison to help Max Winters bust a car theft ring, Max learns that if you want to catch a thief, you have to get in bed with one. (978-1-62639-239-7)

Dragon Horse War by D. Jackson Leigh. A priestess of peace and a fiery warrior must defeat a vicious uprising that entwines their destinies and ultimately their hearts. (978-1-62639-240-3)

For the Love of Cake by Erin Dutton. When everything is on the line and one taste can break a heart, will pastry chefs Maya and Shannon take a chance on reality? (978-1-62639-241-0)

Betting on Love by Alyssa Linn Palmer. A quiet country girl at heart and a live-life-to-the-fullest biker take a risk at offering each other their hearts. (978-1-62639-242-7)

The Deadening by Yvonne Heidt. The lines between good and evil, right and wrong, have always been blurry for Shade. When Raven's actions force her to choose, which side will she come out on? (978-1-62639-243-4)

One Last Thing by Kim Baldwin & Xenia Alexiou. Blood is thicker than pride. The final book in the Elite Operative Series brings together foes, family, and friends to start a new order. (978-1-62639-230-4)

Songs Unfinished by Holly Stratimore. Two aspiring rock stars learn that falling in love while pursuing their dreams can be harmonious—if they can only keep their pasts from throwing them out of tune. (978-1-62639-231-1)

Beyond the Ridge by L.T. Marie. Will a contractor and a horse rancher overcome their family differences and find common ground to build a life together? (978-1-62639-232-8)

Swordfish by Andrea Bramhall. Four women battle the demons from their pasts. Will they learn to let go, or will happiness be forever beyond their grasp? (978-1-62639-233-5)

The Fiend Queen by Barbara Ann Wright. Princess Katya and her consort Starbride must turn evil against evil in order to banish Fiendish power from their kingdom, and only love will pull them back from the brink. (978-1-62639-234-2)

Up the Ante by PJ Trebelhorn. When Jordan Stryker and Ashley Noble meet again fifteen years after a short-lived affair, is either of them prepared to gamble on a chance at love? (978-1-62639-237-3)

Speakeasy by MJ Williamz. When mob leader Helen Byrne sets her sights on the girlfriend of Al Capone's right-hand man, passion and tempers flare on the streets of Chicago. (978-1-62639-238-0)

Myth and Magic: Queer Fairy Tales, edited by Radclyffe and Stacia Seaman. Myth, magic, and monsters—the stuff of childhood dreams (or nightmares) and adult fantasies. (978-1-62639-225-0)

A Spark of Heavenly Fire by Kathleen Knowles. Kerry and Beth are building their life together, but unexpected circumstances could destroy their happiness. (978-1-62639-212-0)

Venus in Love by Tina Michele. Morgan Blake can't afford any distractions and Ainsley Dencourt can't afford to lose control—but the beauty of life and art usually lies in the unpredictable strokes of the artist's brush. (978-1-62639-220-5)

Rules of Revenge by AJ Quinn. When a lethal operative on a collision course with her past agrees to help a CIA analyst on a critical assignment, the encounter proves explosive in ways neither woman anticipated. (978-1-62639-221-2)

The Romance Vote by Ali Vali. Chili Alexander is a sought-after campaign consultant who isn't prepared when her boss's daughter, Samantha Pellegrin, comes to work at the firm and shakes up Chili's life from the first day. (978-1-62639-222-9)

Advance by Gun Brooke. Admiral Dael Caydoc's mission to find a new homeworld for the Oconodian people is hazardous, but working with the infuriating Commander Aniwyn "Spinner" Seclan endangers her heart and soul. (978-1-62639-224-3)

UnCatholic Conduct by Stevie Mikayne. Jil Kidd goes undercover to investigate fraud at St. Marguerite's Catholic School, but life gets complicated when her student is killed—and she begins to fall for her prime target. (978-1-62639-304-2)

Season's Meetings by Amy Dunne. Catherine Birch reluctantly ventures on the festive road trip from hell with beautiful stranger Holly Daniels only to discover the road to true love has its own obstacles to maneuver. (978-1-62639-227-4)

Courtship by Carsen Taite. Love and Justice—a lethal mix or a perfect match? (978-1-62639-210-6)

Against Doctor's Orders by Radclyffe. Corporate financier Presley Worth wants to shut down Argyle Community Hospital, but Dr. Harper Rivers will fight her every step of the way, if she can also fight their growing attraction. (978-1-62639-211-3)

Never Too Late by Julie Blair. When Dr. Jamie Hammond is forced to hire a new office manager, she's shocked to come face-to-face with Carla Grant and memories from her past. (978-1-62639-213-7)

Widow by Martha Miller. Judge Bertha Brannon must solve the murder of her lover, a policewoman she thought she'd grow old with. As more bodies pile up, the murderer starts coming for her. (978-1-62639-214-4)